# RED WINTER

# RED WINTER

## Dan Smith

PEGASUS CRIME

NEW YORK  LONDON

RED WINTER

Pegasus Crime is an Imprint of
Pegasus Books LLC
80 Broad Street, 5th Floor
New York, NY 10004

First Pegasus Books hardcover edition 2014

ISBN: 978-1-60598-609-8

10 9 8 7 8 6 5 4 3 2 1

Printed in the United States of America
Distributed by W. W. Norton & Company, Inc.

*For Helen and Laura*

Once upon a time there was a smith.

'Well now,' says he. 'I've never set my eyes on any harm. They say there's evil in the world. I'll go and seek me out evil.'

So he went and had a goodish drink, and then started in search of evil. On the way he met a tailor.

Well, they walked and walked till they reached a dark, dense forest. In it, they found a small path, and along it they went – along the narrow path. They walked and walked, and at last they saw a large cottage standing before them. It was night; there was nowhere else to go.

In they went. There was nobody there. All looked bare and squalid. Presently in came a tall woman, lank, crooked, with only one eye.

'Ah!' says she. 'I've visitors. Good day to you.'

'Good day, grandmother. We've come to pass the night under your roof.'

'Very good. I shall have something to sup on.'

Thereupon they were greatly terrified. As for her, she went and fetched a great heap of firewood, flung it into the stove and set it alight. Then she went up to the two men, took one of them – the tailor – cut his throat, trussed him and put him in the oven.

From *One-Eyed Likho*, a traditional *skazka*,
translated by W. R. S. Ralston

I

November 1920

# Central Russia

# 1

The village cowered with doors closed and windows shuttered. The street was empty. The cold air was quiet.

Kashtan sidestepped beneath me, shaking her head and blowing hard through flared nostrils. I leaned forward and rubbed her neck. 'You feel it too, girl?'

There should have been voices. A dog barking. Women coming in from the field. There should have been children, but I heard only the wind in the forest behind and the murmur of the river before me.

I stayed in the trees and watched the village, but nothing moved.

'You think they're hiding from us?' I spoke to my brother. 'Or do you think . . . ?' I stared at the back of his head and let my words trail away. 'I promised to get you home, Alek. Look.' I raised my eyes once more and studied the log-built *izbas* across the river. 'Home.' But there was no light in any of the windows.

Kashtan moved again, something making her uneasy.

'Come on.' I nudged her forward into the water. 'Let's have a look.'

I knew I should have waited until dark, but I'd been travelling a long time. For days we had kept to the trees to avoid the colourful armies that had battled over our country in civil war since the revolution, and now the people from my dreams needed to be made real. I had to reassure myself that my family wasn't an illusion; that I hadn't imagined them just to give everything a purpose.

Somewhere a crow called into the darkening afternoon and I

snatched my head up in the direction of the sound. For a moment I saw nothing; then a black shape rose from the bare fingers of the tallest tree behind the houses. It wheeled and dived, skimming the wooden roofs before it passed over me and disappeared from view.

I took one hand from the reins and rested it on my thigh, close to the revolver in my pocket. The mare faltered, reluctant to enter the cold river, but I encouraged her into the shallows, where she struggled to find her footing on the stones below. I pressed her on until my boots were soaked through, but as the water swelled round my knees, leaching my warmth and carrying it away towards the lake, Kashtan tossed her head and stopped in the deepest part as if she had come to an unseen barrier. She wanted to turn, to be away from here. She had scented something that troubled her.

'What is it?' I said, looking at Alek, but he gave no answer. 'Come on, girl.' I spurred Kashtan into motion. 'Don't give up on me now.'

We came out onto the bank close to the windmill and passed beneath the sails, leaving a dark, wet trail in our wake. Kashtan's hooves were hollow on the hardened dirt of the track, and her breathing was heavy, the two sounds falling into rhythm as we walked between the *izbas* and onto the road cutting through the village.

Once there, we stopped and waited, the cold air biting at my legs.

'Hello?'

My voice was dead and out of place.

'Hello? It's us. Nikolai and . . .'

I waited a while longer, watching, but nothing stirred, so I swung my leg over and dismounted. The sound was abrasive in the silence, and as soon as I was down, I stopped still, listening. I scanned the houses, wondering if anyone was watching me from the hush behind the closed doors. I glanced back at the forest, the trees black against the bruised sky, and thought perhaps I had been too eager to leave its protection. I had spent many days in there and now I felt exposed. But although it had hidden me well, the forest was a forbidding place that made it easy to believe in demons.

'Hello?' I called again, but still there was no answer. Doors and windows remained closed. 'It's Nikolai and Alek Levitsky.' My voice was flat and without echo. 'You can come out. We won't harm you.'

With a deepening sense of unease, I drew my revolver and led Kashtan to my home, moving slowly. I hitched the reins round the fence and put a hand to her muzzle. 'Stay here,' I whispered, before forcing myself to look up at Alek. 'I'll come back for you in a minute,' I told him. 'We're home now.'

The front door was closed but unbolted. It yielded to my first push, opening in to the gloom inside.

'Marianna?'

The click of my boot heels was obtrusive on the wooden floor. I took a deep breath, expecting the smell of home, but instead there was something else. Not explicit, but a faint smell of decay that lingered in my nostrils.

'Marianna?'

I had imagined the *pich* would be alight – the clay oven was the heart of our home, the place to cook, and the source of heat in winter. There would be bread baking in its furnace. Marianna would be smiling at Pavel, who would be playing with the little wooden figures my father had carved for me when I was a boy. Our eldest son, Misha, would be carrying logs in from outside. I had hoped for the warmth of a fire on an early winter evening, the faint lilt of a *garmoshka* being played in one of the other *izbas*.

But I found none of those things. No warmth. No life. Nothing.

The house was empty.

# 2

I stood for a long time in the half-darkness of my home. I called their names – Marianna's and the boys' – but no one came. The *pich* remained cold, and the house remained empty.

River water ran from me, dripping onto the floor, leaving a stain round my feet. The drips were the only sound and it felt for a moment as if this was another of my dreams. Perhaps I hadn't reached home at all but was still beneath some grotesque tree in the forest, sheltering from the weather under its twisted branches, hiding from those who would see me dead. Or perhaps this was only a nightmare of what I thought I might find when I returned home.

But I knew it was real. The cold told me that. The *fear* told me that.

The weak sun of approaching winter had dropped by the time I forced myself to move, so that only a grey, grainy light slipped through the windows as I went to the *pich* and put a hand to it, feeling the coldness of the iron door, which lay open, and the hardened clay that surrounded it. In the depth of winter, we often slept above the oven, all four of us sharing the benefit of its heat, but now white ash slumped in a heap inside where it had burned itself out. Beside it, cooking implements leaned against the wall, ready to be used. Sprigs of dried plants hung from a narrow beam over my head, and one or two leaves had been pulled free and lain on the wooden surround. A neat pile of fresh logs and kindling was stacked in the corner.

On the table, four plates lay in no particular arrangement, as if they were about to be set out. The underlying smell in the room pointed to the presence of rotting food, but I saw nothing to indicate where the odour was coming from – nothing in the oven or on any of the plates – and the only food left in the cupboard was a handful of potatoes, some pickled cabbage and a few strips of dried pork.

In the centre of the table, a half-burned candle was glued with its own wax to a chipped bowl and I remembered how it was when the candle was aflame and voices filled the room. It was always warm and light, even in the deepest days of winter, when the *pich* was burning and my family was together.

As a soldier, I rarely had the opportunity to come home; my visits were sporadic and often came less than once a year. The last time I was inside this room was more than six months ago. It was early spring, and my unit was close, meeting with a larger force for resupply, so I took a week to visit home. Alek came too, and we sat at this table that first night and saw how Marianna and the boys coped with what little they had. Whites and Reds had been through the village more than once, taking what provisions they could find, leaving them with almost nothing, but I was thankful my wife and children had been left unharmed. Misha and Pavel were proud to show off the rabbits they had snared in the forest and the fish they had taken from the lake, just as Alek and I had snared and fished when we were younger.

Now I stared at the table and imagined them round it, as they had been that night, and I felt an overwhelming sense of what had been. The togetherness that had filled me was more than any sense of brotherhood I felt with my comrades-in-arms, and it confirmed my growing doubts about the war and all that it stood for. Being with my own children, my own wife, had brought visions of those who now lay wasted in the fields and forests and burned towns and villages of our country. And when our meal was done and the night had grown dark and the children slept, Marianna and I had come together in a way that made me want her more than ever. Lying with her, feeling her beside me, I had found myself longing for a means to leave the horror behind and return to the family she had held together so well. I had known then that coming home was my only chance for redemption; my only chance to fill the emptiness.

My eyes drifted to the bent nails beside the door. I had put them there a thousand years ago, hammering the iron into the thick wooden wall because Marianna wanted somewhere to hang our winter coats, but now those coats were gone and the nails were naked.

I wondered what it meant. Had they taken their coats because they hadn't expected to return? Already the early winter winds had risen and the snow was not far away. Only a fool would leave without her coat when the land was preparing to sleep. With that in mind, I took the absence of coats as a good sign. Wherever they had gone, my wife and children had the foresight to prepare for cold weather.

Running the fingers of my left hand along the edge of the table, I moved to the door that stood open to the bedroom.

'Marianna?'

Shivering from the damp cold in my legs, I pushed the door open a little further and crept in. There was a heavy atmosphere; a sense that I should remain unnoticed. This was my house, yet I felt like a stranger – a thief stealing in during the night.

The beds were made and pushed against opposite walls, just as they had always been. The one below the window was the bed Marianna and I had slept in for years, the other for my sons, Misha and Pavel.

A translucent and frayed curtain hung from a crooked rail, allowing the last light of the day to filter through, and there was a rug hanging on the back wall, red and black, but faded with age. A chest of drawers painted white, and a small, round table with a piece of old lace thrown across to protect its surface. A single chair with a towel over its back. Above the table, a small icon hung on a nail. Everything was in exactly the same place as it had been when I left. Nothing had moved. It was as if, at any moment now, Marianna and the children would come into the house and life would return to normal. But something had happened here; I could *feel* it.

I went to the table where some of Marianna's belongings lay and ran my fingers through the teeth of her hairbrush, one or two hairs still caught there as if to prove her existence. They were long and golden, the colour of ripe winter wheat. It was a trait she had hoped for our children to inherit – fair hair and eyes as blue as the summer sky – but my own darkness had won over. Misha had her fine features, her narrow face, her mannerisms and her strength, but his hair was the colour of burned sugar, and he had dark and serious eyes. Pavel's colouring was lighter, with hazel eyes. His hair had the same hue as the acorns Alek and I used to collect from the forest floor when we were boys, and it always seemed to smell fresh and clean no matter what. I used to love putting my nose to the top of his head in the pretence of kissing him, just to breathe that smell. Pavel's temperament was closer to mine – he was more reserved than his brother – and I always understood him better than Marianna did.

I pulled the hairs from the brush, holding them between finger and thumb, hoping for a sense of closeness to my wife, but feeling no change to the empty silence. I picked up Marianna's *chotki*, the knotted prayer rope she tied herself from lambswool, and turned it in my hand just as I saw a flurry of motion from the corner of my eye.

A dark shape moving. The swish of material and a solid thump on the wooden floor.

I dropped the prayer rope and whipped round, raising the revolver and sinking to one knee to make myself low. My heart pounded and it was almost impossible to breathe. In a fraction of a second I had to choose whether or not to fire. It might be an enemy. It might be my wife. Or perhaps this *was* one of my dreams and it was something darker come to claim me for the terrible things I had done.

No more sign of movement from the shape behind the door. I relaxed my fingers and breathed deeply, keeping the revolver levelled at the object as I approached, seeing almost at once that it was not a person or anything more sinister. It was only a coat I had dislodged from its hook on the back of the door. Just a black woollen coat.

I bent to take it in my fingers, and when I lifted it to the dim light from the window, my heart stopped. This wasn't just any coat. It was my wife's.

It was Marianna's winter coat. She must have hung it here, in the bedroom, but why had she not taken it with her?

I sat on the bed and leaned forward, holding the revolver so tight my fingers began to ache.

'Where are you?' The frustration was almost unbearable. 'Why aren't you here?'

I had come so far and risked so much, and all I had found was this.

When Alek and I had run, our unit had been moving north-east to Tambov, called to aid in the destruction of the peasant rebellion that had begun in August, rising out of the unrest caused by the harsh grain requisition laws and their heavy-handed implementation by the Red Army. Already the peasant militia was calling itself Blue and numbered more than fifty thousand fighters. It had even attracted defectors from the Red Army, so some units were ordered back from fighting the Whites in Ukraine to bring it under control and intensify the Red Terror that would subdue the masses. It was on that journey north-east, heading towards Tambov, that Alek and I had finally seen an opportunity to break away; to escape the endless progression of violence and horror that had become our second nature.

We knew that two men on horseback would be a target for the units hunting deserters, but we ran anyway, taking almost three weeks to travel the hundred or so kilometres home. We avoided the open roads and the steppes as much as we could, keeping to the forests even though it made for difficult travel and nights that were long and cold and lonely. We took hard feed for the horses wherever we could find it, stealing from farms, afraid to be seen. Any soldier would shoot us for the honour, and any peasant would betray us for a handful of grain or a little mercy, but we had stayed out of sight and it had slowed us down. Alek was stronger than I could have imagined. As his wound worsened, I had wanted to take to the road, but he wouldn't let me, and now I couldn't help wondering if I should have done it anyway. We would have arrived sooner and perhaps Marianna would still be here. Perhaps . . . perhaps many things would be different.

I gritted my teeth and bowed my head. I needed my family. Only they could cast away the shadow that grew darker across my soul every day. They had to be here somewhere. I had to find them.

I closed my eyes and took deep breaths, forcing the emotions away. I placed the revolver on the bed and ran my hands across my head and face, rubbing life and sense into them.

'Pull yourself together,' I said aloud, finding comfort in my own voice.

With fresh purpose, I strengthened my resolve and went to the chest of drawers to rummage for fresh clothes, which I laid on the bed beside the revolver. Shucking off my boots, I dragged the wet trousers from my legs and used the towel from the back of the chair to dry. I had to take care of myself before anything else. Damp and cold and driven to madness, I was useless.

Redressed, I fastened my coat and pulled on my cold, wet boots, collecting the revolver before heading back to the front door and pulling it open to the night. The sky was clear of cloud now and any last traces of warmth were stolen away. The countless stars looked on, and the half-moon washed everything in silver.

Kashtan nickered and snorted as soon as she saw me, and I scanned each way along the street, listening, before I stepped out and went to her. She nuzzled my chest and I put a hand to the blaze on her face.

'A moment longer,' I whispered, putting my nose close to hers and feeling the heat of her sweet breath. 'I'll get you out of sight. Somewhere warm. Find you something to eat if I can.'

I patted her neck and moved round her, casting my eyes to the black shape of the forest on the other side of the river. Among the trees, the night was dark, and after a while it played tricks on even the strongest mind. I would be glad to sleep under a proper roof tonight and thanked my luck for that small mercy.

'You did well,' I told her. 'You've been brave.'

She had been in battle, she knew the smell of blood, but it had still frightened her to have Alek on her back. Without Kashtan I never would have made it home. She was a good friend.

I loosened the binding that had kept my brother from falling and pulled him towards me, dragging him over my shoulder as I took his weight. I carried him into the house and leaned him against the wall by the *pich*, collapsing beside him, breathing heavily from the effort. We sat side by side as if we'd settled for a cigarette and a talk about old times.

'You're home,' I told him. 'More or less.'

Alek didn't live with me; he lived in the house next door with his wife, Irina, but she had died childless the year before the revolution, and this was where he spent much of his time when he was here in Belev, so it was more of a home than anywhere else. And this was the house he had grown up in, the house Papa had built himself and that Mama ran with a firm hand and a warm smile, the house we had played and argued and fought in as boys; the house he had left to be with Irina, the beauty of the village. Everyone said she'd marry Semyon Petrovich, but she'd never been interested in anyone other than Alek. He once said to me that Irina loved the way he played the *garmoshka*, that's why she had married him, but I told him it couldn't be true. His playing was tuneless, and his *garmoshka* was so worn and shabby it wheezed like an old man smoking his last pipe.

I stared at his sturdy boots, then looked down at my own – cold and damp and uncomfortable. 'You don't need them now,' I whispered, and sat up to tug them from his feet.

Leaving my own in a heap by the *pich*, I felt a wave of sadness as I pulled on Alek's socks and boots, but they were a better fit than my own and were of no use to a dead man. He would want me to have them.

'Wait here for me,' I said, unable to look at his face.

Back outside, I unhitched Kashtan and led her to the

outbuilding at the back of the *izba*. In the past, we had used it for storing grain and livestock, but now I was beginning to wonder if there might be something else in there, and as I came close to the door, I imagined I would open it to find the bodies of my children hanging from the rafters, with nooses tight about their necks. I'd seen such things already on my journey home, and the darkness of those images had been a constant passenger in my thoughts, but I had not expected that I would find such things here. I had only seen hope and warmth when I thought of home, and now I tightened my jaw and tried to push away the ghosts of my more recent memories. But those bleaker images crept into my thoughts like shadowy apparitions, smothering the light I longed for.

I passed my old two-wheeled cart and swallowed hard as I prepared for the worst – if it was even *possible* to prepare for the terrible things I could imagine. I took a deep breath and braced myself, but when I put a foot to the door and pushed it open, raising the revolver, I found the outbuilding to be as empty as the house.

I stood for a while and allowed my breath to escape me in a long sigh, forcing my fingers to relax as I lowered my arm. A wave of relief washed over me with a suddenness that brought with it the surprise that I could have felt so much more afraid and helpless than I had realised. But that relief was tempered with something else; this time, at least, my fears were unfounded, but the absence of my family here was both a blessing and a curse. They were still missing and I damned the experiences that now sent me visions of the worst.

Any livestock that had once been kept in the outbuilding was long gone, but the scent of animals remained. The fenced-off section to the left of the door was bereft of any food stocks and I assumed the requisitions had been as harsh here as anywhere else. Perhaps Marianna and the children had moved on to find a place where they could feed themselves better. Or perhaps they had forgotten me and run from the war, looking for something safer.

15

But there was the coat. Marianna would never leave without her coat.

The floor was covered with straw, and there was a small pile of hay at the far end beside a shallow trough containing a few inches of rainwater that fed in from a pipe coming through the roof. When I led Kashtan in, she followed without trouble, going straight to the hay.

I removed the few pieces of kit I had collected on my journey and slipped the saddle from her back, dumping it on the ground by the door. There were surface scratches across her flanks, ragged scrapes from our ride through the forest. She'd been reluctant to go where the trees grew so thick – the closeness of them had spooked her, and the scent of wild animals had troubled her – but she'd gone on. She'd been brave and I owed her for that.

I took a rag from one of my saddlebags and soaked it in the trough before cleaning the dried blood from her skin, drying her and leaving her to the warmth of the outbuilding. I closed the door behind me and stood in the silence of the night, looking across at the field where the moonlight washed over the regular wave of the unplanted furrows.

The beginnings of a frost crunched beneath my feet as I slipped to the other end of the yard and climbed over the fence into my brother's property. Holding the revolver ready in front of me, I tried to block the emotions that had plagued me when I was alone in my family bedroom. I had to forget the sadness and the worry and the anger. I had to do what I did best and subdue my emotions, empty myself, leaving only what I needed. And when they were gone, there was just fear; and it was fear that kept my senses keen as I moved in the shadows, heading to the outbuilding behind Alek's house. Finding it empty, I passed along the line of houses, checking each outbuilding in turn and finding no livestock, no grain, nothing.

On this side of the road, there was a line of nine *izbas*, built with enough space between each to prevent the spread of fire. I checked every yard and outbuilding before moving on to the road that ran between the houses.

I listened for a while, shivering as the temperature dropped and my breath misted around me, then moved from home to home, summoning the courage to enter each one but finding them all empty. I headed across the road and searched the windmill, the church, and the houses that backed onto the river, but found nothing other than what I had found in my own home. There were plates on tables, a few bits and pieces of food in cupboards, and all the signs that people had been going about their business, but the people themselves were missing. It was as if they had been plucked from their homes by invisible hands, or left in a hurry without time to do much more than pick up their coats. Except it was only the *children's* coats; wherever they had gone, the adults had not taken their winter coats with them.

As the night matured, the cold bit harder and the wind played among the highest branches in the forest, teasing the sails of the windmill so the air was filled with the creak and groan of old wood.

I returned to check on Kashtan one last time and took my supplies back to the house, but even when I closed the door and pushed the bolt across, it felt as if the forest demons had slipped inside with me. After jamming a chair under the door handle, I went to the windows and considered drawing the curtains but decided against it. If anyone came in the night, they would bring lights, and I wanted to be able to see them.

Eventually I went to my brother and slumped beside him as before.

'There's no one here,' I whispered, staring at the door, feeling more alone than ever. 'They've all gone. *Everyone*. Where the hell are they? What's happened to them?' I couldn't bring myself to look at him, to remind myself that he had gone too.

I placed the revolver in my lap and concentrated on the significance of the winter coats. It bothered me that the children's were missing but not the adults', and I couldn't think of a good reason why it would be so. I went over it again and again, but I was worn out and my thoughts began to blur and swim. I told myself I would look again tomorrow, try to find an explanation.

Somewhere in the night, exhaustion overcame me and I slept a while beside my dead brother. I woke when I thought I heard my wife's gentle laughter and I sat up, forgetting where I was.

'Marianna?'

But then there was the emptiness of remembering she wasn't there, and I leaned back and rubbed my eyes.

The wind had strengthened further and it probed the house, searching for a way in, plucking at the windows, shaking the door and rattling the bolt. I wondered if it might be safe to light a fire. No one would see the smoke in the dark, and I could keep the oven door shut, pull the curtains across the windows. The warmth would be a welcome relief.

I stood and rubbed the stiffness from my neck before going to the range, breaking kindling and arranging it in the oven. Reaching for the bundle of matches and taking one from the roll, though, something stopped me from striking it. A voice whispering in my head. Whatever had taken the people of Belev might come for me too, and how would I ever help them then? What use would I be to my wife and children if I were to disappear the way they had?

I replaced the match in the roll of cloth and put it on the table, my fingers reluctant to let it go. I wanted that fire so much my heart sank at how close I had been to having it; how close I had come to that one small comfort. A huge sadness welled inside me – for the loss of my brother, for Marianna and the boys, for everything I had done and seen. It surged in a great wave and I squeezed my eyes shut, pressing my fingers against them.

Standing like that, I prayed for my family. Prayed for some sign of them.

But my prayer was disturbed by a scraping and shuffling from deeper in the room. At first, I thought I was imagining the noise, but when it came again, I opened my eyes and turned back to my brother. My vision was impaired, blurred because I had been rubbing my eyes, and I thought it was playing tricks on me when

I saw a dark shadow rising in the room. The spectre was taking shape, emerging from the ground in the murky darkness, as if Alek had woken from the dead and was standing to greet me. I tried to tell myself it was my imagination. It was nothing more than an eerie mix of light and dark. As my sight cleared, however, I knew it was no trick. Someone or something was there.

I was not alone in the house.

# 3

A blinding white light of panic and fear exploded in my mind. A quick flash, a fraction of a second and then it was gone. After that, everything was instinct. The revolver lay on the floor beside my brother and was of no use to me now, so I launched myself at the figure, thinking to protect myself by attacking first. I had no idea who had come into my home, but in the fragment of time it took to make my first movement, I remembered that I had bolted the door. The windows were closed, and the door was locked, so it was impossible that anyone could have come in while I was asleep. The only way anybody could be inside the house was if they had already been here when I returned from searching the village. They had waited for me to fall asleep and they had emerged from their hiding place to do whatever it was they had done to the other villagers.

Three steps were all it took for me to cross the distance between us.

Three wide, quick steps.

My boots clicked on the wooden floor and the figure remained as it was. It made no attempt to move or defend itself and I barrelled into it with all my strength. My natural impulse was to use as much force as I could, to destroy this threat without delay. I had seen and suffered things that gave a man the inclination to destroy and kill before waiting for horrors to be committed upon himself. I had extinguished life before, and tonight I would do the same.

There was no resistance.

As soon as I put my arms round it and forced it to the ground, I knew the figure was thin and weak. It was well padded with clothing, but beneath the materials, bones protruded hard against flesh. Skin was old and dry. Muscle was weak. It made hardly a sound when it hit the floor and took my full weight as I came down on top of it. There was just an escape of air and a muffled grunt, and then I was astride the shape, pinning it to the floor. I put my hands out, finding the narrow throat and circling my fingers round it, pressing my thumbs into the soft hollow, squeezing the life out of it, crushing the cartilage.

The smell that issued from the bag of bones beneath me was hellish. The odour of damp earth and human waste filled my nostrils and clotted my throat. The stink of decay washed over this awful creature like a disease, making me gag, but I knew it was human. It had to be. I could feel its neck crushing in my grip.

It raised its hands to my face, touching me with bony fingers, long nails raking at my cheeks. Then, as life began to leave it and its body began to relax, it managed a word. It opened its mouth and spoke a single word, which came out in a long, hot breath.

'Alek.'

And with that word, my senses returned to me. I was killing something I could not see. I might have been strangling my own wife on the floor of our home.

I released my grip and jumped back from the creature, crawling to where my brother lay. I ran my hands around the floorboards, searching for the revolver, and when my fingers stumbled on its cold metal, I snatched it up and pointed it at the shape that lay coughing in a heap. It had turned onto its front and was spluttering and hacking like an old hag.

'Who are you?' I asked, but the creature didn't reply. It stayed as it was, fighting for life, drawing air into its lungs in short, wheezing gasps.

I waited, trying to keep the revolver steady in my shaking hands, the stink of the creature thick around me. And when its breathing eventually settled to a rhythmic rasp and whistle, it spoke again.

'Alek?' the creature said. 'Is that you, Alek?'

'Who *are* you?' I asked for a second time, but I was almost too afraid to hear the answer. I knew this was no witch or spectre; this was a person who was looking for shelter and safety, just as I was. I also knew it was a woman – the voice told me that much – but I was afraid to know which woman. The thought that my wife might have become this creature was almost too much to bear.

When she didn't answer, I raised my voice and asked once more, 'Who are you? Speak now or I'll shoot.'

'No,' she said. 'No, Alek.' She shifted on the floor and turned towards me. All I could make out in the darkness was the shape of her, but I saw she was holding a hand out to me. Whether she wanted me to take it or she was just trying to reach out to me, I didn't know, but I couldn't bring myself to touch her even if it was what she wanted. The way she smelled and the way she had felt in my fingers made my skin crawl.

'Tell me your name,' I said.

'Is that you, Alek?'

'No. It's Kolya. Nikolai. Alek's brother. Who are *you*?'

There was a moment of silence as if she were trying to remember.

'Galina,' she said. 'Galina, Galina, Galina.'

Galina Ivanovna Petrova was a friend of my mother. At least, she had been until Mama died, the summer before the revolution. Mama went to the river to wash clothes one morning and didn't return. When Alek and I went looking for her, we found the clothes but no sign of Mama, so we searched up and down the bank, finding nothing until we came to the lake where the water washed from the river. We swam there when the weather was warm. The lake was a good size, with a small, marshy island close to the far shore where my brother and I played as children. We had an old rowing boat with a tin for baling out the water that leaked through the joins in the wood. At its deepest point, the lake was deeper than any of us ever cared to find out. As children, we would dare each other to swim down and touch the bottom, but the darkness closed around you quickly in the murky water, and the weeds reached up to tangle your hands and feet. Nobody I knew had ever touched the bottom.

Mama was in the lake when we found her. She was floating face up, as if the river's current had turned her to face the sky. Her skirt billowed around her, rippling with the surface water, and her headscarf had come loose so her hair was spread out in tendrils. A deep gash marred her forehead, cleaned by the current and the fish so that it was an empty, ragged scar.

We could only guess that she had slipped from the riverbank and hit her head on one of the many rocks. If the blow hadn't killed her, it was the cold water that had taken her life, swirling about her, drowning her as she lay unconscious.

We never found Mama's headscarf.

We buried her the next day, in the patch of land behind the small church. Papa had been there a long time already, and tomorrow morning, I would bury my brother beside them.

'Galina Ivanovna?' I said, pushing to my knees. I could hardly believe the creature that had risen from the darkness was the old woman I had known all my life. She was the woman who used to give Alek and me *pampushki*, still warm from the oven and laced with enough garlic to burn your tongue.

She was one of the women who had mourned at my mother's funeral.

'Alek. Thank God. Please. Help me.'

'It's Kolya,' I said without thinking. I got to my feet and took a tentative step towards her. 'What are you doing here?'

'Help me,' she said again, and this time I went right to her, reeling at the stink as if coming against a barrier that I had to force myself through. I knelt beside her, feeling the loosened floorboards as I did so.

'You were under the floor?' I asked.

'Always under,' she said. 'Hiding. It's not safe when someone comes.'

I shivered when she touched my wrist. Her grip was stronger than I expected and she squeezed tight as she pulled herself up. Her skin was cold and damp.

'When who comes, Galina Ivanovna?'

'*Anyone.* So I hide and watch and I see everything.'

'From under the floor?'

'From under it and above it. From outside and in. From the forest. I saw you coming, riding your horse, and I knew you had come to help me.'

'Help you how?'

'Help me with the others, of course. You can take care of them now.'

'The others? Where are they? I've been looking—'

'Gone,' she said. 'All gone.'

With that single word, an icy fist punched through me and clawed its fingers round my heart. 'Gone where?'

Galina Ivanovna kept her grip tight on my wrist, and her breathing wheezed in and out, in and out. 'Is it over now?' she asked. 'The war? Is that why you came home?'

'Where have they gone?' I pulled my hand away, loath to feel her touch. 'When?'

'Hmm? Oh. A long time,' she said. 'Days, weeks. I don't know.'

Judging by the way she smelled, I guessed it was weeks rather than days.

'Can you remember what happened here, Galina Ivanovna? I can't find anyone and it's important that you tell me where everyone is. I want to help you.' I wished I could tear the truth out of her, but she was confused and hardly seemed to know what she was saying.

Galina put her hand to her head and tapped it with the gnarled knuckle of one finger. 'Remember,' she said. 'Remember, remember, remember. Oh.' Her movement was sudden and she reached out to grab me once more. This time she grasped my forearm with one hand and reached up with the other to touch my cheek. She brought her face close to mine. 'Don't let him take me too.'

'Who?'

She spoke with urgency, lowering her voice and putting her lips to my ear. 'Don't let him make me go with the others.'

'Where did they go?' I asked, trying to keep my voice calm despite the questions spinning in my head. 'Who are you talking about?'

She loosened her grip on me and put a hand to her mouth. 'Don't let him take me.'

'Who's *he*? Can you remember? You have to tell me—'

'Koschei,' she said. 'The Deathless One.'

She had lost her mind. I understood that as soon as she started whispering about Koschei the Deathless. Gaunt and cruel and brandishing his sword, Koschei was as much an embodiment of evil as Baba Yaga, the cruel witch who lived deep in the forest in a shabby house surrounded by a fence made from the bones of her victims. But Koschei was just a monster from the *skazkas* we told our children. He was no more real than the forest demons, and he couldn't have been in our village, but something had happened here in Belev that had driven Galina Ivanovna out of her mind. Though she rambled like a lunatic and smelled like death, she was my kin of sorts and it was my responsibility to take care of her. And whatever she had survived, I needed to hear about it; I needed to know what had happened to my family. If I was to be of any use at all to my wife and children, I needed to know whatever Galina could tell me.

I calmed her and sat her in a chair at the table. A shaft of moonlight came through the side window to touch the far corner of the kitchen, dust motes dancing in its weak glow, but it was still too dark to see much. I could tell that Galina was bundled thick with clothes to keep out the weather, and when I touched her, her whole body trembled. Whether it was age or fear or just the deep cold that made her shiver, though, I couldn't tell.

I had left the curtains open so I could see into the night, but now I pulled them across and Galina started to protest when I struck a match and put it to the fire I'd prepared in the *pich*.

'It's fine,' I told her. 'You're safe. And this'll make you more comfortable.' I was prepared to risk it. The old woman, my mother's friend, needed some warmth, and for me, it was an excuse to make the fire I had so wanted just a short while ago. Perhaps the flames would chase away some of the demons.

When the *pich* was lit, I boiled the last of the water from my canteen and poured it into two bowls, bringing them to the table. My hands shook as I placed the revolver close to me and put a match to the candle.

The light it shed was weak and orange, and it cast a strange hue across Galina's face, but I immediately saw why she smelled so awful. Her skin was pale and lifeless, with the waxy pallor of the dead. Her grey hair would have once been groomed and tied beneath a headscarf, but now it hung damp and ragged, matted in twists and clumped with dirt. Her right eye reflected the flicker of the candle, but her left was missing. Where there should have been sight there was, instead, a moist and glistening wound.

I fought the urge to turn away.

Galina Ivanovna, once my mother's friend, the woman who had been so smitten by my brother's sweet smile, was dying, rotting while she still lived. She sat with me like One-Eyed Likho and I had a fleeting memory of the tale my mother used to tell me – the one Marianna had, in turn, told our children. I could see Marianna telling it now, sitting at the side of the bed while our children lay with the blankets pulled to their chin. In the heart of our home, the *pich* was burning and a fire crackled, while outside, the wind blew the snow across the field and the water froze thick on the lake.

Marianna would hush her voice and bring the candle close as she told of the two men, a tailor and a smith, on a swaggering journey to find evil. She always paused to swallow and look around before she explained how the two men stumbled upon a cabin where they found the hag known as One-Eyed Likho. Dressed in black, all skin and bone and blind in one eye, Likho made the men at home, put them at ease, and when they were relaxed, she cut open the tailor's throat. Marianna would draw her finger across her neck when she recounted that part; both boys would giggle as she widened her eyes in mock terror and scraped her nail across her perfect skin. Pavel's laughter, though, was never as genuine as his brother's, and he cast glances at Misha and furrowed his brow when Marianna told how Likho cooked the tailor and picked his bones clean, just as Baba Yaga liked to do with the lost children she enticed into her shack.

When the tale was told, Marianna would brush the hair from Pavel's brow and kiss his forehead before doing the same to our eldest, Misha, and we would sit in the outer room and drink tea if we had it and listen to them talking in whispers, sniggering at the horror of the old hags who inhabited the forest. And when their voices grew quiet and the night moved on, it was Pavel who would appear at the bedroom door, looking for reassurance that we were still there, sitting by the warmth of the fire.

I dismissed the image out of mind and forced myself to put my hand on Galina's. 'Tell me what happened.'

Galina shook her head and smiled, revealing broken teeth. 'Alek, you were always a good boy. Do you remember how you used to come to me for *blinis* and *pampushki*?'

'I'm Kolya,' I said. 'Alek's little brother.'

'Of course,' she nodded. 'Little Kolya.' She looked about, growing more confused. 'Where's Alek? I thought I saw him. I have to show him something.'

I glanced across at where Alek lay propped against the wall. 'Alek is dead,' I told her.

'Oh.' She closed her eye and thought about that for a long time. She pursed her lips and raised her eyebrows, and when she opened her eye again, she looked at me. 'Sasha is in the forest, Alek.'

'Your husband Sasha?' I started to stand up. 'Can you take me to . . . ?' I paused as the weight of realisation settled over me. 'Is he all right?'

'I tried to wake him. I tried to put him back together, but . . .' She put a bony knuckle to her lips and closed her eye once more.

I eased back into the chair as the numbness worked through me. 'What about the others?'

Galina shook her head.

'I want you to show me.'

'Now?'

'Yes, now,' I said.

'But the forest is so dark. And Koschei is always watching.'

'There is no Koschei,' I said. 'He's just a story. I need to see *now*. Take me to see Sasha.'

'He took all the children, you know. Into the forest.'

Another stab at my heart. 'Why don't you show me?' My mouth was dry, and my stomach burned. I hadn't eaten properly for days and now bile rose in my throat.

Galina put a hand to her face and rubbed her good eye before looking at me. For a moment a sparkle of lucidity came to her and there was recognition in her expression as she sat up straighter. 'Kolya,' she said. 'Nikolai Levitsky.'

'Yes, it's me.' I leaned closer, seeing a chance to learn something from her.

'How long is it since I last saw you? You look older. The war has been . . .' she started to say before her expression changed. 'You have to help them,' she said. 'I think he took them away.'

'Took them where? Do you know?'

She shook her head. 'They called him Koschei, but he . . .'

'He what?'

'He took them all,' she said, grief beginning to overwhelm her. She put a hand to her mouth as if she were reliving it again, remembering it as if it were new to her. 'Oh. Yes.' She tapped her forehead with her bony knuckle, as she had done before. 'I was watching from the woods. Yes, that's right. I was watching from the woods and I saw . . .' She stopped tapping and put her hand over her mouth, muffling her words. 'I saw what he did to Sasha. And then they saw me. I tried to stop them and they saw me and . . .' She paused.

'And what, Galina Ivanovna? What happened then?'

She looked up at me and the light went from her eye and I knew I had lost her once more. 'Koschei,' she whispered.

'Can you show me now?' I asked. 'Take me to Sasha.'

'But it's dark.'

'The moon is half full. We'll see well enough.'

28

'And there are things in the woods . . .' She looked at the door. 'Such things . . .'

'You'll be safe with me.'

The old woman took my hand and muttered to herself as we crossed the road and followed the riverbank. She hadn't wanted to leave the *izba*, but now we were outside, she was eager to show me her secret.

'The lake,' she said. 'The lake.'

She was unsteady and we moved slowly past the place where I had come across the water that afternoon, heading to the far end of the village, where a small footbridge spanned the river. It was a simple wooden construction that leaned to one side as if it were about to collapse into the water. Many of the crosspieces were long gone, leaving gaps in the bridge, and the ones that were still in place were now coated with the oncoming frost. Like a forgotten jewel-encrusted bridge from one world into another, it spanned the murmuring river from the hardening mud on this side to the dark forest beyond. The wind had died away and an ethereal mist had settled along the banks, flooding the trees and shrubs, drifting in the breeze, and I felt the same apprehension I had felt as I entered the silent village.

Galina hesitated and glanced at me.

'It's all right,' I said. 'I'm here.' But a chill settled over me as we went on, Galina still grasping my hand, and I looked ahead, afraid to find what was waiting for me.

I used my free hand to hold the bridge rail, but as soon as we reached the shadowy mouth of the path through the forest, I let it fall to rest against the revolver in my coat pocket. The trees were naked, withdrawn from life while they endured the onset of winter. Their damp bark was black in places, but in others it was dusted with frost, glistening in the moonlight that broke through twisted and crooked branches. When I glanced down at Galina's fingers closed round my own, I saw a similarity in the way her swollen, arthritic knuckles bulged beneath old skin and once again I remembered One-Eyed Likho and how the smith had fled

29

from her through the forest to avoid the tailor's fate, eventually cutting away his own arm to escape her.

We shuffled along the narrowing path, besieged on all sides by the oak and sycamore and hornbeam. Roots rose and fell from the frozen ground; rotting autumn-flamed leaves shifted across the forest floor as the wind crawled and swirled among the trunks. Somewhere close by came the cawing of many crows. Stark, agitated calls to the night.

When I heard those black birds, I thought I knew what was lying in wait in the darkness. The civil war had cut through the country like the Reaper himself had swept across it, and everywhere he cast his glance he left the dead lying in the fields and villages and forests. And wherever the dead fell so the crows came, obscuring the grass, turning everything black.

My steps faltered and I felt Galina grip my hand harder so that now it was she who was leading me. I shook myself, trying to lose the sickening feeling that swelled in my chest, and told myself I had to go on. I had to see. In the back of my mind, though, a voice told me that I *didn't* need to see. Knowing was enough. *I didn't need to see.*

When we broke from the forest into the clearing before the lake, the stars looked down with indifference and the trees stood silent.

The crows rose into the sky as one when Galina stepped forward, shooing them away. Their raucous complaints shattered the quiet of the forest like screams in the night and I knew what must have brought them here in such numbers. While their presence in fields far from here indicated sights against which I had hardened my heart, the massing of carrion birds so close to home filled me with dread.

Moonlight fell across the clearing, reflecting from the paper-thin ice on the surface of the lake, washing the area in a silvery glow, but even in daylight I would not have been able to make out the features of the man who lay in the frozen grass.

'Sasha,' Galina said, falling to her knees beside him. 'My Sasha.' She put her hand on her husband's face as if she didn't notice what the crows had done to him. 'I tried to make him whole again.'

The body was dressed in black trousers and a shirt that had once been white but was decorated now with a dark stain across the chest. The skin was marked from the attention of the crows, and there was a dark sore in the centre of his forehead. As I came closer, I saw that when she stroked her husband's damaged cheek, his head rolled in an unnatural way, falling to face us and revealing the place where it had been separated from his neck.

I took an involuntary step back and reached a hand inside my pocket to find the reassurance of the revolver's handle. I scanned the clearing, watching the dark shadows on the periphery, searching for any sign of who might have done this. I had seen bodies before, but not often like this, and I knew this man.

A coldness froze my stomach as unwanted images of the possible fate of my family invaded my thoughts.

'What . . . what about the others?' I asked. 'Where's everybody else?'

I knew she'd been alone too long, that this must have happened some time ago, judging by the marks the crows had left on him, but it was almost impossible to know how long unless she told me. There was no smell, meaning the body had decomposed almost not at all, so it could have been quite fresh, but the weather was cold and I had to allow that as a factor. This execution could have taken place two days or two weeks ago.

'Are they dead too?' I asked, looking for other shapes in the clearing before turning my attention to Galina once more.

She cut a sorry figure in the gentle mist that diffused the moonlight. Shabby and pitiful. Her clothes upon clothes were dirty and ragged, making her bigger than she really was. Her lank hair, muddied and unkempt, writhed about her head like a witch's. And in her madness, she sat at her husband's side believing his head could be returned to his shoulders and that he would get up and walk.

'Someone saw them coming.' As before, there was a sudden clarity in her voice, as if she might have stepped from her madness into a moment of sanity. 'A week ago, perhaps a little more. It was early and I was in the forest looking for mushrooms, just coming back as they were sending the children across the river to hide in the woods. That's what we always did when they came, to stop them from taking the boys and . . . and using the girls. But they knew. They must have seen. I waited in the woods and watched them order everyone out of their houses and across the bridge.' She brushed a hand over her husband's clotted hair. Her fingers trembled. 'They lined up the men and made them kneel, and then he drew his sword and said he would kill them, one at a time, until the children came out.'

'Who was it?' I almost didn't dare speak. Galina was like a sensitive switch that had settled on sanity for a moment and I feared that if I disturbed her now, she would slip back to the confusion and bewilderment she'd shown before.

'The men shouted to the children, telling them to run, but they didn't. They came out because they were so afraid and . . .' She took her hand away from Sasha's forehead as if realising for the first time that he was dead. 'And then he killed my poor Sasha anyway. He swung his sword over and over and over, and the children were screaming, and there was so much blood, and . . .' She hung her head and sobbed, and I had to resist my need to press her.

'I had a knife,' she said, but I could barely hear her voice now. 'For the mushrooms. I came out of the woods behind him. I should have done it earlier, but I thought he would stop. I thought he would stop before he did this to my Sasha, but he didn't and then I had . . . I had nothing to lose anymore. He took my Sasha, so I came out of the woods and stuck it in him, but it just made him angry. The knife went in and came out, and there was blood, but all it did was make him angry.' She ran her fingers along her dead husband's leg and I saw the pain she felt at his loss. I had felt it too, with the passing of my brother, Alek, and I faced it again with the disappearance of my family.

'I couldn't save anyone. He just took my knife and did this . . .' She turned to me, raising a hand to touch the cheek beneath her

32

empty socket, and with that action, and the way the darkness fell across her face, the injury was obscured so that she was no longer a hag. Now she was just a helpless and distraught old woman who was forced to mourn her husband.

'I should have buried him,' she said. 'I should have . . . You'll do it, won't you, Alek? You're a good man.'

'Of course. But tell me about the others. What happened to everybody else? The women and the children?'

She turned to look at me, her brow wrinkling in puzzlement. 'They must have thought I was dead. I heard him say, "Throw her in the lake," but I couldn't see. There was too much blood and pain, and I tried to tell them I was still alive, but I couldn't speak. I might have screamed. There was screaming, I'm sure, but it's like I was dead already and then their hands were on me and I felt the water and . . .' Galina stopped. 'Oh.' She said. 'The lake. The water.'

'What *then*?' I saw that I was losing her. The lucidity was leaving her. 'What happened then, Galina?'

'*You* have to look after them now,' she said. 'You have to take care of them. Bury Sasha and find the others. And find Koschei. Find his death.'

'Where are they? Can you tell me any—'

'Koschei took them.'

'Where? Where did he take them?' I wanted to rip the memories out of her.

'Please,' she said, reaching out to touch the pocket where she had seen me put the revolver. 'Use it. Use your pistol and let me go to my husband. I've done what I had to. I've told you what happened. Now it's up to you. Please, Alek, let me be with Sasha.'

'No.' I knocked her hand away. 'Tell me about the others.' I grabbed her by the shoulders and shook her. 'What happened to the others?' I was losing control of myself, desperate to wrestle the answer out of her. I had been patient enough. I had waited long enough. I had earned my answers.

But Galina just dropped her head, saying, 'No. No. No,' and

33

when I saw the blank expression in her eye, I knew I was only driving her madness deeper.

When I released her, Galina turned towards the lake without looking at me. I watched her approach the edge of the water. It was still early winter and the ice was only a thin crust, so it broke when she put the toes of her boots to it. Then she took another step, her foot crunching into the freezing water.

'What are you doing?' I called. 'Galina?'

Before I could reach her, Galina had waded into the lake so she was knee deep in the water, fragments of broken ice floating about her, tangling with the skirt that spread about her on the surface.

I stopped at the edge and waited for her to turn round, but instead she began to take off her coat.

'Galina?'

She dropped the coat to one side and unbuttoned her cardigan.

'Galina.' I waded into the water, but as soon as I touched her, she snatched away.

'Leave me,' she hissed. 'Let me go.'

I tried to pull her back once more, but she resisted, trying to push me from her.

'So much pain,' she said. 'Let it be gone. *You're* here now. *You* can look after them. I can go.'

'Don't do this,' I said, putting my arms around her from behind, preventing her from going any deeper.

'Let me go, Alek,' she cried. 'Please.'

'Tell me about the others,' I shouted. 'Where are they?'

'They're gone.' Galina struggled. 'All gone. Let me go too. Let me be with them.'

I held on to her, pleading with her until I knew it was useless. She had told me all she would – all she was *able* to – and she had made up her mind what she wanted. Something inside me didn't blame her for wanting it, but there was something else too: a dirty thought telling me Galina would be a burden, that this way would be better for both of us. It was a notion that left a bitter taste in my mouth, but I had learned long ago to find priorities, to shut out

34

emotion and put some thoughts and actions before others. There was nothing I could do for Galina now and nothing she could do for me. I had to think of Marianna and the boys. They were all that mattered. Everything I did had to be for them.

Perhaps this was better for both of us.

So, with a heavy heart, I released Galina and stood back, half expecting her to turn and curse me, but all she did was take off her cardigan and drop it into the water.

'All of them gone.' She was lost to the world now and moved deeper into the water, removing her clothing as she went, breaking through the wafer-thin layer of crust. 'All gone.'

By the time she was waist deep, her upper body was naked. Her arms were thin, and her spine protruded from her back. There was almost nothing of her and I wondered how she could have survived alone.

She pushed out into the water and disappeared beneath the ice.

I waited a long time to see if she would resurface. Visions of my own mother in the water haunted me, her hair washing about her head.

But the lake settled, the ice came together, and Galina was gone.

# 4

The light was enough to search the clearing, but I found no evidence of the women and children or the other men from the village. I ventured a little further into the woods, following the sound of the crows, which cawed unseen among the tangled branches. Something was attracting them, but the trees were dense here and it was too dark to see. Alone like that, it was easy to feel eyes watching me, the demons of the forest waiting for me to lose my bearings. Koschei himself might be waiting in there with his sword, and the thought of it unnerved me, making me draw my revolver and stare into the darkness.

I floundered in the impenetrable night among the knotted and crowded trunks for only a short time before I lost my nerve. I would come back in the morning to look again. I had to find *something* to tell me where Marianna and the children had gone, but now was not the time. I tried not to think what might have happened to them, ignoring the crows and telling myself they were still alive. There were no other bodies by the lake, nothing in the village, and I would find them in the morning. The cold reality of the day would lead me to them.

Or perhaps the black birds would show me the way.

I hurried home as if the night terrors of the forest were close on my heels, and I drew the bolts tight. I checked the *izba* for uninvited guests then I changed into dry clothes and put Alek's boots by the oven before I hung my coat and satchel by the door. I inspected the place where the floorboards were missing, bringing the candle close to the hole and kneeling to look in at the small crawlspace beneath the house where Galina had been hiding. I'd been in villages where peasants had made similar hiding places to hold back grain stores from requisitioning units, or to conceal sons and deserters. I wondered for which purpose Marianna had built this one. Perhaps I had inspired it on my last visit with my guarded talk of wanting to come home and of my loss of faith in the revolution. Or maybe it had been to hide Misha and Pavel, to protect them from forced recruitment into the army. Whatever it had been, it seems it had not been enough.

There was a lingering smell in there that reminded me of Galina, so I refitted the floorboards, pushing them down into place before I went back to the table and sat facing my brother.

'There's a dead man in the forest,' I told him. 'You remember Sasha Petrova? Galina's husband? They cut off his head. And I think there may be more. Not just one or two like . . .' *Like when we did it.* I closed my eyes and shook my head. 'I'm afraid it might be all of them, Alek.' We had never done that. Never like that. 'I'll take you to Mama and Papa tomorrow.' I looked at him. 'Then I'll find the others.'

I had only a few snatches of sleep during the night. I put my head on the table and jumped at every sound, every bluster of wind. Sometime in the early hours, a fox screamed from the forest. The noise tore through me like a blunt saw, filling me with a kind of terror I hadn't felt since I was a child, and I sat for a long time before fetching blankets from the bedroom and returning to watch the fire in the *pich* burn itself out. I couldn't risk it still being alight when the day broke, else someone might see the smoke. In the forest, the suspicions of being followed and watched had been a constant companion for Alek and me, and it had increased with Alek's passing and my growing sense of loneliness. Deep down, I knew it had been a mistake to light the fire for Galina, but the warmth had been a blessing. Now, though, I had to focus on staying alive and free for Marianna and the boys. I had to be unseen.

By dawn, it was freezing inside the house. The walls retained some of the heat, but the night had been harsh, and when I dared look from the window, a thick frost had grown across the land.

There was great beauty in it. The sparkle of the weak winter sun on the dappled layer of crystal. The dusting on the roofs of the houses and the dark trees beyond the river. The sails of the windmill glistened, and the mud in the road had frozen hard in peaks. Last night's faint mist still swirled in the air as if I were seeing the world through cataracts.

My breath steamed against the window as I watched the morning rise and wondered at the strangeness of the world. The country was turning against itself, filled with anger and confusion. Men killed men, brutalised women and children, looked for ways to maim and destroy. There were fields where a thousand bodies lay frozen in death, yet the world seemed not to notice. The sun still rose, the frost still came, the rivers still flowed, and the dark forest still watched. When we were all gone, buried or burned, the trees would live on without us, watching the next generation grow in the place where the last had fallen. The river would give life to new people, the fields would feed them, and the sun would warm them in the summer. It didn't make any difference what we did. We were only here for a few moments and all that mattered was making those small moments bearable; being where we wanted to be.

I wrapped my arms around myself and turned to look down at my brother.

'The ground will be hard,' I said.

Outside, the frost touched everything. It glittered on the steps and took on the prints of my boots when I went down onto the road. The air was fresh, and the wind carried a purity, as if it might be able to wipe everything clean with its freezing breath. It pinched at my cheeks and froze the hairs in my nostrils.

I looked each way along the road, but the village was as deserted as it had been when I arrived, so I went round the back, crunching the hard frost as I crossed the yard towards the outbuilding. I had to tug hard to pull open the door, which had frozen in place.

Kashtan nickered as I came in, and she moved over to greet me. The inside of the shed was warm, she had left her smell in there,

38

and it gave me a good feeling to be close to her. Her bright chestnut coat was alive and vibrant, while everything else around me was grey and stripped of life.

I rubbed her nose and put my face against it, taking a deep breath and closing my eyes. I imagined climbing onto her right then, riding away from the silent village and whatever horror waited in the forest, but I couldn't leave without checking for any sign of where Marianna and the others might be.

Something was attracting the crows; something more than a single beheaded man.

If I found nothing, I would head north to Dolinsk on the only track from the village and put my faith in God or fate or whatever it was that had so far forsaken me, but I had to look.

And I had another duty to perform. I had to bury my brother.

'You stay here, Kashtan. I won't make you carry him again. I have to do this. It's my turn.'

Returning to the *izba*, I took Alek under the arms and hefted him up. For a moment we were face to face, almost as if we were about to embrace one another, and strong memories flooded me, making me pause to look at his face, to remember him as he had been. The older brother I had loved and hated as a child, just as brothers do.

I saw the sharp whiteness of the scar over his blanched upper lip, where he had fallen against the fence when he was eleven years old. The mottled marks on his neck caused by shrapnel he took in the Great War. His hair cut close against his scalp, a perfect job made by the company barber from the army I had encouraged him to join. Alek had wanted to come home then, even though he'd already received a letter about Irina's passing, but I had persuaded him to join me in the revolution. He probably would have been conscripted anyway, as most men were, but I couldn't help thinking that I had brought him to this.

'I'm sorry,' I said. Then I put him over my shoulder and stumbled and staggered along the road with him on my back. His joints were stiff, and his muscles were hard, and he seemed to weigh even more today. I fell to my knees in the frozen mud and dropped my brother more than once, and when I came to the church steps, I rested for a moment before going inside.

The church was hardly a church at all. It had no bell or tower, no cross mounted on its roof. It was little more than a house like all the others, except the door was carved with a crude cross and it was built, if anything, from lighter materials than the other homes – as if the original builders had trusted to God that it would stay warm and not be destroyed by the weather. Even though I had searched it last night, I felt compelled to go in, perhaps to show my brother to whatever remnants of God might be left, before I broke the ground for him and covered him in frozen soil. Or perhaps it was a pilgrimage; a penance for letting him die, just as it had been a kind of penance to carry him here from our home. A way to absolve myself of the guilt I felt for his death.

I struggled with Alek, feeling the pinch in my back as I summoned whatever strength I had to lift him. I crouched and hefted him onto my shoulder, using the fence to help me to my feet, then I stood and took Alek into the church, the door creaking on cold hinges.

Empty chairs faced an altar covered with a threadbare cloth upon which stood two large red candles, one at either end. There was a holder for smaller candles, a pair of icons and a wooden crucifix with three cross-beams. There were other icons on the walls too, faded and cracked, exactly as I remembered them.

I put Alek in front of the altar and took a seat, breathing hard as I fought to regain my breath. Despite the cold, I was sweating under my clothes and I felt the moisture chill on my skin, making me shiver.

'Not what we were expecting, is it?' I said aloud. 'We come all this way, get through so much and . . .' I leaned back and looked up at the ceiling. 'I thought Marianna would be waiting. Misha and Pavel. I should have known.' I sniffed hard and looked at my brother again. 'You knew, didn't you? That's why you gave up.'

I wished I had never gone to war. I wished I had stayed at home and cherished every moment with my family. Misha was nine years old when I first left, Pavel just seven, and my time with them since then had been limited to that which I was able to spend away from soldiering. The babies I had once cradled with just one hand were now grown almost as tall as their mama, and I had wasted so much of that time.

'Maybe this is my punishment – to live for *this*.' I looked up at the cross. 'Is that it? Are you punishing me?'

Behind me, the door creaked.

I reached for my weapon and turned to see a figure standing silhouetted against the morning. Bulked by a winter coat and hat, rifle in hand, he cut an impressive figure. His breath clouded about his face, and he stood unmoving, watching.

I stayed as I was, one hand on my revolver.

'What have you done?'

# 5

Everything about her demeanour had made me think she was a man. Only when she spoke did I realise that her imposing profile had deceived me. She had the almost lazy bearing of someone who had nothing to lose; someone for whom violence was a part of life. A certainty. And when she took a step into the church, the muzzle of her rifle pointed at the floor, she looked comfortable and without fear. I'd seen young men hold a rifle with trepidation, even after training, but this woman held it like she meant to use it.

'What have you got there?' She inclined her head to one side. 'Behind the seat? You're armed?'

'I am.'

She nodded as if she had expected as much. 'And you killed him?' She glanced at Alek, lying in front of the altar.

'Not really.'

The woman studied me, perhaps looking for lies, but it was hard to see her expression. She had the advantage of the light behind her, so her face was in shadow, like a closed book.

She came further into the church, taking another two or three steps along the aisle between the seats, until she was no more than an arm's length from me. At this range, her rifle would be of little use to her. We were so close that the length of the barrel would prohibit her from raising it enough to shoot at me.

Despite the cold, my fingers sweated on the pistol grip, and my skin felt clammy, but I was ready to use it if I had to.

'You're alone?' she asked.

I didn't answer.

'You *are* alone,' she said. 'We've been watching the village since first light.'

'We?'

The woman nodded and raised her hand to point behind me.

For a moment I didn't move. I wondered if it was a trick to make me look away. I used to do something similar with Misha and Pavel at dinnertime, a ruse to steal food from their plates. When someone spoke from behind me, though, I knew it was no trick.

'We've been right through the village from the other end.' The voice betrayed some tension in the speaker. A touch of barely restrained hostility. 'As soon as we saw you leave the house with him. Where's everyone else?'

I turned to see another woman standing behind me and guessed she must have come in through the back while I was watching the other. I cursed myself for having been so easily duped.

'You've been following me?' I wondered if Alek and I had been right when we'd thought there had been eyes watching us in the forest.

'Not following, watching.'

'Where are you from? Not here.'

'No. Not here.'

This woman was slight in build, wearing trousers and a long winter coat. At this angle, I could see her more clearly than the other woman: the light was on her face. She wore a dark lambs-wool hat, like a Kuban Cossack might wear, pulled low on her forehead with just a hint of blonde hair hanging below its rim, the fringe cut short and straight. Cold blue eyes gave away none of her thoughts, and her angular, handsome features were set in a permanent frown. Brow furrowed, lips pursed tight, jaw clenched, she had the appearance of someone whose expression was a product of the experiences she had lived through.

She wore a rifle slung over her shoulder and held a com-missar's pistol in her hand, but there wasn't any surprise in

43

seeing armed women any more than seeing armed men. Some of the strongest soldiers I'd known had been women.

I looked for any evidence of affiliation but saw nothing to suggest which army or ideology held her allegiance, other than the pistol in her hand.

'Where did you steal that?' I asked. 'Or has it always been yours?' If it belonged to her, and she had shed her uniform, then perhaps she had been in the Red Army, like me.

'Mine?' She shook her head. 'No. I don't remember where it came from.' But I didn't believe her. If it wasn't hers, then she had taken it from a body – either one she had found or one she had killed – and that was something she'd remember.

I looked down at my revolver, sensing the woman's tension as I turned it. 'No reason for anyone to get hurt,' I said, returning the weapon to my pocket. I had no intention of giving it up to them, but I wanted them to see I was not a threat. They had me at a disadvantage, so it was in my interest to give them the impression of submission without appearing weak.

'I agree,' she said, sitting on the altar step in front of me, resting her forearms on her knees so that the pistol dangled between them.

The woman behind me moved away, finding a distance more suited to the long weapon she was carrying. She'd done her job distracting me and now her duty was to protect the woman in front of me.

'So you're in charge?' I said to the woman in the lambswool hat.

'In charge of what?'

I shrugged. 'The rifle behind me. Any others you might have outside. How many *do* you have outside?'

'Who *are* you?' she asked.

'No one.'

She smiled, but it didn't change her face much. It didn't touch her eyes; it was just a movement of her mouth, those full lips turning up at the corners, a hint of teeth too white for a common peasant. 'Just like me. No one.' She inclined her head toward

Alek. 'And him? When my comrade asked if you killed him, you said, "Not really." What did you mean by that?'

'I meant no.' I looked down at Alek and wished I could have done more for him. It had been my decision to run like that, even though he was hurt. It was the best time, the only way to make it work, but if we had gone back, things might have been different. Alek might still have been alive. 'He's my brother,' I said.

'In arms?'

'In blood.' I looked at the woman. 'My name is Kolya. This is Alek.'

'Kolya.'

I nodded.

'Then you can call me Tanya. And this is Lyudmila.' No patronymic. No surname.

With the pistol in her left hand, she reached into her pocket and took out a small leather pouch. She contemplated it, realising she needed both hands, so rested the pistol beside her and opened the pouch. She removed a cigarette paper, which she put on her thigh to keep steady while she took a pinch of dry tobacco between finger and thumb. To my eyes, her fingers and hands seemed too delicate to be those of a farmer's wife or a soldier, but they looked firm enough when they were wrapped round the handle of her pistol.

There was something precious about the softness in the bend of her wrist when she sprinkled the tobacco along the paper, and when she had rolled the cigarette and licked it to stick it down, she tore the corner from an empty booklet of papers and made a small tube with the scrap. She inserted this makeshift filter into the end of the cigarette in an odd and affected quirk I'd never seen before. There was something about her I couldn't quite put my finger on. She was somehow different from the usual peasants and soldiers I dealt with.

She put the cigarette in the corner of her mouth and was in the process of replacing the pouch in her pocket when she stopped. She looked up and then leaned across, offering it to me.

'Thank you,' I said, taking it.

45

Alek and I had been travelling alone for close to three weeks. The journey had been long and difficult. Some days, we hadn't moved at all, only daring to travel at night through the forest, when it was almost impossible to navigate. Other days, Alek had been too weak to go far. We had come a long way from our unit after what happened, living on the sparse supplies we had, bolstered by whatever we could hunt and forage. We kept to the forest as much as possible, avoiding the roads and the search parties that used them. The tobacco had run out after the first week.

I rolled one for myself, and when I handed the pouch back, she struck a match on the step and leaned across to offer me the flame. I glanced at the weapon by her side, thinking I could take it. I could kill her in a blink, but there was a rifle trained on my back. I was quick, but maybe not quick enough, and I wasn't inclined to fight right now. I was here to bury my brother.

I accepted the light, and the first drag on the cigarette was like a blessing. I realised how low I had fallen for it to be such a singular pleasure. Other than the warmth from the oven last night, it was the closest thing I'd had to comfort for longer than I cared to remember.

I tipped my head back, blew the smoke at the ceiling and stayed that way for a while. I closed my eyes and ignored the women as if they had never been there. Then I remembered Alek lying at my feet. He would have enjoyed this moment, and an image came to me of the times we would go to the lake at dawn to fish because it was the best time, and we would sit in silence, smoking and listening to the water washing the shore. What happened to Mama didn't stop us; we couldn't allow it to. The lake had ugly memories, but it had beautiful ones too. Memories of Alek. Memories of being there in the summer with Marianna.

The lake gave life just as it took it away.

'Where's everybody else?' Lyudmila asked. 'There's no one here.'

'You tell me.' The memories faded into the grey light.

'What have you done with them?' Her insistence suggested she didn't know what had happened here, and I had seen so many lies

46

and betrayals that it would take a good act to fool me. My training and experience had shaped me into not just a soldier capable of great cruelty but also into a reasonable reader of intentions.

'Nothing. This is my home. I don't know where—'

'Are you a soldier?' Tanya asked.

I opened my eyes and looked at her.

'Which colour are you?' The pistol was in her hand again. The barrel was pointing to the floor, but all she had to do was move it a hair's breadth and she could put holes right through me. It was not a threat, but she was ready for whatever might come.

'Which colour are *you*?' I asked.

Tanya showed me the non-smile again and shook her head. 'It doesn't work that way.'

'I'm on my side,' I said. 'Yours. No one's.'

'But you're a soldier. All men are soldiers, aren't they? For one side or another.'

'Red or White makes no difference to me,' I said. 'Nor Black, or Blue, Green.' There were too many colours to keep track of. The Black Army of anarchists in Ukraine, spontaneous Green armies rising out of the peasantry to protect their lands and livestock, and the Blues spawned from the uprising in Tambov.

'I don't care about those things,' I said. 'I just want to bury my brother.'

'He's really your brother? Your real brother?'

'Yes.'

'I'm sorry.' She wiped the back of her hand across her forehead, smoke encircling her face. 'Where are you from?'

'I already told you. *This* is my home. But what about you?' I asked. 'Where are *you* from? How do I know you didn't have something to do with what's happened here?'

'What *has* happened here?' Tanya looked at the woman behind her and there was a flash of something difficult to read in her expression. Recognition? Fear? Perhaps both.

'You know something?' I asked.

'About what?'

'About where everyone has gone,' I said. 'About the dead man lying back there in the forest.'

'Dead man?' She stood and I could see from her reaction that she didn't know about Galina's husband. 'Show me.'

I dragged on the thin cigarette and glanced at the pistol in her hand. 'You don't need that.'

'Tell me where the man is and—'

'Put that away,' I said, 'and let me bury my brother.'

'No, you need to—'

'Let me bury my brother,' I insisted. 'Then I'll take you.' I was eager to press on too, but the thought of what I might find was unsettling me, and I had to honour my brother; I couldn't leave him here like this.

Tanya considered the pistol for a moment before she looked up, nodded once and holstered it. When she did that, I knew our dynamic had shifted. I had something she wanted and she had just complied with *my* demand, soft as it was. She was less of a threat to me than I had first thought.

I turned to see that the woman behind me had followed Tanya's lead and lowered her rifle to point at the floor.

'The ground will be hard,' Lyudmila said, 'for a burial.'

'I have an axe. It won't take long.' I stood up, making Tanya lean back and reach towards the pistol once more.

I raised both hands in front of me. 'Please. Trust me.'

'Trust is a hard thing to come by these days,' she said.

In some ways, it was good to have the company. Galina had been too touched by madness to offer any companionship, and Alek had been incoherent for much of our journey. His wound had festered and I had done what I could, but it hadn't been enough. I couldn't help but blame myself for that. Perhaps if we had stayed with the unit, our medic, Nevsky, could have saved him. There might have been *something* he could do.

'I'm not a threat to you,' I said. I needed to get back to the lake and look for my wife and sons. I had to find some clue of what had happened to them.

'Where are you going to go?' she asked. 'After you bury him. Back to your unit?'

I ignored her and went to my brother.

'No. I think you're avoiding that. You're a deserter.'

It was the first time that word had been thrown at me – a word laced with betrayal and disgrace – and it cut me more deeply than I expected. I knew what I was, and deserter wasn't the worst of it, but I was reminded of the men I had hunted for the same crime, men whose only real offence was to want something better.

I clamped the cigarette between my teeth and the smoke stung my eyes as I crouched beside my brother to put my hands under his arms, turning him over and pulling him across my shoulder. I struggled with him, wishing I were stronger, wishing he were alive, wishing so many things, but none of it helped me and I felt myself weakening. My brother was dead, and my family was lost, and I was alone.

'You came home and there's no one here, is that it? I want you to tell me what happened.'

'Later.' I grunted as my strength failed me and I laid Alek on the floor and sat beside his body, trying to forget the women were there. I bit hard on the cigarette and fought back the shame and the guilt and the fear that threatened to overwhelm me. I had no time for it. I couldn't afford it. I had a job to do and I needed to do it quickly. I would finish my duty to my brother and then I would do my duty to my family.

I steeled myself once more and prepared to lift my brother again.

'Let me help you.' Tanya came round me and crouched by Alek's bare feet.

'I can do it.'

'I know. But it's easier with two.'

She pushed back her hat and looked at me through the hair that fell across her brow, and in that fraction of time, I had a glimpse of the woman she might have been before the war. The look in her eye softened to one more sympathetic, as if she had read my emotions. The frown faded, her jaw softened, and I saw what might be the real Tanya rather than the mask she wore. She wasn't beautiful, but there was something attractive in her features – the way her lips bowed, the upturn of her nose, the sharpness of her cheekbones.

'Thank you,' I said.

We carried Alek through the church, to the plot where the people of Belev had always buried their dead. A small area surrounded by a failing fence and a thicket of trees that shaded the cemetery in the summer. Picking through the simple wooden grave markers, we shuffled to a place close to the back and put Alek down.

In the field on the other side of the fence, two horses grazed at the wintry grass and it surprised me I hadn't heard them approach. The women must have kept to the softest ground and I had been inattentive, but their tactics would have left prints in the frost that could be found and followed by anyone who might be tracking me. I'd seen no concrete evidence yet, but the constant sense of being trailed refused to leave me, and two riders on horseback could easily be mistaken for Alek and me.

I stretched my back and took a last drag on the cigarette before pinching away the glowing end and putting it in my pocket. It would be greedy to smoke it all at once, so I would keep the rest for another time.

'This is where my parents are buried.' I pointed at the two markers in front of us. They were simple, like all the others; just wooden orthodox crosses painted white, faded and cracked by the weather. If the markers were to be removed, there would be almost no sign at all that anyone was buried here.

Lyudmila, the woman with the rifle, had followed us into the cemetery with her weapon in one hand and the axe in the other. I removed my coat and jacket, took the axe from her and began to break the earth beside Mama and Papa, swinging the heavy tool backwards and forwards, backwards and forwards.

As I worked and the women watched, the sky blackened, and when a rumbling cracked in the distance, Tanya looked across at her comrade. 'Thunder?'

'Or artillery?'

'Thunder,' I told them. 'Just thunder.'

By the time I had shovelled out the loose soil and dug a grave deep enough for my brother, the first of the sleet began to fall. Down and down.

Thick and cold, it pelted us, so Tanya and Lyudmila went to the overhang at the back of the church and sheltered from the worst of it, while I struggled to put Alek in the ground. Their sympathy did not stretch as far as allowing themselves to be soaked, but I would have done the same. Cold and wet was no way to be at this time of year, and if they were going back out there, on the road, it could mean a long, slow death.

The black dirt loosened into a dark rain as I threw it over my brother, showering across his lifeless body, and I watched as he disappeared from the world. The patter of the soil on his body was the saddest sound I had ever heard, and the hardest shovelful was the one that hid his face. It settled into his nostrils, his eyes, on his lips and across his pale skin. And then Alek was gone.

I put on my jacket and picked up my coat and satchel, walking back through the crosses and memorials towards the women.

'I've nothing to mark his grave,' I said, as the sleet fell around me.

'That can't be helped,' Tanya replied.

I nodded and stopped to stare at the place where I had buried my brother. He was gone now, but would always be with me.

'Now I'll show you what you want to see,' I said, turning from the grave and walking away without looking back. 'Then I'm going to find my wife and sons.' Perhaps I would have to bury them too.

I had entered the church before Tanya called after me, but I didn't stop. I had done my duty to my brother now, and I wanted to get back to the lake, to the forest, to follow the call of the crows. I had delayed too long already.

'Hold on,' Tanya said, following behind me.

I passed through the church, putting on my coat, and was close to the front door when Tanya came alongside me, walking quickly.

'What do you mean about finding your wife and sons?'

I continued out into the empty road.

'What did you mean?' she asked again.

'Come with me if you want to see.'

# 6

Tanya said nothing, but she fell back a few paces, walking behind me.

Last night, the mist had washed over the bridge and lay across the path and undergrowth like forest spirits waiting to form, but now the wisps had vanished and all that remained were patches of frost and the hardening sleet. It crunched under our boots as we tramped to the far end of the village towards the footbridge.

The crows. They were still here, calling their bleak cries to the morning. From time to time their cawing became more agitated, and some would rise into the air over the trees beyond the lake, then they would settle once more and the sky would be still.

Tanya and I stopped at the mouth of the bridge and waited for Lyudmila to bring the horses.

'They look tired,' I said, as she came from the back of the church and led them along the road towards us.

'They're tough enough,' Tanya replied.

'And the bridge won't take their weight.'

'It won't have to.'

When Lyudmila caught up with us, Tanya took the reins of one of the horses, holding them out to the side so the animal could negotiate the river while she used the bridge.

'After you,' she said to me, so I crossed the bridge with the women following, and the horses splashed through the icy water beside us.

We took the narrow path beyond, the branches reaching across on either side as if trying to touch us. It was less ghostly now than it had been last night, but there was something impersonal and unfeeling about it. As if we didn't belong here.

The horses came without complaint, the water dripping from their bellies as we went on into the forest, the soft thump of their hooves on the lonely path. There were tracks there, below the frost, the coming and going of many feet, but there was no telling how long they had been there.

I knew what to expect when we came out into the clearing by the lake, but it still stopped me in my tracks.

The sight of Galina's husband lying dead on the grass was even starker than I remembered it. It had been softened by the moonlight, but now it was hard and cold and cruel. I was no stranger to the vile things that one man can do to another, but something about this made my flesh crawl. Perhaps because I had known this man.

He had been a part of my life.

The body lay in the centre of the clearing, surrounded only by the last red leaves of autumn, now frosted and glittering with the touch of winter. There was no mistaking the separation of his head now, his face turned towards us. And there was something I hadn't noticed last night. The angry mark in the centre of the old man's forehead that I thought was caused by the attention of crows was not a random and jagged wound. Just above his eyebrows, and regular in design, the wound could only have been a burn.

In the shape of a five-pointed star.

Tanya came to a stop behind me and took a short breath. 'Koschei,' she said.

The name was like a nail driven into my chest and I turned to watch her staring at the headless man. 'What did you say?'

Tanya's eyes didn't move. She was frozen in place by the scene, her whole body rigid.

'Did she say, "Koschei"?' I realised that perhaps Galina hadn't been as confused as I had thought, and it dawned on me that whoever had done this, whoever had killed the old woman's husband, really *was* calling himself Koschei, just as Galina had insisted. Whether he had taken the name for anonymity or notoriety I couldn't tell, but it was a name that unsettled and disturbed. Koschei the Deathless was a hateful and cruel symbol of evil.

Tanya's horse stepped back, shying away from the grim tableau, so she released her grip on the reins, and while the animal moved away towards the lake, Tanya took a few slow steps across the frosted clearing until she was standing over Galina's husband. She stopped, turning her head to look away at the trees, and set her expression firm before looking back at the dead man, studying him.

'What do you know about Koschei?' I asked her. My voice was out of place in the quiet solitude of the forest.

Tanya said nothing, so I turned to Lyudmila behind me. There was a watery glaze to her eyes, but it wasn't the cold that was bringing the tears.

'You've seen this before?' I asked. 'This burn?'

She took a few steps forward, coming to stand beside me. 'More than once. Where are the others?'

I looked back without thinking, raising my eyes to the naked treetops on the other side of the lake. If there were others, that was where they would be. Where the crows had congregated.

I was almost too afraid to go there.

'What do you know about Koschei?' I asked again. 'Who is he?'

Lyudmila shook her head. 'Where were you when this happened?'

'Not here,' I said. 'I came home last night and this is what I found.'

The sound of footsteps made me turn to see Tanya coming back to us.

'So you came just last night?' Lyudmila asked. 'And the village was empty?'

'Yes. But you know that. You said you were watching me.'

Tanya was just a few paces away and still coming with intent. I could see her expression now and her eyes were fixed on me. The corner of her mouth curled, and her hand was reaching for her

55

weapon. I wasn't sure what was going to happen here, but I knew it wasn't good. I had just a fraction of a second to read the situation before Tanya reached me.

I put a hand to my own weapon, but as soon as I did, Lyudmila clamped hers on my wrist. She wasn't as strong as I was, but it was enough to slow me down, and before I could shake her off, Tanya had drawn her pistol and was standing in front of me, pointing it at my chest.

'Tell me who you are.'

She was different now.

Before, in the cemetery, Tanya had been efficient, but there had been an undertone of melancholy and defeat. In the church, when she had helped me with Alek, I had seen beneath the hardened shell, but now there was a menace in her voice and anger in her eyes that made me think she meant to kill me.

'I'm no one,' I said. 'Just a man who came home to his family.'

'So what about this?' She yanked the pistol from my pocket and held it up for me to see. 'Where did you get this?'

'I stole it. Where did you get yours?'

'Don't pretend you're not a soldier.'

'I won't pretend,' I said. 'I *am* a soldier. Or I was.'

'Only officers carry weapons like this.' She stuffed it into her coat pocket.

'I could say the same to you.'

Tanya raised her hand and brought the butt of her pistol down on the side of my neck. She wasn't so fast that I didn't see it coming, but it was as hard as I had ever been struck and I went down on one knee, pain flashing in my vision. As soon as I was down, Lyudmila knocked the hat from my head and took a fistful of my hair, yanking my head back until I was facing the sky. It was difficult to breathe with my head in that position and my throat stretched, pulling my mouth open. Tanya put the barrel of her pistol between my teeth and pressed it against my tongue.

She stared down at me, the rage clear in those cold blue eyes. I had no idea what she had been through, but if it was anything like my experiences, I could understand why the anger had risen in

56

her. I had felt it too. Sometimes it was difficult to control, always boiling just under the surface. But now I was going to die.

I would never be able to find and protect Marianna and the boys.

'You people are like poison. You spread death wherever you go.' It was Lyudmila who spoke to me, and there was hate in her voice. 'Kill him, Tanya.'

Tanya seemed to hear the contradiction in her friend's words and she tried to push away the demon that had seized her. She withdrew the pistol, scraping the steel against my teeth. 'Who *are* you?' she asked.

'I didn't do this,' I said. 'This is my home. I promise you.'

Lyudmila tugged harder on my hair, and Tanya shifted as she tightened her grip on the pistol and pointed it at the bridge of my nose. 'Give me one good reason why I shouldn't just kill you now.'

'What's changed?' I asked. 'From before. What's changed? You know I didn't do this.'

'Just kill him,' Lyudmila said. 'He's Red – I can smell it – and they're all the same. All of them.'

'You're wrong,' I told her. 'We're not all the same.'

'Is that your one good reason?' asked Tanya.

'You need a reason not to kill me?'

Tanya said nothing.

'You lost someone?' I asked. 'To this Koschei?'

Tanya narrowed her eyes and glanced at Lyudmila.

'I have lost *everyone*,' I said. 'Two sons. Misha is fourteen. And Pavel . . . Pavel is just twelve years old.'

Tanya brought her left hand up to steady the pistol and she touched it to my forehead.

'And my wife,' I said, looking her in the eye. 'She's missing too. Her name is Marianna.'

Tanya glanced away to the lake and then back at me again.

'So I have *three* good reasons,' I said. 'Not just one. Is that enough for you?'

Tanya took a step back and lowered the pistol a fraction.

'I want to find them,' I told her. 'Just like you want to find whoever it is you're looking for. That's why you're here, right? You're looking for someone?'

She let her arm drop to her side, the pistol pointing at the ground, and she wiped her other sleeve across her mouth and nose, sniffing hard. 'Let him go.'

Lyudmila gripped harder, squeezing my hair in her fist and tugging as if she wanted to rip it out of my scalp. 'But he's a—'

'Let him go, Lyuda.'

She hesitated a moment longer, then pushed my head away, throwing it forward.

I rubbed the back of my neck and stayed as I was. 'Maybe we can help each other.'

'We don't need your help,' Tanya said.

'Perhaps I need yours.'

'Then you'll have to manage without it.'

'At least help me find the others,' I said. I had been alone in the forest for many days already, and had grown accustomed to being without company, but there was something about the prospect of heading deeper into the trees alone today that I didn't want to face. I was afraid of what I might find there.

Tanya looked at the ground and pursed her lips as if she were thinking about it.

'We don't know anything about him,' Lyudmila said. 'Maybe he even did this.'

Tanya shook her head. 'He didn't. We know that.'

'People *like* him, then. Or maybe he's one of them.'

'One of who? Are you talking about Koschei?'

'What do you know about him?' Tanya turned her attention on me, the fire relighting in her eyes. 'Where is he? You know his real name?'

'No,' I said, getting to my feet. 'I don't . . . Galina told me about him. She said he—'

'Who's Galina?' Tanya asked. 'Where is she now?'

I picked up my hat. 'There was an old woman here last night, one of the villagers. I knew her. She was a friend of my mother.

Galina. She said someone called Koschei did this and I thought . . . I thought she was confused. I thought . . .' I looked across at the old man's body. 'This was her husband, Sasha. Now I have to look for the others —' I swallowed hard '– and I'm afraid of what I'll find.'

'Where is this old woman? I want to talk to her.'

'Galina?' I ran a hand through my hair and pulled on my hat, staring out at the lake. 'She went into the water. Drowned herself.'

'Drowned *herself*?' Lyudmila asked.

'Yes.' When I looked at them, I saw the way the women watched me, something like suspicion in their eyes. 'It's the truth,' I said. 'Her husband dead, the others gone . . . I tried to stop her, but it's what she wanted. I *knew* her. She was my mother's friend.'

'But you let her go?'

'It's what she wanted. To be with the others.'

'With the others?' Tanya said, and she and Lyudmila glanced at one another, then they both looked out at the water. For a while neither of them said anything. All three of us were alone in that moment; each of us retreated into our own thoughts.

'He likes to drown the women,' Tanya said in a quiet voice. 'Koschei. I'm sorry.'

It took a moment for her words to register. As she spoke them, they were just sounds without meaning, but as they unravelled in my mind, they brought a numbness, a crushing white weight bearing down on me.

*He likes to drown the women.*

The words repeated like an echo of themselves and I saw Galina entering the lake, breaking the thin ice, disrobing, sinking and disappearing. Before she went under, though, she turned and looked at me and I saw that it wasn't Galina. It was Marianna's face that looked back at me from the water. Then she was gone, sinking, falling among the reeds and the dark unknown at the bottom of the lake.

'—about Koschei?' One of the women was speaking but the

voice was like a distant whisper. An unimportant inconvenience. All that mattered was Marianna, and I began walking, moving towards the lake. It came to me that she might still be in there, moving gently in the depths with the other women, their faces white and bloated. Like my own mother, the lake had taken her in its watery embrace.

I repeated her name as I approached the water, saying it over and over, feeling the tightness of my heart and the overwhelming need to be with my wife.

The forest was no longer there. The wind stopped. The crows vanished. Nothing existed anymore. Only me; the lake and Marianna.

*He likes to drown the women.*

I was almost at the water's edge when hands gripped my arms and pulled me back.

'There's nothing you can do,' Tanya was saying. 'I'm sorry.'

I fought against her for a moment, stumbling back and falling so that I was sitting, looking out at the lake as if I had come to watch it on a warm spring afternoon.

'There's nothing you can do,' Tanya said again.

'You think she's in there? Marianna?'

'Maybe it was different here,' Tanya said. 'Maybe . . .' but she didn't finish. There was nothing she could say to change what had or hadn't happened, and there was nothing I could do to find Marianna. If she was in the depths of the lake, she was gone for ever.

I pulled my coat tight against the cold.

'Did the old woman tell you what he looks like? What's his real name?' Lyudmila spoke to me, but I kept my eyes on Tanya as I shook my head.

'She said nothing at all?' Lyudmila asked.

'Nothing.' I looked out at the lake again and wished the world were different. 'I have to look for the others now.'

For a moment there was no sound but those that should be there: the sigh of the breeze in the trees; the gentle lapping of the water at the bank; the trickle of the river flowing into the lake.

'Will you come with me?' I asked. 'To find the others?'

Tanya turned to the forest and raised her eyes to the treetops. 'There's nothing in there for me,' she said. 'All that matters is finding Koschei.'

'Maybe he's still there,' Lyudmila suggested.

'No, he'll be long gone.'

'And when you find him?' I asked.

'I'm going to kill him.'

They walked away, going to their horses and mounting up.

'Which way will you go?' I asked as they came back towards the path.

'North,' Tanya said, stopping her horse and looking down at me. 'So far we've been following him north. What's the next town from here?'

'Dolinsk.'

'Anything else?'

'A few villages between here and there. Farms. Nothing else.'

Tanya considered me for a long moment then pulled my revolver from her pocket and dropped it on the ground beside me. 'Good luck, Kolya,' she said.

I didn't turn to watch them leave. I stayed where I was, staring out at the lake, dreading what I would find deeper in the forest.

# 7

So it was that I went to my family home for the last time, crossing the bridge and walking the lonely road through the village. I found myself at my own front door, acting only on instinct as I went into the darkness within. I didn't have a coherent plan in mind, but took a basket from the shelf at the far end of the room and collected every scrap of food I could find. In the drawer, I found a good knife that went into the basket, along with the food, a handful of matches wrapped in a cloth, candles and a single spoon. I collected the saddlebag I had brought from the out-building and threw it over my shoulder before picking up the blankets that had covered me during the night. Arms full, I walked back to the front door and pulled it wide, but something stopped me and I stood like that, with my back to the room, the door open to the cold.

I needed a reminder.

Of Marianna. Of Misha and Pavel. Of everything I was leaving behind and everything I had once been. Something was beginning and I had to prepare for it in the right way.

Closing the door, I put everything on the floor beside it and went through to the bedroom. I picked up Marianna's *chotki* and wrapped it round my right wrist, tucking it into my sleeve, mouthing the words 'Have mercy on me, the sinner', just as Marianna would have done. Then I vowed to find my family, no matter what it took. And when I had found them, alive or dead, I would follow Tanya's path to Koschei and I would kill him.

'Nothing will stand in my way,' I whispered.

Taking the small icon from the wall above the table and putting it in my satchel, I returned to the kitchen and sat down just as Marianna would have wanted. This was the traditional way. It was bad luck to go on a journey without sitting for a moment. Marianna made me do it every time I left to go anywhere and I had always come back.

I was anxious that Tanya and Lyudmila would already be off the road and hidden in the forest – they were my best lead to Koschei and I didn't want to lose them – but I would take this time. It was the kind of superstition I used to tease Marianna about, but it had served me well enough until now. My parents had always done it, my grandparents too. Marianna said it was to trick the evil spirits into thinking the travellers had decided to stay, but whatever the reason for the tradition, I could spare a few moments if it was going to bring me luck.

I sat at the table and closed my eyes, and that simple act helped me to relax and rearrange my thoughts.

I focused first on Marianna and the boys. I touched the *chotki* on my wrist and prayed that they were not dead, as my worst fears tried to suggest, but that they were somehow safe and would stay that way until I reached them. I pictured each of them in my mind as best as I could. It was difficult, though, to hold an image of their faces in my thoughts. I focused instead on the quiet sound of Marianna's understated laughter. I wrapped myself in the way I had felt the last time we had been together in our bed, her naked skin against mine. I remembered the way she scolded me for bringing dirty boots into the house and how I laughed when she broke up the boys' squabbling by chasing them with a wooden spoon. I breathed deep and recalled the smell of Pavel's hair, the smoothness of his cheeks, the brightness of his grin, the seriousness of Misha's furrowed brow and the delight in my eldest son's eyes when he first pulled a fish from the lake. I remembered my brother too, how he had been before the war, not as I had seen him this morning when throwing the cold dirt over his face. I remembered him as he was when we were boys and we ventured deeper into the forest than we were allowed, and the

63

time when he was fifteen and stole vodka, which he drank until he was sick.

Then my thoughts turned to the darkness that had smothered this village.

For me, he was a shadow. Galina had called him Koschei the Deathless. She had put a knife in him and it had done him no harm, but the Deathless One was no more real than One-Eyed Likho, and no one is immune to the blade of a knife. She must have made a mistake.

Anyone can die. I had seen that often enough.

Even in the *skazka*, Koschei had a weakness. This one would have one too, and once I knew what had happened to my wife and sons, I would be sure to find it.

# 8

Kashtan was glad to see me. She'd been alone in the outbuilding for a while and she missed my company. She was a sociable animal and felt the loss of Alek's horse. For days the two animals had shared the journey, walking side by side, and at night, they had been tethered close to one another. They had grazed and slept together.

When Alek died, there'd been no choice other than to cut his horse free. Navigating the dense forest and keeping out of sight was difficult enough without having to lead a second horse, and hard feed was not easy to find. Alek's saddle now lay hidden in the forest, and I had salvaged all the kit and supplies before unbridling his horse and setting her free. The animal was valuable and there was a sense of cruelty in releasing her like that, leaving her in the forest, but at least she would have a chance. It was fair to give her that, rather than put a bullet in her. She had followed us for a while before she began to fall behind and then she was lost among the trees. If she was lucky, she'd make it out to the steppe and stumble upon someone who would take her in. If not, she'd have to face the winter alone, but she would survive, I was sure of that; our horses were hardy animals, as good for hard work as they were for riding long distances or taking in to battle. These animals could survive the cold, grazing on frozen grass two metres under the snow.

I saddled Kashtan and secured the blankets and other kit before leading her to the front of my house and mounting up. I took one last, long look at my home; then we moved away, leaving it behind.

There was a place beyond the bridge where the river widened and became shallow, a good spot to ford it and cross into the forest. Already the day was cold, and short as it was, it was now half gone and soon the feeble sun would drop behind the trees, dropping the temperature even further. I would be sleeping in the forest again tonight, and neither I nor Kashtan could afford to be wet. Yesterday, I had been in a hurry to get home, but today, I had to be more wary.

There were faint prints on the track from Tanya and Lyudmila's horses. I followed them past the bridge, thinking about the two women. They hadn't told me what had set them on their path to find Koschei. Like me, they had been reluctant to give any clue about who they were or where they were from. Such was the nature of our country; no one could trust anyone. Not neighbours, not friends, not even people joined by the same need. Everyone was afraid. But their experience of him must have been similar to mine. Their desire to *find* him was similar to mine, and I hoped we would meet again before that happened. Tanya had not told me her reasons for wanting him, but she had made her intentions clear. When she found Koschei, she was going to kill him, and I couldn't let that happen. I needed him to tell me what had happened to my wife and sons, but the dead cannot talk.

When we came to the bridge, I considered the place where the women's horses had crossed, but it was deep there and would come well past my knees. I didn't relish the thought of travelling with wet clothes, so we went on a little further before I turned Kashtan closer to the river, looking for the shallowest place.

'You're not going to like this,' I said to her, as she picked her way down the bank and cracked through the thin ice that had formed over the still waters at the edge.

I made myself look up at the trees. 'I think we're going to find things in there that *neither* of us will like.'

We kept to the shallows, following the river as it eased westwards into the forest, and I let Kashtan choose her route as she

66

moved further into the course, finding her footing. She didn't stumble and didn't complain as she pushed out into the water, moving deeper and deeper until the surface of the river was almost touching the soles of my boots. Then she was coming out again, the water running from her belly as she took us up the other side.

'Good girl.' I leaned back as she climbed the far bank and headed into the trees.

The forest was silent here but for the river chattering as it slipped towards the lake, slowed by the build-up of ice. Soon the whole course of it would be frozen here, as a silvery serpent lying in wait in the black forest.

The ground beneath Kashtan's hooves was a carpet of decaying leaves, and the air was scented with a damp earthiness that filtered through the cold and caught in my nostrils. It reminded me of so many things and a clutter of half-memories flitted through my mind like summer swallows, giving me just a glimpse but nothing I could latch on to.

Childhood winters, Alek and I daring one another into the darkest parts of the forest, knowing we would never go much further than a few paces into the shadows because the threat of what lay within was too much for us. Babushka filling our heads with stories of the mischievous *leshii* – the woodland spirits that resented travellers in their domain, causing them to lose their bearings, leaving them lost among the trees, ripe for Baba Yaga. And then, when I was older, sneaking out with Marianna, finding places where we could be alone. Snatched kisses from cold lips. The touch of perfect skin.

Then there was the taste of fire, the smell of blood and gunpowder, and the fear returned. The fear of being found. The fear of death. The scream of men calling for their wives and mothers. All of those things passed through my thoughts now as I returned to the forest, wishing I was out on the steppe, where the air smelled only of the cold.

I leaned forward, put my face close to Kashtan's neck and took a deep breath. The heat radiated from her skin and the warm smell that came off her helped to clear my mind.

'I'm lucky I have you,' I said. 'If I didn't have you, I think I'd be out of my mind by now.'

Kashtan snorted as if in reply and continued among the trees, the two of us working to find a route that was safe for her, until we came out into the clearing where Galina's husband lay dead and coated with frost.

We stayed close to the edge of the lake as we passed across the open ground. Kashtan twitched a little, tried to look over at the far side, knowing something was there, but I kept her straight, muttering soothing words. The old man was almost hidden from sight, but I knew he was there, beheaded and branded. I didn't need to see him again. I had promised Galina that I would bury him, but I had neither the time nor the stomach for another burial. I would bear the guilt of that too.

Beside us, the lake rippled in the breeze that skimmed its surface, the low waves lapping against the frozen edges, thickening the ice. In the depth of winter, the lake would be frozen right through to the bottom, and Galina's body would be crushed by the hardening water.

Babushka would have said that Galina would remain a *rusalka* now, an unquiet spirit that would only rest once she was avenged, and for an awful second I imagined her roaming the clearing moaning for her husband. It seemed to me, though, that we had too many stories and too many spirits, that the things we really needed to be afraid of were far more real.

*He likes to drown the women.*

Tanya's words taunted me and I couldn't help seeing an image of Marianna frozen in the ice, but . . . no. No. Marianna was alive. She had to be. If she were in the lake, I would know it.

We came to a halt at the far side of the clearing and looked for a good way into the trees. They were thicker here than by the river, some of them as close as an arm's length apart.

'Be strong,' I told Kashtan, but I waited a few moments be-

68

fore entering. The words were for me as much as they were for her.

A noise behind me in the distance. Something undistinguishable. I whipped round, half expecting to see a *rusalka* coming across the clearing to avenge the lives *I* had taken. With eyes wild, long hair flowing, limbs jerking in spasmodic movement, it would pursue me without rest, but when I looked, there was nothing there. Only the glistening grass bent over in the places where I had walked with Tanya and Lyudmila. Only the faint trail where Kashtan and I had ridden. Only the ripples on the lake.

'Seeing ghosts now.' I shook my head at myself and went back to looking at the trees just in front of me, but the base of my neck tingled as if a cold finger traced a line there and I couldn't help glancing back, feeling as if malevolent eyes watched me from every shadow.

Another sound, but this time it was further away. Perhaps out on the road. I cocked my head to one side and pushed back my hat so I could listen. Kashtan's ears twisted and I knew I hadn't imagined the sound.

'You hear that too?' I said. 'Was that a horse in the village?'

Kashtan replied only by turning her ears this way and that, searching for the source of the sound.

'You think they came back for me? Tanya and Lyudmila?' But I knew they wouldn't have come back.

The sound came again. Hooves on hard dirt.

'Definitely a horse,' I said. 'Or horses.'

I remembered the sensation I'd had of being watched. Those lonely days in the forest with my dying brother, wondering if I was being followed. Hunted. There were some who prided themselves on finding deserters and bringing them in for public execution. I imagined they would do the same for me if they thought me to be still alive.

I had ridden along streams where I could, stayed in the forest, doubled-back to cover my tracks. I had done everything I could to remain untraceable, but the sounds were clear behind me. Someone was in the village. I glanced over my shoulder, looking for any hint of movement, but saw nothing other than the unsympathetic trees, the silent brushwood and the glistening frost.

Then a voice. A sound that jolted me and filled me with dread.

I looked back again, wondering for a moment if it might be Marianna and the boys. I fought the sudden urge to return to the road, telling myself it could not be them. And when I stared across the clearing to the trees that hid the road from view, I saw the passing of shadows and heard the sound of men's voices and knew I had to move quickly. I could not afford to be seen by anyone.

'Come on.' I nudged Kashtan with my heels and together we melted into the forest.

We had left a trail. It was almost impossible not to. In the village, there was evidence of the horses, but the tracks would be muddled. Footprints across the bridge, hoof prints leading into and out of the village. There were Kashtan's tracks too, travelling beyond the bridge right up to the river and out on the other side. If there was someone in the village now, they would see all of that evidence, but it would be confusing. My best chance was that if they chose to follow anyone, they would follow the women. Theirs would be the clearest trail.

But if someone or something *had* been tracking me in the forest as I had journeyed home, then they would not follow the women. They would follow the single horse. The man alone.

If they were hunting me, they would follow Kashtan's trail right to the clearing and beyond. It would take them a while to decipher the tracks, though. I still had time to elude them.

It was difficult to navigate through the dense forest, but it could work in our favour. Kashtan would have to be brave and move quickly, but it would be easy to leave a confused trail here, so we weaved among the trees, heading deeper, closer to the place where the crows had gathered. I could not leave until I had seen what was here. I had to know.

I heard no more evidence of anyone following. Kashtan breathed hard, but her tread was light and there was little sound to our movement. The occasional creak of the saddle or the slap of my kit against Kashtan's hide, but other than that, we were quiet, moving through the forest like a ghost from one of Marianna's stories, until the trees began to thin out once more and we came to the place of crows.

# 9

Kashtan could smell it before we came to that place. She grew more agitated the closer we rode, and she reared as soon as we broke into the small clearing and laid eyes on the victims lying about it. The sight of them seared itself into my mind.

Kashtan shook her head and rolled her eyes and tried to turn away.

Startled by our arrival, the crows cawed and flew up into the trees in a flurry of agitation and displeasure.

'All right,' I told her, as I looked away and strengthened my nerve. 'All right.'

I turned her to the right and rode further into the forest, and once we were out of sight and Kashtan grew calm, I stopped and dismounted, hitching her to a sturdy tree branch.

'I have to look at them,' I told her. 'I have to know.'

She nuzzled my chest and blew in my face, then I stepped away and stood for a moment, closing my eyes, touching the fingers of my left hand to the *chotki* round my right wrist and offering a clumsy prayer of hope. I was not much of a believer; it was not part of the new thinking. Marianna had been the one to keep the faith and perhaps that was why the *chotki* gave me some comfort. It had been round her wrist and would still bear traces of her, bringing us closer. And because she believed, then I would carry that for her, and if there was anything that could give me strength enough for this, something that might answer my prayer, then I was willing to give it a chance.

I took a deep breath and removed the rifle from my back, grasping it tight as I picked my way back towards the horror.

I was overcome with numbness as I made my return to where the bodies lay. My vision was tunnelled, so I only saw what was right before me: my path through the sleeping trees. I could no longer smell the decaying leaves at my feet, or the damp bark that surrounded me. To my ears, the forest was silent but for the pounding of my own blood as it pumped through my veins. And when I came to the massacre, that pounding faltered before gathering speed and I fought to make myself strong.

All I had to do was identify the people; to satisfy myself that my children and wife were not among them. Once that was done, I would leave.

Two men lay on the ground close to the cold remains of a small fire. They were naked, victims of the same fate as Galina's husband, except their heads were nowhere to be seen. Judging by the shape and size of their bodies, they were older men, so I passed them by and steeled myself as I approached another man, who was slumped against a tree, his face swollen and beaten beyond recognition. His hands had been flayed, and in the centre of his chest was branded a star, just as I had seen on Sasha. The swollen welt of seared flesh was pink now, but would have been angry when it was first burned. The star would have been a bold, patriotic red.

I turned away and went to another man, nailed to a tree, his head dropped so that his chin rested on his chest. He was just out of reach, so I put the barrel of my rifle under his chin and pushed up his head. Maxim Mikhailovich. In the centre of his forehead was branded a five-pointed star.

Other men were there, all of them older, and I forced myself to detach. I had to view them not as people I knew, not even as people at all, but as something else. Something less valuable. Something unimportant. Callous as it seemed, I had learned it was the only way to cope when faced with people whose skin was flayed from their hands, whose throats were cut, whose necks were punctured by bullets.

Each man had the five-pointed star branded into the skin somewhere on his naked body. I had never seen anything like it

73

and I found myself wondering if it had been done before or after death.

If it had been done to my sons.

I saw no children at all, though, no women, and that gave me a glimmer of guilty hope as I went from body to body, identifying each one, finding neither Misha nor Pavel, but many of the people I had grown up with. I told myself that my sons were still alive, and that until I knew for certain, I had to believe that Marianna was too. I refused to accept that she was drowned in the lake. So I kept on, forcing myself to look at each body, trying not to remember their names and their families, and only when I came to the last of them did the full horror of this place sink in. Now that I had satisfied myself that my family wasn't here, the evil of this place began to overcome me. It was like a malevolent spirit wrapping its arms around me and dragging me into its despair. My hands began to shake, and my breathing quickened. Only now did I realise how dry my throat was, that I had been clamping my teeth together so hard my jaw ached.

The tableau of death before me was as shocking as anything I had seen during the course of the war. I had grown all too aware of the appalling things that one person could do to another, but I had never seen such a variety of atrocity in once place. Most perpetrators of this kind of extermination tended to stick to a preferred method. There were those who flayed their victims while they were still alive. Others opted for crucifixion or hanging or a simple bullet to the back of the neck. Some liked to impale their victims or roll them naked in barrels punched through with nails. I had even heard of men and women forced to stand naked in the cold while water was poured over them, a few drops at a time, until they became ice statues frozen in death.

The one thing I believed these victims had in common was that they had been visited by the cruellest enforcers of Bolshevism: Chekists. The men tasked with bringing the populace into line by spreading fear in their campaign of Red Terror. That was the only conclusion I could come to, looking at the massacre before me. This was not the work of some supernatural being; this was the work of men.

I could only imagine why the perpetrators had brought their victims this deep into the forest. As far as I knew, this kind of thing was not usually kept hidden, but displayed for the world to see. After all, what use would there be for Red Terror if not to terrorise? Perhaps they had been brought here to maximise their fear. I would probably never know, but the end result was the same.

My chest burned as I drew shallow breaths. The sweat was cold on my brow, and my body trembled as the world fell away from me, spinning into the abyss. I backed away, shaking my head, and suddenly the forest was alive with noise. Everything darkened, my mind spun in confusion, and I moved away further, afraid to take my eyes from the carnage in case the bodies should rise against me for the things *I* had done.

I stumbled over something hidden in a tuft of grass, putting my hands out to stop myself, but there was nothing there for me to grab. I dropped my rifle as my arms wheeled in the air and I fell, collapsing into the cold grass, turning immediately, afraid to be so vulnerable. The frozen undergrowth brushed against my face as I searched on my hands and knees for my rifle.

'Where is it?' I said, over and over. 'Where is it? Where is it?'

My hands pushed against something hard and cold. I recoiled in horror at the sight of a human head lost in the foliage. I turned, desperate to find my rifle, desperate to be away from here.

When my fingers finally curled round the weapon, I pushed to my feet and began to run.

I ran and ran, stumbling and faltering, the low branches tearing at my face as I passed them. I felt the breath of the dead on the back of my neck, forcing me on, always threatening to catch me, and when I finally reached Kashtan, I fumbled with her reins and climbed onto her, panic and grief and guilt and revulsion all boiling in my veins.

I kicked her hard and drove her through the forest, not daring to look back. I bent low towards her neck, an instinct to streamline myself and avoid the branches that flashed past as she wove in and out of the trees, obeying my furious commands to run faster and faster. Her hooves pounded the hard ground, and her body moved this way and that, fluid as she twisted and turned, finding the most accessible route ahead. I kept urging her on, digging my heels hard, frantic to be away from here, anxious to be in the open and to see the light of the day.

The forest floor was treacherous, though, and when Kashtan slipped, I felt a different kind of panic. Her hooves caught on something hard, a protruding tree root or a rock, and she stumbled to one side, her flanks thumping into the trunk of a nearby tree. Her cry of pain penetrated the shock that had taken control of me. I could not survive without her. I was driving her too hard.

Kashtan's stride was uneven now, her steps faltering. I pulled back on her reins, but she felt my fear as if we were one being and she surged on through the forest. I struggled to bring her under control, speaking to her, slowing her.

'Good girl.' I stroked her neck. 'It's all right now. We're safe.' Once again I realised that when I was speaking to her, I was speaking to myself. 'We'll take it slowly now.'

I looked back, seeing the place where she had bumped the tree, then I inspected her flanks where there was a dusting of moss and bark. 'No broken skin. That's lucky.' I reached back and brushed it away. 'You'll have a bruise, though.'

But there was a difference in her step, she dipped more to one side, and I suspected straight away that she had thrown a shoe during our race through the forest. I brought her to a halt and she stood, breathing hard, her chest expanding and relaxing, the smell of sweat oozing from her well-lathered coat. I climbed down and soothed her before lifting her left front leg.

'We'll have to get it looked at. Can't go far like that.' The shoe was missing, and as well as there being a stone lodged in her hoof, a small chunk was missing on the outer edge of the wall. If the damage worsened, it could lead to serious bruising and even lameness.

I placed her foot on the ground and looked back into the forest, turning about, searching for any signs of followers. I had that inkling once again, that something was closing in on me, and that whatever it was, I would never outrun it.

'I'll do what I can,' I said, still watching, 'but it'll have to be quick.'

From one of the rear saddlebags I took a hoof pick and checked each of Kashtan's hooves in turn, removing any stones and clearing the dirt from around the frog. I should have done it before I had saddled her, as well as checking her shoes, but I had been in too much of a hurry.

As I worked, I felt a constant unease, as if I were being watched.

I untied the roll of blankets from home and cut a square large enough to put round Kashtan's damaged hoof. I secured it with a short piece of twine round her fetlock before cutting another square, this time from the small tarpaulin that acted as my rain cover when sleeping outdoors. This, too, I tied round her hoof.

'It should do for now,' I said, hoping it would prevent any further damage.

When that was done, I rested for a few minutes, sitting on the tarpaulin and leaning back against a tree, trying not to think about what I had left behind in the forest. Kashtan stood close and I watched her for any sign that her hoof was bothering her.

'I don't know where we are,' I said to her.

Just as Babushka had told us, so Marianna had told our boys that the woodland spirits would try to lead them astray in the forest by covering their tracks so they couldn't follow them home, or by calling to them, enticing them deeper into the trees, always at the edge of their vision, always tricking. I hadn't needed the *leshii* to confuse me – I'd had my own demons to do that – but I couldn't help looking around. Alone, it was easy to imagine that something malevolent was waiting out there, hiding just out of view.

I struggled not to think about such things. There were no *rusalkas*. No vengeful spirits of the dead surrounded me, preparing to descend on me from the darkness. I was alone with Kashtan. Nothing else was here.

And yet the disquiet would not leave me.

'We need to move,' I said to her, fishing a small compass from my satchel and tapping the dirty glass cover. 'Need to get away from here.' I held it out to the light so I could read it better and shook my head. 'We're heading in the wrong direction.' I looked over my shoulder, then put the compass away, touching the tobacco pouch in my satchel and wishing I had enough for a cigarette. It would have helped to calm my nerves, but the half-smoked stub from Tanya lay forgotten in my pocket.

'What now, though?' I had intended to further investigate the forest beyond the lake before returning to follow the treeline close to the road the women had taken, but hearing horses in the village had put a stop to that. I wouldn't be able to return to the road yet.

'We'll go north,' I said to Kashtan. 'That's where they said they were headed, so we'll keep going that way until we're out of the forest. Then we'll think again. Maybe even look for the road.' I tried to sound hopeful. 'Perhaps find Tanya and Lyudmila. God knows I could use the company.' And they had been following Koschei for some time. We could work together to find him.

'They weren't there,' I said. 'My boys. They weren't there. I'm sure of that.' I stood and put my face against Kashtan's. 'That means they might still be alive. Maybe even Marianna too.'

*He likes to drown the women.*

No. I couldn't let myself believe that.

'You think they're out here somewhere on their own? That they got away?' I turned and looked behind me. 'Maybe we *should* double-back. Lay a false trail and . . . They might be hiding in the forest right now. Or they might have gone home to wait and . . .' The possibilities tore at my resolve and I wished I could split myself and go in different directions, but I could make only one

78

choice, so I *had* to assume Koschei had them. It was the most likely of all the alternatives that tumbled through my mind, and I made myself concentrate on why I believed that.

Koschei had visited the village a week ago, maybe a little longer, according to Galina in one of her rare moments of lucidity. If Marianna and the boys *had* managed to escape, I was sure they would have returned home by now, but I had seen no sign of recent activity there. Nor had I found their bodies – not of any of the women or children – and I couldn't afford to run blind through the forest searching for them while Koschei moved further and further from me. Returning would waste precious time and increase the possibility of coming face to face with whoever might be following me.

Pursuing Koschei was my only choice.

'God, I hope they took prisoners. You think they took prisoners?' I touched the *chotki* on my wrist.

Please let them have taken prisoners.

I stood back and looked at Kashtan, my only friend. 'I'm sorry I scared you. You ready to go now? You ready to help me find them?'

Kashtan snorted, bowing her head up and down as if she had understood me.

She looked fine, so I rolled the blankets and tarpaulin, securing them behind the saddle, then climbed onto her back, but it wasn't long before she began to favour her right foot, her head bobbing down each time she put pressure on the left.

My own weight was adding to her pain, so I climbed down and led her through the forest, checking the compass every now and then to make sure we were headed the right way.

We turned this way and that, never moving in a straight line, stopping from time to time to cover any tracks we had left. If anyone *had* found our trail in Belev and was following us, it would be difficult for them to hunt us in here, and there would be breaks in our trail, places where we seemed to simply disappear. Our erratic journey through the trees would make it almost impossible to pick up the trail once more. Travelling like that took longer and was more tiring, but if it threw potential hunters off our tracks, it would be worth it.

I was of no use to Marianna and the boys if I were dead.

# 10

Passing from the gloom into the dull evening light after hours in the forest was like emerging from the underworld. Leaving that darkness was a blessing and the relief was tangible. The air tasted fresher, the expansive sky spread above, and the steppe stretched out before me, a vast sea of frosted grass and thistle and dandelion, scattered with lonely islands of hawthorn and oak. There was cover to be found among the trees behind me, but right now it felt safer to be in the open. In there, anyone following was invisible, and there was a constant sensation of being watched, of being pursued. On the steppe, nothing could hide.

Out here, I could kill my enemies; in there, they were just wisps of imagination.

I estimated there was still an hour or so of daylight left, so we pressed on.

I led Kashtan across the steppe, moving north towards a cluster of trees and elderberry shrubs, and we walked for half an hour before the distant copse began to take shape. A small collection of barren oak and maple, their naked branches laden with the dark and tangled balls of crows' nests. Seeing the first sign of a rooftop just to the east of them, I stopped and took the binoculars from my saddlebag.

'Let's see what we have,' I spoke aloud, as I put the cold lenses to my eyes and scanned west to east.

The isolated farm was still too far away to see much, but there were at least two buildings: a small, one-roomed farmhouse, not much more than a hovel, and what looked like a barn. In front of them, a field with the late crop rows of alternating green and brown.

'There might be tools,' I said to Kashtan. 'A new shoe. Somewhere for you to rest. We'll have to get closer.' I lowered the binoculars and narrowed my eyes against the cold. 'See if anyone's there.'

It was a risk to venture close to anywhere occupied. There was no certainty of finding sympathy from anyone. If the farm was occupied, we were as likely to be run off by angry, frightened peasants as we were to be welcomed, but we had no choice. Kashtan needed help. We both needed to rest.

We carried on as the light faded and the temperature dropped. As night approached, so the wind picked up, moaning as it wheeled across the steppe, a lilting tone, deep and mournful.

I wrapped my scarf tight and walked with my head down to cut through it, stopping from time to time to watch the farm.

Coming closer, I saw the smoke from one of the buildings, caught in the wind and almost horizontal as it streamed from the chimney, but there was no other sign the place was occupied. No horses, no activity, and we continued until I could smell the faint odour of burning wood in the breeze.

The wind was a constant nuisance, as if its intention was to hinder us, and the long, frosty grass was difficult to tread, so our progress was slow, and the closer we came to the farm, the more eager I was to find a warm welcome. But as we reached the edge of the field, scattering a flock of scavenging crows into the air with a raucous cry, I stopped and checked my revolver. I tested the action on my rifle and unfastened two coat buttons so I would be able to slip my hand inside and reach for the knife on my belt if necessary.

If the reception we received was hostile, I was more than ready to meet it.

When I was satisfied my weapons were good, I raised the binoculars to scan the buildings once more, this time seeing a single figure emerge from the house.

The man crossed the yard towards the barn and was almost

there when the door to the farmhouse opened again and a second figure, a child, came running out to join him. The child was followed by a dog, which stopped on the threshold and looked towards me. Black-haired and long-legged, it looked almost like a wolf, and when the man turned to look at the boy, he noticed the dog, then followed the direction of its attention, catching sight of Kashtan and me on the other side of the field. He froze for a second before reaching out and pulling the boy close. I held the two of them in the magnified lenses of the binoculars and studied them, wishing I could see them better.

They looked to be peasants, farmers, not soldiers, but it was impossible to be sure. Without my rifle and my pistol, my own clothes would belie what I really was, just as theirs might be doing right now. Regardless of that, they had seen us and I had a decision to make. The man could be unfriendly, and he and the boy might not be alone.

I lowered the binoculars and looked at Kashtan's foot. 'Or maybe he can help,' I said, and knew I had to go on. I would deal with whatever situation presented itself.

If I had to kill them, that's what I would do.

At the farm, the dog had left the threshold and run across the yard. It didn't bark and circle its tail as a dog would usually do, but stood still and watched us as the man and the boy returned to the house, disappearing inside and closing the door.

I strained my eyes to see them as we walked, and when we came to the edge of the field, I took off my gloves to free my hands for swift action. I inspected the farm once more with the lenses, then forged on, hoping for the best but prepared for the worst.

The crows alighted in the field behind us as I led Kashtan towards the buildings that nestled by the desolate trees, picking our way along the furrows between the rows of turnips that grew as large as two of my fists, the swollen white roots bulging from the soil.

The dog continued to watch and I could feel Kashtan's nervousness, but the beast didn't venture beyond the yard, and I spoke encouraging words into Kashtan's ear.

We slowed down as we came closer, and the man emerged from the house to stand in the same place as before, at the front of his yard, just behind a fence that I hadn't seen from further away. He was like a statue, feet apart and holding a weapon in both hands. The dog came to sit close to him, but not right beside him. It was as if they were not together. Neither master and dog nor friends, but separate.

When we arrived at the fence, the dog stood, and although there was no overt display of aggression, it was alert to danger, its ears pricked and its body tensed. Close to, it still looked wolf-like with its long legs and large paws. It had a narrow snout, and the fur was thick round its neck, but it was not as black as it had seemed from a distance. There were flecks of brindle in its coat and the first hint of grey around its muzzle. There was a promise of wildness about the animal and its presence made Kashtan uneasy.

The man shifted the shotgun but didn't pull it to his shoulder in a show of hostility. Instead he held it at waist height in front of him, the barrel pointing just to one side of us. He was scared and he wanted me to think him dangerous, but at the same time, he didn't want to provoke a fight.

'Good evening,' I said, glancing at the weapon, then studying the man's eyes instead.

They were hazelnut brown, pale and watery from the cold. Narrowed in suspicion but nervous, as if he wasn't sure whether to look me in the eye or watch my hands. His features were soft, not the rugged complexion of a farmer who had seen many harvests, but I guessed he was similar in age to me, no more than late thirties. He wore a cap and was bearded like a Cossack, the hair wild about his chin and neck, black as the devil but gunpowder grey around the edges. His coat was knee length, belted at the waist, dirty and flecked with pieces of straw. His boots were in poor shape, repaired and patched and bound to his feet with twine.

'Is this your place?' I asked, glancing at the dog.

He nodded once and I wondered how he must see me, a

stranger riding out of the steppe, no uniform, no insignia, but armed and leading a horse. I must have looked as wild to him as he did to me. I was dirty from days of living rough, and the last shave I'd had was from a company barber. Now my beard was thickening and growing untidy.

'Good crop,' I said, making conversation, settling him. 'Must have been ready to harvest a few weeks ago.'

'Your horse?' He looked at Kashtan.

I nodded.

'Did you steal her?'

I shrugged. 'It's quiet here. It must get lonely.'

He reaffirmed his grip on the shotgun and hefted it as if it were growing heavier. 'Are you asking if I'm alone or if I've seen anyone passing?'

I shrugged again. 'Both. Who's the boy?'

'No one.' The man shifted his feet and tilted his chin at Kashtan. 'What happened to her foot?'

'She threw a shoe and chipped her hoof.' I glanced across at the barn. 'You have tools I can use?'

'You know how?'

'I know a bit,' I said. 'Do you?'

He followed my gaze and lowered the shotgun a little. 'Maybe.'

I had the impression that he didn't intend to use the weapon unless he felt I was a threat. His intention was only a protective one. His land. His boy. Perhaps a wife hiding in fear in the warmth of the farmhouse. He was a danger to me if he thought I aimed to harm them, and my instinct was to eliminate that threat right away, but I thought about Marianna and the boys, how they must have felt when Koschei came, and I felt sympathy for this man. He was only doing his duty to those he loved, and I was in a far better position to understand that now. In the past, I had overlooked the humanity of that, seeing only revolutionaries and counter-revolutionaries. I had been so deep in the war, I had closed my eyes to anything else, and it had taken something wicked to prise them open and make me see more clearly.

'I don't want any trouble,' I said, holding out my hands. 'I only

85

want to fix my horse and be on my way. I'm not here for your animals or anything else you might have in there.'

'What else would I have in here?'

'I saw the boy. I know he's in the house.'

The shotgun barrel rose a touch as the man's fingers tightened. 'You stay away from—'

'I have sons,' I said. 'Children of my own. I don't mean any harm, I swear it.'

The man thought about that, watching my eyes for any sign of deceit. He said nothing for a long while, then breathed in and relaxed a little. 'You've done a good job on that foot,' he said. 'Good binding.'

The dog sat now, but its attention was still on us.

'It's not enough,' I said. 'I have a long way to go.'

'How far?'

I shook my head and something like a smile appeared on his lips.

'It's like a game,' he said. 'Answer a question with a question. Don't give anything away. What happened to the days when one man could pass the time of day with another without the threat of . . . ?' He tipped his head at the rifle, hanging muzzle down over my shoulder.

'I mean you no harm,' I told him.

'Nor I you.'

'And yet here we are,' I said, 'at an impasse. You have *your* weapon, remember.'

'Impasse. Such a simple word with a complicated meaning.' He sighed and shook his head as if he despaired at the sorry state in which our world had found itself. 'Are you a religious man?'

'What?'

'The *chotki* on your wrist.'

My hands were slightly raised, the sleeves of my coat pulled down to reveal the lambswool prayer rope. 'My wife's,' I said.

'She's not with you?'

'No.'

The man nodded as if he knew what I was saying. 'Let me

offer an olive branch.' He lowered the shotgun a touch further and nodded at Kashtan. 'I can fix her for you,' he said. 'The horse. And there's some oats in the barn. Not much, but enough. For one rouble she'll be as good as new and you can be on your way.'

I glanced up at the grey sky and wondered if it might snow tonight. The frost, at least, would be heavy and deep. I wanted to push on, to gain some ground after having lost so much in the forest, but I was exhausted and so was Kashtan. The father and husband in me wanted to move on regardless, but the soldier told me that a night of rest would serve me well. Tomorrow, I would move faster and make up for lost time.

'What about a hot meal?' I asked. 'I'll pay you three for that and to sleep in the barn tonight.'

He took a deep breath and puffed his cheeks as he blew out. 'I don't know . . .'

'I've been travelling a long time. I'm hungry. Cold. Please.'

The man stared at me, thinking it over. 'We'll fix the horse first,' he said. 'Then we'll see.'

'All right,' I said, stepping closer to the fence and putting out my hand. 'My name is Kolya.'

The man looked at my hand as if he didn't know what to do. To not take it would be an insult, but the alternative would bring him close to me.

I waited for him to make up his mind, standing with my arm stretched across the fence until he finally stepped forward and took it, shaking once and saying, 'Lev.' It was in that moment of friendship and peace, when he had lowered his guard, that I could have killed him.

It would have been the easiest thing in the world for me to pull him towards me, slip the revolver from my pocket and shoot him dead, or take the knife from inside my coat and put the steel in him. Instead I looked him in the eye and felt the warmth of his hand and the hesitant offer of friendship.

Then we broke away and he stepped back.

'Stay there,' he said.

He backed off to the *izba*, eyes still on me, only stopping when he reached the front door. He knocked once and the door eased open, just a crack.

I moved my hands towards my coat pocket, seeking the reassurance of my pistol, anticipating danger. I almost expected soldiers to burst from the house, but all I saw was a glimpse of Lev's son at the opening.

They spoke for a second, then the door shut and I heard bolts being drawn across. Lev returned, standing on the other side of the fence as if he was reconsidering his offer.

'Please,' I said. 'My horse will go lame without help. I mean no harm. I swear it.'

'On the lives of your children?' he asked. 'Devil take you?'

It was a serious request, especially considering I didn't know where Misha and Pavel were, but I *really* didn't mean this man and his son any harm.

'On their lives,' I said, letting him see how solemn this vow was. 'Devil take me.'

Lev nodded and swung the gate open, stepping back, gesturing towards the barn. 'Come,' he said.

'And the dog?'

'I don't think he'll hurt you.'

I stepped towards the animal, holding out my hand, and he came forward to take my scent. He was just over knee height on me, solid-looking, but his stomach was becoming hollow and his ribs were beginning to show through his coat. He showed me no more aggression, allowing me to run my hand over his head and rub one of his ears in my fingers.

Satisfied the dog was comfortable with me, I led Kashtan through the gate towards the closed door of the barn. She had known dogs in her time but seemed a little nervous of this one. If he came too close, he might frighten her, so I kept her head forward and away from the animal.

Lev might have shaken my hand, but he wasn't naive enough to trust me. He walked behind us, shotgun in hand, exactly as I would have done in his position. The nape of my neck tingled with anticipation and I told myself to relax. I was accustomed to dealing with threat, rather than deferring to it, but I needed Kashtan to stay calm. If she detected my anxiety, it would heighten her own. I also understood Lev's need to protect what was his.

'Open it,' he said.

I stopped, slipping a hand into my pocket and curling my fingers round my revolver. I had no idea what was in that barn. It might be filled with soldiers waiting to hang me from the nearest tree or flay the skin from my back.

'Something wrong?' he asked.

I looked up at Kashtan to see if she showed any sign of fear. She was a good judge of a situation and she communicated her feelings with a turn of her ears or a swish of her tail, but she seemed more relaxed than she had been for a while and I took it as a good sign.

'Nothing,' I said. 'It's been a long ride.' I took my hand from my pocket and gripped the door handle, taking a deep breath and pulling it wide.

It took a moment for my eyes to adjust to the darkness inside the barn, but Kashtan showed no hesitation. She pushed past me and went in where it was warm and there was a heavy smell of horses. When I followed, I looked about, seeing armatures on the near wall, one of which had a saddle on it and others that held assorted tack – halters, bridles, stirrups – some of which looked old and unusable. There was a door in the rear wall of the barn, bolted shut from the inside, and close to it, a second horse grazed on hay piled in the corner. Another mare, taller than Kashtan, almost black and with white socks on her front feet. She hardly even looked up at us, just a quick glance that displayed the white blaze on her nose.

'She's beautiful,' I said.

'Light that.' Lev pointed to a lamp hanging from a nail in one of the barn's supports, then pushed past and went to Kashtan.

I closed the door, shutting out the bleak landscape I had travelled through that day, and put a match to the wick. A warm glow filled the area about us, contrasting with the harsh greys and blacks that had filled my day. It was the most comfort I had felt since the fire last night, and I allowed myself a moment to enjoy the relative safety, hidden from the dangers outside.

Lev told me to stay there. 'Where I can see you,' he said.

The big dog lay down close to me, his head up and his tongue lolling from one side of his mouth.

Lev turned Kashtan so she was between us, protecting him from anything I might do, then he placed his shotgun within easy reach and lifted her foot to remove the binding. He had made an attempt to shield himself using my horse, but he was not accustomed to situations like this. If our roles were reversed, I would have remained armed while I told the other man to remove the binding. Lev was not a soldier, I was sure of that, but neither did he have the complexion of a farmer. And that suggested he didn't belong here any more than I did.

He looked over at me time and again as he worked, afraid to take his eyes off me as he inspected the damage to Kashtan's hoof. He never once turned his back on me, always kept Kashtan between us, and whenever he moved, he brought the shotgun with him, keeping it close to hand at all times. He was a sensible man. Though I had extended a hand of friendship, he was still wary of the dangers I might present, and his fear made me nervous. I wondered what small act it would take for me to make him feel he needed to use that weapon. Perhaps just a movement in the wrong direction.

'I'd be happier if you put the shotgun away,' I said. 'You don't need it.'

'I'll keep it with me for now.' He paused, watching me. 'You have your rifle.'

'I don't need it.' I shrugged it off my shoulder, making him lift the shotgun. 'I'm just putting it down,' I said, holding it out in front of me with one hand and placing it on the floor before step-ping away from it. 'There. It's down.'

The dog came to see what I had put on the floor, sniffing it before going back to lie in the straw, this time putting his head on his paws as if bored by what was happening in the barn. Kashtan watched the animal, but was less bothered than before. She saw that I was not afraid of him and that bolstered her confidence.

Lev lowered the shotgun and took a deep breath. 'This hoof's not too bad. I can fix this.'

'And shoe her?'

'Of course.'

'While holding a shotgun?'

Lev said nothing.

'I'm sorry. Look, I really don't mean any harm.' I turned to one side so he couldn't see as I took a fold of money from my coat pocket, counting off three roubles before tucking the rest away and holding the notes out to him. 'For the work, some oats for my horse . . . and for a meal and a bed.'

'We'll talk about that later.'

'Whatever you say.'

'Put it on the table.' He tipped his head towards the side of the barn where a sturdy wooden table was laid with an assortment of tools. There were others hanging on the wall, resting on well-placed nails, and there were ropes and pieces of leather and a heavy black anvil to one side of the table, beside a wooden crate filled with loose horseshoes.

'You're a blacksmith?' I asked, laying the notes beside a set of iron tongs. But his hands were not blacksmith's hands.

'Something like that. And you? A soldier?'

'Something like that,' I echoed his own words, and backed away from the table.

When he had finished checking Kashtan, he came over to take the notes, stuffing them into his pocket before examining the tools, standing sideways so he could watch me. He kept the shotgun in one hand as he hunted for the right implements, looking up at those on the wall, then returning his attention to the ones in front of him, moving some of them about and half bending to look under the table.

'Lost something?' I asked.

'Hmm?'

'Have you lost something?'

He shook his head in dismissal, distracted by his search. I thought it strange that he couldn't find what he was looking for. When Papa used to take Alek and me to the blacksmith in Dolinsk, I spent my time studying the neat rows of clean tools. Every implement was returned to the place from which it had been taken as soon as it had been used. And in the army, the company blacksmith was almost obsessive about his tools. In the same way that soldiers kept their weapons clean, so blacksmiths took care of their implements. They were their livelihood. As I watched Lev searching, I thought about the turnip field outside, the vegetables swollen and past harvesting, and something occurred to me that I hadn't thought of before.

'This isn't your barn, is it?' I asked.

Lev stopped.

'It doesn't matter,' I said. 'It's not my business. All I want is to fix my horse.'

He started to straighten now, bringing the shotgun up as he did, the barrel rising in my direction. 'Who *are* you?'

The intonation of his voice made the dog sit upright.

'You really don't need that,' I said, taking a step towards him and putting my hands out to the side. 'I'd feel much better if you put it down.'

His eyes followed the movement of my hands and I seized the opportunity to act while he was distracted. I took just one more step, turning to the side so that if he fired, it would miss me, and I grabbed the barrel of his weapon in both hands, pulling hard with a sudden jerk. The force of it, combined with his awkward positioning, unbalanced him and dragged him forwards. I snatched the weapon from his grasp and let him fall to the floor, where he scrambled in the straw to turn onto his back and look up at me. With the suddenness of the movement, the dog sprang to his feet. I turned the shotgun on him, but he did not rush to Lev's aid. He stood and growled, lowering his head and raising his shoulders, but made no attempt to attack me or protect Lev. The dog's reaction seemed more to warn me away from himself, and the impression I had was that the creature did not belong to Lev.

'Don't kill me.' Lev raised his hands and shrank back.

'I don't want to kill you,' I told him, sharing my attention between him and the dog. 'I want you to help me.'

Lev opened his mouth but said nothing.

'So you don't need this.' I broke the shotgun open, picked out the cartridges and put them in my pocket before laying the weapon on the table and stepping away. 'I told you,' I said, holding out a hand to help him up, 'I just want to fix my horse and have something to eat. Sleep somewhere warm for a change.'

Lev propped himself up on his elbows and looked at my outstretched hand. 'Fine.' He reached out to take it. 'Fine.'

'Leave him alone.' A childish voice spoke to my right and I turned to see that the door was open and Lev's son was standing just inside with his back to the last of the light. He was holding an axe over his shoulder as if about to take a swing. 'Get away from him.'

'I'm just helping him up,' I said, taking Lev's weight and pulling.

The child cocked the axe back a little further and stepped into the barn and I saw that he was not Lev's son at all. Dressed in trousers and a quilted jacket, and with a boyish frame, it was no wonder I had mistaken this child for a boy, but when she came closer, I saw her for what she was: a frightened but determined girl. Her dark hair fell in a messy plait from beneath the back of her cap. Her skin was pale and smooth, her cheeks reddened by the cold. Her features were fine, but she had tightened her face into a hard look of aggression.

'Put it down, Anna.'

The girl hesitated with the axe held high, looking first at her father then at me.

'It's all right,' Lev said, crossing to her and taking hold of the

93

axe, setting it against the wall. 'Kolya is our friend.' He glanced at me. 'Isn't that right?'

'Yes.' I went to the door and looked out, scanning the horizon, then closing it to keep the warmth inside. 'That's right.'

# 11

Lev was nervous, his hands shaking as he gathered the tools he needed, and there was sweat on his brow despite the cold. As soon as he started working on Kashtan, though, he began to relax. He lifted her leg between his knees and cleared the hoof before rasping it and clipping away any loose pieces that might catch and tear.

Anna stayed close to him, her dark eyes watching me with suspicion. She was probably no more than twelve years old, but she had a hard expression, like someone who had seen too much of life, and she stood still, passing a hoof knife from one hand to the other, moving only when Lev asked her to fetch or hold something for him.

The dog lay with his chin between his paws, his eyebrows twitching as he watched us. He behaved as if he had no particular bond to any of us and was only interested in protecting himself but, for some reason, preferred to be in our company. He wasn't the only one who didn't want to be alone.

'You look like you know what you're doing,' I said to Lev.

'I've done it before,' he replied without looking up.

'But you're not a blacksmith.'

'No,' he said. 'Not here.' He passed the nippers to Anna and ran his hardened fingers round the edge of Kashtan's hoof. 'The damage isn't too bad. Maybe a little bruising, but with a bit of tidying up and a new shoe, she'll be fine.'

He put down Kashtan's foot and went to the box of shoes beside the table, glancing at the shotgun as he passed it. Anna

95

followed close behind him, taking her eyes off me only to check she wasn't going to bump into something.

'If not here, then where?' I asked, going to the door and opening it just enough to look out. The dog followed my movements as I watched the horizon, but for now everything looked clear.

'Different places. Nowhere.' He took a number of shoes and went back to Kashtan, testing for a good fit.

'No one is from anywhere now,' I said. 'No one is anybody.' I closed the door and watched him return to the anvil to hammer the chosen shoe for a better fit. 'No one wants to *be* anyone in case it gets them into trouble.' The chime of the hammer reminded me of being with the other men of my unit, drinking and talking while the blacksmith prepared the horses for moving on.

'Is that what you are?' he asked, placing the shoe on Kashtan's hoof and checking the fit, feeling for unevenness. 'No one?'

'Exactly.'

Satisfied it was right, he gestured for Anna to put out her hand. She stuffed the hoof knife into her pocket, and Lev placed a number of nails on her outstretched palm, then began to fit the shoe, hammering the first nail into place.

'You look like a soldier to me,' Anna said, closing her fist round the nails. 'Is that what you are?'

'Sh.' Lev shook his head and spoke to her in a quiet tone. 'Don't ask questions.'

'He looks like a soldier,' she said under her breath. Then, 'You look like a soldier.' Staring at me. Defiant.

'Do I?'

'You have a gun.'

'Anna.' Lev cast her a sideways glance. 'Angel, don't—'

'It's all right,' I told him, then turned to his daughter. 'Lots of people have guns. *Too many* people. Your father has a gun.'

'For shooting pheasants,' she said. 'And crows on the crops.'

'But not these crops, eh?' I said. 'Because these ones are not yours.'

Anna shrugged. 'They are now. No one else wants them. No one else was here apart from—'

'We found it empty,' Lev said, glancing up at his daughter, and I saw a connection between them as if they could communicate their thoughts to one another with just a look. 'It was a good place to stay.'

I watched them, wondering what they were hiding from me, what they had done. Something Lev wasn't proud of, from the look of him. 'Empty, eh? Lucky for you,' I said. 'Maybe not so lucky for whoever lived here before.'

Lev nodded and tapped his daughter's hand so she opened it for him to take another nail.

'Are you a deserter?' Anna asked.

'What do you know about deserters?'

'Nothing,' Lev replied for her, and another look passed between them. This was one of warning, though – I could see that right away. She was outspoken and he didn't want it to bring them trouble. 'We don't know anything about anything.'

'It's the safest way,' I agreed, smiling at Anna to reassure her I meant no harm. I opened the door a touch and looked out again. It was almost dark now and the distant trees were little more than a dark smudge on the horizon.

'I know they get shot,' she said. 'Or hanged.'

'Anna.' Lev shook his head at her as he tapped her hand harder than necessary and took another nail.

'We saw someone hanged,' she said, ignoring him.

'Where?' I asked, pushing the door shut and turning to face them.

'A farm we passed.'

'Just one person?'

She shook her head. 'Two. And they had stars right here.' She tapped her own forehead, right in the centre. 'We even saw—'

'That's enough,' Lev told her.

'No, that's not enough,' I said, raising my voice, making both Lev and the dog look up in surprise. 'Did you say "stars"? Here?' I

97

stepped closer to her and touched my forehead just like Anna had done.

The girl's whole body tensed and she backed away from me, moving nearer to her father.

'Did you say "stars"?' I repeated, taking another step.

'Yes,' Lev said, dropping Kashtan's hoof and moving in front of his daughter. He held the driving hammer tight in his right hand. 'You're frightening her.'

'Like they were branded?'

'What?'

'Did it look like they had been branded? Burned? The hanged—'

'Yes,' he said. 'I suppose so, yes.'

I made a calming gesture with my hands and tried to relax. I took a deep breath and nodded. 'All right. Good. I'm sorry, Anna. Sorry if I scared you.' I took a step back and spoke to the girl. 'I'm sorry, but it's important you and your papa tell me everything you saw.' I tried to keep my voice even and looked at Lev. 'Please. When was it?'

'It was days ago.' Lev put out his left hand to bring Anna further behind him. 'I don't know where it was, what the place was called.'

Lev's chest rose and fell, his body having begun to prepare itself for defence. His brow glistened with sweat, and his eyes were wide, reflecting the lamplight, his fist tight round the driving hammer. When he spoke, saying, 'South,' his tongue clicked in a dry mouth.

'Carry on working,' I said, thinking it might help him to relax, give him something else to concentrate on. 'Tell me when you're ready, but I need to know.'

I moved to stand beside the door, giving him plenty of space, showing him I meant no harm, and he watched me for a long while before he crouched and put his arms around Anna. He whispered something in her ear and she nodded and hugged him in return, all the while keeping her eyes on me. When they broke apart, she stepped back and Lev picked up Kashtan's hoof once more, gripping it between his knees as he returned to work.

He took nails from Anna, one by one, hammering the shoe in place then he nipped away the nail ends that protruded.

'We'd been travelling a while,' he said after some time. 'We saw a farm much like this one but closer to the road.' He took a rasp and filed the nail ends flat as he spoke. 'There were men there. With horses.'

'Soldiers?'

'We weren't close, but . . . probably.'

'Chekists?'

'Maybe.'

'You didn't see their faces?' I wondered if it was the same men who had been in Belev. The branding was the same – the red star. I had never seen it before, never heard of anyone doing such a thing, so I was sure it was the same man. Perhaps Lev and Anna had seen Koschei.

He shook his head.

It had been too much to hope for. 'How many were there?'

'I don't remember. Maybe as many as ten.'

'What were they doing?'

'Leaving. They were mounting up when we saw them, so we let them ride away. We thought . . .' He rasped around Kashtan's hoof, smoothing the edges to match the shoe. 'We thought we might find something to eat there. That they might have left something.'

'Did they have anyone with them?' Having not found any women or children in the forest, I was hoping that he had taken them with him. Tanya said Koschei liked to drown the women, but I had to believe there was a chance for Marianna, and when villages were attacked in the way Belev had been, people were often taken away.

'You mean prisoners?' Lev asked.

'Yes.'

Boys of any age could be indoctrinated and taught to fight, or they could be sent to labour camps to work. Women and girls

99

were also forced to work and fight, but men at war had other uses for them. I could only hope my family had been taken for labour. If that were the case, I could still find them. I could still bring them home.

Lev shook his head, saying, 'No. Nothing like that,' and a little of my hope fell away. Maybe Koschei took no prisoners. I tried not to believe that Tanya was right, that Marianna was at the bottom of the lake, and I began to regret my flight from the woods. Koschei had taken the men into the trees beyond the village to torture and execute them. Perhaps he had done the same to the boys. I should have searched further, hunted deeper, and I despaired at the thought of my boys lying out there in the decaying leaves on the floor of the dying forest. I looked to the door, seeing through it and beyond to the forest, considering whether or not I should go back, but Koschei was ahead of me and I was growing certain that there were men following me. I had covered my tracks, but I had to consider that it might not have been enough.

There was no point going back to look for the dead. I had to go on, look for the living, and cling to the smallest hope.

'How long ago was this?' I asked.

'I don't know. A week maybe. There was nothing at the farm for us, and when I saw them hanging, we moved on.' He returned to his work. 'We've seen some strange things. One village was empty. No one there at all. After that, we kept away from the villages and towns. Until we found this place.'

'Belev?' I said.

'Hmm?'

'Was the village called Belev? The empty one?'

'I don't know. Is it important? Is it where you're from?' he asked.

I shook my head. 'Somewhere I passed through. Did you see the bodies before or after the deserted village?'

'Before.'

So perhaps Koschei didn't take prisoners until Belev. It was possible, and I was willing to cling to any hope.

'Are you all right?' Lev asked.

'Hmm?'

'You look . . .' He didn't finish, and when I turned to look at him, our eyes met.

'Have you heard of Koschei?' I asked.

He was confused. 'The Deathless? It's a story, isn't it? Wasn't he in a place called Buyan? The island of Buyan, or . . . No, that's where his soul was . . . Why d'you—'

'But you haven't heard of a man by that name?'

'A man?' Lev paused as he watched me and a long silence passed before he broke the spell and said, 'No.' He ran the rasp once more round Kashtan's hoof, then set it down. 'Good as new. Have a look.'

I went forward to inspect it, nodding at the cleanness of his work. 'It's good,' I said in a flat tone. 'The best I've seen in a long time. Thank you.'

'I'll do the others if you want.' He looked at me. 'And thank *you*.'

'For what?'

'For not killing me,' he said.

And his words confirmed for me what a terrible country this had become, where a man thanked another for letting him live.

# 12

With Kashtan reshod, Anna put half a bucket of oats into a raised wooden trough for each horse and we closed the barn, leaving them stabled for the night. Lev led the way back to the house, Anna sticking close by him, the dog running ahead in expectation. Anna held the lamp from the barn to light the way.

'Turn it off,' I told her. 'We can see well enough until we get inside.'

She waited for her father to nod in agreement, then did as I asked, saying nothing as she stepped up and pushed open the door. The dog slinked in first, eager to be in the warmth. Once Anna and her father were inside, I stood on the threshold and looked out at the night. Towards the brooding forest, there was nothing to see but darkness, but above us, the sky was so cold and clear it glittered with countless stars.

'We'll cover the windows,' I said, '*then* we'll light the lamp.'

'Is someone following you?' Lev asked.

'Hmm?'

'In the barn, you kept looking out. And again now. Are you expecting someone?'

I didn't reply. I just stepped in and closed the door.

The farmhouse was small, with bare wooden walls and a modest *pich* at the far end. To the right of it, primitive wooden platforms, one above the other, provided sleeping berths, each one scattered with straw for comfort. To the left, the *krasny ugol* – the beautiful corner – had been arranged with a collection of modest icons and a small wooden cross. This was a traditional way for peasants to show their faith, but most had removed their icons for fear of being reported to the authorities. Religion was not part of the new way, and Chekists were already rounding up the priests. Bolshevism was the new religion, with Lenin as its god and the persecution of counter-revolutionaries as its ceremony.

There was a dilapidated table in the centre of the room, and benches fixed around the walls. A cabinet was the only other piece of furniture, an old *garmoshka* lying on top of it, the decorative paint faded and chipped. Seeing the instrument brought a mixture of sadness and warmth as I pictured my brother playing it and remembered his insistence that Irina had loved him for his music.

The *pich* was topped with a chimney, which poked through a hole cut in the thatched roof, but the interior of the *izba* still carried a smoky smell, as if the place had been cured with years of burning straw and wood and dung. Despite the heavy odour, there was a homely feel to the place. It was warm and dry, and I was blessed with being out of the forest at least for one night. Looking at Lev and Anna, I knew I would be glad for the company. Though Lev might have been hiding something, I didn't think he was dangerous. He struck me as a good man, and his daughter was spirited and strong. Being with them here in the warmth reminded me of being with my own family.

As soon as he was inside, Lev bowed once to the *krasny ugol* and made the sign of the cross over his body with his right hand.

'You think He sees you?' I asked, propping Lev's shotgun by the door.

Lev looked over his shoulder and shrugged. 'What does it hurt?'

I smiled and followed his lead, thinking that if God was looking down on us, it wouldn't hurt to have Him on my side, but the irony wasn't lost on me. I had tied the *chotki* round my wrist, I carried the family icon in my satchel, and now I was crossing myself at the *krasny ugol* and thought I might have even whispered a prayer when I was stumbling about in the forest. Yet I was a revolutionary and I had done unspeakable things in the name of strengthening the crop.

*My* belief had been that to make the motherland stronger, it was vital to remove the disease that threatened to decay the new vision. I wasn't supposed to believe in God. God was *part* of the disease, one of the things that stopped the common man from being free from his restraints. And yet here I was, carrying Him in my pocket and round my wrist, finding comfort in His totems while I had purged myself of all the symbols of the revolution. There wasn't a red star anywhere about my person and I didn't feel the worse for it. And right there, in front of the *krasny ugol*, my changing beliefs were only reinforced. It wasn't God who had taken my children. He hadn't tortured those people in the forest. Men had done that. And I was certain those men would have been wearing red stars on their caps.

There were no blankets in the *izba*, no sheets or cloth of any kind, so I unrolled my blankets and tarpaulin, fixing them over the two small windows before telling Anna to relight the lamp. When the interior was filled with a cosy orange glow, I circled the table, checking the floor and pressing hard on any floorboards that felt loose.

The dog found a good spot close to the *pich*, while Lev and Anna stood with confused expressions as I banged my heel down on an area that sounded hollow. I got to my knees and studied the boards.

'You'd be surprised,' I said.

Lev shook his head and took off his coat, throwing it across one of the benches along the wall. Underneath, he wore a dark jacket, which matched his trousers and might have once been smart but was now faded and dirty. He went to the *pich* and used a wooden paddle to take a clay pot from inside.

I went to the cabinet and put my fingers to the *garmoshka*, running them along the concertinaed mid-section.

'You play?' Lev asked. 'It would be good to hear a tune.'

'No.' I shook my head. 'My brother, Alek, used to play, but not very well.' I smiled as a thought came to me. 'My wife fancied she could sing, but the pair of them were as bad as each other.

Sometimes he'd play and she'd sing and the only thing that made it bearable was a lot of vodka.'

Lev smiled and banged the wooden paddle on the side of the pot. 'Hungry?' he asked. 'It's not much, but there should be enough.'

He set it on the table and removed the lid, letting the steam rise above it.

'The best thing I've smelled in a long time,' I said, leaning my rifle against the end of the table and hanging my satchel over a chair before taking off my jacket. I sat so I was facing the door and waited for Anna to bring three wooden bowls and a heel of black bread. She pulled her chair round so she was close to her father.

'So you've been travelling a long time?' I asked Lev as he spooned soup into the bowls. It looked to be full of turnip and pieces of dried fish, but not much else.

'You could say that.' He pushed a bowl of salt towards me and I took a pinch for my soup before tearing a piece of bread.

'And that's all you're going to tell me?' I asked, lifting the spoon to my mouth.

'Who's Koschei?' Anna asked.

Her words took me by surprise and the hot soup caught in my throat, making me cough and bringing tears to my eyes.

'He's from a story, my angel, a *skazka*. And don't pry,' her father told her, as he pushed away from the table and went to the cabinet.

'But you asked as if he was someone real,' she went on. 'Who is he?'

Lev came back from the cabinet carrying a bottle and two small bowls that served as cups.

'I can see she obeys your every command.' I smiled.

Lev sighed and shook his head as he uncorked the bottle, pouring a small amount of the clear liquid into each cup before pushing one towards me. 'Just like her mother. If I said "shaved", she'd say "cut".' He looked across at Anna with the strongest expression of love I had seen for close to six months.

'I used to say the same thing about my wife.' I smiled again and lifted the cup to sniff at it. 'Vodka?'

'Or something like it.' He put his close to his lips and looked over at me. 'So what do we drink to?'

'A safe night.'

Lev nodded. 'A safe night.'

The vodka burned as it went down, warming my chest, and I took a deep breath to feel its full effect. When I put the cup down, Lev had drained his too, so he refilled them both.

'So who's Koschei?' Anna leaned forward and watched me, expecting an answer.

'Your mother never told her the stories?' I asked.

Lev tore a piece of bread. 'She died.'

'I'm sorry.'

'Typhus,' he said.

I sat back and put down my spoon.

'No. A long time ago,' he said. 'Just after Anna was born. She knew all the stories, but I can never remember them. All I remember is that Koschei's soul was on the island of Buyan, inside an egg that was inside some other animal inside a chest . . . or something like that. You had to find his death to kill him.'

'That's *one* of the stories,' I said. 'He's in more than one.'

'Do you have children?' Anna asked.

'I have two sons.'

'Then you'll know the stories. Tell me one.' She tried her soup once more, but it was still too hot for her, so she left the spoon in the bowl and sat back, crossing her arms.

'It doesn't always work like that,' Lev said, watching me. 'Perhaps Kolya has been away from home for a while . . .'

'I have,' I admitted, 'but I still remember bits and pieces.'

'Then tell me one,' Anna said.

'I'm no storyteller. That was always . . .' My words caught in my throat and I stopped myself from finishing. Storytelling had always been Marianna's love – that's what I was going to say, but a flood of emotions had surged with that thought and threatened

106

to overcome me. In the warmth of the small house, with the lamp burning, and sitting with Lev and Anna, I couldn't help but remember the way Marianna told the stories to the boys, the way she revelled in the telling and they delighted in the hearing. The old *skazkas*. Mama and Babushka had both loved those stories, always filled with princes and princesses, witches and wives and devils and some poor peasant wandering back from the tavern.

'Please.' Anna shuffled on her seat.

When she had come into the house, she had removed her cap and jacket, making her look smaller. She had a slight, boyish frame draped in a shirt that was too big for her – or perhaps it had once been a perfect fit. Her skin was as white as the delicate flowers of the thimbleweed that rose from the forest floor in spring, and while there were dark circles under her green eyes, there was also the sparkle of a bright young girl burning in them. The plait in her hair had loosened further, strands protruding in all directions, and there was a look about her that suggested Lev had done the best he could for her, given their circumstances.

'Have you heard about Marya Morevna?' I asked.

Anna shook her head.

I dipped my bread in the soup and took a bite. I chewed it well, tasting every crumb, savouring the heat of it as I tried to remember the story.

All eyes were on me. Waiting. Expecting. Marianna would have enjoyed this. She would have drawn it out, turned down the lamp, leaned in to the table and lowered her voice. I saw her now, her blue eyes sparkling, the lamplight glistening on her golden hair, her fine features alive with the pictures she painted with words. I was no match for her in this, but I looked at each of them in turn as I finished the bread and ran my tongue round my teeth.

'A long time ago,' I said, 'there was a prince. Ivan, he was called, and he was young and bold, as princes always are in the stories, and he had three beautiful sisters with shining black hair. But the tsar and his queen were ill, and as they lay dying, they made Ivan promise to look after his sisters and make sure they married well. He agreed, of course, and when they died, they died happy, knowing Ivan would take care of their daughters. Ivan and his sisters buried their mother and father in the palace grounds, and on the way back, a great storm arose. Black clouds covered the sky, and lightning flashed. Ivan and his sisters hurried home, and when they arrived in the great hall, there was a huge clap of thunder and a falcon flew into the room. When it landed, it turned into a handsome prince, who asked for one of the princesses in marriage. Ivan thought he was a good man, so he agreed.'

'Princes and princesses,' Anna said with disdain. 'I want to know about Koschei.'

'We haven't come to him yet,' I told her, taking another bite of bread. 'We have to get past the princes and princesses first. You want me to stop?'

Anna shook her head.

I waited, recalling the story, and when I was ready, I hunched lower to the table and began speaking in a quieter voice. 'So, three years in a row, three different princes came in a clap of thunder and a flash of lightning – first as a falcon, then as an eagle, then as a raven – and each time, Ivan sent his sisters away to get married. When they were all gone, he was left alone in the palace.'

'Does that mean he was the tsar now?'

'I suppose it does,' I said. 'Does that matter?'

Anna screwed up her mouth and thought. 'Aren't the tsars bad?'

'You're a revolutionary?' I asked, and the image of a branded red star flashed in my mind.

'Not really.'

'Well. In this story, the tsars are good.'

Across the table, Lev held up his cup. 'Your health.'

I lifted my own. 'And yours.'

We drank and Lev refilled the cups as I continued. I was feeling good now. The *izba* was warm, the soup was nourishing, and the vodka was softening my thoughts.

'So Prince Ivan was alone in the palace,' I said.

'That wouldn't be so bad.' Anna looked around. 'Better than here.'

'Better than without your family?' I asked.

She looked into her bowl and took a spoonful of soup, blowing on it before tasting.

'So he decided to go travelling,' I said, 'to visit his sisters. Only, the first thing he came across was a battlefield and a whole army lying dead on the steppe. Bodies everywhere. But he found one man alive among them, just one, and when he asked who had done this—'

'Koschei?' Anna asked.

'No,' I told her. 'Not yet. The man told Ivan that the fair princess Marya Morevna had done it.'

'A *princess* killed all those people?'

'She did.'

'Why?'

'I don't know, but when Ivan found her, he must have been impressed because he fell in love with her and she with him.'

'Just like that,' Lev said.

'Just like that,' I agreed. 'So they got married and lived together for a while until Marya Morevna grew bored and decided to go warring again, leaving Ivan alone in the castle. When she left, she told Ivan not to look inside her secret room, but, well, you know what it's like when someone tells you not to look or touch or listen. He just couldn't help himself, and one day, when he was bored, he opened the room and found a man bound by chains. He was tall and thin and gaunt and terrible-looking. A *monster*.'

'*That's* Koschei,' Anna said. She stopped, spoon in mid-air, and sat upright with a pleased but concerned look.

'You're too clever,' I said.

'Go on.'

I lowered my voice again, starting to enjoy the telling, forgetting, for just a moment, about the real Koschei, somewhere out there.

'Ivan thought the man was ugly and frightening, but he was a good prince and felt sorry for him when the man asked for a drink, so he brought him a bucket of water. The chained man drank it down and kept asking for more until he had drunk three whole buckets, but the water gave him his strength back and he snapped the chains like they were twigs and told Ivan he would sooner see his own ears than see Marya Morevna again. Then Koschei left in a whirlwind of smoke and fire and blazing eyes, and he found the princess. He snatched her up and threw her on his skeletal horse and took her away to his kingdom.'

'Sooner see his own ears?' Anna said. 'All he'd have to do is look in the mirror. He's a prince – he must have a mirror.'

'There's no fooling you, eh?' I stopped and took the last spoonful of soup, wiping the crust of the bread round the bowl before looking over at the dog sitting by the *pich*. He had not moved from his warm spot, but his eyes were always on us. From time to time he closed them, but the slightest change in the rhythm of our voices caused him to lift his nose and check the room. I threw the crust of bread over to him and in an instant he was on his feet, chewing it down and licking his lips.

'That was a good meal,' I said to Lev. 'Thank you. I think he liked it too.'

Lev took a packet of papirosa cigarettes from his pocket, offering them across to me. There were only three left in the packet and I hesitated, but he gestured for me to take one. 'Please.'

I looked him in the eye and nodded once before taking it. Then I struck a match on the tabletop and lit both, savouring the first lungful.

'Then what happened?' Anna asked. 'Did Ivan find Marya?'

The dog left his place, claws ticking on the wooden floor, and came to sit beside me, putting his chin on my lap. I ruffled his head, guessing no one had ever thrown him a scrap from the table before.

'Does he have a name?' I asked.

'He's not ours.' Lev shrugged. 'He was already here.'

'He looks like he might have some wolf in him.'

Anna yawned and put out a hand to stroke his fur. 'What happened to Marya?'

'Where was I?'

'Koschei took Marya.'

'Oh yes,' I said, sitting back and waving a hand. 'Well, Prince Ivan looked for her, of course. He looked for a long time, but the first thing he found was one of his sisters. She and her prince told Ivan to give up on Marya Morevna because Koschei the Deathless would surely kill him, but he wouldn't give up on his wife, so he left and went on his way. Before he went, though, he gave them his silver spoon and told them that if it turned black, then it meant something had happened to him and they should come to look for him. When he found his second sister, she tried to stop him too, but he went on, giving her his silver fork, and to the third sister he gave his silver snuffbox. Then finally he found the place where Koschei the Deathless was keeping Marya Morevna.'

Anna stopped stroking the dog and went to sit on her papa's knee. Lev put his arms around her and held her tight. Beside me, the dog moved, turning in a circle several times before flopping on the floor at my feet, making me look down and see my brother's boots.

They waited for me to go on.

'Koschei was out hunting,' I said, trying not to think about Alek lying under the ground, 'so Ivan took Marya and they rode away on his horse, but Koschei knew.'

'How?'

'I don't know. He just *knew*. So he went after them, and though his horse was like a skeleton, it was much faster, so he caught up with them.'

'Did he kill the prince?' she asked.

'No, he took pity on him, just as Ivan had once taken pity on him.'

'So he let him go?'

'Yes, he did, but not Marya Morevna. He kept her, so Ivan stole her twice more when Koschei was out hunting, and each time Koschei's horse was too fast and each time Koschei forgave him. In fact, he forgave him three times because Ivan had given him three buckets of water, but after that, he decided enough was enough and he flew into a whirling rage. He jumped on his hellish horse and came crashing from the forest, sword raised, eyes blazing, and cut Prince Ivan into little pieces.' I brought the edge of my hand down on the table in a chopping motion.

Anna halted mid-yawn and sat up straight. 'But he's the prince.'

I took a drag on the cigarette. 'Yes, he is.'

'And the prince always wins.'

'Does he?' I asked.

'Of course he does. He's—' She stopped herself and shook her head at me, giving me the same stern look her father had given her earlier in the barn. There was something strangely inclusive about that, as if she had accepted me. 'I know what you mean,' she said, 'but this is different.'

Anna was young, but not too young to know the fate of our own tsar, executed just two years ago, along with everyone in his family. She didn't see any irony in the fact that the hero, Ivan, was now a tsar, though. She saw a *skazka*, a hero and a villain, that was all. 'This is just a *story*,' she said. 'It's not here; it's . . . somewhere else. And in the *stories*, the prince *always* wins and the monster is *always* burned or drowned in the lake or killed with a sword.' She shrugged. 'That's just how it always is.'

'Not in this story,' I said, narrowing my eyes and leaning closer. 'I'm sorry. But this is the part my boys always love. Pavel especially. And Marianna loves telling it. You see, I'm afraid Koschei really does chop Ivan into pieces and he puts all the bits of Prince Ivan in a barrel and smears it with pitch. Then he binds it with iron hoops and throws it in the sea.' I stopped and looked at Anna. 'Are you scared?'

'Of course not.'

'He doesn't die,' I said.

'How can he not die after all that?'

'Because he's the prince, of course –' I winked '– and the prince always wins.'

Lev lifted his cup. 'To the prince,' he said.

'To the prince.' I smiled and drank, feeling the effects of the vodka. It was the best I had felt in a long time.

'You shouldn't worry,' I said to Anna, 'because when the spoon and the fork and the snuffbox turned black, so the falcon and the eagle and the raven came to help. One of them dragged the barrel from the sea, while another went to fetch the water of life, and another to find the water of death. They broke open the barrel, put the pieces of the prince together and sprinkled them with the water of death to make everything stick together. Then they used the water of life to bring back Ivan. Straight away Prince Ivan set off in search of Marya Morevna again, but this time, instead of taking her, he told her to find out where Koschei got his horse from.'

Anna stifled another yawn.

'Tired?' I asked.

'Maybe you can hear the rest another time.' Lev started to stand.

'Please,' she begged.

'Maybe the short version,' Lev suggested.

'All right. The short version.' I took the last drag of the cigarette and put it out in my empty bowl. 'In the short version, Ivan discovers that Koschei's horse is from Baba Yaga's herd.'

'Baba Yaga.' Anna pretended to shiver. 'I know her. She's the witch with the house that has legs like a chicken. She eats children.'

'Hmm. But only juicy ones, eh?' I licked my lips at her. 'Now, on the way to her hut, across the fiery river, Ivan grows very hungry, but every time he finds an animal to eat, the animal begs him not to eat it, and when he eventually finds Baba Yaga and asks her for a horse, she says she will give him one only if he can perform an almost impossible task – which he manages to do because the animals help him in return for his mercy.'

'Like Koschei gave *him* mercy?'

'I suppose,' I agreed. 'But Baba Yaga tries to betray Ivan anyway, so he tricks her and gets away with a horse, and this time when he steals Marya Morevna away, Koschei finds it hard to catch him.'

'So he gets away?'

'Not quite. You see, Prince Ivan and Marya Morevna stop to rest, and that's when Koschei catches up with them and he takes out his sword to chop them into pieces.' I pretended to draw a sword from my belt and brandish it.

'So *that's* when the prince kills him?'

'Well, the prince's horse kicks Koschei in the head and then Ivan finishes him off with a club before building a pyre and burning his terrible body. And *that's* the end of him.'

'So why do they call him "the Deathless"?' she asked. 'He isn't deathless, is he?'

'No,' I said. 'He isn't.'

'And why are you looking for him? Is there a *real* Koschei?'

'In a way,' I said.

'A man?' She waited for a reply, watching me intently.

'I think so.'

Anna nodded as if she had just come to a long-awaited conclusion to something that had puzzled her for a long time. 'Papa always said there were no monsters, but there are, aren't there?'

I wanted to tell her she was wrong, but I couldn't. There really were monsters, but they didn't hide in lakes and graveyards and under beds. Instead they hid in uniforms.

'Come on.' Lev eased Anna from his lap. 'Time to sleep.'

With tired reluctance, Anna headed to the sleeping berth above the *pich* and Lev helped her up. He kissed her and I saw the love they shared and I remembered kissing my sons goodnight; how I used to make them giggle by rubbing my whiskers on their cheeks.

I stood and went to them, giving Lev one of the blankets I had brought from home. 'To keep her warm,' I said.

'Thank you.'

'You didn't say why you're looking for Koschei,' Anna said before she climbed up to bed.

'Because he took my sons,' I told her. 'And my wife.'

114

'Like he took Marya Morevna?'

'Yes.'

'And you're Prince Ivan?'

'I'm no prince.'

'But your horse is fast?'

'Kashtan? She's as fast as the wind.'

'And when you find him, are you going to kill him?'

'That's not something for you to be—'

'*Are* you?' she asked again, and I saw that she needed to hear the answer.

'When I've found my wife and sons . . .' I said, '. . . yes. Yes, I am.'

# 13

When Lev came back to the table, he poured us another drink.

'To your daughter,' I said, raising my cup. 'You're a lucky man.'

'And to your sons.' He raised his own and drank with me.

I drained the vodka and put my hands on the table to look at them, seeing bloodstains that were no longer there. I was reminded of the wicked things I had made these hands do, in days when I had been blinded by what I thought was the righteousness of my actions. Now there were other things to fill my thoughts, things that crammed into my mind, pushing everything else aside. Never had I felt such fear. Not in fighting a hundred battles or witnessing countless deaths had I felt anything close to the dread and apprehension in not knowing what had happened to my wife and sons, not knowing where they really were. Perhaps they were even dead already.

*He likes to drown the women.*

Except I could not allow that idea to poison my thoughts. They were dark enough already without that to cloud them further.

'What's your story, Kolya?' He spoke quietly so as not to disturb his daughter. 'You seem like a good man to me.'

I looked up at him and forced a smile. 'No one is ever quite what they seem.'

'Well . . . a good man is a good man.'

I liked his sentiment but wasn't sure if I agreed. 'There's good and bad in all of us.' I ran a hand across my face as if to wash away the day's events. It felt as if I had been awake for weeks. 'It's finding the right balance that's hard.'

'You look tired,' he said. 'How long have you been travelling?'

'Longer than I want to think about. How about you?'

'The same. We've been here a few days, though. It's a good place to stay.'

'But you haven't seen anyone?'

'No one.'

The dog grunted beside me and scratched himself.

'How about two women on horseback?' I asked. 'Have you seen them?'

He shook his head. 'No one at all. The road is further east; we can't see much of anything from here.'

'Which means no one can see this farm from the road.'

'It works well for us,' he said.

Perhaps Tanya and Lyudmila had passed along that road, and Koschei before them, but for now they were out of sight, out of reach, and might as well have been across the sea in some country where the revolution was just words in a newspaper.

'So how did you find it?' I asked.

Lev pulled an empty chair towards him and put his feet on it. 'We were lucky, I suppose. We kept away from the roads, spotted this in the distance and came closer to see what was here. We were hungry and cold, so it was worth taking the risk.' It was his turn to look down at his hands now, making me wonder what he had made them do.

'And it was empty?' My words caused him to glance up at me, but he didn't hold my gaze. His eyes shifted to look at the *pich* where Anna was sleeping, then back to his hands again.

His mouth tightened and he swallowed. 'Yes. Empty.' He took the bottle and poured again, splashing a few drops on the table. 'Who knows what happened to whoever lived here, but they hadn't been here for a while – months, I'd say. Maybe a husband fighting, a wife who couldn't look after a farm alone.' He shrugged. 'Who knows?'

'Who knows?' I agreed, lifting the cup to my lips. 'To our children,' I said, knocking it back and feeling it burn my throat.

'Our children.' Lev drank it and wiped his mouth with the back of his hand without putting the cup on the table. He stared into the bottom of it.

'And the horse?' I asked.

'The horse is mine.' This time he looked me right in the eye and I knew it was the truth.

'But you're not a blacksmith.'

He placed the cup on the table and picked dirt from under his fingernail. 'No, not a blacksmith, but we always had horses. My father always had them.'

'So you're . . . ?'

'I'm a teacher,' he said. 'At least, I *was* a teacher. Mathematics. You think I always looked like this? Like a beggar?' He swept a hand towards his chest in a false flourish, but when he noticed them shaking, he clasped them together to make them stop. 'I was always so smart, so tidy. I wore a good suit and—' He stopped himself as if he were suddenly aware of our differences. A teacher telling a revolutionary how well dressed he used to be. 'I don't know what I am anymore.' He hung his head. 'The things I've had to do to take care of Anna.'

'I don't care what you had to do to get here,' I said.

'Not even if I killed a man?'

'Is that what you've done?' I watched him closely, wondering what might have driven Lev to kill, but it didn't take much to work it out. I had seen how he loved his daughter.

'I'm a *teacher*, for God's sake.' He tightened both hands into fists. 'A teacher. And look at me now. Stealing and begging. Dirty and cold and hungry. I used to be smart and respectable and . . . I never hurt anyone, had never even hit a man until . . .' He shook his head.

I waited for him to go on, thought about pressing him to tell me more, but it was better to leave him. It didn't matter what he had done, and if he wanted to talk about it, he would do it when he was ready.

'I was always a soldier,' I said. 'Well, it feels that way. I thought that was respectable too, but not anymore. Not really. I joined to fight the Great War, and when that was finished, I wanted a better country for Marianna and the boys, so I continued to fight. For them, at first, and then for me, because it was, I don't know, it was what I did. Sometimes it's hard to leave the path you're on.'

Lev wiped his eyes with his fingers, leaving damps streaks in the dirt on his face. Streaks that glistened in the lamplight. 'And now? Are you still a soldier?'

'Now I'm a father. A husband.' I thought for a moment. 'And a soldier still.'

'But you left the army?'

'Deserted.' The word still felt wrong on my tongue and left a bitter taste in my mouth. 'I've always believed that was a bad thing. Cowardly.' There were many deserters who had been executed because I once held that belief so strongly, but I didn't tell him that. 'Now, though, all that matters is finding my family.' I told Lev about what I had found in Belev, what Galina said she had done and what she had called the man she stabbed. I had thought it was the ramblings of an insane old woman, but then Tanya and Lyudmila had come and they had known the name 'Koschei' too.

And I told him about the star branded into men's skin, just as he had seen himself.

'So you think this man Koschei has taken them?' he asked.

'I didn't find them, so I have to believe that, otherwise . . .' I smiled a melancholy smile and turned the cup in my hand. 'Otherwise I'll need a lot more of this.' I showed him my empty cup.

'Your sons,' he said, refilling us. 'Are they fighting age?'

'Depends on your idea of fighting age. Pavel is just twelve . . .'

'The same age as Anna.'

'. . . and Misha is fourteen, but I've known armies take boys as young as ten.'

Lev closed his eyes and shook his head at the sadness of it. 'And if they don't take them to fight, they want to send them away to labour camps, right?'

I put my head back and closed my eyes.

'I'm sorry,' he said. 'I didn't mean to . . . I was thinking aloud. It was stupid of me.'

'It's all right.' I waved away the comment with the back of my hand. 'I've thought of that already.'

'So who do you think he is?' he asked.

'Well, he might seem like a ghost, but I'm sure he's no fairy tale.' I concentrated on the darkness behind my eyelids as I spoke to him. 'He uses the name to frighten people maybe, but I've seen what he leaves in his wake, so he's real enough. A man.'

'But who?'

'The exact man, I have no idea, but the *type* of man?' I looked at him. 'You already know.'

Lev sat back and ran a hand over his head. 'Chekists?' he whispered.

I said nothing.

He cleared his throat and stared into the top corner of the room behind me. He couldn't hide what he was thinking. 'The worst of humanity.' He said the words with a quietness that made me shiver. Even here, just the two of us, he was afraid to speak ill of them aloud, such was their reputation.

With Lenin's sanction, the All-Russian Extraordinary Commission – the Cheka – was put together by Dzerzhinsky to combat those who would undermine the revolution. It was a political army to safeguard the toiling masses, the ordinary man, but after Kaplan tried to kill Lenin more than two years ago, Stalin recommended using the harsh tactics he had employed to crush counter-revolutionary resistance in Tsaritsyn. And so the Red Terror was born.

Landholders and the wealthy classes who refused to fall into line were the first targets, but the definition of wealth had become hazy and the Cheka units, made up of Communist leaders and former convicts and soldiers, were left as both police and executioner. Peasants were targeted as often as anyone else, and some units primed themselves on drugs and alcohol before raids, while others used artillery to bombard towns into dust. Dzerzhinsky himself said the units stood for organised terror, to keep the people under control, and with the peasant uprising in Tambov that started in August, the Chekists had been sent out with units to create that terror. They hunted deserters, burned villages, tortured peasants for refusing to give up their crops and gassed rebels who took refuge in the forests. They took young men for recruitment and deported thousands to labour camps across the country. Cheka agents were even secreted in Red Army units to report on their comrades. They were darker and more frightening than any fairy-tale monster.

They were worse than devils.

Lev poured us another drink without speaking. It was as if he was giving us both a moment to deal with the thought of such atrocity, giving *me* a moment to compose myself after voicing my concern for my family.

When our cups were full, he sat back and cleared his throat. 'So you deserted before you knew what happened in your village? What made you leave?' He didn't ask what unit I had come from.

'This isn't a war anymore; it's just people killing people and I didn't want to be a part of it. I had to go home.' He didn't need to know the rest of it, the *real* reason.

'So you ran? Just like that? Don't the Bolsheviks hunt deserters?'

'It was early morning,' I said. 'We entered a village to . . . Anyway, we were ambushed by fighters.'

'You don't need to tell me.'

'My brother was wounded.' I put a hand to my stomach without even thinking about it, remembering the place where Alek had been hit. 'I tried to make it look as if we were killed in the fighting – swapped our uniforms with men who were already dead, left our papers in their pockets and . . . it was mayhem. Screaming, shooting, grenades exploding in the houses. People dying. It was all so . . . so out of control. I couldn't do it anymore. I had to get away. Undressing the dead peasants was easy, but getting them into our uniforms was hard. We left them in a ditch just outside the village we were fighting in, more or less where they died, but we had to make them unrecognisable. No one could know.' Of all

121

the things I'd had to do, that was the hardest. Bringing the rock down on them again and again. Over and over. Rubbing them from the world. I pushed the image away and reached for the bottle.

'What made you do it?'

'So many things.' I thought for a moment, trying to put it into words. Alek and I hadn't ever voiced it so bluntly to one another. For us, it was a succession of utterances, of exchanged glances, of silent understandings. We didn't dare discuss it, because the illegality and wrongness of it were so ingrained in us. We had punished men simply for thinking such things and knew what would happen to us if we expressed the thoughts aloud.

'All the killing,' I said. 'All the suffering. All the terrible things I'd done.' I glanced at Lev but couldn't look him in the eye. I had terrorised people like him. 'I didn't know myself anymore. I was . . .' I shook my head and let the thought trail away. 'My brother and I went home six months ago. It was . . . so good to be there, with Marianna and my sons. Things were hard for them, just like anyone, and Marianna was so *strong*, the way she took care of Misha and Pavel, but I should have been there for them. *That* was my place. Being with them reminded me of that.'

'Marianna persuaded you?' Lev asked.

'Without needing to. I *felt* it. Her need for me, and mine for her and my sons. It was so good to feel something other than the numbness that I had once forced myself to feel but now came like second nature. Like I can be two people. And when Misha, my oldest, started talking about how he wanted to join the fight, I saw . . .' I looked away and tried to find the right words. 'I saw a never-ending war. Children of fourteen taking up rifles and doing the things I had done. It was too much.'

'And that was the first time you considered getting out?'

'Not really. The idea had always been there, but I suppose I was too afraid even to think it in case I gave myself away, so I crushed it like I crushed every other feeling. Then Misha asked to join Alek and me when we went back to our unit and I remember looking across the table at my brother and that's when we knew.

If there was a single moment that brought everything into focus, it was *that* one. I couldn't take my son into that world to see what I saw. I couldn't even bear the thought of him knowing the things I'd done. And there, with my family around me, my eyes opened to what really mattered.'

Lev remained silent, but his expression told me that he understood, and when he reached across the table to pat my arm in a simple gesture of sympathy, the warmth I took from that small connection threatened to choke me.

'If they thought we were dead, they wouldn't think twice about us.' My voice cracked as I spoke, but I cleared my throat and composed myself. 'That's what we hoped. But once we were in the forest and we finally talked about what we were going to do, things became so complicated. Maybe we couldn't just go home and be with Marianna and the boys. Maybe someone would come looking for us. Maybe someone would denounce us. Maybe we would have to take them and leave, find somewhere else to live. Alek's wound made things worse and . . . there were too many possibilities.'

'But you had to try.'

'We decided we'd get to Belev and watch from the forest and make a decision then. Perhaps take Marianna and the boys out under cover of darkness, find somewhere to go. Anywhere.' I looked up at Lev. 'Like you did.'

Lev nodded.

'But my village was empty and my family was gone, and now I'm not sure if our deception worked,' I said, filling our cups, hands trembling. 'There have been times, in the forest, when I thought I was being followed.'

Immediately Lev's eyes went to Anna and I could see his concern.

He watched her for a moment, then took the last cigarette from the packet and lit it, shaking the match and placing it carefully on the table. He sucked the smoke into his lungs, then leaned forward to pass it to me. 'That's why you kept looking across the field. You think they'll follow you here?'

'Maybe. I don't know. I was in the forest all day; it would be difficult to track me.'

'But we should leave.' His worry was clear to me. 'It's not safe for us here anymore?'

'Maybe I imagined it.' It was the most I could say to reassure him.

'You're not afraid?'

'I'm always afraid.'

He nodded in agreement, and for a while we sat in silence as we shared the last cigarette and drank to families and peace and to not being found.

'We ran away from the fighting in Tambov,' Lev said, wiping his lips on his sleeve. 'With the war and then the uprising, it was like the world had gone mad. Nowhere was safe, and we had nothing left after the requisitions. We joked that the chickens had been drafted into the war, but it wasn't funny. Not really. Anyway, I had a daughter to protect and thought if we kept off the roads, we could get to Moscow and—'

'Why Moscow? That's a long way.'

He shrugged. 'I thought there might be work for a teacher or . . . I don't know. Maybe I never really believed we'd get there. We just had to get away. Then we found this place and decided to stay for a while. There's food. Shelter.'

'And the man you killed?' I asked. 'He was here? You want to tell me about it?'

He looked down at the table.

'Did Anna see? Does she know?'

'It was about two weeks ago.' He continued to stare at the table. 'We were coming through a village and some people tried to pull us off the horse. We hadn't been on the road long and were looking for shelter, but soldiers had been there and the people were hungry. They just wanted something to eat and . . . one of them grabbed Anna's leg and she was shouting for me to do something. More and more of them came, people crowding round us. They were going to pull us down, getting nasty, calling us selfish, and Anna was screaming and I was afraid and . . .' He shook his head. 'I didn't know what else to do. I shot him. Right here.' He looked up at me and patted his chest. 'I didn't wait to see what happened. The people stood back and we rode away.'

'Maybe he lived,' I tried to reassure him.

'No.'

'What about Anna?'

'She never mentions it. I tried to talk to her about it, but she won't. Maybe it's better that way.'

I reached across the table and put my hand on his arm. I didn't know what to say to him. I tried to remember how I had felt the first time I had taken a life, but it was so long ago and so much had come between that I felt nothing.

Lev forced himself to smile. 'I did it for Anna.'

'Of course,' I said. 'That's the only reason to do something like that – for our children.'

I knew that I would do anything to bring mine home. Anything at all. Even if it meant I would burn for eternity.

# 14

My concerns about being followed had worried Lev, so we agreed to sleep in shifts. He insisted on taking the first watch, saying I was more in need of the sleep, and I accepted his offer as another kindness. So with the vodka and tobacco gone, and the state of our country lamented, I went to my bed while Lev blew out the lamp and sat at the table with his shotgun by his side.

It was as dark as any night could be inside the smoky *izba*, and I settled on the straw in one of the berths and held my rifle close as if it were my lover. Beside my head, within easy reach, my revolver.

I believed Lev was a good man, but too many people hid their true colour, so I tried to remain wary and stay awake as long as I could. The vodka had taken its effect on me, though, as had the days of travel and little sleep, and my eyes closed with almost no resistance. And when the dog climbed up onto my bunk and curled himself against my legs, I did nothing to dissuade him.

There was a simple comfort in being with other people, sharing a meal, lying in a bed beneath a roof in the warmth, and so sleep threw herself around me.

The wind was shrill as it rushed across the steppe, slipping over the grass and humming through the furrows. It swirled about the *izba*, lifting the roof and rattling the doors and windows as if all the devils and spirits had come to batter this small refuge. The trees in the copse groaned and creaked, the cantankerous crows complaining from time to time, and in that chaos of the land's breath, I dreamed of nothing and everything.

Images of the gaunt rider, immense on the back of his horse, raising his sword to cut me into a thousand pieces. I saw the men in the forest, crucified, hanged, and I turned away in horror when their faces became those of my sons and their eyes were empty sockets burned in the shape of a five-pointed star.

In a moment of waking, I swore I heard wolves howling in the forest and I opened my eyes to stare at the blackness, not even the faintest hint of light, wondering where I was before I remembered Lev and Anna.

'Lev?' I spoke into the darkness.

'I'm here.'

'Isn't it my turn to—'

'It's not time,' he said. 'Sleep, Kolya. I'll wake you.'

'But surely—'

'Go to sleep,' he repeated.

The dog whined his alertness to the sounds outside, but I patted him and he settled, pressing against me, sharing his warmth while we listened to the wolf song, far away, mingling with the whistle of the wind and the spatter of sleet against the thatched roof. Sleep came quickly once more, and when I woke again, there was a grey light around the blankets covering the window, and Anna was shaking me, calling my name.

'Kolya,' she was saying. 'You have to get up.'

There was an urgency in her voice and I was moving right away, annoyed for having slept so long.

There was no time for a slow awakening, no time for the hangover already thumping at the back of my head. Hands on my revolver, I swung my legs to the floor.

In an instant I was alert. Prepared. Ready to fight.

Anna took a step back and put up her hands in fear. 'Papa told me.'

'What?'

'Papa said to get you.' She took another step back and turned her body away from me as if she was expecting to be hurt.

I looked down at the revolver in my hands, the muzzle pointed at her, and it took a second for the implication of that to sink in.

'No,' I said, moving it. 'I won't hurt you.'

'Papa said to get you,' she repeated. 'He saw someone.'

'Saw someone?' I said, hurrying to the window and snatching away the blanket. 'Who? Where?'

'Across the field. Where you came from.'

The day had barely begun; there was less than an hour's daylight in the sky, so everything had a grey hue to it. To make matters worse, the glass was uneven and distorted everything outside. In some places, the fields were magnified, in others almost impossible to see due to the grime that had collected on the window.

'I don't see anybody.'

'Papa said—'

'Where is he?'

'With the horses.'

'Get my coat,' I said, and when I had pulled on my boots, I took it from her, leaving it unbuttoned. I put my rifle over my shoulder and hurried about, gathering my belongings, ignoring the dog that now followed at my heels. I stripped the remaining blankets away from the windows and put them in Anna's arms, saying, 'Hold these,' before taking my satchel and the saddlebags I had brought in. 'Wait here.'

I went out first, startling a pair of magpies that was sitting on the fence, the dog following me out into the yard. I ignored the flurry of black and white, and scanned the horizon beyond the field but saw no one.

I beckoned Anna out, telling her to hurry. 'The barn,' I said. 'Quick.'

She ran ahead of me, small and afraid, clutching my blankets, and I spent a few more seconds looking into the distance, then followed, skidding on the ice that had formed during the night.

In the barn, Lev had already saddled Kashtan and prepared her for me to leave.

'What did you see?' I asked as I ran in.

Lev took the blankets from Anna and spread them into my

tarpaulin. 'A man on the horizon,' he said. 'The same direction you came from.'

'Alone?'

'Yes.' He folded and rolled the blankets as I secured my saddlebags.

'On horseback?'

Lev lifted the roll onto Kashtan. 'I came to check on the horses and there he was.'

'How far?'

'As far as he could be. Any further and I wouldn't have seen him.'

'And you're sure it was just one rider?'

'That's all I saw, but there could be more.'

'Why didn't you wake me last night?' I asked. 'We were going to share the watch.'

'You needed the sleep more than I did.'

I ran a hand across my face, feeling the growth of my beard. 'You should come with me.'

Lev shook his head. 'Whoever it was, they could have seen me. If we're not here, they'll come after us, think we've got something to run from.'

'Maybe you have,' I said. Running was no life for a child, but if the rider on the horizon was hunting me, then he could be a Chekist, and who knew what might be in store for Lev and Anna? 'You should come with me.'

'We're just a poor farmer and his daughter,' Lev said. 'They'll leave us alone. If it's you they want . . .' He shrugged.

I tried to convince myself that Lev was right. Whoever he had seen, they were coming after *me*.

'Maybe they won't even stop,' I said, thinking I would be much faster without them. If I took them with me, it might cost Marianna and the boys their lives. 'They won't want to waste time, lose my trail.'

'Exactly,' Lev replied. 'We'll tell them you gave us no choice. That you threatened Anna.'

I nodded, allowing him to persuade me it was the right thing to do, knowing it would be too dangerous for them to come with me. Where I was going, I foresaw only blood and death.

'I hope you have found the peace you're looking for,' I said to Lev, holding out my hand. It was what he wanted – for me to go and for him and his daughter to be left in peace. It was what a part of me wanted too – to be free from any bonds or responsibilities, to leave them right now and continue my search unhindered by anyone else.

But my eyes met with Anna's and something about it didn't feel right.

'And I hope you do too,' Lev replied, ignoring the hand and putting his arms around me. 'Perhaps we'll meet again, Kolya,' he said into the fur of my hat as he embraced me. 'When all of this is over.'

With the sense that I was abandoning this man and his child, I returned the embrace, enjoying the friendship but hating the other, darker feelings that plagued me.

'When they come, leave the shotgun above the *pich*,' I said, as I put my foot in the stirrup. 'Keep the dog calm and tell them I forced you to . . .' Kashtan pressed herself towards me, eager to be out ' . . . to give me a bed for the night. I ate your food, drank your vodka and threatened to kill you. You're lucky to be alive.' I pushed up and swung my leg across, looking down at the teacher and his daughter. 'Give them whatever they want.'

'Come,' Lev said, jogging to the back of the barn. 'This way they won't see you leave.' He drew back the bolt on the rear door and pushed it outwards before beckoning me with both hands.

'Lev Andreyevich Filatov,' he said, as I passed him. 'That's my name. Will you remember it?'

'Yes.'

Kashtan stepped out, the dog following as if he intended to go wherever I went. Anna ran alongside, coming out into the cold air and crossing to the fence at the far side of the rear yard. When she opened the back gate, I stopped to look down at her.

'I hope you find Koschei,' she said.

'I will. And . . . look after each other. Be safe.'

'What's your name?' Lev asked, coming to put his arm around his daughter's shoulder. 'Who are you really?'

'It's better you don't know,' I told him. 'If you did, you'd wish you hadn't asked.'

# 15

There was no sign of the rider as I took Kashtan from the barn and headed across the field. Before us, last night's rain and sleet had frozen in the furrows, lying like glass between the turnip leaves. Beyond that, the plain stretched on with only the slightest undulation in the near distance, but further away, perhaps two kilometres, the land rose in a sharp and rocky eruption where the steppe changed level on a new plateau. Above it, the air was muddled by a thin mist.

I glanced down at the dog running with us. 'You stay here too,' I said to him. 'You can't keep up with us.' Then I put my heels into Kashtan's ribs and she responded straight away, trotting through the turnips, reaching the sea of grass and thistle in just a few minutes. Here, the plants were laden with the hoarfrost, their stalks and leaves weighted and feathered with the shining crystals. I glanced back at our wake, knowing there was no way of hiding our progress. Whoever the riders were – for I found it hard to believe there could be only one – they would find my trail with ease. They had managed to track me through the forest despite my efforts, so this trail would offer no challenge.

The only advantage I had now was speed. Kashtan was rested and fresh. She had slept and eaten well and felt like a new animal. My pursuers would be tired from their night in the forest. The cold would be gnawing at them just as it was gnawing at their horses.

I pulled a scarf over my mouth and spurred Kashtan into a gallop, hoping the cold night had not darkened my pursuers' tempers or else Lev and Anna would bear the brunt of it. I leaned into her, watching her head bobbing, her mane rippling, as we rushed past the clusters of trees that stood like sentinels, leaning away from the prevailing wind, unclothed and stark against the clear sky and the glistening grass. The cold wind was hard on me, like riding through something more solid than air, and I narrowed my eyes, feeling the tears squeezing out and freezing in the creases in my skin.

As I moved with Kashtan, confident to let her race on and choose the best route ahead, I began to wonder if I should have brought Lev and Anna with me. If anything happened to them, it would lay on *my* conscience, but I told myself I had my own family to consider, and they had to come first. Lev and Anna would slow me down, giving my hunters time to make ground, and if something happened to me, Marianna and the boys would have no one to come for them. They would be left alone to their fate, just as Lev and Anna were now left alone to theirs. I'd had to choose between my own family and another.

A teacher and a little girl.

And if the people who were coming to their place of refuge knew who I was – if they were men who had learned of my attempted deception and had followed me from the village where Alek and I had left our uniforms – then they were hunters of men. They were torturers and murderers. Violent individuals charged with the dispersal of terror. Not unlike the men *I* was following; the men who had taken the peasants of Belev into the forest and . . .

I pulled back on Kashtan's reins and called to her, telling her to slow down. I rose in the saddle and twisted to look back at the farm. There was no sign of Lev and Anna, but they would be there, waiting for the approach of the devils. I knew now, just as I had known when I left, that they were not safe. I had done a terrible thing. Though I had tried to ignore it, I had known that if the men following me were the kind I expected them to be, they would not ride past and leave Lev and Anna alone. They would execute them for their collusion with a counter-revolutionary. A deserter. They would show no mercy. They would do what they had probably done a hundred times. They would kill and burn.

I had left them to die.

The seconds passed like hours as these things went through my mind. The cold air clawed at my throat, and the ice crackled around my eyes. I felt the ghost of Lev's embrace and saw Anna looking up at me that last time.

'We have to go back,' I said to Kashtan, and though I could hardly believe I was going to do it, I felt a great joy in it. They would make me slow. They would be a responsibility I didn't need, but I couldn't leave them. I couldn't go on to find my own family knowing I had left another behind to die.

I turned Kashtan and gave her the spur, pushing her hard so that we raced through the hoarfrost. The wind was cruel in my eyes as I watched for any sign of the rider Lev had seen, but so far, there was nothing.

There was a thickening mist that obscured the trees on the distant horizon, but I could still see a little way beyond the farm to the empty steppe. If the rider had been an advance scout, he would have returned for the rest of his party. He must have seen Lev and thought it might be me, preparing an ambush for them. He knew who I was and would not want to approach alone. Or perhaps they had split up to follow my confused trail through the forest and he was waiting for the others to catch up. Whatever the reason, I was glad for it, and I lifted my eyes to the sky and prayed once more to the God I had never trusted.

I asked Him to find us more time, to slow the riders down, and if He didn't help, then to hell with Him. I would deal with it myself.

Halfway back, Kashtan's hooves pounding, I spotted the dog following the flattened path of our trail. He had stopped, ears pricked and neck stretched, his whole body alert.

'Wrong way, dog,' I shouted as we reached him, forcing him to leap out of our way. 'We left something behind.'

He turned his head as he watched us pass; then he was behind us and out of sight.

Kashtan felt my urgency and she didn't let up, crossing the field at a gallop. She was probably glad for the chance to run without the restriction of the forest she'd had to cope with so much these past days.

Once across the field, she cleared the fence in an easy jump, and then her hooves were thumping on the compacted dirt of the yard and I was shouting for Lev and the girl.

'Come out,' I called as Kashtan turned in a circle, snorting with excitement. 'It's me. Kolya.'

I took Kashtan towards the rear of the barn and dismounted as Lev and Anna came out of the farmhouse. I pulled open the barn door and took Kashtan inside.

'What's going on?' Lev asked, running in behind me. 'I thought you—'

'Close the door. You have to come with me,' I said, grabbing tack from an armature on the wall. 'Get this on your horse. Now.' I thrust the saddle into his arms and went to Anna. 'I want you to go to the door and open it just enough to look out, do you understand?'

She nodded.

'Good. Now, it's important you don't go outside. Just open it a crack – enough to watch the horizon – and if you see anyone there, let me know straight away, all right?'

Anna nodded again and ran to the door.

'What the hell is this, Kolya?' Lev asked when I returned to him. He kept his voice quiet so as not to alarm Anna, but I could hear the edge in it. He worked as he spoke, lifting the saddle onto the horse's back, setting it in the right position over the pad that was already in place.

'Is she fast?' I asked. 'Your horse.'

'Fast enough for what?'

'You were wrong,' I told him, taking the front cinch. 'What you said about just being a peasant and his daughter. If the man you saw was one of the men I think are following me . . .' I pulled the cinch tight under the horse's belly and looked up at him. 'If he was one of them, there will be more. And they won't be forgiving. You helped me. You could die for that.'

Lev stopped what he was doing and stared at me. 'Who are you?'

'Keep working,' I told him. 'Get the bridle on.'

He didn't move right away. Something was going through his mind, and I was sure I knew what it was. He was thinking about how I had left them, knowing what might happen to them.

'The bridle,' I said, looking up. 'We don't have time for—'

It was Anna who brought it, hurrying back from the door and snatching up the bridle as she came. She thrust it into her father's hands, saying, 'We'll be all right, Papa.'

'Yes, we will,' I told her.

'Kolya came back to help us,' she said.

'Right. Now get back there and keep watch. And you need to get that bridle on. Quickly.'

As Anna returned to the door, Lev did as I asked, putting the bit between the horse's teeth and slipping the bridle over her head.

'I'm sorry. I told myself you'd be all right.' I bent to take the rear cinch and fasten it. 'I listened to what you said and let myself believe you were right.'

'What changed?' The horse resisted the bridle as if she felt the tension in us, but Lev held her steady.

'I had time to think about it,' I said, standing and checking the saddle was firm. 'And I realised you were wrong. *I* was wrong. I'm sorry. Sorry for putting you in danger.'

Lev was fitting the throatlatch when Anna shouted back to us. 'They're coming,' she said. 'I see them.'

'How many?' I asked, jogging to the door and looking out.

'Three.'

'We have to go,' I said to Lev, seeing three riders in the distance. Not much more than dots on the horizon, made hazy by the mist. 'You ready?'

'Let me get my shotgun,' he said, but I held him back, closing the door and telling him to leave it. There was nothing they needed. Nothing that was worth dying for.

'Just mount up,' I said, as I ran to the back of the barn and pulled open the rear door. If we left that way, it would make us invisible from the direction of the advancing riders. We wouldn't be able to hide our tracks across the steppe behind us, but at least it would earn us a little extra time if they didn't see us leave. By the time the riders arrived, we would have reached the plateau I spotted earlier. They would probably approach slowly, watching for an ambush, and they would spend a while investigating the farm before discovering our trail. With a bit of luck, we would be in the trees beyond the plateau by then and we could better hide our tracks.

'Hurry,' I said, coming back to help Anna onto the horse. I lifted her up and Lev held her as she swung her leg over so she was sitting in front of him. 'Go.' I shooed them out of the barn, taking Kashtan's reins and leading her outside before I shut the door behind us. 'Come on. Quick.' I continued to shout commands at them, feeling my nervousness increase with the added responsibility they brought.

I yanked open the back gate and ushered everyone through before closing it behind us and climbing onto Kashtan's back.

'As fast as you can,' I shouted, kicking my heels into Kashtan and holding tight as she broke into a gallop without further persuasion. Like always, she was in tune with my emotions and my needs, and she responded exactly as required.

We raced across the field, Lev and Anna riding well and in close pursuit, and when we passed the dog for a second time, I looked back at him, seeing him change direction and follow once again.

On the other side of the furrowed field, there were patches of hawthorn and elderberry and places where the brambles had grown wild, but Kashtan avoided them, pressing on across the steppe until we came to the rise almost without me having noticed. I brought her to a stop and turned to look back at the farm in the distance, but it was no more than a dark smudge now, made indistinguishable by the trees around it. If I hadn't known it was there, I would not have spotted it from this angle.

'Are you both all right?' I asked as Lev came to a halt beside us.

'Fine.' He was out of breath, and his skin was as flushed as Anna's, both of them almost glowing in the grey and white that surrounded us.

'Do you have scarfs? You should cover your faces.'

'We only have what you see,' Lev said. 'Everything else is at the farm. We're lucky to have coats and hats.'

'Anna's cap isn't enough,' I said.

'It's all we have.' There was a hint of resentment in Lev's tone.

'I'm sorry,' I told him. 'I'm sorry I ever came to the farm. I've dragged you into this now and . . .'

Lev blinked long and hard, shaking his head. 'No. I should be thanking you for coming back. We were already in this. Everybody is. You didn't have to come back for us.'

'We should keep moving,' I said. 'We're not safe yet.'

I leaned down and patted Kashtan's neck. 'Well done.' I praised my friend and encouraged her to find a good route to pick her way to the top of the rise. In places, it was almost sheer, while in others, the gradient was gentle and easy to navigate, and when we were at the top, we were perhaps ten metres above the part of the steppe we had just ridden across.

The top of the ridge was busy with a confused tangle of twigs and thorns, but we found a way through, coming out onto a steppe that rose into the distance where the forest erupted from its soil once more. Somewhere close to those trees, the road from Belev snaked its way to Dolinsk, and that was where I intended to head next – to follow Tanya and Lyudmila; to find Koschei. There was something I wanted to see, though, before moving on. I needed to assess the scale of what followed in our wake, so I dismounted, knowing we were out of sight from the farm.

I told Lev to stay and rest for a moment, and Kashtan wandered a few paces away, nuzzling the frost, searching for grass, while I went back to the undergrowth, finding a gap and lying down on my stomach. Crystals showered me as I pulled myself through, some finding their way down the back of my neck, but I ignored them and kept moving to the edge of the outcrop. From this elevated position, there was a clear view of the steppe, the farm and the land beyond it.

With the naked eye, it would have been impossible to see the men approaching the farm, but with the binoculars, the shapes were visible on the steppe between the distant forest and the field I had first seen yesterday.

Seven of them, approaching the farm in a line.

I shivered as I watched them, but I was not afraid now as I had been before. In the forest, there had been a sense of the unknown, but now I had confirmation. I *was* being followed, and that was easier to deal with than not knowing. My concerns were no longer washed in the shadow, and though I was still fearful of being caught, of failing Marianna and the boys and Lev and Anna, those seven riders were men. And men could be outsmarted, or confronted and killed if necessary.

They must have set out at first light; they couldn't have navigated the dense forest at night, and they were tracking me, which would have been too difficult in the dark. But they had gained ground faster than I had anticipated.

I put the lenses to my eyes again, propping myself on my elbows and watching the figures coming closer to the farm. It was impossible to see them as anything other than riders, and I would have liked to know exactly who they were.

Which of my former comrades had betrayed me?

If I knew that, then perhaps I could face them. I was armed, skilled, and had a good position here on the ridge, but if they were seven men with the skills I had, then a confrontation might not swing in my favour. I would be of no use to Marianna and the boys if I was lying dead in the hoarfrost, waiting for the snow to bury me, and I had Lev and Anna to think about now, waiting just a stone's throw behind me.

My life would be easier without them and the responsibility I had for them, but it would be poorer in other ways and I was glad they were here. As I watched those seven riders inch across the steppe, I knew I had done the right thing. The men following me would be well armed and expecting trouble – some of them would even be *hoping* for trouble, as I had once done. They might hardly even have needed an excuse to murder Lev and Anna.

The rider at the centre rode slightly ahead of the others and was the first to reach the gate, but the others were soon alongside him so that all seven riders were in a line facing the yard.

From here to there was a frozen sea of glittering hoarfrost on the thistle and feathergrass and shrubs of the wild steppe. With the wind dying, the mist was thickening, changing the light, threatening to shroud the landscape in a dense cover, and it was impossible even to tell what colour the horses were. They were just dark smudges. The men were faceless shadows and that made them all the more frightening.

As if on command, the men dismounted and came over the fence into the yard. Four broke off to one side, heading to the barn, while the remaining three made their way towards the house.

Having seen enough, I lowered the binoculars, but something caught my eye, making me raise them once more. In the near distance, there was movement on the steppe, a dark shape moving in our trail.

The dog, I said to myself. He's persistent.

I watched him for a few seconds, nose to the ground; then I crawled back through the undergrowth and returned to Lev, brushing the ice from my clothes.

'Seven men,' I told him.

'*Seven?* My God, who are you that they need seven men?'

'It won't take them long to find our trail. With a bit of luck, they won't come after us straight away.' I looked around. 'This mist is getting thick and they won't want to lose our trail out here. If they stray off it in the mist, they'll waste time finding it again, but if they stay at the farm . . . well, the trail isn't going anywhere. If it was me, I'd rest.'

I couldn't be certain, though. Whoever they were, they had been following me for a while now, at least since Belev, and that meant they were good trackers. They would have to be resilient too: the route I took through the forest hadn't been easy and I'd worked hard to disguise my trail. It was possible that they wouldn't stop; that they wouldn't risk losing me.

I didn't want to tell Lev that, though. I didn't want to scare him and Anna.

'So you think they'll stay at the farm?'

'They'll be tired. Their animals too. They must be tough to have followed me this far, but it's no fun sleeping in the forest every night. It gets tiring. They'll be glad of a fire and something warm to eat, just like I was. I think they'll rest.'

'Are you sure?' Anna asked, watching me closely.

'I can't be sure of anything.' Kashtan's saddle creaked as I climbed up. 'That's why we need to keep moving; get as far ahead as we can. We have to try to lose them.'

# 16

The mist stole the radiance of the hoarfrost on the thistles. It settled its damp and delicate fingers over everything, smothering the land in a bewildering half-light that lowered the sky and folded in around us. It gave its allegiance to no one. It favoured no colour. Just as it kept us hidden from our pursuers, so it kept them hidden from us. If they had chosen to continue after us, we had no way of knowing.

Kashtan walked on without seeming to notice, but there was nothing visible ahead of us now other than a few metres of frozen grassland. When I turned to look back, there was nothing to see behind us either. We were alone in our pocket of the world, isolated from whatever might be lurking beyond the wall of mist. Marianna would have known the name of some spirit or devil that was out there, protecting its home or punishing the wicked, but my concern was for something more human. My mind was on the seven riders and I kept us moving at a good pace, ever afraid they might appear as wraiths from the gloom.

'You keep looking back,' Anna said, breaking the almost lifeless calm. 'You think they're following.'

'I think it's possible.'

'It's all right,' Lev said, holding her tight. 'Don't be scared.'

'I'm *not* scared.'

'We'll be fine,' I told her. 'We'll be in the trees soon and then we can hide our trail better.'

'Who are they?' Lev asked. 'Why do they want you so much?'

'Chekists, probably. I deserted, so they want to—'

'But who are *you* that they're so desperate to catch you? That it needs seven men? And to follow you like—'

'I'm no one,' I said, and it occurred to me that when we reached the trees, perhaps I should let Lev and Anna go ahead. I could stay behind and make a stand; try to pick them off from the treeline. But the men following me were well trained and experienced and I was haunted by the image of leaving Marianna and the boys without anyone to come for them. I had to keep going for their sake.

As we continued into the mist and the crushing silence ahead, I pulled my scarf up to cover my mouth. My head was never still, always moving, my eyes always searching, watching for shadows, but there was nothing. We were the only living things on that steppe. The regular crunch of horses' hooves breaking the frost, the occasional dull clink of a bridle were the only sounds.

'Find the way,' I said to Kashtan. 'Find the way, girl.'

She snorted and nodded and kept on moving.

On and on.

We saw nothing. No one. We might have been moving through a dream.

I estimated we were riding for two hours, steady but slow, when I caught sight of the forest, sinister and imposing. It was a shadow, a presence that darkened the mist and stood like an uninviting guard across our path. Coming close enough to make out the individual trees, I spotted the track just a few paces ahead of us. It was almost indistinguishable from the sea of white we had just come through. Seldom used, the ice and the frost had claimed the rutted track in the same way it had claimed everything else.

'Well done,' I said, bringing Kashtan to a stop when we were on the road. I looked both ways, but there was nothing to see, so I climbed down and inspected the track, walking a few steps in either direction.

'The road to Dolinsk,' I said when Lev dismounted and came to join me. Anna stayed close to him.

'You think the dog's all right?' she asked.

143

I glanced back into the mist. 'I'm sure he's fine. He has our scent. If he wanted to, he could find us in the dark.'

On the road, there were many clear marks in the mud from horses that had passed this way, prints on either side of the track too, close to the trees, as if large numbers of animals had used this route together. Armies had been crossing this part of the country for years now and these tracks might have been here for as long as that, or they might have been fresh just a few days ago. Frozen in time as they were, myriad prints intermingling, it was almost impossible to tell.

'Nothing recent,' I said, seeing how the ice had formed hard in the marks and the latest frost had left its crystal calling card. If Tanya and Lyudmila had come this way, they would have kept within the forest – like me, they wanted to avoid any confrontation – but some of those prints could have been made by Koschei and his men. He could have been in this exact spot. Perhaps Marianna had even stood here; Misha or Pavel might have put their feet in the place where mine were now. I crouched and took off my glove to put my fingers onto the frozen mud as if it might somehow bring me closer to my wife and children, but there was no consolation to be taken from the hard ground.

I stood and pulled down my scarf so that I could put my face against Kashtan's and she pushed her nose into my chest. 'What would I do without you?' I said, taking her reins and turning to look at the forest. 'Come on.'

I led her forward, right to the trees, so that I could smell the damp earthiness, but something made me stop.

'What is it?' Lev asked. 'What's the matter?'

'It's safer for us in there, out of sight –' I glanced at Kashtan and put a hand to her cheek '– but . . .' Staring into the misty gloom between the crowded trunks, I was reminded of the horrors I had witnessed among the trees close to Belev. The blood and burned flesh, and the sense of something terrible lying in wait for me. 'We'll stay out here a while longer,' I said, turning north and following the treeline. For now we would use the weather as our friend; we could enter the forest later, when there was no other choice.

I glanced down at the multitude of hoof and boot and cart prints in the ground at our feet. 'Stay in these tracks. It shouldn't be long before they freeze over like all the others. It'll make us harder to follow.'

So we went on, heads down, using the forest and the road as our guide. With poor visibility it was difficult to estimate how far behind us Belev was, and how far ahead Dolinsk lay, but at least we were heading north again, following the trail Koschei had taken. Assuming Tanya and Lyudmila had been telling the truth.

We curved east and then west, cutting between more pockets of forest so that at times we were flanked on either side by the dark sentinels of oak and birch and maple and spruce. I checked my compass from time to time, knowing the more direct route to Dolinsk would be straight through the trees, so as soon as they began to thin out, we entered the forest.

The mist still drifted among the contorted trunks and twisted branches, but behind us, it had thinned and I stopped to raise the binoculars to my eyes and scan the steppe. The farm was far behind us now, as if it had never existed, but I half expected seven dark smudges to appear, hazy and indistinct. I wished I could see through the mist, know how far away they were, see what course of action they had chosen, but all I could do was guess.

Guess and keep moving.

'Are they coming?' Anna asked. 'Can you see anything?'

'Nothing yet –' I lowered the lenses '– but we should go into the woods now.'

'Let me see.' Lev reached out for the field glasses and I let him take them.

'What about the dog?' Anna asked. 'Any sign of him?'

'No,' I said. 'Sorry.'

'Could they follow him?' Lev scanned the distance. 'Could he lead them to us?'

'They don't need him to lead them across the steppe – our trail is clear enough – and they can move much faster than him. My

145

guess is . . . if he's still following us, and they are too, then he'd be a long way behind those riders by now. He looked half starved to me; he'll be slow.'

'But if they lose our trail, they could wait for him to catch up and take our scent.'

'They could – if he hasn't given up or exhausted himself. Anyway, there are ways to muddle our tracks once we're in the trees, make it hard for them.'

'Is that what you did before?' Lev asked.

'They're good trackers,' I admitted, 'but we'll confuse them. It will be easier to do that with two horses.' They had followed me this far, though, and I was beginning to wonder if I could ever lose them.

Lev handed the binoculars back to me and put his hand on my shoulder. 'We'll be fine, then.' He forced a smile.

'Of course we will.'

And with that, we turned and entered the shadow of the forest.

The trees were tight together on the edge of the wood, brought closer by the shrubs and bushes, which grew in twisted thickets between them, but once we were inside, they separated to a comfortable distance apart. They were too close for a horse-drawn sled or cart, but fine for a single rider. Once we moved past the treeline, the bracken and undergrowth thinned out, making our progress easier, so we mounted up and let Kashtan find the way, steering her on a different course from time to time, doubling back on ourselves, avoiding areas where we might displace the vegetation or leave visible prints. We separated at times, creating different trails, confused signs, clearing away the horses' dung when they dropped it, and when we found a small stream, we used it as our path for a while, breaking our scent and hiding our tracks.

As Kashtan took us on, deeper and deeper into the mist, time passing almost unnoticed, the sound of something alien arose in the distance.

A clatter and clank of metal. The hiss of steam and the thunder of rolling wheels.

It resonated through the trees, an unnatural and intrusive discord in the wilderness.

Anna gripped her father tighter and he, in turn, released the reins with one hand so that he could put his other hand on hers for reassurance.

He looked across at me, opening his mouth to speak but flinching as a shrill scream cut through the cold air, snatching away his words.

His horse lurched beneath him, her legs locking for a moment, jerking Lev and Anna forwards before she backed away, head turning from side to side, searching for sight of the danger she could hear. Her muscles flexed, and she turned in a tight circle, desperate to escape the unnatural sound. She snorted hard, her breath coming in great clouds of steam.

'Whoa.' Lev calmed her, stroked her neck while the scream faded to an echo and then to nothing, allowing the rhythmic clatter and clank to rise from behind and threaten to fill our world.

# 17

I had not forgotten that the railway line cut through the road between Belev and Dolinsk, bypassing both towns so that any passenger was oblivious even to their existence. I had seen the trains many times before. It was always something of an attraction, almost as if it were from another world. The great metal beast that steamed through the forest, scattering the snow in winter. Sometimes they were immense, and as boys, Alek and I would count the seconds it took for the wagons to roll past. We would put our hands on our ears as the ground shook, and laugh at the exhilaration of being close to something so large and powerful.

But I did not feel the same exhilaration now as I heard the familiar sounds of approach. It grew louder, the squeal of metal on metal cutting into the quiet of the forest.

'A train,' I reassured Anna. 'Just a train.'

'Which direction is that coming from?' Lev asked, raising his voice and turning his head to catch the sound. It was disorientating here among the trees. Everything looked the same from every angle, and the sound seemed to wrap round us as if it came from everywhere at once.

Anna pushed tighter against her father, eyes wide at the approaching sound, and Kashtan moved her ears, searching for the source of it.

'Keep going,' I told her. 'Don't be nervous.' She had seen trains before, but here it was just a terrible noise somewhere out of sight. And it is always the unseen that holds the most fear.

We moved on as the sound grew louder, and when I spotted the track in a shallow cutting between the trees a few metres ahead of us, we dismounted and brought the horses into the shadow of a thick-trunked ash to hide us from the train as it passed. I considered forcing Kashtan to lie down, but thought the effort and discomfort to her were not worth it. The train would be here and gone in just a few seconds, so the trees would be adequate cover.

As the train approached, though, it seemed to be travelling slowly, and when it finally broke from the mist with a swirl of steam, I knew it was slowing down.

I let Kashtan rest her chin on my shoulder and I wrapped my hand round her muzzle to hold her tight as it came closer. She moved against me, snorting with anxiety, but I calmed her and glanced at Lev, who was doing the same. With his other hand, he held his daughter close to him. He was half turning her head, pulling her face into his chest as if trying to protect her, but despite a hint of fear, there was also a spark of curiosity and excitement in her eyes.

The metal beast passed by at walking pace, travelling south on the line, giving us a clear view of the armoured engine at the front, its lights winking in the mist, the red star on its nose grimy yet still unmissable.

When that symbol of the revolution led the war machine from the gloom, it stood as a stark reminder of what I had once followed. I had marched under a banner with such a symbol on it, I had worn the red star on my uniform, and more recently, I had seen it turned to a different purpose: to burn its mark into skin, searing flesh as if it were a calling card. I had once associated that symbol with a better life for people like Marianna and the boys, like Lev and Anna, but now it was something to revile and hate.

The procession of carriages continued past, sullen and brooding, out of place in this bleak and beautiful wilderness; a blunt sign of the war that was throttling our country.

Coupled behind the reinforced engine was a blinded wagon, plated with metal, riveted and welded and cut with slits for riflemen to fire at all angles from within. The open wagon directly behind that was small and provided a platform for a Maxim machine gun, which was unmanned but accessible from the armoured car. The following wagons were an assortment of passenger cars and red cattle-cars, at least ten, and they rattled and clattered past us as if limping back from battle. At the end of this war train was another blind wagon with firing slits, and the final carriage was open and mounted with a Putilov field gun, which was capable of firing a variety of shells over great distance.

Some of the passenger cars had glass windows steamed opaque, while others were shuttered or covered with metal mesh so it was impossible to see what or who was inside. There were holes punched into the woodwork, splintered boards in the wagon sides, blackened patches where it had been burned or caught with the blast of explosives. On the roof of each wagon, there was a multitude of boxes, bags and crates of ammunition, weapons and supplies and man piled upon man in chaotic disorder. The soldiers were sitting, standing, lying wherever they could find space. Some of them were wounded, some were dead, and some were dying.

There was an air of tiredness and defeat about this limping monster.

'What is this?' Lev asked. 'Where are they coming from?'

I shook my head, still watching this ragged convoy limping past. It was not the monstrosity we had thought when we heard its approach. Now it seemed more tragic than terrible.

'Looks like they're retreating from something,' I said.

'I thought the fighting was further south,' Lev replied. 'They're going in the wrong direction, heading right into it. That doesn't make sense.'

The train was moving at just a crawl now, and we waited for it to pass before I told Lev, 'Stay here.'

I mounted Kashtan and approached the railway line, watching the field gun retreat and then disappear into the mist, leaving a swirling vortex that shifted and twisted and then settled. The noise of the train continued, but it slowed further, as if the beast were dying.

'It's stopping,' I said to Kashtan. 'Maybe we should go and look.'

I turned her about and went back to Lev and Anna, telling them my intention.

'Shouldn't we just keep moving?' Lev asked. 'That train is loaded with soldiers.'

'We'll stay hidden,' I said. 'You can even stay here if you want, but I have to look.'

'Why? Why can't we just keep going? Those men are behind us and—'

'Because I'm looking for my wife and sons, and this train is coming from the north. Some of those carriages might contain prisoners bound for labour camps, or someone aboard might be able to give me some information about Koschei. Maybe they heard something, saw something. Maybe they know who he is.'

'But the men behind us . . .' Lev looked over his shoulder, staring into the forest.

'I *have* to look,' I said. 'Don't you understand? If that train is carrying prisoners on their way to labour camps, then Marianna might be with them. My wife. My sons too. Misha and Pavel.'

'I'm sorry,' Lev said. 'I didn't think. But this is a war train, isn't it?'

'Any one of those closed carriages might have my family inside it,' I argued. 'I have to know there are no prisoners. I *have* to.'

Lev looked as though he wanted to say something else, but he understood how desperate I was. I couldn't leave this possibility uninvestigated.

'Look,' I said, 'if you want to go on without me, I'll catch you up.'

Lev thought about it, his agitation clear. He was afraid of the men following us, and he was afraid of the men on the train, but he didn't want to be alone in the forest with his daughter. He was a teacher, not a soldier. It would be easy for him to lose his way.

'All right,' he conceded. 'We'll come.'

So we followed the iron track, moving off it when it became

clear the train had stopped. If I were going to investigate, I would have to do it carefully. I was a deserter, a wanted man.

We trailed the noise of the idling train and the smell of burning coal left in its wake, keeping the track visible to one side, while listening to the shouts that came out of the mist. At first, they were intermittent, the occasional order snapped from the mouth of someone in charge, punctuated by the hiss of released steam from the engine.

'Out!' the voice was shouting. 'Out!'

Then other voices joined it so that a chorus of them was yelling orders.

Nearer still, the train not yet visible in the mist, other sounds began to prevail. Many of these were quieter and lower, but they were infinitely more disturbing. An almost perpetual groaning hummed in the air, deadened by the stillness of the forest. A bustle of hushed voices.

Murmuring and whispering was coming from all sides, as if the spirits had risen and were closing in on us.

'What *is* that?' Anna asked.

Lev glanced at me, waiting for an answer.

'Sounds like ghosts,' Anna said. 'I don't like it.'

'It's wounded men,' I told them. 'That's what the battlefield sounds like after a fight.'

We kept on, moving closer until the shape of the train was just visible and the deep moaning had grown louder.

'You two should stay here.' I stopped and inspected our surroundings.

At some time, a path for the track had been cleared through the forest, but it had not been well maintained and already there were saplings, taller than a man, pushing from the earth close to the rails. Grass and thistles grew in the spaces between the sleepers, nature threatening to reclaim what had once been hers. A little further back, there was an area where the trees were thick and the brushwood and brambles were unruly.

'Over here,' I said, leading Kashtan away from the track.

I hitched her to a tree, Lev doing the same, asking, 'What are you going to do?'

'I'll have a look around, come back as soon as I can.'

'Are you sure it's safe?'

'It should be fine. I won't be long, but don't come near the train. If I'm longer than an hour, go on without me, covering your trail just like we've been doing. Keep going north to Dolinsk; you'll be fine there.' I gave him my best reassuring look and winked at Anna, crouching in front of her and pulling down my scarf so she could see my face. 'Look after Kashtan for me.'

'I will.'

'Good girl.'

When I stood, Lev pointed to my rifle. 'You can't take that with you. We both know civilians are outlawed from carrying weapons.'

I looked at the rifle, reluctant to leave it behind, but knowing he was right. 'You know how to use it?' I asked him.

When he nodded, I handed it to him and he started to put it over his shoulder.

'No,' I said. 'Keep it out of the way. Hide it somewhere you can get to if you need it, but don't let anyone see you with it. And don't make any noise.' I started to walk away but stopped and lifted a finger. 'Make sure you stay right here. Don't go anywhere. And no—'

'It's all right,' Lev said. 'I understand. We'll wait right here.'

'Good. I'll be back soon.'

And with that, I went on, enveloped by the sound of dying, as if I was walking into hell.

# 18

The train had not stopped at a station, but hunched in the shallow cutting through the forest as if it had paused for breath before continuing its journey. From all along its length, men spilled onto the trackside. The wounded stumbled from every door, like the walking dead. Comrade helped comrade as they fell and limped and crawled away from the train. Officers patrolled the length of the track shouting orders, telling the injured to stand clear, to get away from the train, and from the roofs of the carriages, soldiers passed down the corpses of the men who had perished during the journey.

The mist swirled about them, mingling with the smoke, burned away in places by the steam that hissed and jetted from beneath the wheels of the engine. The length of the train was shrouded in a nightmarish whirlpool of cloud, and the stink of burning coal, and there was that awful sound underlying everything; that terrible moaning.

Few men had the energy to speak, but those who did spoke in heightened voices, confused chatter, edgy with panic that began to build, smothering the monotonous groan of the wounded and the dying.

And with the wind so still and the air so cold, there was another dimension to the horror of this train. When the doors were opened, so the atmosphere from within the carriages was released, and warmed by the wood-burning stoves within, the tepid air that escaped was sweet with the scent of decay.

Watching from my place in the woods, it occurred to me that

this whole land was dying, and I wondered if anything could revive it.

The chaos grew as more and more soldiers disembarked from the train until there were three or four hundred of them littering the forest. Many lay down as soon as they were clear of the metal beast, dropping wherever they could until bodies covered every part of the frosted ground. There were men with their arms in slings, others with bandaged heads or chests, men with missing limbs, diseased men resigned to their fate. Others were becoming more vociferous, calling to their commanders, asking what was happening, what was to become of them. The commanders ignored them and carried on with their task of emptying the train and setting able men to clear the dead from the roofs.

So it was into this sea of uniformed men that I went unnoticed, stepping from the trees and going among them, searching for any alert enough to answer my questions.

Crouching to speak to one man, I asked where they were coming from, had he heard of Koschei? But he just stared through me as if I wasn't there, so I moved to the next man and then the next and the next, stepping over and among them, asking the same question but receiving no response other than the blank stare of men who have seen enough.

Up ahead, close to the front of the train, a soldier faced the carriages, ordering men down from the roof. I took him for a commander of some sort because he assumed an air of authority. He was dressed in a good winter coat and wore a thick hat. Round his shoulder he wore a leather strap from which hung the wooden case of his pistol. He had sturdy boots on his feet, and he moved back to avoid the poorly dressed men who tumbled from the roof and limped from the doors.

When I was three carriages away, the commander looked in my direction and our eyes met. He had a severe face, mean and hardened by war, only now it displayed a hint of confusion, his eyes narrowing as if he recognised me or wondered at my purpose. When he moved, though, starting to come towards me, one of the disembarking soldiers fell against him, jostling him backwards. The commander regained his footing and held the man firm with both hands, turning him and helping him to sit on the ground by the track.

I pulled my hat low to cover my brow and tugged the scarf over my mouth to hide my face as I continued, picking my way among them. I watched the commander squat by the wounded man and light a cigarette for him, looking up in my direction, just as someone reached out and grabbed the hem of my coat.

I stopped and turned to look down at him.

'Are you a doctor?' he asked. 'They said there would be doctors.'

He was sitting cross-legged, his cap tipped to one side, his coat unbuttoned. The dressing on the left side of his face had once been white but was now a dirty brown. Beside him, a younger man sat with the head of another comrade face down on his lap. He was turned towards the forest, staring at the bones of the trees while running his hand through his comrade's hair as if to comfort him.

I crouched beside the soldier who had grabbed my coat.

'Are they going to leave us here?' he asked.

'Of course not.'

'Then why are they making us leave the train? They said there would be doctors; that they were taking us to the doctors.'

'They will,' I said, glancing around at the commanders walking the length of the train, checking doors and roofs, ordering the last stragglers from the cars. 'Are there prisoners here?' I asked. 'In any of these carriages?'

'Are we there? Is this where the doctors are? Is that what *you* are?'

'No. Listen to me.' I kept control of my temper. I had to remain discreet. 'Are there any prisoners on this train? Women and children? Are you headed for any camps?'

'They don't tell us anything,' he said.

'But you must have *seen*.' I felt as if I wasn't getting through to him, but I needed to find out what he knew.

'I've seen no prisoners. Just soldiers.'

I didn't know whether to be relieved or disappointed. 'You're sure?'

'Sure as I can be.'

I nodded and took a deep breath to calm my nerves. 'Where are you coming from?' I asked. 'What happened to you?'

'Tambov.'

'But you're going the wrong way. You're heading *towards* Tambov.'

'No.' He shook his head and looked about. 'No, that can't be right. We came from there. Fighting the Greens . . . Or was it the Blues? I can never remember.'

'Do you know Koschei?' I asked him.

'Koschei?' He looked confused. 'Why do you—'

'Do you know him?'

'From the *skazka*? You want me to tell you a story?' His voice was thick with sarcasm.

'Or do you mean the man?' A voice spoke beside me and I turned to look at the young soldier who was staring into the forest. His face was streaked with blood, and his uniform was caked with dirt, but he didn't appear to be wounded. He continued to look into the trees while running his fingers through the dark hair of the man resting his head in his lap.

'Yes,' I said, moving closer to him. 'Yes. The man. Do you know who he is?'

'No.' He turned his head but still didn't seem to be looking at me. His eyes were vacant, as if unseeing. 'But I've heard of him.'

'How? What do you know?'

'That he's like the devil. They say he boiled a priest and made the monks eat the soup.'

'What?'

'Stas would have told you. He knew him.'

'Stas?'

The soldier looked down at the man lying in his lap. 'He died on the train.'

I shifted and reached out to touch the dead man. I knelt in the dirt and hefted him so that his face was to the sky. The young soldier made no move to help, but also made no complaint.

I brushed the dead man's hair away from his face and recognised him straight away.

'Dotsenko,' I whispered.

Now the soldier looked at me. He leaned in so his foul breath was in my face. 'You knew him?'

I took my hand away from Stanislav Dotsenko's body, wondering how he had come to be on this train. 'I fought with him.'

'You fought with him?'

'Yes.'

'So you're a—'

'Did he say a name?' I asked. 'Did he say who Koschei is?'

'Nikolai Levitsky,' the man whispered.

'What?' The shock of hearing my own name was like being charged with electricity. Any regret or sadness I felt for Stanislav Dotsenko was shattered and I was suddenly aware of everything around me. My senses heightened, as if I saw better, heard better. But he couldn't have said my name. I must have misheard. 'What did you say?'

'Nikolai Levitsky.'

'No.' I sat back. 'No. That's not right.' I looked around, hoping no one else had heard it. From having been just another man in a crowd of men, I now felt singled out. I knew it wasn't so, but it was as if all eyes and thoughts were on me.

'He didn't say that Koschei is Nikolai Levitsky,' I pressed him. 'Tell me he didn't say that.'

'He didn't say that.'

'Then what *did* he say?'

'He said that someone called Levitsky let it happen.'

'What?' His accusation was somehow even worse: that I could have somehow unchained this monster.

'Levitsky made Koschei. He let him loose, is what he said. It didn't make any sense, but he kept saying it, over and over, and that he was sorry.'

'What for?'

'How should I know? I hardly knew him. He just needed someone to die on.'

A comrade to share his last minutes. None of us wants to die alone. I could understand that, but not the meaning of his final words. How could I have been responsible for Koschei? How could I have had anything to do with his actions?

I grabbed the soldier's lapels with both hands and shook him, pulling him so close that our noses touched.

'What's his name?' I asked. 'Who is Koschei?'

'I don't know.' The soldier displayed no fear. No emotion. No resistance. His expression remained blank, as if I were shaking a doll. 'I don't know.'

I released him, pushing him away so that he fell back and Stanislav slipped from his lap. I looked down at the dead soldier and felt the sting of shame and anger that now followed me wherever I went, always festering just beneath the surface. I stood and backed off, suddenly wanting to be away from here, back out on the steppe, just as I had done when I found the place of bones close to Belev. I took a deep breath and controlled myself, made myself remain calm. I didn't want to attract attention. I wanted to slip back among the trees and go to Kashtan, find comfort in her companionship. I wanted to see Anna's small, pale face and know there was something better in this world. I wanted to press on in search of my beautiful Marianna and my growing boys.

As I turned to pick my way back through the mass of the dead and the dying, though, I found my way obstructed by the commander who had noticed me earlier.

He looked me up and down as if to highlight my lack of uniform. 'Who are you?' he asked. 'What are you doing?'

'I'm a doctor,' I said.

'There are no doctors on this train.'

'And yet here I am.'

'So where are your . . . your things? Your bag. Your medicines.'

'Stolen,' I said, looking back in pretence. 'I put them down and now they're gone.'

'Do you want me to find them? We can turn these men inside out and—'

'No.' I put out my hands. 'Please. That's not necessary. Don't you think these men have suffered enough, Comrade Commander?'

'Most definitely. Thank you.' The soldier cast his eyes over the sea of men and sighed. 'The division commander is wounded,' he said. 'If you're a doctor, you can fix him.'

'I have no—'

'We have supplies in the division commander's cabin.'

I had to think quickly. I had to get away.

'What about these other men?' I turned and swept my arm about me, taking the chance to peer into the forest and make sure Lev and Anna were well hidden. 'They need a doctor too.'

'More than the division commander does?' His voice darkened and he stepped closer to me. 'Do I need to remind you that—'

'No,' I said, turning back to him. 'Of course not, Comrade Commander.'

He stiffened his back and pushed out his chest as he stared at me. 'Then come with me,' he said. 'Now.'

I didn't have time for this; there were men pursuing me, and ahead, time might be running out for my family if they were still alive. I was trapped here in the middle, but I had no choice other than to follow him. Although I was armed, my revolver heavy in my pocket, he was surrounded by men who would do his bidding without a second thought. Questioning orders in this people's army could result in the most severe of penalties.

I risked another glance back at the forest to reassure myself that Lev and Anna were still hidden by the mist and the trees; then I did as I had been ordered.

The commander led me to the blind carriage directly behind the engine and we stepped through the steam that billowed from the undercarriage. He moved to one side, instructing me to climb aboard, so I pulled myself onto the steps and waited for him to follow and open the door into the car.

The interior was basic. Slatted plank walls, some of them

reinforced with more wood nailed into place at random. The outer sides of the carriage were clad with welded metal plates, but the designer had clearly not anticipated attack from below because the floor had been left as it was. Some light crept through the firing slits cut into the walls, and yet more found its way through the cracks in the floorboards. Looking down, I could see the track below us. Benches lined the walls, and there were still one or two soldiers occupying places on them, but there was, by no means, a full complement of men aboard.

The men looked up at us as we came in, but paid us no more attention than that, going back to rolling cigarettes and drinking tea from metal cups.

In the centre of the carriage, an iron stove burned, warming the air to an almost bearable temperature, but the chimney, which fed through the roof, was cracked in places, and grey smoke swirled in the draught that cut in through the firing slits. The scent of burning wood and coal and decay was thick and sweet, almost covering the unwashed smell of the countless soldiers who had sat in here.

The inside of the carriage was stunted, though, smaller than it had looked from the outside, and I realised right away that it had been separated into two compartments.

'There,' the commander said, pushing past and marching to the door at the far end of the car, his boots clicking on the wooden floor.

I hesitated, glancing at the men seated on the benches, then followed, making my way past the stove and the pile of loose coal on the floor. The commander knocked on the door as I reached him and pushed it open without waiting for an answer.

'Doctor for you, Division Commander Orlov,' he said, ushering me in. Then he backed out and closed the door behind me.

There was the same odour of smoke and decay in here, but the room was more comfortable than the one I had just walked through. The bench at the side of this compartment was cushioned and upholstered with red fabric. There were no windows or firing slits here. Instead the walls were adorned with colourful maps of the Tambov area, nailed to the woodwork. Fingers of natural light filtered up through the cracks in the floorboards, smoke and dust swirling and eddying like magic in its glow.

In the far corner a small stove, this one in full working order, and beside it a stool with a colourful samovar balanced on it. In the centre of the compartment there was a table laid with maps and papers, a collection of used glasses, a lamp, a bottle of vodka and a pistol.

The large man who sat behind the table was Division Commander Orlov, whom I knew by reputation and had met once, a long time ago. I hoped he would not recognise me and was glad for the hat and scarf to cover my face.

Everything about him seemed square, from his shoulders to his chest and his short legs, and he would have been powerful in his youth, sturdy and well built, but he had aged a lot since I had last seen him. There was a beaten look about him now; a strained weariness reflected from him, filling the room. His hair was cropped close to his head, but there was little growth there anyway, and his cheeks were shaved clean. He still had the thick moustache I remembered, dropping at the corners of his mouth and pointing to the edge of his square jaw, except now the whiskers had turned from black to grey.

Commander Orlov leaned back in his chair, tunic open to reveal a dirty white shirt beneath, with his right foot propped on a stool. He wore no boot on that foot, and the material of his trousers had been split to the waist so that it hung loose to display the wound that festered in the meat of his calf.

A young soldier knelt on the floor, fumbling with a collection of medical supplies. Unravelling a bandage, it was clear the boy had no idea what he was doing.

Behind the commander, hanging on the wall, a clock told me it was just after ten, but it had to be at least midday by now.

'So you're a doctor?' Orlov said, looking up and beckoning me over. 'I didn't know we had any doctors on this train.'

I pulled my hat down further and lowered my head.

'When did you get on?'

I thought for a moment, trying to think where the train might have been coming from, where it might have stopped, but it would be dangerous for me to guess.

'Doesn't matter,' he said, before I could answer. 'We've picked up all manner of stragglers. Every time we stop, a whole lot more climb aboard. Don't they know we're going to hell?' He slurred his words and I guessed the vodka on the table was his way of killing the pain. 'Get over here before this boy keels over from the smell. He's useless anyway.'

Orlov shooed the boy away with one hand and reached for his glass with the other. The boy stumbled past me, making me step back, and hurried from the compartment, closing the door behind him so that I was left alone with the commander. I stared at the door for a moment, hoping that Lev and Anna had stayed where they were; that they had done as I had instructed.

'Come on,' he said. 'Fix me up.'

I turned and glanced around the carriage, my eyes settling on the pistol resting on the table for a second, then I approached the commander, pulling the other chair towards me and rummaging among the medical supplies. My fingers worked quickly as I looked for the supplies I needed to dress the wound. The sooner I was back with Lev and Anna, the better.

Close to the commander, the stink of his wound was nauseating, even through my scarf, and I tried to take only shallow breaths.

'Take off your hat,' Orlov said. 'Let me see your face.'

Without looking at him, I reached up and removed my hat. I placed it on the floor beside me, continuing to search through the bandages and field dressings. Outside, the muffled calls of soldiers shouting orders was beginning to die down.

'The scarf,' he said, taking a drink from the dirty glass, slurping the liquid.

I pulled down the scarf and looked up at him, our eyes meeting. For a long moment he held that look, breathing heavily, running his tongue round his teeth. His face glistened with

163

sweat, and his whole demeanour was that of a man struggling with a fever.

When he spoke, his lips were wet with vodka, and flecks of spittle fell onto his chin. 'Do I know you?'

I shook my head.

'We've never met?'

'No, Comrade Commander.'

'You look familiar.' He drank again, staring at me over the rim of the glass as he drained it. He swallowed hard and wiped his sleeve across his mouth. 'There was a time I never forgot a face.' He shook his head and sniffed. 'Now I see so many damned faces I don't know how I ever remember any of them.' He reached for the bottle and refilled his glass. 'Most of them don't live long anyway, so there's no reason to remember them all, is there? But you . . .' he said, pointing with the hand holding his drink. 'For some reason I feel I should know you.'

'I'm just a doctor,' I said, leaning over and making a pretence of looking through the medical supplies. I was trying to decide what was my best course of action. I could dress the wound and leave – I knew how to do that, but he might decide to keep me as his personal physician. I could simply leave the carriage. Orlov was wounded, probably dying from the infection, so he was in no shape to come after me, but his pistol was close to hand; he could shoot me before I was at the door. I had my own revolver, but even if I could take it from my pocket before he could reach for his own, I couldn't shoot him, not with soldiers just a few paces away, in the other part of the carriage. They would be in here in an instant, and when I was lying on the floor, bleeding and full of lead, I would have failed my children and my wife. Lev and Anna would be forced to continue into the forest alone.

I would have to overcome him silently, kill him without a sound if I were to escape from here unharmed. Perhaps I could reach the knife inside my coat, but I would have to be fast – his pistol was within easy reach.

In my contemplation, I had looked up without realising it and

Orlov followed my attention, putting his hand over the pistol. He dragged it towards him and held it in his lap.

'You're not a doctor, are you?'

I stopped what I was doing.

'You don't even look like a doctor. Don't act like one.'

I took my hand away from the supplies.

'All the doctors I ever met were soft intellectuals. Weak and spongy men who never did a proper day's work. Soft hands and waxy skin.'

I sat up and looked at him.

'Not you, though. You move like a soldier – I saw that the second you stepped through that door. I'm not too old and blind to see that. Your hands have done too much work – *killing* work, I would say, judging by the way your fingers reach for the button of your coat. What do you have in there? A knife would be my guess. The pistol in your pocket would draw too much attention, but the knife . . . ah . . . that would be quiet, wouldn't it?'

I hadn't even noticed my hand move, but there it was, ready to unfasten the button and reach inside for the blade.

'But it's your eyes that really tell me what you are.' Orlov drained his glass once more. 'It's always the eyes that give it away. I can see your *intent* just by looking into them. I can see you sizing me up.'

He leaned over to put his glass on the table, then lifted the pistol, staring at it. 'Pour us both a drink,' he said, 'but keep those killing hands where I can see them, eh? This wound in my leg makes me . . . twitchy. It shames me. I've been in more battles than I can count and this is where I get shot. It couldn't have been the heart or the brain – a good clean death – it had to be here so I can die slowly while my men watch. I might as well have been shot in the arse.'

I reached across the table and put two glasses together, looking over to the side of the carriage, wishing I could see through the metal plating, beyond the crowds of men and to the place where Lev and Anna were hiding in the forest. I wanted to get back to them, to be on with our journey. I envied the connection they had to one another, and I had enjoyed what little of it they had been prepared to share with me so far. It had left me wanting more; to be with them, in the presence of warmth and love, rather than here where there was only death.

'Something out there?' Orlov's voice snapped me back to the moment.

'Hmm?'

'You were looking at the window. Where there *was* a window anyway. Is there something out there demanding your attention?'

'No.' I shook my head. 'No.'

Orlov watched me as if he didn't believe me, pushing out his neck so that his face was closer to mine. He put two fingers to his eyes and narrowed them at me. 'It's all there,' he said. 'They give it all away.' Then he leaned back again, wincing in pain and slapping his hand on the table.

'Probably just as well you're not a doctor,' he said, recovering. 'You'd only want to cut it off. The whole leg. To get rid of the infection, you'd say. Just . . .' He made a sawing motion with one hand across the top of his thigh. 'I'd only be half a man then, and what's the point of that? What use would I be then? Maybe it's just as well there are no doctors here – I'd have a train full of cripples.'

I said nothing and glanced at the clock. It was still just after ten, the hands stuck in the position they'd been in when the clock stopped.

'So have you come to kill me?' he asked as I picked up the bottle. 'To give me a good clean death?'

'No.'

'Then why are you here?'

'I'm looking for someone.' I had to tell him something and perhaps this was the best thing. He might have information I could use.

He made an impatient gesture over the glasses. 'Pour. Pour.' When he put his hand down, he studied me with unblinking eyes. 'Looking for someone? Someone you *do* want to kill?'

'Maybe.' I poured vodka into each glass and pushed one across to him.

Orlov nodded and glanced at the glass but left it where it was. 'You know, there's someone *I* want to kill,' he said.

I waited for him to go on.

'We've been fighting in Tambov. Trying to put down this damn rebellion.' He turned the pistol in his hand as if looking for the secrets of life in its design. 'Returning with the wounded, picking up men along the way.'

'But you're heading *towards* Tambov,' I said.

Orlov looked up. 'Excellent observation. And that's who I want to kill – the man who issued that order. I get this far, bringing my injured men and anyone else who cares to catch a ride with us, and they send new orders. Turn back, they say. They need the train, they say. Drop off the wounded and come back, they say. So I drop them here, in the forest. To die.' He sniffed hard. 'What else can I do?'

'Disobey?'

Orlov waved his hand as if that didn't deserve a reply. He picked up his glass and raised it to me. 'The wounded,' he said.

I toasted with him and took a sip. Orlov drained the glass and indicated I should refill it. He continued to talk as I poured, vodka glistening on his moustache. 'Did you know that this man Antonov – the one who they say started this peasant uprising – he's a petty criminal? Put in prison for stealing from railway station offices of all things, and when the revolution pardons him, what does he do but go to war against us.' Orlov scoffed and shook his head. 'What a bloody mess. This whole damn country has gone to hell and we can't even pick our enemies properly. Too many colours to choose from, I say. *Tokmakov* is the real leader of this uprising, though, a former Imperialist. A decorated soldier, no less.'

Commander Orlov winced in pain and lifted his glass to his lips, stopping as he was about to drink. 'Damn Imperialists,' he smiled. 'I was one myself once.' He paused for thought. 'You know the uprising began when some soldiers beat up an old man in Khitrovo?' he said. 'I went there and it was just like anywhere else. Just another unimportant town.'

I had been there too, but I didn't tell Orlov that.

'As if we don't have enough trouble with all the other damn armies who want to stop the people's revolution. This isn't war; this is chaos. No one knows what the hell is going on. We push the White Army down to Crimea, send Wrangel to the dogs, deal with the Blacks, and now our own people are rising against us. Now we have a Blue Army to fight.'

'The Whites are defeated?'

'More or less. Wrangel and his men disappeared into the Black Sea, going to who knows where, and now there's just all these other colours to finish off – Blue, Green, a whole *rainbow* of colours – but they might as well all be brown for the shit this country has gone to.' He seemed pleased with that analogy and smiled to himself before tipping back his head and swallowing the vodka.

'They say they're diverting men who are coming back home from Perekop,' he said, wiping his moustache on his sleeve and looking at me, 'but they'll be as useless as the men I've just kicked off this train. Every one of them battle-weary or wounded, and I am ordered to leave them here rather than take them to a place where they can be treated, which is what I promised them.' He nodded at me. 'Drink.'

I put the glass to my lips and sipped again.

'All of it. Drink it all,' he said, so I drained the glass and put it down beside his.

'More.' Orlov waved the pistol in my direction.

When I had refilled the glasses, he fell into a sombre silence, shaking his head every now and then, staring at the pistol. Outside, the sounds of the men had settled. No more orders were shouted. There was only the occasional voice that lifted above the constant murmur and moan.

I watched Orlov, wondering if now was the time for me to leave. He was so deep in thought I might have been able to slip from the carriage without him noticing. Or perhaps I could get to my knife and put an end to him, but I realised I had no reason to want to harm him. He had done nothing to me. He was a wounded commander trying to do his job, and it was refreshing to see the remorse he felt at having to leave his men to die. It would take huge courage for him to defy his orders, and looking at the state of the men outside, many of them would be dead before long anyway.

'Nikolai Levitsky.' The words came at me like a slap. It was the second time today that someone had spoken my name and I missed a breath, my hand tightening round the glass, some of it spilling over and running through my fist.

'Nikolai Levitsky,' he said again, this time turning his head to stare at me. 'You've heard of him?' He looked me up and down as if assessing me with new interest.

'No.'

'A hero of the revolution. Recipient of the Order of the Red Banner.' Orlov shifted in his chair, pushing himself up a little straighter. 'He was an Imperialist, just like me, but after the war with the Germans, he joined the Red Army and—'

'Why are you telling me this?'

Orlov shrugged. 'Not much longer than a month ago, Nikolai Levitsky and three men fought three hundred attackers in the village of Grivino. Armed with just their Mosin-Nagant rifles, they held the Blues back until reinforcements arrived. Earned himself the Order of the Red Banner. Now that's a hero,' Orlov said. 'Fighting for the people. Not like this man Tokmakov, leading his peasants against the revolution.'

It hadn't been that way, though. We hadn't been fighting for the people; we had been fighting for our lives. And there hadn't been three of us; there had been ten, including my brother, Alek. And we had a *tachanka*. Peasants with a few rifles and pitchforks were no match for trained soldiers with good weapons and a horse-drawn machine gun. We gave them a chance to surrender, but they refused, so we gunned down every man, woman or boy they sent at us. Not three hundred, though; there can't have been more than a hundred and fifty. And there were no reinforcements

169

coming to help us; we didn't need them. The battle lasted no longer than twenty minutes before the peasants finally saw the futility of their attacks and scattered back into the forest around Grivino. We didn't follow them in, but sent a few gas grenades into the trees to finish off any stragglers.

Only one of us died in that battle, and that was because his own rifle exploded, the barrel fragmenting and firing a piece of shrapnel into his head. But the real story was no inspiration to Bolshevik soldiers. They needed heroes, not men who slaughtered women and children. So the propaganda machine changed our story and put medals on our chests, right over our heavy hearts, and the more I had thought about it, the more ashamed I grew. It had been a burden to my brother too. He never spoke of it, but I had seen it every day in his eyes.

'You know, they say Levitsky was killed in Ulyanov. Ambushed by guerrillas and shot dead. Left in a ditch with his face smashed in.'

'Is that right?'

Orlov shrugged. 'Maybe. Others say he deserted. Left his unit like a coward.'

'Maybe he just wanted to go home.'

'And who would blame him?' Orlov said. 'Don't we all just want to go home? Except it isn't permitted.'

'He doesn't sound like a coward to me.'

'Nor to me. And yet they say that men from his own unit are hunting him down to bring him to justice. Just like you're looking for someone,' he said. 'Who *are* you looking for, *Doctor*?'

I put the glass down without emptying its contents. I had drunk enough already, and I needed to keep my wits about me. The alcohol would slow me, diminishing my chances of leaving the carriage alive. Outside, Lev and Anna were expecting my quick return, relying on me to lead them to safety. I would not let them down.

'Well?' Orlov waited for a reply.

I held my hands together to stop them from shaking and met his stare, wondering if he was going to shoot me or call for me to be arrested. But he had come from north of here; perhaps he knew something that could help me. 'I'm looking for a man who calls himself Koschei.'

'Like the story?'

I nodded and told myself to relax. I breathed steadily, loosened my hands and let them separate to hang by my sides, ready to act.

'I never understood that story,' Orlov said. 'Why they called him "the Deathless". Every story I ever heard about him, he dies at the end. I suppose that's the truth, isn't it? Eventually everybody dies, no matter who we are. Even me.'

I said nothing and the commander shifted round in his chair a little more, the pistol still in his hand, the muzzle towards me. All it would take was for his finger to twitch.

'I've heard of a man who call himself by that name,' he said. 'A Chekist.'

And with those words, my attention sharpened. 'Do you know who he is?'

'Nobody. Somebody.' Orlov shook his head. 'I overhear the men talking when I'm sitting in here, but I've heard so many names. Krukov, Levitsky . . .' He watched me for a reaction. 'Other names I forget.'

'Krukov?'

Orlov shrugged. 'That's a name I heard.'

I knew Krukov: we were from the same unit. I had fought alongside him, and now I saw his face. Lean and gaunt. I could understand why men might call him Koschei. Like the spectre in the *skazka*, Krukov was tall and thin and drawn. His beard was long enough to touch his chest, and he carried a sword, too. But if Orlov was right – if Koschei and Krukov were the same man – then what the young soldier outside had said could be true. Perhaps I *had* been responsible for loosing Koschei upon the world. If I had not deserted, he would never have been able to perpetrate such acts as he had.

Belev would have been safe.

If Alek and I had stayed with our unit, Koschei might never have gone into our village, and that sense of responsibility was like a weight crushing down on me. My mind reeled as it followed the thread of events that could have led to Krukov's metamorphosis into Koschei. If I had not run, so much would be different.

'You know where he is?' My mouth was dry, my throat tight. My skin crawled and grew cold. The smoky air suddenly felt thick and claustrophobic.

'No idea. First I even heard of him was a few weeks ago, but it was just stories. Hearsay about the things he had done. Yesterday, we took one of his men on board. Maybe he could give you—'

'I saw him.' My voice seemed to come from someone else. 'He's dead. What else can you tell me?'

'Not much. My commanders are afraid of the Cheka, so they don't ask too many questions, but he said he was with a small group escorting prisoners to a camp north of Dolinsk. His own men turned on him for some reason.'

'Prisoners? You're sure?' I couldn't hide my concern.

Orlov raised his eyebrows in interest. 'Mm-hmm. It's what he said.'

'Women and children?'

'I think so.'

*Prisoners.* It was a single word that gave me renewed hope. If Stanislav Dotsenko had been with Koschei and was then transporting prisoners, there was a greater chance for Marianna and the boys.

'From what they say, I think a lot of people would want to kill this man Koschei, but why do *you* want to kill him?'

'He took my family.'

'Then I can see why you're interested to hear about prisoners, and why you'd want to find him.' Orlov nodded. 'I have a family – a wife and son in Moscow. So far away.'

'You're wounded; you can go back to them.'

'Maybe,' he said. 'Maybe if I could walk like you can. Maybe if this damned leg wasn't so rotten.' He snatched his glass from the table and stared into it.

'Do you have any prisoners on board this train?' I asked.

'You mean civilians?'

I nodded.

'You mean, did the Chekists give their prisoners to us?'

I nodded once more.

'No,' he said. 'Your family is not here. You have my word on that.'

I felt a mix of emotions at this news. There was relief that Marianna and the boys were not cooped up and starving inside one of the carriages, and there was disappointment because I still didn't know where they were. But Koschei *did* have prisoners – Orlov had told me that much – and that gave me more hope that they were still alive.

'You know what I would do if I found Nikolai Levitsky?' Orlov said. 'If, for instance, he walked into my carriage right here on this train and told me he was looking for his family? Like you are, I mean.'

'No. What would you say?'

'I'd tell him to keep running. To keep looking. To find this man Koschei and tear out his heart for taking his family.'

'Why?'

'Because now I understand what is important. Not fighting. Not war. Not revolution. None of this shit. *Family*. Family is what matters. In all this mess . . .' Holding the pistol, he swept his hand around him. 'In all this mess, nothing matters anymore except family. Not the revolution, not Lenin and definitely not the idiot who ordered me back to Tambov.'

His words were enough to warrant execution.

'I'll never see my family again,' he said, lowering his voice and becoming reflective. 'With this leg, I won't last more than another week. I'm rotting away right here in this carriage and they're sending me back south to die.'

'I can still dress it for you,' I said. 'I know how.'

'I imagine you've seen a few wounds in your time.'

'Maybe you'll find a surgeon who—'

'A surgeon?' he sneered. 'Out here? Not a chance. Anyway, I don't want to be half a man. I'm a soldier.' Commander Orlov looked up at me. 'But if I knew that a man like Nikolai Levitsky was out there looking for his family, I would tell him to find them and take them somewhere small.'

'Small?'

'Somewhere unimportant. Invisible. Because even when this war is won – and it will be the Bolsheviks who win it, I'm sure of that – there still won't be any peace. Not for anyone.' He raised his glass and toasted, saying, 'Family.'

Orlov placed the glass on the table, then turned the pistol once more in his hands. 'Time for you to go,' he said. 'We both have things to do.'

'Thank you, Commander.' I stepped out and closed the door.

Returning through the carriage, the soldiers hardly watched me pass, but I was relieved to reach the far end and come out into the fresh air. I wanted to be back on Koschei's trail straight away. Commander Orlov's information had given me greater hope and I felt a renewed urgency. I was eager to return to Kashtan, to Lev and Anna, and to be away from this place.

But I hadn't escaped yet.

As I turned to descend the iron steps, I saw something that changed my mood in an instant.

I stood for a moment, trying to process what was happening.

The commander who had taken me aboard the train was picking his way through the wounded men, coming towards the carriage with a grim expression of determination on his face. As he came, he drew his pistol from the wooden holster, raising it to point at me, and when I glanced up to look behind him, beyond the sea of wounded soldiers, I understood why.

Close to the trees, two men with rifles stood guarding Kashtan. Lev's horse grazed beside her. And there, between the soldiers, Lev and Anna stood prisoner.

# 19

The commander stopped a few paces from the bottom step, standing in the sea of wounded men, and looked up at me, aiming his pistol. 'Come down.'

My only choice was to go back to Commander Orlov. It was he who had let me go, and so he might do it again, but there was a chance he would change his mind. When he sent me away, we were alone, with no one to know his actions, but when others were involved, he might not be so ready to do the same. Even a man like him could be accused as an enemy of the Bolsheviks, which was why he hadn't disobeyed the order to dump his wounded and return to Tambov. On the other hand, when I had just left him, he was a broken, dying man. Perhaps he had reached the end of his allegiance. Maybe he would release us anyway. He was our only hope.

'Please,' I said, holding out my hands. 'Come and talk to Commander Orlov. He—'

'You're no doctor,' the commander said, sending a wave of interest flowing among the wounded men behind him. 'Who the hell are you?'

'Please. Come and talk to Commander Orlov. He'll tell you—'

'Get down.'

I stood for a moment, looking at him, wondering what was the best course of action, but there weren't many options open to me. It would be easy for him to shoot, and he wouldn't need much more reason than my failure to obey. I would have to comply for now.

But as I put my feet on the ground, so the first voice spoke among the soldiers.

'Doctor?' It was impossible to tell who said it: there were hundreds of men lying or sitting on the trackside.

'He's a doctor?' A different voice this time. 'Please. Help me.'

'Get down here, now,' the commander ordered.

'Did someone say "doctor"?' More voices joined the chorus. 'Where? Where's the doctor?'

The men around the commander's feet were the ones in the worst condition, left closest to the train to avoid carrying them too far, but the men further back were more able and a ripple of movement broke through them. A few began to struggle to their feet, some saying, 'Over here, Doctor. Over here,' and more and more of them called for me, adding their voices to the discord as they stood and began to shuffle towards me.

'Stay back, everyone,' the commander said without taking his eyes off me. 'Sit down. Stay where you are.'

Two or three of the other able-bodied soldiers were coming to the commander's aid, pushing into the gathering crowd, telling the men to get back. They forced some of them away, shoving them against other men, so they were falling over one another, but already the hope of treatment had lodged itself in the minds of the wounded men. Commander Orlov said that they had been promised doctors and now they thought the promise was being fulfilled, so they stood and they came, joining the growing mob of injured men coming towards me, jostling each other, surging around the guards, approaching the place where the commander and I stood.

'Back!' he shouted, but the men paid him no attention. They were dying. Their comrades were dying. They were in pain. They wanted help. And so they shambled on, swarming around the guards who tried to stop them, hemming them in, crushing them with the force of their number.

The commander came closer to me, stepping over the dying, keeping the pistol level, saying, 'Get back on the train.'

But the first of the wounded men had already reached us. This young soldier wore a bandage at an angle round his head, covering one eye, and he forced his way past the commander, reaching out his hands to touch me, to beg me to help him. Just behind him, another man pushed through, this one holding a bloodied arm to his chest, and then others shoved in from all sides. Men horded about us, bloody and dazed and sick, so that we were surrounded by them, in danger of being crushed by them, the commander becoming frantic as he tried to turn me and force me back onto the train. At the top of the steps, one of the guards had come out to see what was happening, and as I looked up at him, a sound came from within the carriage that stopped everything.

A single, muffled gunshot.

It was as if someone had frozen time. Nobody moved. Nobody spoke. We stood in the mist, our minds cleared by that single report, and for a brief few heartbeats, no one thought of anything else. Except for me. Because I knew who had fired that shot, and I knew that Commander Orlov had taken his leave of the war.

I seized the distraction, grabbing the commander's pistol and twisting it from his grip with my right hand while slamming my left elbow into his jaw as hard as I could. His legs buckled underneath him, and as he dropped, I pushed him hard into the crowd of wounded men. He looked at me in surprise as he staggered backwards, putting out his arms for balance, but he only succeeded in taking more men down with him. The soldiers behind him were weak with injury and provided no support at all, falling into others, pushing the whole crowd back, smothering the guards who had come to the commander's aid.

As they collapsed onto one another, I identified the clearest route and began pushing my way through the men. Hands clawed at me and I dropped the commander's pistol as they grabbed at my coat, snatched at my arms, tried to grasp my legs, and I shoved and kicked and slapped them away as I broke through.

Some of the men called for me, shouting, 'Doctor, please,' but I had to get away from this hell.

Bursting free from the clutching hands, stumbling away from the men, I raced towards Lev and Anna.

Only one of the guards remained with them, but he was confused by the surge of bodies in front of him, everybody desperate to follow me, and I was on him before he could react. I grabbed him by the front of his coat and used all my strength to turn and throw him back into the crowd.

'Get on your horse,' I shouted to Lev and Anna, who were struck dumb by what they were witnessing. Although Lev had moved to stand in front of his daughter, he watched in horror, as if hypnotised by the crowd of walking dead that surged towards us.

'Get on your horse,' I shouted again, snapping him out of his trance as I came to his side. '*Now.*'

'Yes,' he said, gripping Anna with one hand and turning to his horse. 'Yes.'

Every second was valuable now. The wounded men were closer, and the guards were recovering, preparing their weapons.

Kashtan had begun to retreat from the advancing horde, but Lev's horse was terrified. Her eyes were wide, her teeth bared and her ears pinned back. Her hindquarters were tensed, the muscles knotting under her coat, and she tried to bolt. The reins jerked in Lev's hand and he tried to keep hold of them, losing his footing and stumbling as the leather tore from his grip.

Seeing her father's struggle and watching the advancing horde of men, Anna backed away, wanting to be with her father. She saw him as her protector, but he was preoccupied with taking control of his horse and she didn't know what to do. Her distress was clear, her mouth opening and closing, her head turning from side to side as she looked for a way out.

I knew Lev would struggle to settle his horse and climb onto her, and with Anna to consider, it would be even more difficult for him, so I went straight to her, sweeping her off the ground and swinging her high, lifting her onto Kashtan.

'Papa!' she called out to him, struggling against me, reaching out as if she would be able to touch him. 'Papa!'

Lev spun round when he heard her cry, his face contorted with panic.

'I've got her,' I told him, and when he saw that she was safe with me, he shouted to us, saying, 'Go!' then turned back to the horse that was trying to escape the mayhem.

Anna squirmed in the saddle, still leaning out towards Lev, still shouting for him, saying, 'Papa! Papa!' Her voice rose in pitch as she became more and more afraid for him.

I held her tight with one hand to keep her from slipping out of the saddle, controlling Kashtan with the other.

'Stay there,' I pleaded with Anna as I encouraged Kashtan to turn. 'There's nothing you can do. He'll be fine. He's coming. Don't worry.'

Kashtan knew me like we were part of one another and she responded well to my instruction, turning to face into the forest, no longer staring into the mob of soldiers. She prepared to run.

With only himself to consider, Lev managed to grasp the reins of his own horse and hold her steady enough to climb up, the animal rearing as the men surged around us. The horse's actions deterred the wounded soldiers for a moment, giving Lev a chance to spur his animal on towards the trees, but then they were coming forward again, so I kicked the man closest to me, pushing others away, clearing enough space for me to put my foot in the stirrup.

Kashtan didn't wait any longer. She was forging into the undergrowth, just behind Lev's horse, even as I was swinging myself up into the saddle.

I held Anna tight, feeling the tension in her, hearing her sobs as I glanced back to see the commander standing in the crowd, holding a rifle to his shoulder. Further along the train, other soldiers were also raising weapons. The commander leaned this way, then that, trying to find a shot at us, but he was frustrated by the men obscuring his line of sight, and when he finally chose to fire, his bullet struck one of his own soldiers from behind. The man's head snapped forward and he went down as the gunshot echoed in the mist, but the commander didn't stop. He worked the bolt and fired again, his second shot crackling into the undergrowth to one side as Kashtan carried us away.

And then we were out of sight, among the trees, running from the barrage of gunfire that erupted behind us.

Bullets ripped through the brushwood. They sang in the air, whistled and whined, thudded as they tore into the trees, powdering bark and ice. The sound of the shooting was accompanied by the shouts of the soldiers, the calls of help from the wounded, and then a single long blast from the train's whistle as a call to arms for all men.

I gripped Kashtan's reins with both hands, leaning into Anna to press myself against her and stop her from falling. She, in turn, had taken fistfuls of Kashtan's mane and was holding tight. We thumped together with every step Kashtan took.

Lev's horse crashed through the forest ahead of us. She was out of control, bumping into low-hanging branches, her hind legs throwing up broken twigs and dead leaves as she careered among the dark trunks. Lev was bent low, leaning right down along her neck to protect himself from the tree limbs that whipped and snatched at him, and I could see he was trying to calm the horse, pulling the reins hard, but to no effect.

I spurred Kashtan on, thinking I might be able to catch up with Lev, somehow help to bring his horse under control, but as we came closer, a bullet smacked into the horse's right shoulder with a loud slap. The animal let out an awful scream as her front legs twisted beneath her, then she crumpled to her knees, her head going down as she skidded forwards, throwing Lev from the saddle.

Lev was in the air for less than a second before he hit a frosted tree, crashing through a low branch, striking the trunk and showering a white cloud of ice around him.

His body was limp when it hit the ground.

# 20

Anna called for him. She *screamed* for him.

'Papa!'

It was the single most terrible thing I had ever heard.

Behind us, the soldiers continued to shoot. They didn't know who they were shooting at or what they might hit, but they shot anyway, over and over again, their bullets peppering the forest.

'Papa!'

Lev's horse writhed and kicked in the undergrowth, the black hide around her shoulder glistening with the dampness of her blood. She screamed and rolled her eyes, adding to the already nightmarish sounds that enveloped us.

'Papa!'

Kashtan tried to choose a new route to avoid the fallen animal, so I resisted her, slowing her as we approached the spot where Lev had fallen. It was the most natural thing in the world for me to want to reunite Anna with her father, but as soon as we were close enough to see him, I knew there was nothing to be gained from it. We couldn't help Lev now, and if we stopped, we would be in greater danger from the soldiers behind us who might already be advancing into the forest.

I spurred Kashtan on and put one hand around Anna, pulling her to me as we passed the place where her father now lay.

Lev wasn't moving.

He was on his front, his head turned at an awkward angle, his face pressed against the base of the tree he had struck.

Underneath him, a fallen branch, one of its broken fingers piercing his neck just under the chin.

There was no doubt that he was dead.

# 21

As soon as she realised I wasn't going to stop, Anna began to struggle. She wriggled to get away from me, calling for her papa, trying to turn and look back, but I held her firm. Strong and wild though she was, she couldn't match my strength, and even when she bit down on me, her teeth crushing through the cloth of my coat, all she succeeded in doing was pinching the skin of my forearm. So she took to pummelling my arms with her fists, begging me to stop, crying out again and again for her papa, but I resisted her. I focused my thoughts on what lay ahead and concentrated on leaving the train behind us, on keeping Anna safe.

There was nothing for me to take Anna back to except the pain of seeing her broken father once more. The soldiers would have reached the place where he fell and they would shoot at us on sight, but I doubted they would come after us. Even if there were horses on the train, they wouldn't use them to chase us. They had instructions to go to Tambov, so someone would bring order to them and slip into Commander Orlov's role quickly enough.

There were other riders to think about, though. The seven men on our trail.

And we had delayed long enough, so I kept on.

I held Anna, wishing I had the words to soothe her, and I turned Kashtan north and kept on.

She moved quickly. The forest passed us by, tree after tree after tree. The mist showed no sign of clearing and we pressed further into it. Disappearing further and further into the forest, on and on until Kashtan grew tired and could run no more.

She slowed her pace to a trot, and eventually we were walking through the forest.

Anna was silent now. She had exhausted herself and no longer fought against me. She had ceased calling for her papa too, but I still held her tight, my arm aching, and she swayed with Kashtan's movement. When I spoke her name, there was no response and I suspected she had descended into shock.

I wanted so much to be able to return her father to her. I wanted to rewind time and somehow save him from his fate, but I had to content myself with Anna's safety. I considered how lucky it was that I had put her onto Kashtan's back, otherwise she too would be lying dead in the forest behind me. And, thinking that, I held her even tighter.

We had been travelling for an hour, maybe more, when we stopped. Kashtan was too tired to carry us much further without rest, and we had come to a small stream, which was a good place for her to drink.

I dismounted and lifted Anna down, telling her to sit at the base of a nearby oak. She complied without a word, sitting with her knees pulled to her chest, arms wrapped around them as if she were curling herself into a ball. She looked even smaller like that.

I put two of the blankets around her, making sure she was well covered, then hitched Kashtan close to the stream and broke the surface ice with my boot heel. While she drank the chilly water, I took a few things from the saddlebag and returned to Anna's side.

I stood for a moment, wondering what to say to her. I wanted to give her some words of comfort, tell her something that might alleviate at least some of her pain, but there was nothing I could say. No words could make her feel better about what had happened. The only thing I could do was be with her. Protect her and keep her safe.

'You should eat something,' I said, kneeling beside her and unfolding a piece of cloth containing a few strips of dried meat – the last of a deer my brother and I had cured over a fire when we were heading for Belev.

Looking at those strips of meat reminded me of Alek and the loss I had felt. My brother and I had been close, and his passing had been hard, but what Anna was feeling would be worse.

'I'm sorry,' I said, staring at the thin, dark pieces of dried venison. 'About your papa. We couldn't have stopped for him, though, you know that, don't you?'

It was important to me that she understood. Not for selfish reasons – it wasn't because I didn't want her to think ill of me – but because I wanted her to know I hadn't let her down. That I *wouldn't* let her down. That I would keep her safe.

'It was too dangerous to stop, and he was already . . .' I sighed. 'It was quick. There wasn't anything we could do.'

'You could have let me stay with him.'

'No. It wasn't safe for you there.'

'Will he be with Mama now?' Her voice was almost inaudible and she seemed so small and vulnerable.

'I don't know. Maybe.' I refolded the cloth without taking any of the venison. Neither of us could face the thought of food.

The forest was quiet, the mist still hanging in the air, the sky darkening. The days were short now, the sun quickly falling below the horizon.

Anna looked up as though she'd had a sudden revelation. 'We should go back. Maybe Papa is all right. Maybe he's—'

'No, Anna, you saw him,' I spoke gently. 'Your papa is dead.' It was a cruel thing to say, and I felt terrible saying it, but she had to accept what had happened. I didn't want her to persuade herself that we had left him to die alone instead of helping him, or that he would somehow survive and come for her. I knew men who had let themselves believe they had left wounded friends behind rather than dead ones, and the guilt they suffered for the thoughts of not going back was a heavy burden to them. She had to know he was gone and that there was no coming back.

Better to suffer the grief and move forward.

'Will they come after us now?' she asked, looking up at me. Her skin was ashen, her eyes red from her tears.

'I don't think so. I didn't see any horses, and they won't follow on foot. We should be safe here for now.'

'It was my fault,' she said.

'No. It was an accident. You can't—'

'Papa said you'd been gone too long.' Her lips hardly moved as she spoke. 'He said that something must have happened and that we should leave, just like you told us to.'

Her voice was quiet, almost a whisper.

'But I wouldn't let him. I said you helped us, so we should help *you*. I made him bring the rifle.'

My heart almost broke for this brave little girl.

'You came to look,' I said.

She nodded.

'And the soldiers saw you.'

'He did it for me.' Her face crumpled, her shoulders hitched, and she sobbed in silence, tears falling down her cheeks.

'It wasn't your fault,' I said, putting my arms around her. 'We should never have stopped there. Blame me. Blame me for what happened. I should never have made you stop there. It was *my* fault.'

She could hate *me* if she wanted something to hate, so I gave her a reason, but while I was angry and upset about what had happened to Lev, I wasn't angry with myself for going to the train. I had come away from there knowing that Koschei had taken prisoners. I now had some hope that Marianna and Misha and Pavel were still alive, even if that hope was tainted by what had happened to Lev.

I pulled Anna to my chest, as I had done with my own children when they needed comfort, and I lowered my head so it was touching hers. I closed my eyes to the world and felt her pain, wanting to make it go away, but knowing I was helpless.

'I'll take care of you,' I told her, but the words sounded weak when I spoke them. I was no replacement for her father.

I don't know how long we stayed there by the tree. An hour, perhaps, maybe more. We hardly moved. I kept my arms around Anna as her sobbing slowed and finally stopped, and then we just

186

sat together, watching and listening to the forest. We stayed close, huddled together for warmth and comfort, and my exhausted mind wandered, drifting close to sleep. We might have been the only two people in the world.

A slight wind stirred in the treetops, swaying the weaker branches, rubbing them against one another. There came the creak of ancient trees, the swirl and hush of the breeze spiriting through the undergrowth, stirring the amber and red blaze of fallen leaves. The gentle trickle of the stream. The pull and tear of Kashtan's grazing, the clink of her tack. All these things just at the edge of my consciousness as I came closer and closer to sleep.

And then something else. A more regular disturbance in the forest. A shuffling and crashing that came to me as if in a dream. But I had been too long in the forest to dismiss anything and sleep was immediately brushed aside. My eyes were open in an instant, my mind was alert to my surroundings, and straight away I looked to Kashtan. If there was any danger out there, she would have heard it long before me; she would be showing the signs. What I saw confirmed that the noise had not been in my imagination.

Kashtan had stopped grazing and raised her head, turning her ears, waiting for the sound to come once again.

Together we listened.

The wind picked up, blustering in the trees, but that was not what had woken me. I had heard something more substantial, something more—

Then it came again. The sound of movement in the undergrowth. Something close.

'Wake up.' I shook Anna. 'Wake up.' I was loath to steal her from her sleep. At least there she would rest. Awake she would only remember her papa.

'What?' Her voice was loud and sleepy when she spoke.

'Sh.' I put a hand over her mouth and leaned away from her, shaking my head. I pointed out into the woods, then used my teeth to pull off one glove. I spat it aside and put a finger to my lips.

Her eyes widened and she stared at the place where I had pointed. Right now there was nothing to see but the frost-covered trunks and the tangle of brambles and deadwood.

'Have they come for us?' she whispered when I took my hand away from her mouth.

'I don't know.' I reached for the revolver in my pocket. 'Stay right here. Don't go anywhere.' As I said it, I had a fleeting memory of the last time I had spoken almost exactly the same words to her, when she had still been with her father and I had gone to the train.

'Don't leave me,' she said, panic in her eyes. 'Please.'

'I won't leave you. I promise.'

I had been sitting for some time and my muscles and joints were stiff as I got to my feet. I ignored the pain in them and raised the revolver towards the source of the sound, but it was quiet now.

I glanced back at Kashtan, wondering if we had time to ride away before whatever it was reached us, but then the noise came again, not more than a few metres away.

'Stay down,' I told Anna, as I moved in front of her, protecting her from whatever was coming.

'Is it them?' she asked, but I could only shake my head. I had no idea who it was. I had told Anna the men from the train wouldn't follow us on foot, but perhaps they *had*. If one of the carriages had been transporting horses, they might have ridden after us. Or maybe it was something else. Maybe the seven riders had caught up with us.

But then Anna said something that made a chill run through me.

'Is it *him*?' she asked. 'Is it Koschei?'

I shivered but kept my arms steady. I tried to still my breathing and not picture the whirling, terrifying figure of the gaunt rider crashing from the forest, sword raised, eyes blazing. I set my resolve as hard as cold iron and stood with one foot in front of the other, revolver extended, finger touching the trigger. Whatever was out there, I would kill it. Whether it was the men from the train or the seven riders, or Koschei himself, I didn't care. I was protecting two of us now, and whatever came out of those trees would have to be prepared to fight hard because I intended to shoot until I had no more bullets, and then I would draw my knife and do whatever was necessary to defend Anna and myself.

Above all, I would not let her see my fear.

I steadied the revolver, aiming it at head height, and thumbed back the hammer as the sound drew nearer. Movement in the undergrowth.

Coming closer.

Not the heavy sound of horses.

I pushed my shoulders forward, braced for the recoil.

Perhaps a single man.

I focused, slowed my breathing and prepared to react.

It was just a few paces away now, but something felt wrong. The pattern of movement was unusual.

I let nothing break my concentration. There was just me and my enemy.

And then the dark shape broke from the undergrowth.

In that instant, it was nothing more than a black blur, confused against the background of the messy brushwood and brambles. It was a shadow, movement in my peripheral vision. It was much smaller than I had anticipated, low to the ground, and my aim altered without thinking. I bent my knees, my arms moving at the shoulders, dropping the aim of the weapon, and as my finger tightened on the trigger, I realised what I was seeing.

The dog had found us.

He padded towards me, tail wagging, tongue lolling, but I gave him little more than a glance. I returned my aim to the forest and waited to see what might follow him out of the trees.

With the arrival of the dog, many unanswerable questions began to form in my mind, the most important of which was whether or not the seven riders were behind him.

'Go to Kashtan,' I said to Anna.

I didn't turn to watch her, but backed away from the wall of undergrowth, listening.

The dog whined as if to remind me he was there, but I ignored him, remaining intent on what was in front of me.

'Are they coming?' Anna asked.

'Just go to Kashtan,' I told her. 'Now.'

I heard her moving behind me and risked a glance at her, seeing her do as I had asked, before I returned my attention to the forest in front of me. I kept the revolver aimed as I shuffled backwards, careful not to fall. The dog followed me, tongue lolling as if it were a game, and when he came close, I pushed him away with my foot.

'Get away. Get lost.'

But each time he just regained his footing and came again. Always following.

'What's the matter with you? Don't you know when you're not wanted? Go on. Go away.'

I waved my free hand at him, kicked at him, but still he followed.

When I reached the place by the stream where Anna and Kashtan were waiting, I pocketed the revolver and took Anna under the arms to lift her up. Once she was settled, I took the revolver from my pocket once more and pointed it at the dog's head. I admired his resolve and he had done well to follow us, but he was a risk. No matter what we did to hide our tracks, he had a good nose, he'd proved that. He would find us no matter what action we took to cover our progress.

'What are you doing?' Anna asked.

'Don't look,' I told her.

'You can't.'

'There are people following me, Anna. The dog could lead them right to us if he hasn't already.'

'But you can't just shoot him.'

'I'm sorry, Anna. I know it's—'

'But you *can't*. And where are they?' she said. 'If he's led them to us, then where are they?'

I shook my head. 'Maybe he didn't, but he *could*.'

'They passed him – you said so yourself. Before we came into the forest. So maybe . . . maybe they got lost and he didn't. Maybe he went past them. Maybe they're *still* lost. Or maybe they're at the train. Or . . .'

'That's too many "maybes", Anna.' Even so, I had thought the same thing myself. They might still be far behind us.

'You *can't*.' She swung her leg over Kashtan's back and held on to the saddle to lower herself to the ground. 'Please.' She came to stand beside me, looking up into my face. 'And they might hear. They might be close and they'll hear.'

I looked at her, the way she watched me with such intensity. Her eyes were pleading with me as hard as her words and I wondered why she felt the need to save this dog. At the farm, I had not seen her show him any affection. Neither she nor Lev even threw him a scrap of food. I believed it was me the dog had followed, not them, and yet she was the one begging for his life.

'If they're close, they'll hear all right, but they won't know where it's coming from. No, I have to do this.'

The dog sat on his haunches watching with interest, as if he had no idea what we were discussing. He didn't know how close to death he was. All I had to do was squeeze the trigger.

Anna moved in front of me now, crouching by the dog's side and putting her arms around him. He leaned into her, more because she was pulling him than because he wanted to, and Anna pressed her face into the fur that bunched at the side of his neck.

'Get away from him.'

'Please don't kill him.'

And then I realised this was all she had left of her father. A dog that had not even belonged to him. I had never seen Lev scratch the dog's ear, and he hadn't even given him a name, but in Anna's mind he was her only remaining link to her father. Everything she and Lev owned had been on the horse that we had left behind. There was nothing else but this dog.

I lowered the revolver.

'Thank you,' Anna said. 'Thank you.'

'He'll have to keep up with us.' I put the weapon away. 'We're not going slow for this dog.' I pointed at him. 'And he's not eating our food.'

When I went back to Kashtan, the dog broke away from Anna and trotted towards me, oblivious to her having just saved his life.

# 22

We were still in the forest at nightfall. We left the place where the dog found us, covering our tracks as much as we could, and moved on. We alternated between riding and walking, giving Kashtan a break from time to time, and the dog kept up with us.

For Anna, the dog was a reminder of her father and their time at the farm, a place where they were safe for a while. For me, he was a reminder of what followed in our wake. Anna's reasoning had been good – it was possible that the men following us had been confused by our trail and become lost while the dog had passed them by, but I was still concerned he might have led the riders to us. They might be hanging back, waiting for a better time to make their attack. If it were me, I might wait until we were out in the open, or I might come in the night when my quarry was asleep. Or perhaps I would split my men, try to get some of them ahead so that we could attack from multiple sides.

With those thoughts in my mind, we went on. Even as the darkness filled the forest, we went on. There was almost no light, the cloud too thick to allow the moon to provide for us, and still the mist endured, but we went on and on, because every hour I was not with my wife and children was an hour in which they might be branded with that red star.

When Anna was too tired to put one foot in front of the other, I lifted her onto Kashtan's back and walked alongside her, but there came a time when I, too, was exhausted, so I finally decided to stop.

It was too dangerous to light a fire, so Anna and I sat close together, wedged between the protruding roots of a giant maple. I

193

kept the revolver close to hand and pulled the blankets over us for added heat, while Kashtan stood by and the dog came to curl beside me. I was thankful for his warmth and his vigilance – between them, he and Kashtan were excellent guards – and when he put his chin on my knee, I was glad Anna had stopped me from shooting him.

I didn't sleep much. Not much more than snatches. Every sound in the forest had me peering into the darkness. Every time the dog twitched and looked up, I did the same. When I did close my eyes, I had an agonising vision of Marianna and Misha and Pavel, backing away from a branding iron in the shape of a five-pointed star. Or of my brother's face, sullied with a dusting of soil. Or of Lev lying by the tree, thrown from his horse.

On one occasion, the dog growled, an ugly sound deep in his throat, and I sat up straight, gripping the revolver, widening my eyes, trying to see into the misty gloom, but the night was silent except for the creak of a bough or the rattle of a falling twig. Something small scurried in the darkness, a quick scampering of tiny feet, and the dog growled again, so I put my hand on his head and rubbed his soft fur.

'Good boy,' I whispered, 'but it's just a rabbit or something. Nothing more than that.'

Anna stirred beside me. 'Are you awake?'

'Yes.'

She said nothing for a while and then, 'What's going to happen to me?'

'I'll keep you safe.'

'But . . . later.'

'I'll keep you safe,' I said again. 'For as long as you want.'

'I wish Papa was here.'

'So do I.' I had liked Lev, he was warm and kind-spirited. He and I would have become good friends in a time when friends were a rarity.

'Thank you for saving the dog,' she said.

'We should give him a name.'

'Like what?'

'I'm no good at thinking of things like that.' Marianna would have chosen a good name. Perhaps a character from one of her *skazkas*. 'We had a cat when I was a boy. Well, it was my brother's really. Vaska.'

'It was called Vaska?' Anna turned to look up at me and I put my arm around her.

'Mm-hmm. He was beautiful. Black as soot and so quiet you'd step on him before you realised he was there. He knew how to catch a mouse too. Mama used to hate him leaving those things on the step and she used to shout at Alek – that's my brother – so that you could hear her from the other end of the village. Papa said he was so ashamed when he heard her yelling that he'd have to leave the village and never come back.' I smiled to myself.

'Where's your brother now?'

'Gone,' I said, disappointed not to dwell longer on the memory.

'And the cat?'

'Who knows. He went missing a long time ago, but I always thought he'd be fine. He knew how to survive – he was half wild anyway. Mama said he probably moved in with some witch out there in the forest.' I looked down at Anna when I said it, hoping I hadn't scared her.

'Is Vaska a good name for a dog?'

'I don't know. Probably not. I don't know any good names for a dog. Anyway, maybe he already has one.'

'He can't tell us what it is, though,' she said.

'Maybe we should just call him Dog. It's easy to remember.'

Anna didn't comment, so we sat without speaking, all three of us pressed together between the roots of the tree. The breeze picked up, swaying the branches overhead, creaking the primeval boughs and moaning as it vibrated the brushwood. Kashtan nickered and snorted, and the dog lifted his head to listen, a short whine escaping him as he pushed harder against me. None of us wanted to be so far from comfort.

The wind swept the clouds from the sky, revealing a half-moon and allowing its light to flood into the forest. It filtered through

195

the twisted fingers above us, and I looked down at Anna beside me, her face small and pale, moonlight glittering in her eyes.

'You think you can walk some more?' I asked.

'Yes.'

I was glad to be moving again. I was tired, but I wanted to press on towards Dolinsk and hoped I would find some clue as to where Koschei had gone. I didn't know why he was heading north; most of the Cheka units in this area would be heading towards Tambov rather than away from it. Like Commander Orlov, their orders would be to crush the rebellion, and yet Tanya and Lyudmila had said that Koschei was heading north. Always north. I hoped that was still the case; that he hadn't turned in a different direction, leaving us to follow a false trail. I needed to find some civilisation now, some way of knowing if I was still heading the right way.

As we moved, I reflected on Commander Orlov's words, seeing how his eyes had been opened to the chaos, just as mine had. His escape had been on a different path from the one I intended to take, but his words had put an idea in my head; one that showed me a hint of what my future might be. To find somewhere quiet, a place where the eyes of the world might overlook me. Before that could happen, though, I had to escape my pursuers and find Marianna and the boys. As Orlov had said, they were the most important thing now, and without them I was nothing but the soldier I no longer wanted to be. Father and husband were the roles I saw in my new future, but it was the soldier who could make them happen.

Stanislav's comrade had said something, however, that troubled me. I had tried to put it out of mind, but it scratched at my subconscious, from somewhere beyond coherent thought, and I couldn't help returning to it over and over again. He had said that Nikolai Levitsky made Koschei, that *I* had made him. I contemplated on how that was possible and the only explanation that came to me was linked to the name Commander Orlov had given me. Or rather, a name he had mentioned.

Krukov.

If any man I knew bore any resemblance to Koschei, it was

Krukov, and if it was he who had murdered the old men of Belev and taken the women and children away, then Stanislav might have been right. Perhaps I *was* responsible for him in some way. And perhaps the men of Belev would still be alive if Alek and I had not deserted. We had been in the same unit as Krukov and would have steered him away from Belev without him even coming close to it.

That was a notion that wrapped itself round my heart and squeezed hard. That I could be to blame for my family's fate was beyond anything I could live with. If I discovered it to be true, and if my family lost their lives because of it, would I want to take the path that Commander Orlov had chosen?

But when I looked at Anna, I knew I had another responsibility. I could no longer choose the path that was best for me; I had to take the one that was best for both of us.

# 23

When morning finally broke, the low sun was bright and good. It was as welcome as any morning had ever been, and though its light lacked heat, there was enough for it to burn away what was left of the mist. Our spirits were lifted even further when we came to the edge of the forest and stepped out into the open. There was a greater chance of being seen, and we would be easier to follow, but it was a relief to be away from the forest once more, and we would move quicker, taking us further from our pursuers and closer to our goal.

Kashtan's pleasure was clear; she liked the forest even less than I did. It was an unnatural place to her, primordial and full of hidden threat, and she was happiest where she could see approaching danger and where there was space for her to run. When we climbed into the saddle, she needed no more encouragement than a quick nudge for her to race out into the steppe. She thundered through the hoarfrost, scattering the ice dust, and there was a great sense of freedom in her movement. The air was clear, as fresh as I had ever known it, and I couldn't help smiling at the joy of that moment. In those brief minutes, everything was forgotten and I knew that Anna felt it too.

As Kashtan began to tire, she slowed to a trot and Anna turned to me. She wasn't smiling – happiness was still beyond her – but something had lightened in her.

'What about the dog?' she asked, looking back at the trees. They were some way behind us now, and I wished it was as easy to put other things behind us. How simple life would be if we could forget the things in our past.

'He'll catch up,' I said. 'He did last time.'

'We should call him Tuzik. Mama said that if she had a dog, she would call it that. She said it was a good name for a dog.'

'Tuzik.' I nodded. 'It *is* a good name.'

With little available cover, we stayed close to the road, and when Anna asked if we shouldn't try to cover our tracks, I explained that it would be easy to follow us in the open, whichever route we took, so we might as well take the most direct one. At least on the road, our prints could mingle with the many others. I didn't need to tell her that if the riders had been able to follow us through the night, they would see us almost as soon as they came out of the trees, but I knew she hoped, as I did, that they had not. We had been able to travel a good distance during the night, but it would have been impossible for anyone to track us.

Around midday, we came into a small village, just six houses set back to one side of the road. The *izbas* were in various states of ruin, but none of them was untouched by fire. We had watched from a distance, seeing nothing moving and decided it was safe to approach.

'Horse droppings,' I said, pointing to dung scattered on the road in front of the houses. 'Looks quite fresh.' I dismounted and went to look at it, moving it with the toe of my boot. It was still soft, a little damp, and a smell came off it too. 'There are tracks here. Maybe a couple of horses.' I squatted to study the hard ground, seeing marks where the frost had been disturbed and the mud pressed into hoof prints and boot prints. 'People too. Someone's been here recently.' I looked up at what was left of the buildings. 'Maybe just this morning.'

Neither of us said it, but we were both thinking the same thing. Koschei.

By now Tuzik had caught up with us, and he sniffed the dung, then trailed around the front of the *izba*, testing everything, spending some time around the base of an intact water barrel to one side of the shattered ruin. It was the kind of barrel peasants used to store water brought from the river, or to collect fresh rainwater. Tuzik cocked his leg to mark the base of it, then caught

199

scent of something else and hurried out of sight, nose to the ground.

'What's he found?' Anna asked.

'Probably a rabbit,' I told her. 'Wait here.'

'Don't leave me alone, Kolya.'

'I'll be right where you can see me. I'm not going anywhere. Just stay on Kashtan, and if anything happens, you know how to ride her, right?'

Anna nodded.

'Then stay here.' I pulled the revolver from my pocket and went into the ruin of the first house.

All that remained was the north wall and the *pich*; everything else had crumbled in the heat of the fire. I took a blackened stick and poked in the ashes, looking for anything that might be of use, but found nothing. I raised a hand to Anna, letting her know everything was all right, then I moved on to the next house, but this one was as ruined as the last.

'There's nothing here,' I called to Anna.

'Can we go, then?' She didn't like it when we stopped. It was as if she were more aware of our pursuers than I was. Even now, as she spoke to me, her eyes kept going to the horizon behind us, looking for the seven riders. But, for now they were nowhere to be seen.

'Not yet.'

If Koschei had been here, there would be something to confirm it.

So I told Anna I would check the rest of the houses and moved on to each one, raking through the debris to find some sign, but it wasn't until I ventured into the yard at the back of the last *izba* that I found what I was looking for.

Tuzik had already discovered the bodies and was licking blood from the back of one man's head. He looked more like a wolf than ever when he was standing over those corpses. I stopped, wondering how he would react to me. I didn't blame him for what was instinctive, but I couldn't let him continue, not while I was here, so I slapped my hands together and kicked him in the ribs when he displayed a reluctance to leave. However much wolf he had in him, he had lived with humans long enough to know what a kick meant, so he yelped and skulked away, averse to losing a meal.

There were four bodies lying in the frost, and while the cold made it difficult to tell how long they had been here, I had seen enough dead men to estimate that it had been no more than a few days. Each of them was naked from the waist up, and each of them with the skin flayed from both hands. I could only imagine the terror they must have felt waiting for their turn to be tortured, the pain they would have endured when the skin was peeled away. The perpetrators would have been high on their power and bloodlust while they carried it out. Perhaps drinking to heighten their enjoyment.

Tuzik sat a few paces away, watching as I stood over the bodies.

The flaying reminded me of what I had seen in Belev, but such an act was not unknown elsewhere. Although my instinct told me Koschei had been here, this kind of atrocity did not necessarily point to him. I had seen things like it before when I had still been fighting. It was an effective way to persuade men to confess to almost anything, and it acted as a good deterrent from anti-Soviet activities when witnessed. It was the kind of act that had made me want to leave the army and return home.

However, the loss of skin had not been the cause of death for these men. One of them had suffered the same fate as Galina's husband, while the other three had been shot using a common method of execution for Cheka units. A single bullet fired downwards into the back of the neck was an effective and economical means of despatching large numbers of prisoners. Two of them were lying face down, side by side, but the last body was lying face up, dry, dead eyes staring at the sky, and it was clear this was not the way he had been left by his killers. Whoever had shot him had left him face down like the others, but someone had turned him over. The blood on the ground beside him and the imprint in the frost told me that much.

The man must have been in his fifties when he died, maybe a little younger. He had been a working man, from the look of his complexion, weather-beaten and old beyond his years, so it was difficult to be sure of his age. His beard was thick, but his torso was thin and pale, his ribs visible. His skin was marked all over with bruises, indicating that he had been beaten as well as skinned before he was shot. And in the centre of his chest, an angry red burn in the shape of a five-pointed star. The same star I had seen in Belev, and the same star Lev and Anna had seen.

'Koschei,' I whispered.

I turned the remaining bodies onto their backs, rolling them over and looking at their bruised faces, but I recognised none of them and it occurred to me that whoever had turned the first body had seen all they needed to see. They had moved only one of the men and left the others as they had found them. One look at the red star had been enough for them to know who had done this. They hadn't been here to identify the victims, only the perpetrator.

Perhaps I was following more than just one trail now.

And when I turned to walk away, I saw something that confirmed my suspicions.

# 24

'Did you find something?' Anna asked as I came back to her. 'What is it?'

I stopped and shook my head.

'Dead people?'

I didn't need to answer for Anna to know she was right. Instead I studied the object in my hand, turning it over to see it better in the light.

'What's that?'

I held it up for her to see.

'A cigarette end?'

'Found it over there,' I said. 'Behind the houses.'

'What's so special about it?'

'See this?' I said, holding it up in front of her to look at. 'The way this is rolled with the piece of card?' There might be a thousand, a million people who did the same thing, but I had only ever known one person to do it, and it was too much of a coincidence to find it here. Beside the overturned body. 'I think I know who smoked this.'

'Koschei?' she asked.

'No. Someone else who's looking for him.' And if Tanya had come this way, then it was another clue to confirm I was on the right track. But the red star had been the biggest give away. Koschei had left his mark here.

'Who is it?'

'Someone I met.' It was then that I remembered the cigarette she had given me. The one I had half smoked behind the church and put into my pocket. I took it out now and smelled the end, comparing it to the smell of the one I had found here, but the two just smelled of burned cigarettes.

'Who?' Anna asked.

'Two women I met in Belev. My village. They're called Tanya and Lyudmila. I think they might have been here not long ago. The prints I found.'

'Are they soldiers?'

'I'm not sure.'

Tanya had been here. I was certain. She had been here recently, and she had found the bodies before moving on.

I split the cigarette and brushed the tobacco into my pouch, then replaced it in my satchel and took out the water bottle.

'We're getting closer,' I said, looking back for any sign of the riders while unscrewing the cap. 'We'll follow these prints for now.'

'What about Tuzik?' Anna asked.

I rinsed my mouth and spat water onto the road. 'He'll catch up like always.' I had been able to shoo him away from the bodies while I was there, but he had not left them. Short of burying them, there was nothing I could do to stop him from doing what was natural to him. He would follow us when he was ready.

I didn't want to think about Tuzik's meal, though, so I drank and turned my mind to Tanya and Lyudmila. It was reassuring that they had come this way – I had begun to wonder if I might have passed Koschei, or if he might have turned back towards Tambov, but the signs were clear. Something was making him press north, and I was still on his trail, probably growing closer.

I wondered what orders he might have that would make him travel away from the centre of the fighting, or if something else was driving him north, but for now it didn't matter. The important thing was that I was still headed in the right direction. If this was the way Tanya was coming, then it was the route to finding Koschei. Her desire to find him was strong, and she might have even discovered more about him on her path from Belev. She had come from a different direction, would have found different clues. Perhaps she even knew who he was now. She, too, might have heard the name Krukov in connection with the monster she was following.

I passed the water bottle to Anna, telling her to take as much as she needed.

'We'll fill it up here,' I said when she handed it back to me. I had been trained not to waste any opportunity to replenish my supplies, so I went to the barrel at the side of the nearest *izba* and removed the stone from the top before taking out my knife. The blade slipped under the lid, cracking the icy seal when I twisted, giving enough room for me to take hold of it with my fingertips. I dropped the lid and used the butt of my knife to break the thin layer of ice that had formed on the surface, but as the pieces began to separate, I saw that the water beneath was spoiled. Tendrils of dark algae floated and swirled in the disturbance, like they did in the still parts of the lake during the summer. Before I had time to register the strangeness of such plant life in winter, I caught sight of something else among the chunks of ice and suspended fronds.

Something beneath the surface.

Something so white it was almost glowing in the darkness.

And when I leaned closer, brushing the ice aside with the blade of my knife, I realised it was not algae that hung in the water but hair. And the whiteness was skin.

Her eyes were still open. Her mouth was stretched wide. Her arms were twisted behind her back, her body wedged in place.

*He likes to drown the women.*

I recoiled, dropping the canteen.

'What is it?' Anna asked.

I stared at the barrel as if the woman inside might push to her feet, wet hair falling about her bloated white face.

'What's the matter?'

Was this how Marianna would look?

'Kolya!'

I turned away so I didn't have to see that bloated face as I snatched up the lid, shoving it down on the barrel, closing the woman back in. I pushed it down hard, then lifted the rock into place and stepped away.

'Nothing,' I said as I retrieved the canteen. 'It's nothing. We need to go, that's all. We need to go.'

We stayed on the road, seeing one or two small settlements in the distance on either side, always looking back, always scanning ahead.

'My wife is called Marianna,' I said.

Anna made no comment. I wasn't even sure if she had heard me.

'I sometimes call her Anna. The two of you almost share a name.'

'And you're going to keep looking for her, like Prince Ivan looked for Marya Morevna.'

'Yes. Except I'm no prince.'

'Is she pretty?'

I couldn't see her face in my mind, so I closed my eyes and tried to picture her. I was bothered that I was still unable to see her. I knew she had hair the colour of winter wheat and eyes that were blue like a clear summer sky. I knew her nose was small and sharp and well formed, and that her lips were thin. I even knew that her left front tooth was chipped from the time she fell when she was seventeen, but I couldn't *see* that in my mind.

'Yes,' I said, opening my eyes. 'Like you.'

'What about your sons? What are their names?'

I smiled to myself and imagined them all sitting round the table. Again, I couldn't picture their faces, but I could *feel* them all together, Marianna taking care of them, making our little *izba* a good home. We didn't have much, but we had enough. A house and an outbuilding. A small plot of land.

'Misha is the oldest,' I said. 'Then there's Pavel. He's about your age.'

'What are they like?'

'Serious most of the time, I suppose, but not always.' I remembered how excited and proud they'd been to show me the rabbits and fish they had caught when I was last there. 'They like to be outside in the summer, just like *my* brother and I did, daring each other into the forest, hiding in the wheat, swimming in the . . .' I faltered as the image of the lake came to mind and I pushed it away. 'When we sat for a meal, there was always a lot of talk. Sometimes it was like they'd never stop.'

'So they're good friends?'

'Definitely. They look after each other too. Misha always lets Pavel have the last piece of fruit or the last pinch of sugar, and Pavel lets his brother have the best side of the bed. Misha even tried to carve a wooden horse for his brother once, like the ones my papa used to carve for me.' I smiled at the memory of it. 'Wasn't so good, though,' I laughed. 'Marianna and I thought it looked more like a goat.'

Anna smiled and waited for me to go on.

'They're not perfect, though,' I said 'Boys are boys. They argue sometimes, just like all brothers do. Like I did with mine. They answer back too. You know, when they were younger, my wife used to clip them on the backside with a wooden spoon when they talked back.'

'Didn't it hurt?'

'Probably,' I laughed again, remembering how cross she would get if they dirtied the house or took food without asking. 'But not too much. As they got older, though, they were too quick for her. Misha is like a wolf, the way he slips away from her. One time she chased him out into the road. It was autumn and the mud was thick and she slipped, right in front of the whole village. She was so mad . . . but when everyone laughed, there wasn't anything she could do but laugh herself.'

'Will she hit *me* with a wooden spoon?'

'Of course not.' I nudged her. 'The spoon is only for the boys.'

It was good to think about home as a place filled with warmth and sound and life rather than the empty village I had left behind. I smiled to myself, enjoying the unexpected moment. The thoughts came to me in the way that a patch of cloud might clear on a dull day and let the sun shine through and I allowed myself to bask in them for a while as we continued along the road.

With Anna's next words, though, the clouds reformed and closed around the gap.

'There's another farm.'

I scoped it with the binoculars, but it was in ruins like the last settlement. Just two deserted buildings burned to almost nothing, standing beside a single chestnut tree that had grown to lean away from the wind. In the lenses I saw the bodies hanging from the tree, twisting in the wind.

Anna was afraid to be left alone, but I didn't want to take either her or Kashtan any closer, so we stopped a hundred metres from it and I dismounted to investigate on my own.

When I returned, I had seen more flayed hands, more branded stars, and I mounted without a word, taking Kashtan off the road and steering well clear of the farm before we came back to the road.

We were still on the right track. Koschei had been here.

Kashtan moved on at a steady pace for another hour, and apart from the occasional fresh, clear print in the frozen mud, we had the road to ourselves. Anna and I hardly said a word to one another – both of us were consumed by our own thoughts – and we travelled in silence but for the thump of Kashtan's hooves, the regular rhythm of her breath and the creak and clink of tack.

There was almost no distinction in the landscape of this part of the steppe. The road ahead and behind were the same. The land to either side of us was untouched grass with the occasional field in the distance to east or west, but nothing distinct, and for a long time, the horizon remained unchanged. We saw one other farm, at least a kilometre east of the track, and with the lenses, I watched a single farmer working in the field.

'Are you going to go closer?' There was tension in Anna's voice.

'No.' I was convinced I was heading in the right direction and was sure I would learn more when we reached Dolinsk, so we continued until we reached the top of a rise that looked down at the steppe before us. From here, there was an unbroken sea of frost, with only a hint of forest on the horizon. The road snaked away to our right, cutting down the slope and disappearing in the whitened grass.

'Is that where we're going?' Anna asked.

'Dolinsk,' I said.

In the middle distance, perhaps eight or ten kilometres away, the town settled in the bowl of the shallow valley. Larger than Belev, Dolinsk had grown in a different way. In the centre of the town stood the traditional *izbas*, but they were surrounded by other buildings built from stone and, at the far edge, the blue dome of a modest church.

Remaining in the saddle, I pulled the heavy binoculars from my saddlebag and scanned the steppe beyond. In the magnification, I spotted two dark smudges on the road, moving away from me, directly towards Dolinsk.

'That's them,' I said under my breath.

'Who?'

'The people I told you about – Tanya and Lyudmila.'

'Can I see?'

I put the strap over her neck and let her take the binoculars.

'How can you tell it's them? It just looks like dots to me. Or lines.'

'It's them,' I said. 'I'm sure of it.'

'What if you're wrong, though? What if it's someone else? Koschei . . .'

'If it was him, there would be more of them. No, I'm sure it's Tanya.' It had to be them.

'What's she like?' Anna asked.

'Who?'

'Tanya.'

'I don't really know.' I took the binoculars and watched the two figures for a while, seeing their steady progress, then swung them across to study the steppe on either side of them. Over to the right, there was a shine in the grass and thistles; a trail of bent and broken stems suggesting a larger number of horses had passed either up or down the rise, but without being close enough to see which way the stalks were lying, it was impossible to know which. I wondered if it could be the remnants of Koschei's progress, or something else, but it had been at least a few days ago, judging by the way the grass had started to spring back.

'Do they know where Koschei is?' She couldn't speak his name without a slight tremble in her voice.

'I don't know. Maybe.'

'So are we going after them?'

'Not yet.' I rummaged in one of the saddlebags behind me, taking out a piece of *salo* I'd found in Belev. The thin layer of fat coating the smoked ham had started to yellow and it didn't smell fresh. It would be better than a lot of the things I'd eaten on my journey to Belev, but it would be nothing compared to the meal I had eaten with Lev and Anna. I cut a corner from it and handed it to Anna. 'You haven't eaten since . . . Take it. You need to keep well.'

She looked at it, shaking her head, but took it between finger and thumb as if it might be dangerous.

'Eat.'

She nibbled the tiniest piece and chewed it slowly. I smiled at her and took another bite as I glanced back at the horizon behind us. We had been lucky so far, but I didn't know how long it would last. The men following me were well trained, battle-hardened and driven. They would push on as much as they could, and I found myself touching the *chotki* once more, hoping, *praying* that our tricks to cover our progress had worked.

Kashtan moved off the road as we ate, finding a patch of good grass and lowering her head to graze. The movement tugged the reins, pulling at my arm, but she had done enough to earn it. She had worked hard and the least I could do was allow her to eat. It would keep up her strength.

'Tuzik's coming,' Anna said.

He was trotting along the road, nose to the ground, swerving from side to side as he took the multitude of scents from the dirt.

'He must like us.'

'Maybe,' I said, taking a sip from my canteen. The water was icy cold and washed away the greasy taste of the *salo*, but it made me think of the woman in the barrel.

'Why else would he follow us?'

I gave the canteen to her, glad she hadn't seen that horrible whiteness beneath the water. 'Maybe he doesn't have anywhere else to go.'

Anna wiped the mouth of it with her gloved palm. 'He could have stayed at the train. There were people there.' She tipped back her head and took a sip.

'True.'

'So I think it's because he likes us. Likes *you*.'

'Me?'

'He can see that you're nice.'

'Come on,' I said, replacing the cap. 'Let's get moving.'

We followed the women's tracks, always looking, always aware. I stopped from time to time to scan the surroundings with the binoculars, but never for long. There was a constant fear of danger here, just as there had been in the forest, but this was different. In there, it was the imaginary that played on my mind. It was the shadows and the creak of the trees in the wind. It was the dark fingers of the forest that inspired a more primeval fear. Out here on the steppe, it was the sharpshooter's bullet that concerned me, the scouts of an approaching unit, and I was growing more and more conscious of the riders who might be following. While I was pleased to have caught up with Tanya and Lyudmila, and hoped they might have more information about the man we were following, I was concerned that the devils on our heels may catch up too.

The women had reached the part of the steppe that levelled out towards Dolinsk and they had split up, moving in opposite directions to investigate the outskirts of the town before they went in. There was a chance that Koschei was still there, or perhaps some other army had garrisoned the town for its own purposes, although there was no immediate evidence of that.

Spying the women in the distance, I watched them trot away

from each other and approach the town. They looked as if they knew what they were doing and I was reminded of how well they worked together. If I had been down there with my brother, we might have used the same tactic to approach Dolinsk.

I moved the binoculars up to study the town. We were closer now, everything was clearer in the lenses, and the buildings were better magnified. The stone homes at the edge closest to me were sturdy and standing intact, but some of them were in ruins, perhaps struck by stray artillery fire as if the town had been caught in the crossfire between two forces. There were wooden *izbas* that were little more than blackened piles of charred logs.

'Looks like they had some bad luck,' I said.

'Was it Koschei?' Anna asked. 'Has he been here?'

'He's not responsible for all the bad in the world.'

'But those farms . . .'

'This looks different . . . bigger. I think there were a lot of men here. Some kind of battle, but it must have happened a while ago, judging by the way it's been cleared up.'

Anna tensed in front of me and sat up straight in the saddle. 'There's something there.' She raised a hand and pointed into the distance. 'Further away.'

Kashtan snorted and shifted beneath me again, eager to move on, but I held her steady.

'Where?' I narrowed my eyes.

'There.' Anna gestured with her small, gloved hand, stretching her arm further as if it might help. 'Something in the distance. Behind the town.'

'You have good eyes,' I said, raising the binoculars to look at the horizon. 'Is that . . . ?'

Beyond Dolinsk, the steppe stretched into the distance, the expanse of frosted fields broken by solitary trees standing guard, and at the limit of my vision, where the fields met the pale winter sky, there was movement on the horizon. Dark, indistinct patches coming into view.

I focused on Tanya and Lyudmila once again, judging their distance from Dolinsk. They were almost there, coming back towards each other as if they had decided the town was safe, riding side by side as they made their final approach. They wouldn't be able to see beyond the roofs now. They had no idea that something was coming.

Looking back at the horizon, it was difficult to know for sure what I was looking at, but I could make a good guess. It was shadowy and ill defined, but it was growing, lengthening like a snake uncoiling itself from an unseen lair beyond the horizon.

'That looks like a column to me,' I said. 'What do you think? You're the one with the good eyes.' I held the binoculars in front of Anna and let her take them.

'Soldiers?' she asked. 'Looks like . . . lots of soldiers.'

Kashtan took a step forward, her ears turning, listening.

'Soldiers,' I agreed, taking the binoculars.

I estimated the column might be ten kilometres away, but it was difficult to be sure. They weren't moving quickly, but they were fast enough for me to see the line growing as it marched down into the bowl of the steppe, straight towards Dolinsk. Longer and longer it grew, wider and wider.

'There's a lot of them,' I whispered. 'A small army.' If they rode into Dolinsk, they would run straight into Tanya and Lyudmila. 'I wonder what colour they are.'

'Does it matter?' Anna asked.

I packed the binoculars back into the saddlebag. 'You ready to hold on to your cap, Anna?'

She reached up and tugged it down hard.

'How about you, Tuzik?' He was lying in the grass with his chin between his paws. 'You ready for a good run?'

'Are we going to go fast?' Anna looked back at me.

'Yes, we are. Hold tight.'

I spurred Kashtan into a trot and then pushed her into a gallop. She didn't need too much encouragement, and she was sure-footed as she thundered through the grass, hooves pounding the frozen dirt.

I leaned forward and kept low, holding tight to the reins and pressing Anna lower to Kashtan's neck. I had to get to Tanya. She and Lyudmila would not have seen the army; they would enter Dolinsk thinking it safe. Perhaps even the people of Dolinsk, as many or few as they were, would not spot the advancing soldiers until it was too late for them to do anything. There was a chance the army meant them no harm, but it was unlikely that such a large body of fighters would pass the town without stopping to strip it clean of food and provisions.

There was little I could do for the town or its inhabitants other than warn them, but I had to get Tanya and Lyudmila away. They might have information I needed.

I urged Kashtan faster, feeling the cold air biting at my face and the tears streaming from the corners of my eyes. My kit rattled and jangled, Kashtan's breathing resounded about me, and I felt every step she took. At first, Tuzik kept up, his long legs a black blur, but he tired quickly at that pace and soon fell behind.

'Come on, girl,' I shouted as we raced down into the bottom of the steppe, squinting to see the dark shapes ahead that were Tanya and Lyudmila.

Kashtan gave everything she had. She was sweating hard despite the cold, her breath steaming.

By the time Tanya and Lyudmila were out of sight among the houses, Kashtan began to slow. She had done everything she could, so I let her drop to a walking pace. We had gained good ground, though, and as we reached the bottom of the valley, the houses and buildings of Dolinsk grew in front of us, stretching outwards to replace the steppe beyond. Those solitary trees and the approaching soldiers were now obscured, and all that was visible were the stone houses, the *izbas* and the pale blue church dome at the far end of town.

I reached back and fumbled a rag from my kit, passing it to Anna, saying, 'Dry her neck. It's freezing out here.'

Anna was used to horses. She wiped the sweat from Kashtan's coat without complaint as we pressed on, and I saw the care she took with it, rubbing the cloth along the horse's neck, careful to move with direction of her coat.

We had reached the outskirts of Dolinsk by the time she had

finished and I put the rag away, telling Anna to take the reins for a moment. She barely had to do anything – Kashtan was following the road – but Anna was confident to do as I asked, keeping us moving towards the town. I took off my gloves and dug the revolver from my pocket. I held it behind Anna's back, pointing out into the fields as I opened the cylinder and checked the load. The rifle would have been better – it had a shortened barrel that made it good for use from horseback – but I had given it to Lev and now it was in the hands of the men who had caught him.

'Are we in danger?' Anna asked when she realised what I was doing.

'I just want to be ready,' I told her. I didn't know who was in the town, who might have seen us approaching.

Satisfied the revolver was in good working condition, I tucked it into my belt, keeping it close to hand, and stuffed my gloves into my pocket. It wasn't so cold yet that it would freeze my fingers, and gloved hands would be a hindrance if I needed to use the weapon.

Reaching the edge of town, I took the reins back from Anna and dismounted. 'We'll walk from here.'

Had I been alone, I would have ridden through Dolinsk. Kashtan would have given me an advantage of height and speed if ambushed, but Anna's presence made things more complicated. If we remained on horseback, Anna in front, she would bear the brunt of any attack from ahead, and if we changed positions, she would be in the line of fire from behind. I considered leaving her on the outskirts, but didn't want her to be alone and knew she would object.

'Stay between me and Kashtan,' I said, as I tugged the revolver from my belt. 'Do whatever I tell you.'

# 25

It was almost impossible to follow Tanya's route. Among the houses, the ground was clear of grass, packed hard and ripe for hoof prints, but there were many here already. The paths were a mosaic of prints, and though some looked fresher than others, there was no way of knowing which belonged to Tanya and Lyudmila. Their prints were lost in the throng, just as mine would be, making it more difficult for our pursuers. I had been to Dolinsk before, though, and knew the centre of the town, so that's where I headed, thinking that Tanya would do the same thing. If she was looking for information about the man we were trying to find, the centre of the town would be the most obvious place to gather it.

The silence in Dolinsk was unnatural and troubling. The thump of Kashtan's hooves echoed from the stone houses around us. The closeness of the buildings amplified the heavy sound of her breathing, and I watched her ears turning as she listened to her surroundings. Now I had the added benefit of Tuzik's ears too. He had caught up with us once more and trotted ahead as if scouting the area for us.

There was a temptation to move at speed through the town, but it would be dangerous to barrel round tight corners without knowing what lay unseen beyond. Towns like Dolinsk were perfect for ambush and nightmarish to fight in. Since the uprising in Tambov last August, more and more peasants had been joining the fight. Some took up arms and fought with the peasant armies, while others remained in their hometowns and villages, waiting for units to come their way. Nowhere was free of danger and it was better to be cautious.

As we pressed on through the quiet street, I came to the older part of town where the wooden *izbas* were laid out in much the same way as they were in Belev, except here some of them were blackened ruins. There was no smoke, no smouldering, so it must have happened at least a few days ago, but there was a thick smell of burning in the air. Kashtan snorted and turned her ears, and I felt her reluctance to keep going. She sensed the death here as she had done in Belev.

'It's all right,' I whispered to her. 'Just keep listening.'

Some of the *izbas* still standing had curtains pulled across their windows, but from others faces watched without speaking. Frightened eyes followed our progress through the homes and I began to suspect that Dolinsk had already been subdued. The town was so silent and still I could hear the wind that dropped from the steppe and whistled through the paths between the houses.

Coming closer to the centre of the town, a door opened to our left and I turned, raising my revolver and aiming at the old man who stepped out.

'We have nothing,' he called out to me. 'Leave us.'

A poor man, dressed in a worn jacket and threadbare trousers. He was the first civilian I had encountered since I'd met Lev and Anna. Seeing that he was unarmed, I was tempted to lower my revolver, but it could be a distraction to catch me off guard. I glanced about, looking for any sign of a rifle barrel protruding from a window, but saw nothing.

I moved so I was standing in front of Anna, almost pushing her back against Kashtan. 'Did someone pass by here a short while ago?' I asked.

He looked at the revolver in my hand, then leaned to one side to see Anna.

'Have you seen anyone?'

He studied Anna, then shifted his eyes to my face. 'Two riders,' he said. 'Women.'

'Did they say anything to you?'

'They were looking for someone,' he said.

'What did you tell them?'

He looked at Anna once more, but something distracted him and he backed away from the door. I didn't take my eyes off him, but as soon as the black shape moved into my peripheral vision, I knew what had scared him.

Tuzik came close to the side of the road, just a few paces from the man's home, and settled on his haunches, staring.

'Tell me what you said to them and we'll be on our way.'

The old man stepped further back into his house and began to close the door. It was odd that he would be more afraid of the dog than of me. I was pointing a revolver at him, but there was something primal about Tuzik that made the old man fearful.

'Please,' I said. 'Tell me—'

'They're looking for someone who calls himself Koschei.' He stood with the door half closed, one hand ready to slam it shut.

The name made me bristle. 'What did you tell them?'

'That I don't know anyone called Koschei.'

'What about Krukov?'

'Not Krukov either, but there were some men. Came past here the day before yesterday.'

'Into the town?'

'No. They went past. I told those women the same thing.'

'Soldiers?' I studied the old man's face. His eyes were full of defeat, his posture tired.

He shook his head. 'Chekists maybe.'

'How many?'

He shrugged. 'I didn't count them. Maybe five or six. But they had prisoners and—'

'Prisoners? Women and children?'

'Boys. Some women too.'

It was further confirmation of what Commander Orlov had said. Hope and relief surged in me.

'Did you see them?' I pressed him, trying to stay focused. 'What did they look like?'

The door opened wider now and an old woman came out to stand close beside him. She was bundled thick with clothes, like Galina had been, with a scarf tied tight about her head. 'Devils,' she shouted at me. 'You're all devils, bringing your guns and your bloodshed. Killing old men and dragging children away to fight. You see that?' She pointed to the *izba* opposite, burned to the ground, almost nothing left. 'My sister lived there.'

I sighed and lowered the pistol. 'I'm sorry.'

'What good is "sorry"?' she said. 'Can I eat it? Will it keep me warm? Will it give me my sister back? Will it bring my neighbour's son home and resurrect her husband from the dead?'

I turned my eyes to the ground in shame.

When I looked back at the old woman, she had spotted Anna behind me and was staring at her as if seeing a child for the first time.

'Is he yours?' she asked, taking a step closer. She was unafraid of both Tuzik and the pistol.

I turned my body, an unconscious movement to protect Anna. 'Yes.'

The old woman shuffled closer still, coming out onto the road and pushing past me to get to Anna. 'A girl? I thought you were a boy.' She reached out to put her bony hand on Anna's cheek. 'Beautiful,' she said. 'Beautiful.'

I felt Anna flinch from her and I had to stop myself from warning the old woman away. She meant no harm.

'Look after her,' she said to me. 'Keep her close. Safe.'

'I will.'

She stood with her arm out, her fingers still on Anna's cheek, and her lips moved as if she were whispering some kind of prayer or incantation, then she nodded and turned to shuffle towards the *izba*. She struggled up the step and went inside without looking back.

Anna didn't relax even when the old woman was gone, but she didn't cower behind me either. She stood straight as a broom handle and lifted her chin as she stood by my side.

'Which way did they take the prisoners?' I asked the old man.

He thought for a while, his watery eyes watching me, then he raised his arm and pointed north. 'There were others too.'

'Other soldiers?'

He nodded. 'The day before the ones with the prisoners. Fewer, but they could have been Chekists too.'

I wondered if they were the ones that Lev and Anna had seen. Perhaps Koschei had split his unit, one group riding on ahead while the second brought the prisoners. It would be the second group that Commander Orlov had seen, the same group that Stanislav Dotsenko had been with. It was beginning to make some sense, but I wondered why Koschei wouldn't stay as a complete unit. What was it that was drawing him north in such a hurry?

Always that question. *Why north?*

'They went past?' I asked. 'Without coming into the town?'

He nodded.

'Did you see what *they* looked like?'

'No.'

It had been too much to hope for. It didn't make a great deal of difference if I confirmed that Krukov and Koschei were the same man, but it would settle the question in my mind. It would tell me what Stanislav had meant when he said that I was responsible for his creation.

'Thank you,' I said. 'I'm looking for—'

'I don't want to know.' The old man held up a hand and shook his head. 'Don't tell me.' He began to close the door. 'What I don't know can't hurt me,' he mumbled as he shuffled after his wife.

'There's an army coming,' I called after him. 'From the north. They'll be here within the hour.'

'We have nothing to give them. Nothing they would want. And there's nothing more they could do to us.'

'I'm sorry.' I glanced along the street once more, thinking about the army I had seen on the horizon. 'Within the hour,' I said, turning back to the old man. 'They'll be here soon.'

But he had already closed the door.

For a moment it was as if the old man had shut me away from

the rest of the world, rather than shutting himself in his own house. He understood there was nothing he could do.

They had no one here to defend them. All those people who had gone away to fight for this cause or that cause had, in effect, deserted them. They were of no use when they were fighting in a field far from here, leaving their families unprotected, as I had done. *That* had been my desertion, not my escape from the army.

I stared at the closed door, not seeing the timbers or the cracks but seeing what was happening to our country. While trying to unify itself, it was tearing itself apart, and I could find nothing honourable or just in that. As long as men like Koschei were permitted to commit the crimes that he perpetrated, our country was no better now than it had been before the revolution. We had only swapped one kind of tyranny for another. And I had been a part of it.

We moved on, knowing there was nothing I could do to change the course of these people's lives. I could only ride on and hope for them. The new machine was in motion, and now that the Whites were gone, the Green and Blue and Black would soon fall under the red flag.

# 26

When the wide path between the houses came to an end and opened onto the centre of the village, Tanya and Lyudmila were waiting for us. They had probably seen us on the steppe and had been listening to the approach of Kashtan's hooves among the buildings so had taken defensive positions behind the well that stood almost exactly in the middle of the central market space of Dolinsk. There was no market here to speak of anymore, just a collection of skeletal frames that had once been stalls.

The well was surrounded by a circular wall that rose to waist height and was covered by a pitched wooden roof that housed a draw wheel. On a normal day, this would be a busy place, full of women come to collect water. There would have been traders here too, and locals just coming together to talk about the weather, the crops and the state of the country. Today, however, it was almost deserted.

Behind Tanya and Lyudmila, Dolinsk's church stood taller and larger than the other buildings in the town. It was more impressive than our church in Belev, but it was still not much more than just another *izba* with a domed roof that housed a bell and had a cross mounted at its highest point. The blue paint was worn by the frost and the winds and the autumn rain so that it was cracked and wrinkled like old skin.

A handful of weary people was gathered in the square, mostly older women. They wore heavy skirts and an assortment of coats and shawls to protect them from the cold, headscarves tied in bows under their chins. One of the younger women wore a dress the colour of the pink chamomiles that bloomed in the late spring; a dress that would once have been kept only for special occasions. A girl, perhaps two or three years old, clung to the hem of her skirt, but other than that there was a conspicuous absence of children. There were three men standing by, dressed like common peasants returning from the field, one of them with a pipe clamped between his teeth, but there was not a single young man among them. All were old and beyond fighting age.

They looked our way as we came from between the houses.

Tuzik led, trotting out into the open space and pausing to look back, making sure we were following. He went halfway into the square, then stopped and sat down, watching. I was close behind, a step in front of Anna, leading Kashtan so she would shield Anna as much as possible.

Tanya and Lyudmila's horses were tethered to the frame of one of the wooden stalls and they became agitated by Tuzik's presence, just as Kashtan had done when she first saw him. There was something of the wild still in that big dog and the horses feared him.

I let the revolver hang at my side, visible but not threatening.

'You have to leave,' I called out.

'Where did you get the horse?' Tanya called back. The barrel of her rifle was resting on the edge of the well, muzzle pointed at me. 'And who's the boy?'

I felt Anna stiffen behind me.

'There's an army coming,' I said. 'We should be gone before they get here.'

'An army?' Tanya was hesitant. 'Whose army?'

'Does it matter?'

'It might.'

'All I know is there's a column of men less than an hour's ride from here and they're coming in this direction.'

The locals exchanged glances, and the one wearing the pink dress edged away.

'Wait!' Tanya called, but the woman ignored her and the others began to follow. They moved in silence, like spirits, making for the alleys and tracks that ran off from the centre, disappearing as if they had never been there. One of them, an older man, not so quick on his feet, entered the church and closed the door behind him. The bolts were loud and sounded firm when he pushed them across.

Then we were alone in the square, no sight or sound to suggest there was anyone else in Dolinsk.

'We should leave now.' I raised my voice. 'We can't afford to wait any longer.'

'Who said anything about "we"?' Tanya stood up so the wall of the well came only to her waist. She held her rifle to her shoulder and aimed along the barrel at me.

'If you were going to shoot me, you'd have done it in Belev,' I said. 'Get on your horse.'

Lyudmila stayed where she was, crouched behind the well with her rifle pointed at me, but Tanya lowered hers. 'You didn't say you had a horse.'

'You didn't ask.'

'And who's the boy?'

'I'm not a boy.' Anna stepped to my side, puffing her chest and putting back her shoulders, as she had done just a few minutes ago.

'There'll be time for this later,' I called. 'But not now.'

Tanya sighed and nodded to Lyudmila. 'We'd better go. If he's right—'

In the church tower, the bell began to ring. Slow and baleful, it was more like a funeral toll than a warning.

Tanya looked in the direction of the church, then went to her horse and unhitched it, climbing up into the saddle.

'Come on,' I said to Anna. I pocketed the revolver and put my hands under her arms.

'I can do it myself.' She pulled away.

'All right.' I stepped back. 'After you.'

Lyudmila was the last to move, but she finally lowered the rifle and went to her horse just as Anna put her foot in the stirrup. It was a stretch for her to reach that high and she only just managed it, but once there, she hopped a few times as if to build momentum and then, with a grunt, heaved herself into the saddle.

'Well done,' I said, as I climbed up behind her, and I felt a certain pride that she had managed it. She was resilient. She would survive.

Tanya looked back at me. 'What about these people?'

'There's nothing we can do for them.'

'They've already endured so much,' Lyudmila said.

'And we haven't?' I asked.

Lyudmila held my stare, then looked to Tanya for her orders. Tanya responded by putting her heels to her horse. 'Which way?' she asked.

'Follow me.'

The bell continued to toll its low, mournful beat as we passed more charred *izbas* and homes with broken doors.

'What did they tell you?' I asked Tanya, as we rode through the deserted street. 'Those people back there.'

She ignored my question. 'Who's the boy?'

'I'm a *girl*,' Anna said. I couldn't see her face, but it sounded as if she had spoken through gritted teeth. Perhaps her grief was turning to anger, and while that could be useful in some circumstances, I didn't want her to become awkward.

'A girl?' Tanya came alongside us to see Anna. 'So you are. And is the dog yours?'

'He's called Tuzik,' Anna said. 'He's *ours*.'

Tanya looked at me, raising her eyebrows, and I felt my pride in Anna grow. There was something reassuring about the way she had said 'ours'. We were together now, a partnership.

'So what did they tell you?' I asked again.

'Not much.'

'Then it won't take long for you to tell *me*.'

'Let's get out of here first,' Tanya said. 'Then we'll talk.'

'Keeping it to yourself?' I said. 'Making yourself important to me?'

'Something like that.'

'What if something happens to you? I need to know what you know.'

'You'll have to make sure nothing *does* happen to me.'

Tanya was smart. She knew how to keep herself alive.

'And what can I do to make myself important to you?' I asked.

'Nothing.'

Coming out of the town, we pressed the horses harder, pushing them out of the bowl of the steppe and up towards a cluster of trees on the horizon just west of the town. As we rode, I glanced across to see the column that had halted a kilometre or so north of Dolinsk.

'You believe me now?' I asked.

A little further away from the town, I brought Kashtan to a stop and lifted the binoculars to scan the line of soldiers. Tanya and Lyudmila rode a few steps ahead before they realised I had stopped.

Tanya came back to me, breathing hard, saying, 'Red Army.' She didn't need binoculars to know who it was, because we were above them now, with the sinking winter sun behind us, and they were closer than they had been when I first saw them. The red flags flying over the heads of the vanguard were plain enough.

'Red Army,' I agreed.

'How many?'

'Four hundred,' I guessed. 'Maybe more.' I lifted the binoculars again. 'Maybe a hundred on horseback and the rest on foot. I count . . . five or six *tachankas*.' I passed the binoculars to Tanya. 'They have Putilov guns too.'

The *tachanka* was a powerful weapon in anyone's hands. A horse-drawn mounted machine gun that could be quickly man-oeuvred and deployed without much delay. Four or five of them could be used to tear through a small force in minutes; something I had experienced first hand in Grivino when we'd been fighting the peasants of the Blue Army. Coupled with the Putilov field guns, they were devastating. The peasants had good numbers, but they didn't stand much chance against resources like this.

Tanya shook her head and pulled her own binoculars from the saddlebag behind her. She watched for a while before passing them to Lyudmila.

'Where do you think they're going?' Lyudmila asked.

'Where do *you* think?' I replied.

She lowered the binoculars and stared at me. 'To kill peasants. Farmers. Men and women with pitchforks, maybe a few rifles, against machine guns.'

'Or perhaps to stop the uprising,' I said. 'Not to fight *peasants* but to crush *counter-revolutionaries*. Enemies of the people. It depends which side of the fence you live on.'

'You don't believe that,' Tanya said. 'You can't.'

I had. Once. I had believed it with all my heart. When I fought, I had fought for ideals I held dear. In the Great War, it had been for my country, to protect it from the aggressor, and then, in the revolution, I had fought for the common man. I fought for the worker, the farmer and the peasant. I fought so that my family could have a better life under a fairer regime. I wanted to protect the weak from tyranny and greed. I had been an idealist. I believed in the revolution and the new union, but I believed that there would first have to be blood if we were to build it as glorious as intended. It was vital to remove the counter-revolutionary weeds from the fertile field of our new nation before the soil was at its best and the crops could grow stout and tall. And there was a constant need for maintenance, to keep the weeds at bay. I loved my country and my leader, and I believed in the revolution and was willing to put myself forward to fight for it, just as others were prepared to fight for whatever cause it was they believed in.

So when the peasants began to hoard their grain for themselves, to hide it from the revolutionary army, I saw them as traitors. When they formed their black market and sold their crops to other peasants at high prices, I saw them as elitists taking advantage of the situation to line their own pockets. I was too steeped in revolution, too single-minded to see them as families trying to feed themselves, or as men who'd had their fill of upheaval and war, and just wanted to go home and be with their wives and children. I hadn't understood it until I became weary and wanted the same things for myself.

Tanya was right. I didn't really believe it. Not anymore. The peasants of Tambov, irritating though they were to the Red Army and the bearded men who sat in Moscow, might have been rebels, but they were not enemies of the people. They were just people. Men and women who wanted to be free to work on their farms, feed their children and sleep in their beds without fear of being taken away in the night or burned out of their homes.

The Red Army would crush them, though. Now it was done with the Whites, it would turn its might on the rebels, and armies like the one we were looking at now would seal the Bolsheviks' supremacy. The free peasants would be subdued by the conscripted ones, the country would be red in more ways than one, and the men in Moscow would smile and congratulate themselves on a revolution well won.

The division had halted in the valley, but had sent outriders to scout the surrounding area – a pair was heading directly towards Dolinsk, and others were moving east and west, one pair coming right at us. Two men on horseback, Cossacks from the look of them, riding well, as all Cossacks did. They wore thick coats the colour of grain sacks but ingrained with the dirt of war and emblazoned with red stars on the cuffs. Brown boots, winter hats, rifles over their shoulders and sabres at their belts. These were professional soldiers, not conscripts. They would be a deadly opponent, well used to fighting from horseback and not afraid to kill. If they knew I was a deserter, that Tanya and Lyudmila were . . . whatever they were, the Cossacks would not hesitate to execute us.

'I see them,' she said before I could speak. 'What do you want to do? Shoot them?'

'I'm not so sure that would be a good idea.'

'You don't think?' Her voice was heavy with sarcasm.

'We should just go,' Lyudmila said, turning her horse.

'Go where?' I asked. 'We'd never outrun them. Their horses

will be fit, maybe fitter than ours, and those men will be good shots.'

'Not that good,' Lyudmila argued.

'Maybe not, but do you really want to take that chance?'

'What do you suggest, then?' Tanya asked, fixing me with those cold blue eyes. 'What's stopping them from taking us back to the rest of them? Or from just killing us where we are?'

'I'll go and talk to them,' I said.

'And say what?'

'Something that will make them leave us alone.'

'Really? What could you say that—'

'Can I trust you to look after Anna?' I really had no other choice, and neither did they. There was no way we could try to run.

'She'll be safe with us,' Lyudmila said, and when she looked at Anna, there was the briefest moment when her sullen mask seemed to slip. Just a flash and then it was gone.

'I want to come with you,' Anna said.

'It's better if you stay here. They'll wonder why I have a child with me. It might make them suspicious.' I was sure I could handle the Cossacks, but not with Anna on my horse – that would raise too many questions and undermine the authority I would have to portray to these men. 'And if they decide they don't like me . . .' I shook my head. 'It's better you stay here.'

'Why don't we just ride away?' she said. 'Kashtan will—'

'Please, Anna. Just do as I ask.'

She gritted her teeth to show her displeasure, but swung her leg over and slid from Kashtan's back. 'I'm scared, Kolya.'

'So am I,' I whispered to her, 'but we need to be strong.'

Anna nodded. 'Do you promise to come back?'

'I promise.' I leaned down and put a hand to her face before looking at Tuzik. 'You wait here too. Look after Anna.'

Tuzik cocked his head to one side. He knew I was talking to him, but that was all. He couldn't be told to follow orders.

'Are you sure this is a good idea?' Tanya asked.

'You have a better one? Just make sure you keep your hands off your guns.' I put my own into my belt, within easy reach. 'Unless . . .' I shrugged. 'Well, you know.'

With a creak of saddle leather, I turned Kashtan and set off towards the approaching Cossacks. Tuzik sprang to his feet and followed. 'Stay here,' I said, pointing. 'With *Anna*.'

To my surprise, the big dog stopped and looked back at Anna. He switched his attention a few times, from her to me, as if deciding whether or not to obey. In the end, he chose not to, and when I nudged Kashtan into a gallop, Tuzik ran after us, body low to the ground, just like a wolf.

The outriders drew pistols as they came closer, slowing their horses so we came together a good two hundred metres from where the women waited. They circled round me once and came to halt so they were on either side of me.

Tuzik stood with his muscles tensed and ready to attack, his fur bristling on his neck. His lip lifted to show his teeth and he let out a long, low growl, stirring the Cossacks' horses. These men were good riders, almost born in the saddle, but faced with a threatening predator, their horses backed away to a safe distance.

'Keep your dog under control,' one of them said, and the way he moved his pistol, I knew what he meant.

'He won't do anything unless I tell him.' It wasn't true – I had no power over the dog – but though Tuzik's presence might anger them, it might work in my favour too. He was a distraction, and a vicious dog could be as frightening as a loaded gun.

'Are you heading for Tambov?' I asked once they had calmed their animals.

'Who are you?' This man had a serious face, with a thick beard and a moustache that was turned up at the corners. He wore a sabre across his belly, clipped to an ammunition belt that circled his waist and held his coat together. He also wore cartridge bandoliers criss-crossed over his chest. His hat was thick and pulled tight on his head.

'I'll ask you the same thing,' I said, turning to look at the second man.

This one had his hat pushed back and was without the array of bullets gleaming on his coat. He had a scraped chin, but his moustache was as impressive as his partner's. His eyes, though, betrayed his fear. He didn't take his eyes off Tuzik.

'Who are you?' the first man asked again. 'Let me see your papers.'

'Papers? You're asking me for papers? I am Commander Krukov,' I said, not daring to use my own name in case they had heard of my desertion, 'operating from the Tambov Cheka.' I glanced over my shoulder at Tanya and Lyudmila. 'My comrades and I are working on . . . Chekist business.' The mere mention of the work registered immediately with the two men. 'Put your weapons away,' I said, 'or I will be speaking to your commander.' I stared at him hard. 'I will ask him to turn you men over to me right away.'

The two men shared a hesitant look. They weren't used to being spoken to in such a way.

'I—'

'Let me see *your* papers,' I said, 'so that I know *your* names. I don't have time to deal with your counter-revolutionary behaviour right now, but when I am done, I will come back for you. Maybe put you in a room with my dog.'

Both men looked at Tuzik and he, as if playing to his audience, raised his lip and snarled.

'That won't be necessary, Comrade Commander,' said the first man, lowering his pistol. 'I apologise for the insult. We have to check, you understand. You're not in uniform, so—'

'You think we always wear uniform?'

'I thought—'

'If we always wore our uniforms, you would always know who we are. Sometimes it is better for us to be . . . unseen.'

'Yes, Comrade Commander.'

I looked them both up and down, showing my disdain, then I sighed and softened, letting them feel as if they'd had a lucky escape. 'It's all right,' I said. 'It's been a long day.' An idea came to me. 'There are other Chekists operating in this area, men I sent north with prisoners, have you seen them?'

'No.' The man shook his head. 'Do they have dogs like this?'

'You think there are other dogs like this?'

He shrugged.

'Where are you men coming from?' I asked.

He looked back at the army. 'All over. Most are fresh conscripts, but many have come east from Ukraine, Poland. Some from Riga. They say we're needed here, some kind of rebellion.'

'All right. Well . . .' I glanced down at his pistol. 'You men need to get on with your jobs. Your unit is relying on you.'

'You want us to take you to meet our commander?'

'I don't have time for that, and nor do you – you have a job to do.'

'Yes, Commander.'

The two men even managed a salute, but they didn't ride away. We were all three heading in the same direction, so they rode either side of me, as an escort. When we came closer, I saw the tension in Tanya and Lyudmila's faces and in their body language, but when we reached them, the soldiers each raised a hand in salute again and continued past, moving up the incline towards the cluster of trees Lyudmila had wanted to run to.

Anna stood close to Tanya and Lyudmila, but there was something about her demeanour that made her seem apart from them. They were still on horseback, while she stood in the grass, arms folded, awaiting my return. I didn't think the women were a threat to Anna, but I still hadn't wanted to leave her alone with them. Only now, though, did I realise how torn I had been – as if something had been taken away from me. Anna and I had not been together long, but our bond was firm and now it felt right to be with her. The strength of my feelings surprised me, and it was a great relief to be reunited with her.

Both women turned as the soldiers passed, watching the Cossacks press on, scouting the area around Dolinsk.

Tuzik had escorted me back too, and while we watched the men riding away, he went to stand close to Anna, almost pushing her over as he leaned against her and allowed her to stroke his head.

'What did you say to them?' Tanya eyed me with suspicion as I offered my hand to help Anna.

'Not much.'

Anna took her place in the saddle in front of me, and Tuzik trotted away into the grass to do whatever it was he did when he was alone. When I looked over at Tanya, I saw she was waiting for an answer.

'I told them I'm a Chekist commander and that we're on a covert operation to find counter-revolutionaries.'

'And they believed you?' Lyudmila came closer. 'Why?'

'Why wouldn't they? They don't know anything about me. I could be anyone.'

'Yes, you could be.' Lyudmila narrowed her eyes. 'Who *are* you?'

'I'm Kolya,' I said. 'I already told you that.'

Tanya watched me for a few moments longer as if she was making up her mind about something.

'I don't trust you,' she said.

'And I don't trust you,' I told her, 'but we're going in the same direction, looking for the same thing, so I don't see that we have a choice but to stick together.'

'We should leave them behind,' Lyudmila said. 'We can't travel with someone we don't trust.'

'I'd rather it wasn't this way, but it is, and we have to make what we can of it.' I looked at Tanya when I spoke. She seemed to be the leader; she was the one who made the decisions. Lyudmila was sullen and insular, but Tanya's emotions were more heightened. If they had any information about Koschei, I wanted to know it, and if either of them could be persuaded to impart it, I believed it would be Tanya.

'We'll be stronger together. We can watch out for each other.' And as I spoke my thoughts, so I was persuading myself as much as I was persuading Tanya. 'We should share what we know about

Koschei and find him together. This is not a competition between us.'

'Tanya.' Lyudmila lowered her voice in warning when she spoke to her comrade, and a look passed between them that reminded me of the silent exchanges that used to pass between Alek and me; the kind I had seen shared between Anna and Lev.

Tanya studied her partner for a moment, biting the inside of her lower lip with a gesture that made her look human and vulnerable. 'I don't know . . .' she said, but I could see that she had acknowledged the benefits of us staying together.

'Give us one reason why we should trust you,' Lyudmila challenged me. 'One.'

'I'm just asking you to try. You *have* to see the advantages.'

'And the disadvantages,' Lyudmila added. 'Like waiting for your bullet in my back.'

'Riding ahead of me wouldn't prevent that.'

'Or we could kill you right now.' Lyudmila started to raise her rifle.

'Lyudmila!' her comrade snapped at her, making her jolt in the saddle and turn to look at Tanya.

Tanya inclined her head towards Anna.

Lyudmila lowered her weapon. 'The girl would be safer with us,' she muttered.

'If you were going to kill me, you would have done it in Belev,' I said. 'So I'll give you the same reasons I gave you then. Do it for my family. For my wife, Marianna. For my sons, Misha and Pavel.' I spoke their names clearly so they would remember them. So they would see me as a father and not just a soldier. 'And do it for Anna,' I said.

Lyudmila sighed and looked away.

'All right,' Tanya said. 'For Anna. But I still don't trust you. And this is only for now.'

'Then "for now" it is,' I replied.

# 27

We left the army behind us as they forged on to Dolinsk and we moved in the opposite direction.

'Did they say where they were going?' Tanya asked.

I looked back, but there was nothing behind us except the hoarfrost and the bruised sky streaked with wisps of the palest cloud. 'Tambov. With the Whites gone, that's their priority now.'

'The Whites are gone?' Tanya asked. 'How do you know that?'

'Pushed all the way down to Crimea,' I said, 'and across the sea. A man on a train told me.'

'A train?' Lyudmila asked. 'What train?'

'It's a long story.' I didn't have the inclination to tell them anything. I didn't mind the company – Alek used to say that a journey of a hundred miles was just a few steps with good company – but they wanted me to think they were holding back from me, so I intended to do the same.

'And where did the rest of your party come from?' Tanya looked at Anna.

When I had ridden away to speak to the Cossacks, Anna had kept her distance from Tanya and Lyudmila. I thought she might have taken to them, that, as women, she would have found them more sympathetic or more attractive somehow. I had expected her to want to be with them rather than with me, but that wasn't the case. She had refused to join Tanya on her horse and had barely spoken to her when I wasn't there.

'That's also a long story,' I said. There was no good reason to make Anna relive what had happened to her. Tanya didn't need to know, and she seemed to accept that. She nodded with a slow and thoughtful movement as she watched Anna, and there was a look in her face that I understood. She had children in her life too. Whether or not they were her own I didn't know, and whether they were alive or dead I couldn't tell, but the expression was soft and wistful, and there was sadness in her eyes. Wherever they were she missed them.

We covered some of the distance on foot, leading the animals and stopping from time to time to rest them, but other than that, we kept moving. The steppe was expansive, and none of us liked the exposure of being in the open, so we found protection in small wooded areas whenever we could.

In one such area, where we had stopped to rest and eat, I left Anna sitting with Tuzik and went to speak with Tanya, who was leaning against a tree, surveying the steppe. As before, Anna was reluctant to let me leave her side, and both she and Tuzik had tried to follow, but I told her to stay, pointing to Tanya just a few paces away and reassuring her I wouldn't go any further.

When I was standing beside Tanya, I looked back and raised a hand to Anna. She raised hers in return, but remained sitting upright and unable to relax. I noticed that Tuzik was now between her and Lyudmila, providing a protective barrier. Whether that had been his idea or hers I could only guess.

'We don't have to do this, you know,' I said to her.

'Do what?'

'Treat each other with suspicion. Be enemies. We're all after the same thing.'

'Are we?'

'As far as I can tell.'

'Except you're Red. I can smell it.'

'This has gone beyond colours and . . . ideology. This is about family.' Commander Orlov had been right about that. He had known what was important.

'Family.' Tanya echoed the word and looked at me. She dragged on one of her self-rolled cigarettes and let the smoke drift from her lips.

'Her mother died from typhus,' I said, inclining my head towards Anna but keeping my voice low. 'Years ago. And her father died . . .' I had to think about it; the days had blurred into one. 'Yesterday. He died yesterday.' An image of Lev's broken body came to mind. 'I told her I'd look after her now. And the dog . . . well, he just came along. Maybe he was looking for a new family.'

Tanya said nothing. She took another drag on her cigarette and contemplated the glowing tip before holding it out to me. I kept my eyes on hers as I accepted it and took a long pull on it, the smoke sharp on my throat, tight in my lungs.

'Thank you,' I said.

Standing there, at the edge of the grove, I decided to tell Tanya what she needed to know. If we were going to travel together, the knowledge could prove to be important, and it made sense for us to try to get along, so I gave her the information as both a safeguard and a peace offering. Much like Lev had offered his olive branch of help.

I kept some secrets for myself, but recounted what I had seen in Belev and what had happened at the farm when I met Lev and Anna. I told her about the seven riders, about the bodies we had found on the way to Dolinsk and what Commander Orlov had told me about Krukov and about the prisoners.

As I spoke, Tanya stared into the distance as if she wasn't listening, and I watched her face for any sign of what she was thinking. She remained composed, blank, questioning nothing, but when I mentioned prisoners, I saw something change in her demeanour. A strained expression as if something had caused her pain, then she looked up and tears glistened in her eyes. She sniffed hard and turned her face so that I could no longer see her.

When I finished speaking, Tanya was silent for a long while before she looked at me.

'They're hunting you. I don't like that. It puts Lyudmila and me at greater risk.'

'It doesn't really change anything,' I said. 'You and me . . .

we're following the same trail. We can't avoid each other, so we might as well be together.'

'It's a mistake to think we'll help if they catch up to you,' she warned, but she looked back at Anna and I saw the doubt in her eyes.

'I intend to stay well ahead of them,' I told her. 'Lose them, if we haven't already.'

'But they're persistent.' She turned her face towards me. 'So I'm wondering who are you, Kolya? Who are you really?'

'I'm a deserter.' I shrugged. 'They hunt deserters.'

'So you *are* Red.'

'I'm not anything anymore. I'm just a man who wants to find his family.'

'But you're something more than that. I know it. They don't send seven to catch one. Not unless the one is special. Dangerous, even.'

'I'm nobody,' I said.

'Don't ask? Is that it? I don't ask about you, you won't ask about me?'

'It's better that way. We leave the past behind us; it's easier for us to be friends.'

'I don't think we'll ever be friends, Kolya, and we can only the leave the past behind if it isn't chasing us.' She scanned the steppe as if searching for a glimpse of seven distant riders, and when she looked back at me, I could see she wanted to know more. There were questions in her eyes, on her lips, but things remained unsaid. I didn't tell her what or where I had deserted from, and I didn't disclose my connection to Krukov. Those were things she didn't need to know; things that would almost certainly affect our relationship for the worse and leave one or other of us dead, right there and then in that grove.

While I kept my secrets from Tanya, I knew *nothing* about her. She gave no information willingly, but there were some things she could not hide and I was beginning to suspect that she was not just a simple peasant. The way she ate when we stopped to rest, the way she rolled her cigarette, the sharpness of her thoughts, the questions she asked, the way she spoke, and the words she used. Everything about her behaviour told me that Tanya was educated. She wasn't just a farmer's wife.

'It seems you've learned more about Koschei than I have,' she said eventually. 'There's nothing more I can tell you about him. We've been following his signs, looking for the red star and going north, that's all. But what do you think is drawing him north? Everyone else is going south.'

'I've been wondering the same thing. Maybe the uprising has spread north of here. Maybe something else. They said they had prisoners and that there are holding camps in this area; he could be bringing prisoners here and then he'll go back.'

'What stopped him from killing *them*?' There was something odd in the way she stressed that last word.

'It legitimises what he's doing,' I suggested, but it was just an idea. 'The Red Army always needs new conscripts, and the labour camps need filling. There's a lot of work to be done, so he takes the young ones. But the old men and women . . .'

*He likes to drown the women.*

I took a deep breath and tried not to see the images that flooded my thoughts. '. . . It could be that's why he split his unit. Prisoners would slow them down, so maybe part of the unit went ahead—'

'For what?'

'To find more prisoners? Spread more terror?' I shook my head and speculated about the reasons Koschei might have to split his unit. I thought about telling Tanya that perhaps they hadn't just split into two. That maybe there was a third fraction of Koschei's unit. With the intelligence gleaned at the train, I had convinced myself that Koschei and Krukov were the same man, and it would make sense if a part of *that* unit were now following me. Koschei and his men might not just be in front of us, but behind us too.

'And I think we should stop calling him "Koschei",' I said. 'It makes him . . . less than human. Or *more* than human. But he isn't. He's just a man. We should call him by his name. Krukov.'

239

Tanya looked at me and nodded once. 'And this commander on the train, he was sure about that? About Krukov?'

'He was sure.' When I told Tanya about my conversation with Commander Orlov, I had bent the truth a little in my favour, leaving out the part about him recognising me, so she might not have been as sure as I was, but I was convinced Krukov was Koschei not because Commander Orlov gave the name to a doctor, but because he gave it to Nikolai Levitsky. He had known who I was from the moment he saw me and had made it clear what he thought of me. When he used Krukov's name in connection with Koschei, he was telling me the truth, and my knowledge of Krukov only concreted my certainty of that.

Tanya flicked her cigarette into the frosty grass and looked up at the sky. Grey clouds were moving across it now, the pale winter blue almost entirely gone.

'What did he do to you?' I asked. 'What did Krukov do?'

Tanya turned her back on the steppe and switched her attention to Anna, who was sitting close to Tuzik, one hand buried in the thick fur at his neck. There was a change in Tanya's expression when she looked at Anna. Something of the melancholy I had seen earlier washed across her face like an incoming wave. The sudden softening of her appearance showed me something I'd never witnessed in her before, and for the first time, it occurred to me that her eyes were almost exactly the same colour as Marianna's. Before now, they had always seemed cold and hard, but the softening transformed her.

I felt a stab of anguish, a desperation to be with my wife again, and I stared into Tanya's eyes as if it would give me just a taste of what it would be like to have Marianna here.

But then the lightness of Tanya's countenance was gone again, leaving not a trace. It was a sudden and brief transformation, as if she had swept one personality aside and replaced it with another. Now her face hardened.

'You have children?' I asked.

There was a furrowing of her eyebrows, a clenching of the jaw.

'That's why I want him,' I said. 'You know that. I understand what you're feeling.'

'You understand nothing,' she said. 'What *can* you understand?'

'More than you think.'

'You're a professional soldier; you've got it written all over your face. It's in the way you walk and talk. Everything. I've seen so many damn soldiers, I know what one looks like.'

'So what would you see if you were to look in a mirror?' I asked.

Tanya glanced up at me and sighed before turning her eyes to the ground.

'Whatever I've done,' I said, 'whatever I am, I'm still a father. A husband.'

'When did you last see them?' she asked. 'Your sons? You have two, right? When did you last tell them you love them? When did you last hold your wife?'

There was anger growing in her voice and I knew that when she looked at me, she couldn't see me as anything but a soldier. It was men like me who had shattered her life, whatever colour they had chosen.

'It's a long time, isn't it?' she said. 'Because you've been out there, armed, killing other fathers and sons; mothers and wives too, I'd bet.'

Her stare cut through me just as her words did. She was right about me. There was nothing I could say to change that; nothing I could say to make her think differently.

'He didn't take them prisoner, did he?' I asked. 'Your—'

'No. He slaughtered them. Everyone. My son, just fifteen. My daughter, not much older than . . .' She looked back at Anna and squeezed her eyes shut, determined that her emotion would be anger rather than grief.

'And you? Were you there? How did you—'

'My husband and my father with red stars burned on their skin. Do you know what that does to you? Seeing that?'

'I can imagine it—'

'No, you can't imagine,' she said. 'You can't imagine it at all,

241

because it hasn't happened to you. You have some hope that your family is alive. *Hope*. That's what keeps *you* going. For me, there is only hate. That's what it does to you – it fills you with hate. *That's* what keeps *me* going.'

I wondered what was different about Tanya's family that had made Krukov murder everyone while he took the young people from Belev with him. *Her* son had been fighting age.

Perhaps it was something to do with who she was. I had come to suspect that she wasn't a common peasant – she had developed a hard look to her, but she didn't have the posture or mannerisms or speech traits I expected from a worker. I wondered if she had a background in wealth and education that had riled Koschei into such frenzy. Or maybe there had been some change in the way he operated. Or perhaps he had just had a bad day. It wasn't uncommon for Chekist leaders to lose their minds – perpetrating such horrors, fuelling themselves with drugs and alcohol, it was little surprise.

'You were wealthy?' The words came out before I thought about them.

Tanya didn't reply, but she turned and stared at me with an expression that at least confirmed it.

'And educated,' I said. 'So you're not a soldier?'

Tanya glanced back at Lyudmila, then turned to look out at the steppe once more. 'No.'

'What about her?' I asked. 'Lyudmila? What—'

'If you want to know about Lyudmila, you'll have to ask her yourself.'

But I had a feeling she would tell me even less than Tanya had.

'I'm sorry about your family.' It was a pointless thing to say. Words couldn't bring them back, and they couldn't convey my sympathy for her. Tanya was wrong about something, though. I *could* imagine how she felt, and I understood that there was an important and worrying difference between us.

I was looking for my wife and sons; Tanya was looking only for revenge.

'When we find him,' I said, 'I want to know what happened to my family.'

'You're telling me not to kill him.'

'Not right away.' It was more important now than ever that we stayed together. I couldn't afford for her to find Koschei before me.

'I'll make him tell you what you want to know.' She looked me up and down. 'Though I suspect you'd be good at that yourself.'

I ignored her comment. 'After that, you can do whatever you want.'

'What I *want* is all of them, not just Kosch— Krukov. Not just *Krukov*. I want all of them. Every single one of his men.'

'When was it?' I asked. 'How long have you been looking for him?'

'Thirty-seven days,' she said. 'And out here, that's a long time. It changes you. But we're getting close, I can feel it.'

'When it's done? What will you do then?'

'I haven't seen that far yet.' Tanya adjusted her rifle, moving the strap on her shoulder, then took the tobacco pouch from her pocket. 'But when the time comes,' she said, 'I just hope you're as good at killing as I think you are.'

# 28

It was early evening and we'd seen nobody for hours when we reached a farm.

Already the sun had begun to set, a hazy orange disc behind the grey clouds, and with its setting so the cold had bitten harder and harder.

'It look like snow?' Tanya directed her question at Lyudmila, who stared up at the sky and shook her head.

Lyudmila didn't talk much, but she watched me all the time. She guarded Tanya with jealousy, and I saw the way she grew tense whenever I came close to her. She hated everything about me and I wondered what it was that burned so deeply in her; what tragedy or otherwise had brought her together with Tanya.

Her reaction to Anna was different, though. Lyudmila barely spoke to her; seemed to avoid being close to her, as if she didn't like children or didn't know how to deal with them. Or perhaps she thought it might soften her. I had seen her steal glances at Anna, though, and I knew her coldness didn't run all the way down to her core.

'It'll snow soon enough,' I said. 'Maybe tomorrow, maybe next week, but it's coming.'

We had come through a forested area, thick and dark, and spied the farm from the trees. Taking up position to watch it for some time, we thought it would be good to spend the night here. It was a simple place with two wooden houses standing side by side. The nearest was larger than the one beside it, and while they were both basic constructions with pitched, thatched roofs, the farthest was in bad repair. It looked older and had suffered the onslaught of the weather for many years so that the windows were cracked, the walls were patched with moss, and there were places where the thatch had come away from the roof.

It was almost as I pictured One-Eyed Likho's house to be when Marianna told her *skazkas* to the boys. If I hadn't known better, I might have believed the witch was real and waiting in the house to catch us off guard so she could cut my throat and put me in her oven.

In front of the second house, in the far corner of a yard surrounded by a ramshackle fence, stood an outbuilding, which also had a thatched roof. The yard was empty but for a water trough at one end and a cart, which lay idle in the centre.

Behind the farm was nothing but the forest we used for cover. It was mottled with shadow there now, and the trunks leaned in towards the buildings, the crooked and barren branches extending as if reaching out to smother it and take the farm for its own.

Beyond the yard, though, the fields stretched a long way. On the far side of them, there was a hedgerow and evenly spaced trees, beyond which another farm stood. Only the roofs of the far buildings were visible.

There had been no movement for at least half an hour. No sign at all that the near farm was inhabited. No smoke from the chimney and no light from the windows. The evening closed in on us and the air grew colder and we shivered in our heavy winter coats.

When the darkness smothered us, and the time of forest demons was on us, I felt a chill run through me.

I put my arm around Anna's shoulder and held her close.

Tuzik stood in front of us, Kashtan behind, the four of us inseparable now.

'We should go down there,' I said into the eerie quiet. 'Either that or go back into the forest and find somewhere good to build a fire. It's getting late and I don't want to freeze to death out here.' My breath was white and thick around me.

'Maybe we should keep going,' Tanya said.

'I want to go on as much as you do –' I didn't take my eyes off the farm '– but there's too much cloud to travel at night. And the horses need rest. We all do.'

I felt her turn to me, so I met her gaze. Jagged teeth of hair jutted from the fringe of her hat. Her eyes had a distant look.

'We'll find him,' I said. 'Together. But we need to rest.' Stopping at Lev's place had given my pursuers time to catch up, and I was reluctant to make the same mistake, but we were exhausted and needed to rest. My hunters would need to do the same thing.

She looked away, clenching her jaw and pursing her lips tight.

'It pains me to say this, Tanya, but he's right. I say we go down there.' Lyudmila hadn't spoken for a while and it was a surprise to hear her agree with me. 'There's no one there.'

'And if there is?' Tanya asked. 'What do we do then?'

'If there were soldiers down there, we'd have seen them,' I said. 'There'd be horses, equipment . . . and with three of us, armed, we should be able to deal with any overprotective farmers.'

'And what about the other farm?' Tanya asked, looking out at the rooftops beyond the hedgerow. 'There might be people there.'

'We've seen nothing so far. And if we can't see them, they won't see us.'

So we led the horses out of the trees and headed towards the back of the farm, keeping out of view as much as possible.

When we reached the rear of the two houses, Tuzik padded ahead, nose to the ground, and we followed him round to the front.

'There's no one here,' I said, as we came closer and let the horses through the gate.

As we entered the yard, though, the door to the first building opened, making me snap my head round, my hand reaching for my pocket. I half expected One-Eyed Likho to appear from the house like a crazed old hag, but instead it was an old man who stepped out into the cold.

He was as surprised to see us as we were to see him and we all stopped dead in our tracks.

Tuzik lowered his head and splayed his front legs in one sudden movement, his whole body tense. The fur on his neck rose, his ears went back, and he bared his teeth in warning. The growl that escaped him was feral.

'He's unarmed,' Tanya whispered. 'Don't do anything.'

'What do you think I'm going to do?' I asked, moving in front of Anna. 'Attack an old man?'

Tanya gave me a look to suggest that was exactly what she expected me to do. 'You or your dog,' she said under her breath. 'Keep the damn thing under control.' Then she turned and raised a hand. 'Good evening,' she said.

The old man nodded once with uncertainty and glanced into the house behind him with a worried expression before casting his eyes over us once more.

'Let me talk to him,' Tanya said, handing me the reins of her horse. 'And hold on to that dog.'

I called Tuzik, surprised when he obeyed and came to my side. Anna held on to him as Tanya strode over to the old man and took off her hat, holding it in the fist of her right hand. As she did so, the old man stood a little straighter and took a deep breath.

'What do you want?' He closed the door behind him and took a pace forward to stop Tanya from climbing onto the first step.

'We thought there was no one here.' She hesitated with one foot raised.

'And now you can see there is.' His voice was deep and rattled with phlegm as if he needed to cough.

'We're passing by on our way north. Looking for shelter for the night.' She withdrew her foot.

'And you want to get it here?' He looked down at her, then squinted and peered through the semi-darkness at me and Lyudmila standing with the horses.

'If that's agreeable with you,' Tanya said.

The man's craggy face broke into a smile that displayed blackened teeth. He put back his head and laughed, emitting a croaky, rasping sound more like a death rattle than a laugh.

Tanya took another step back and glanced across at me.

I made an encouraging gesture with my hands, prompting her to speak again, but before she could say anything, the old man stopped laughing as suddenly as he had started and stared down at her with watery eyes.

'Three of you, armed, deserters most likely, with a . . . What is that? A wolf?'

'A dog,' Tanya said.

'A bad-tempered dog, then, and you're asking if it's agreeable with me?' He took a step forward so he was looking right down at Tanya. 'Of course it's not agreeable with me, but since when did anyone care about that?'

'Sir,' I said, coming forward, 'we have food we can share in return for shelter and warmth. We mean you no harm. We're not deserters.'

'Then why are you armed?'

'We're searching for someone.'

'Searching for someone?' The old man scratched the back of his head and furrowed his brow as he looked around me. 'That doesn't mean anything. Who are you? What . . .' As soon as he saw Anna standing with the horses, he stopped scratching. 'You have a child with you.'

'Yes.'

He dropped his hand to his side and puffed his cheeks as he blew out a long breath. For a moment I thought he was going to welcome us in. I thought perhaps the sight of a child had softened his heart, but then his face hardened and his next words were spoken with venom. 'There's nothing for you here. Go away. You should—'

Just then the door to the *izba* opened once more, making him look back in surprise.

'Who's out there?' said a voice, and an old woman came out onto the step, dressed in black and with a shawl draped around her shoulders. She shuffled in an unsettling way, like Galina had done. Like I imagined a witch would.

'It's no one,' said the old man. 'Go back inside.'

'I want to see who it is,' she said. Her voice was coarse and hard and unsympathetic.

'It's no one.'

'Well, it has to be *someone*, you old fool. Who is it?'

The old man sighed and shook his head. 'They say they're looking for someone.'

'Who? Who're they looking for?'

'Chekists,' Tanya said.

It was more than I thought she should have given away, but there was something in the old man's eyes when she said it; some sort of recognition, or perhaps it was just sympathy.

'Well, bring them in, Sergei, bring them in.' The old woman's tone changed, but it still sounded unfriendly. It was as if she were hiding her true nature, like One-Eyed Likho settling the tailor before cutting his throat. 'You can't leave them standing in the cold.'

'Maybe we should let them move on,' he said. 'We can't spare any—'

'Don't be such a miser,' she told him. 'Bring them in, bring them in.' She stepped back and beckoned with gnarled hands.

Sergei rolled his eyes and grumbled.

'We should move on,' Lyudmila said under her breath, and I knew why she said it. We weren't welcome here – the old man made that clear enough – and his wife reminded me too much of Galina and the *skazka* witches. But it was getting colder by the minute and I had to think about Anna. She needed warmth, food and a good night's sleep.

'Look,' I said, taking the piece of *salo* from my satchel and showing it to him as I unwrapped it. 'We can share what we have.'

'They have food?' the old woman said. 'Even better. What are you waiting for? Bring them in.'

The old man studied the piece of *salo*, small as it was, moving his mouth as though he were eating the greasy fat already. He came down the step, making Tanya move out of his way, and he reached out to take my arm and bring the *salo* closer. He looked it over, then leaned in to smell it.

When he had done that, he released me and fixed his eyes on

mine. 'Red, White, I don't care who you are. Are you an *honest* man?' he asked. 'That's what matters.'

'Yes.'

'A man of your word?'

'Yes.'

'And you give me your word you mean no harm here?'

'I swear it.'

He thought for a moment before taking a deep breath and holding out his hand, but he didn't look me in the eye as Lev had done when he offered me his olive branch. His was not a warm greeting, as Lev's had been, and I felt my friend's absence with some pain.

I removed my glove and took the old man's hand in mine, feeling the coarseness of his skin. His fingers were strong, his grip tight, despite his age. And in that moment I felt pity for him. Winter was close, and the war had brought food shortages. The old were vulnerable and exposed. Many would not see the spring.

'There's hay in the barn for your horses,' he said, 'and the dog stays outside. Bring some logs with you when you come in. We light the oven at night.'

The old man stood by the *pich*, pointing to the place where he expected us to pile the logs. The *izba* still held the remnants of warmth from last night's fire, the *pich* having kept its heat well. A good oven was always the heart of any home, and a good *pichniki* was one of the most valuable tradesmen. It took great skill to build a stove with enough passages to channel the smoke and hot air through the bricks to build a good heat. If the old man only lit his oven at night, then the *pichniki* had done a good job – the bricks still gave off enough heat to make it warmer inside than it was outside. The iron door was open to reveal an oven large enough to keep even Baba Yaga or One-Eyed Likho happy – either witch could accommodate a whole adult in there, if need be.

The *pich* was well placed in the room, and there was a good space between its top and the ceiling above it. The corner of a blanket hanging down gave the impression that more were bundled on top of it, and I knew it would be a warm place to sleep.

'You have a good *pich*,' I said, piling dry birch logs on the floor beside it. I couldn't stop myself from leaning to one side to inspect the interior of the oven, as if to reassure myself there weren't any children roasting in its coals. When I saw it was empty, I told myself to stop being so foolish. I'd listened to so many *skazkas* they were starting to affect me the way they were supposed to frighten the children.

I turned to see the old man watching me. His black hair was streaked with grey, bushy around his ears but thinning on top, and his face was almost covered by a thick beard. His eyes were hooded with heavy lids beneath unruly eyebrows, and his nose was bent at an odd angle as if it had once been broken. His clothes looked clean and in half-decent repair.

'The *pichniki* must have been very skilled,' I said.

The old man grunted and spat into the open oven, the gob of saliva arcing into last night's ashes. It was a gesture used to ward off bad luck if a compliment is given.

'He built it himself,' the old woman said from the far corner of the room, 'though he doesn't like to admit it.'

We gathered more logs from the pile outside and returned to the *izba*, Tanya and Lyudmila entering first. Tuzik tried to follow Anna and me up the step, but I pushed him away with my leg, trying to be gentle.

'He would enjoy the *pich*,' I said to Anna, 'but we have to honour the old man's request.'

'Why won't they let him come in?' she whispered.

'Maybe they're scared of dogs.'

'He's not as scary as they are. That woman is so ugly.'

'Sh.' I put a finger to my lips. 'She's just old. Tuzik doesn't seem bothered anyway,' I said. 'Look at him – he doesn't care.'

'Because he can see how scary she is. She looks like a witch.'

I couldn't help smiling. 'I think he wants to stand guard. Maybe even go hunting.' I put the logs inside the door and squatted to let Tuzik bury his head into my armpit. 'Guard us well, my friend,' I told him, as I rubbed his back. 'I'll bring you something to eat later, I promise.'

Tuzik moved back into the yard and watched us go into the house, but he made no more attempt to follow.

'I don't blame him,' Anna said. 'This place is creepy.'

We dumped the logs on the pile, and the old woman stepped out of the shadow as if she'd been lying in wait for us. She came to the table, put a candle in a holder and lit it with a match before putting a glass storm shield round it. The flame flickered for a moment and then grew, lighting the surface of the table and the chairs round it.

The old woman was stooped a little, bent at the waist, and hunched; thin and bony beneath her black dress and woollen shawl. She wore a tight black headscarf to match the dress, and it covered her hair, making it look as if she might be bald beneath it. All I could see were her wrinkled forehead, her watery eyes and veined nose. She had soft shoes on her feet, and when she shuffled over to greet us, her hag-like manner made my skin crawl.

'Pretty girl,' she said, reaching out to pinch Anna's cheek between her hardened thumb and the gnarled knuckle of her first finger.

She smiled, revealing more gum than tooth, and I felt Anna recoil.

The old woman's breath was rancid, like sour milk. She was as repellent to my eyes as she was to Anna's and I kept thinking of Galina with her putrid eye and her unsettling insanity. And the way she touched Anna, it was as if she was testing her tenderness, sizing her up for the pot.

I had to laugh at myself and try to dismiss my unease.

'Very pretty,' she repeated, nodding to herself, and the tip of her tongue slipped out to wet her lips. 'Her name?'

'Anna.' I introduced all of us, giving them our first names, but the old woman only had eyes for Anna right now.

'Your daughter?' she asked.

'In a manner of speaking.'

'In a manner of speaking?' She craned her neck to stare at me. 'Either she is or she isn't. Which one is it, my dear?'

'She is now,' I said.

'An orphan of the war?'

'I'm right here, you know.' Anna pulled away from her.

'She doesn't like to be reminded,' I said.

'Hmm.' The old woman peered at Anna. 'Well . . . sit, sit. Let me see what else you've brought us.'

While Sergei lit the *pich*, the rest of us sat at the table and spread our supplies across its surface. We had left most of our belongings in our saddlebags in the outbuilding, which was just as well because the old woman had hungry eyes and a hungrier stomach. By the time we had unpacked what we'd brought in with us, there was the piece of *salo*, some strips of dried meat, three chunks of sausage and a slab of *kovbyk*. Lyudmila had been reluctant to hand it over, but the old woman hadn't given us much choice. She had taken our satchels and rummaged through them, pushing the ammunition to one side and handing us the knives to hold while she searched for food. It was bad luck to leave a knife on the table and these were superstitious country people.

'We'll sup well tonight,' she said, smiling at Anna for longer than necessary before handing back our satchels.

'There's enough food there for us to eat well for two *days*,' Lyudmila said to Tanya. 'We need that.'

'We can find more,' Tanya replied.

'Where? Where do we find more?'

'The forest is full of things to eat, and we're close now. We can spare it.'

'But—'

'We can spare it,' Tanya said again.

The old woman watched closely as they spoke, as if she was hanging on every word they said, waiting to learn the outcome. And when they had finished speaking, she put out a crooked and liver-spotted hand to touch Tanya's. She patted it once and smiled her near-toothless smile. 'You said there's enough for you for two

253

days.' She looked at Lyudmila. 'Then perhaps there will be enough for nine to eat just one good meal.'

Lyudmila stared back at her as if about to challenge the old woman to explain herself, but I understood what she meant. She and Sergei were not alone on the farm. There were others here too.

The old woman shifted and turned to Sergei, who had finished lighting the oven and was watching from a distance. 'Tell them to come down,' she said.

Sergei hesitated.

'Go on. Go.' She waved a leathery hand. 'It's safe. Kolya won't hurt us.'

I dropped my hand beneath the table and slipped it into my coat pocket. The pistol was still cold when I wrapped my fingers round it.

Sergei looked at the floor as if his feet had become interesting, but his wife snapped his name, making him jump. 'Sergei.'

He looked up.

The old woman sneered at him. 'It's all right, you old fool. Tell them to come down.'

Sergei went into the darkness at the far end of the room and lifted a ladder from its place against the wall. He put it up to the side of the *pich*, placing it carefully.

'You can come down,' he said, but as he spoke, he cast a look in our direction. He wasn't as convinced as his wife that we were harmless.

The first feet to step onto the ladder protruded from the hem of a dark skirt and the woman came into view as she climbed down. For a moment I was taken aback, as I saw my own wife, Marianna, descending those rungs and I had to close my eyes and shake some sense into my head. When I opened them again, the woman was looking at me. She wasn't Marianna, but there was a resemblance. She had hair like Marianna's, and it was tied back in the style that Marianna wore it, loose at the front so that it fell across her forehead. She had a similar build, with a waist that had once been full and healthy but had narrowed as times became harder. She was pale like Marianna too, but not as pretty, and when she stepped into the light, I saw she had dull green eyes, while Marianna's were blue.

'Our daughter, Oksana,' said the old woman, and as she spoke, the first set of children's feet touched the ladder and Oksana stretched up to help the girl down.

'Natasha,' said the old woman with a smile.

The girl, perhaps five or six years old, clung to her mother's skirt as the second child descended the ladder; a boy who looked to be at least ten years old. Both children were pale and thin like Anna, their cheeks almost hollow, dark circles under their eyes.

'And this is Nikolai,' she said, looking at me. 'Your namesake.'

The three of them stood huddled like refugees at the bottom of the ladder, holding each other close, and I imagined Marianna might have looked the same when she tried to protect our sons from Krukov. Except for them, it would have been different, because Marianna would have only been able to hold them for a few seconds before snatching up their coats and ushering them out and across the footbridge to seek the false safety of the forest. I could only imagine how she must have felt, seeing them go, having to return home to wait for the devils, only to be dragged across the road and into the trees, forced to witness the murder of Galina's husband and then . . .

*He likes to drown the women.*

When Oksana came closer, I took my hand from my pocket and acknowledged her with nod and by speaking my name but little else.

Oksana and the old woman made soup, while the children stayed close to them at the *pich* and the rest of us waited at the table. Sergei sat with his hands on the coarse surface, fingers laced together as if in prayer, eyes fixed on the tabletop. He only looked up from time to time, catching my eye and then looking away again.

'It's good of you to take us in,' I said, breaking the uncomfortable silence.

Sergei shrugged.

Behind him, the old woman opened a cupboard to retrieve a bowl of salt and I noticed the cupboard was not as empty as I might have expected it to be. There were bottles lined against the back of it, jars of what looked like pickles, and bundles of cloth like the ones Marianna used to keep dried fish and meat.

'The war hasn't been too unkind to you?' I said, making Sergei raise his eyes and follow my gaze.

'Oh. No. Not too unkind.' He nodded and looked away, embarrassed.

I glanced sideways at Tanya and saw that she had spotted it too. I could almost hear what she was thinking – that these people would take our food when they had plenty of their own – but I gave a small shake of my head, warning her to keep quiet. This was a family trying to stay alive, and they had offered us shelter.

Now that I had seen the well-stocked cupboard, though, I began to notice other things inside the *izba*, such as the boots by the door. I paid them no attention when we came in, but beside the rifles Tanya and Lyudmila had propped against the wall, there were two pairs of good boots that looked hardly used. The woven mat on the floor still had its colours – bold reds and blues and clean whites – and there was another hanging on the wall at the back of the room. There was a shotgun on nails close to the door. The blankets above the *pich* were plentiful. The soft shoes on the old woman's feet were clean and still held their shape, and the clothes they wore were in better condition than I might have expected.

This was the home of poor peasants, so it would have been a surprise they owned so much and lived so comfortably at any time, but especially in these years of confiscation and requisition. Yet they did not have the appearance of people who lived well. Their skin had the waxy pallor of those who have had little nourishment. The children had the sunken and hollow faces of those who were growing close to starvation. Their demeanour didn't match their possessions and their well-stocked cupboards. The acquisition of this food had come recently.

Perhaps they had found this place, like Lev and Anna had

found the farm where I met them. Or perhaps there was another reason. Something darker.

When the meal was ready, Oksana brought it to the table and the old woman served it and we sat together round the table to eat, as if we were a family. The hot broth was good and went well with the cold meat, but nothing about that meal made me feel the security I ever felt at home, or the inclusion I had felt with Lev and Anna when they took me in.

While the old man remained quiet, his wife talked about the revolution and about the war the before it and the war that had come after it.

She leaned forward across the table as if she was going to invite us into a conspiracy. 'They even fired shells at the field just on the other side of the farm.' She nodded her head. 'Men fighting, shooting, killing one another – there was so much noise we hid under the table waiting for it to stop. Full of holes it is now, that field. No use to anyone.'

Sergei looked at his wife as she spoke, his eyes shifting away to watch me and Tanya and Lyudmila in a way that made me nervous. With the light and the warmth and the food and the family sitting about us, I should have been comfortable, but there was an undeniable tension here.

'And no one came to the house?' I asked. 'After the fighting?' I couldn't help look around at the full cupboards, the tidy clothes and the clean boots. There were even enough spoons and bowls for each of us at the table.

The old woman shared a glance with her husband, then shrugged. 'They passed on. Hardly even knew we were here.'

'You went to look, though,' said Tanya. 'You went to see where they had been fighting.'

The old woman nodded. 'It was terrible.'

'That didn't stop you from taking what you could.' It was Lyudmila who spoke this time, and I wondered if she had seen what it was that had filled their cupboards and put fresh clothes on their starving bodies. She understood what was making the old woman and her husband so edgy. They had stolen from the dead.

The old woman looked down at the tabletop. They were ashamed of it. 'Times are hard.'

'I understand,' I told her. 'Nothing can be wasted.'

She nodded.

'We're not bad people,' Sergei said. 'We're just . . .'

'You don't need to explain yourselves,' I said.

Sergei lifted his eyes to look at me across the table before he reached for his pipe and took a healthy pinch of tobacco from a worn but full pouch.

'All of this didn't come from a battlefield,' Lyudmila said, as he packed the tobacco tight and clamped the pipe between his teeth. 'Not all this food.' She cast her eyes around the room.

Sergei shook his head.

'Papa brought us things too,' the boy said, making his mother squeeze him and give him a stern look. Everybody watched him but the old woman. She kept her eyes on the three of us, sitting on the opposite side of the table.

'What's that you said?' Lyudmila sat back and put one hand on her thigh.

'Nikolai misses his papa.' The old woman smiled, displaying blackened teeth, before leaning in and whispering to us. 'He imagines he sees him sometimes. It's very hard for the children, you know.' The stink of her breath soured the air.

'Of course.'

For a moment there was no sound in the room but the fire crackling in the *pich*.

'But tell us about you.' The old woman sat back and raised her voice. 'Where are you from?'

I looked at Tanya and Lyudmila, none of us saying anything.

'I understand,' the old woman said. 'You're deserters – of course you don't want to talk about it.'

'No, we . . .' Tanya stopped.

'It's all right.' The old woman pulled her shawl tighter. 'We won't tell anyone, will we, Sergei?'

'No. No, of course not.'

'So what brings you this way?' she asked. 'You said you're looking for someone.'

There was an awkward silence as we considered what to tell them, what kind of threat they could be to us, or what information they might have.

'We're looking for a man calling himself Koschei,' I said eventually, glancing at Tanya. 'Have you heard of him?'

'Koschei?' Sergei took his pipe from his mouth and studied the glowing tobacco in the bowl as if the answer might be hidden in the embers. With his other hand, he reached up and stroked his beard, smoothing it round his upper lip and running his fingers down its length. 'Like the story?'

'Yes, but this man is real. Have you heard of him?' I asked.

'No,' said the old woman.

'He's a Chekist. His real name is Krukov.'

'I don't know the name.'

'And you haven't seen anyone pass by?' I asked. 'Soldiers taking prisoners? Or maybe—'

'We don't see anybody here.' The old woman spoke a little too suddenly.

'What about your neighbours? Might they have—'

'No one passes by. No one sees anything. It's safer that way.' An edge had crept into her tone and the atmosphere in the room had become more tense. When I looked across at Sergei, he was still staring at the tabletop. Oksana busied herself with her children, stroking their hair and bringing Natasha to sit on her knee, as if she was finding something to do so she didn't have to make eye contact.

'Is there something wrong?' I asked.

'There is always something wrong,' the old woman said.

'We do what we have to.' Sergei looked up with sad eyes. 'What else *can* we do?'

I was about to ask him what he meant by that, but Oksana pushed back her chair and stood up. 'It's late,' she said, making it clear it was time for the conversation to end. 'The children need to

259

sleep, and *you* must be exhausted.' She gave Anna a sympathetic look.

'I'm fine,' Anna said without expression. 'I'm tougher than I look.'

Oksana smiled, but there was sadness in her eyes. 'I'm sure you are.'

'Well, you can sleep in the *izba* next door,' the old woman said. 'The roof's not so good, so it'll get cold, but there are some old blankets, and if you light the fire, you'll be warm enough.'

Before we left, I thanked the old woman for her hospitality and shook Sergei's hand.

'Oksana,' I said, 'may I ask where your husband is?'

'Our son is fighting the war,' the old woman answered for her, filling her chest with pride and standing as straight as she could. 'He's a good boy.'

I didn't ask which uniform he wore.

# 29

The night was bitter and black. The cold had rooted itself deep in the earth, and the frost had thickened. The first few flakes of snow were in the air, small and light and almost nothing, but they lay where they fell.

No breeze stirred in the forest, and the air was silent.

I was the first to step out of the warmth, Anna at my side as always. Tuzik must have jumped to his feet as soon as he heard the door open, because he was trotting over before I had even crossed the threshold. He was almost invisible in the darkness and came without sound, a creature of the night, nuzzling into my hand to take the morsel of food I had promised. As he snapped it down, I felt a wetness in my palm, and when I turned to look at it in the weak light from the lamp Sergei was holding, I saw the blood of a fresh kill.

'Looks like he's already eaten,' I said to Sergei. 'You have one less rabbit to eat your crops.'

Sergei took us to the front door of the empty *izba* next door and stood aside so that Tanya and Lyudmila could go in first. Sergei didn't object when I let Tuzik enter, but when I stepped up to go in, he put his hand on my chest and stopped me.

'Are you sure you want to stay?' he asked. 'The woods make for good shelter if you know how to build a fire.'

'Have we taken advantage of your kindness?' I asked.

'No, it's not that . . .'

'You have no reason to be afraid of us,' I told him.

'I know. It's just . . . you seem like good people.' He looked down at Anna and put out his hand to put it on her head, but he stopped himself, closing his fingers and letting his arm fall to his side.

'What is it?' I asked. 'What's the matter?'

Sergei paused with his mouth open as if the words had caught in his throat, then he shook his head. 'Sleep well,' he said, handing me the lamp. 'And God protect you.'

When he was gone, I bolted the door and turned to Tanya and Lyudmila, who were standing by the table in the cold room. It was dark and dusty, as if no one had been here for a long time, but there was a pile of old blankets on the table just as the old woman had said.

'What do you think?' Tanya said. 'Did anyone else feel uncomfortable in there?'

'They're hiding something,' Lyudmila said.

'*Everyone's* hiding something,' I told her. 'These people are ashamed of stealing from the dead.' I put the lamp on the table and looked around the room, seeing my breath form in clouds. There wasn't much in there to speak of. The table was bare, apart from the blankets, and the shelves were all empty. True to the old woman's word, there was a man-sized hole in the far corner of the roof, just to the right of the *pich*, which explained the temperature in the house, and from time to time a snowflake found its way through and dropped to the floor. It would have been easy enough for a young man to fix if he had the right tools and supplies, but for a man Sergei's age, it would be too much.

'Great,' Tanya said. 'It's snowing inside.'

When I went to the *pich* and looked in, it was clear of ashes. No fire had been burned in there for some time, but there was a pile of logs and kindling, ready to be used.

'You think they were expecting us?' Lyudmila ran her hand along the top blanket. 'Or someone else?'

'You know how to light this?' I asked Anna.

'Yes.'

'Good girl. See if you can give us some heat.' I handed her my small bundle of matches. 'And try to use only one of these. I don't have many left.'

'Not like them,' Tanya said. 'You see how many matches the old woman had?'

'What about everything else?' Lyudmila pulled out a chair and sat at the table. 'All that food in the cupboard. And *these* blankets are more like what you'd expect in their house, not those nice clean ones they had.'

'They swapped their old for new,' Tanya said. 'I suppose it can happen, but . . .'

'They've been looting dead men,' I reminded her. 'They admitted that.'

'Or, at least, it's what they told us.' Lyudmila took out her pistol and put it on the table. 'But they didn't get all that food from dead men.'

'It's possible,' Tanya said. 'Look at the supplies we have with us.'

'We don't have *soft shoes* with us,' Lyudmila said.

Anna went to the *pich* and found a small square of cloth, which she tore into pieces using her teeth before bunching them together and arranging them inside the oven.

'No, they're hiding something.' Lyudmila put her rifle across her knee. 'I'm sure of it. Did you see how they reacted when you mentioned Chekists?'

'Most people would get nervous if you mentioned Chekists,' I told her. 'Some people won't even say the word for fear of what will happen to them. Maybe that's what it is – they're afraid we'll report them.'

'To who?' Lyudmila asked.

'That's what we've come to? People afraid to say words?' Tanya sighed. 'Afraid, maybe, to even think them.'

'Or maybe they're planning on cooking us in that oven and eating us,' Anna said, as she layered small pieces of kindling over the cloth, preparing the fire. 'She *looked* like a witch.'

'This is no joke.' Lyudmila's words were clipped and sharp. 'And there's more to it than them just being scared.' She checked the bolt on her rifle, sliding it back and pushing it forward with the heel of her hand. A cartridge ejected from the breech and she caught it in her left hand. There wasn't much light from the lamp, but I suspect she would have caught the cartridge if there had been no light at all in there. 'We should leave,' she said again.

'Where did you learn to handle a weapon so well?' I asked, making her look up and stare at me. 'You're more comfortable with that than a lot of soldiers I've seen.'

'I always liked shooting.'

'People? You always liked shooting people?'

'Animals,' she said. 'Hunting. Our father taught us. He said girls were better at shooting than boys. That they were calmer and more patient.'

I was searching the single room as we spoke, checking the cupboards and drawers, looking through the windows, while Tuzik made his own inspection, but now I stopped and looked at Lyudmila. It was the most information she had ever offered about herself, and her voice had taken on a hint of warmth when she mentioned her father. It made her seem more human.

'Where is he now?' I asked.

She was still hunched over the rifle, checking and cleaning. 'Gone. And now I just hunt men.'

'What happened to—'

'Enough questions,' she said, glancing up at me with dark eyes before returning to what she was doing.

I knew it was pointless to press her further, so I went back to my search.

The dog's claws ticked on the wooden floor as he poked his nose into every corner, but it didn't take us long to check the room. The *izba* next door, where Sergei lived with his family, was bigger, and I had seen a door into a second room, much like my own home in Belev, but this was smaller even than the one Lev and Anna had made theirs at the farm. Here, there was just the *pich*, a pair of sleeping berths along each sidewall, scattered with old straw, and a small wooden chest that contained only dust and stale air. In the far corner, a dented samovar that looked as if it hadn't been used in a long time. The room was barely big enough for the four of us.

Lyudmila remained at the table, checking her weapons, and Tanya sat beside her, both of them facing the door. Anna managed to get a fire going, feeding it with more kindling, encouraging the flames higher.

'You notice they said Oksana was their daughter —' I went to the front door and tested the bolts once more '— but they said her husband was their son?' I held back the curtain across the window by the door and peered out, seeing nothing but black, spotted with the white of the light flakes that fell like they were a hallucination. 'Which do you think is actually their child? Oksana, or her husband?'

'Does it matter?' Lyudmila asked.

'Probably not.' I looked back at her, thinking I knew almost nothing about her. Even less than I knew about Tanya. We were four strangers thrown together by circumstance. People who, in another time, would never have even known of the others' existence.

Lyudmila picked up Tanya's rifle and started checking it. 'We shouldn't be staying here. We should leave now. I've got a feeling . . .' She shook her head.

'I agree there's something strange,' I said, 'but I don't know about leaving. Where would we go?'

'We could go into the forest.' Lyudmila looked up. 'Keep moving, stop when we're tired. It's always been good enough before.'

'You wanted to come down here,' I said. 'You agreed.'

'That was before.'

'We can't go anywhere tonight,' Tanya said. 'The clouds are too thick for the moon, and it's starting to snow.'

'It's snowing in *here*,' Lyudmila said.

'And Anna's got the fire going.'

'We can light a fire out there.'

'You have to admit, though, the idea of a blanket and a bed is tempting. When was the last time you slept in a bed?' Tanya asked her.

'Right now, it feels as if I *never* slept in a bed, but I'll survive.

265

And remember –' Lyudmila inclined her head in my direction '–
*he's* being followed.'

'Not in the dark,' I said, but I couldn't help wondering if
Lyudmila was right. Something was telling me it might be better
to move on. If it hadn't been for Anna, I might have done just
that, but she needed the warmth and shelter of the house, not the
cold damp of the forest. There might have been a hole in the roof,
but with the fire burning, it would soon warm up.

'So what do we do?' Tanya asked.

'We leave,' Lyudmila said.

'I think we should stay,' Tanya replied. 'We need to rest, and
the horses do too.' She looked at Anna, who was coming back
from the *pich*, great yellow flames roaring behind her. Already the
heat was flooding the room. 'And we have to think about you,
don't we?' She smiled at Anna. 'The forest at night is no place for
you.'

'Don't go soft,' Lyudmila warned her. 'Don't let the child make
you forget who you are.'

'I've already forgotten,' Tanya said. 'That's what Krukov did.
Anna can only help me remember.'

Lyudmila shook her head and went back to checking their
weapons.

'You don't have to stay here because of me,' Anna said, watching Lyudmila. 'If you think we should go . . .'

'We all need to rest,' I told her. 'Don't listen to what Lyudmila
says. Don't be scared of her.'

'I'm not scared of her. I just don't want us all to stay because of
me. If it's not safe.'

'It's safe enough,' Tanya said. 'What can an old man and
woman do? We'll take turns to stay awake,' Tanya said. 'Leave as
soon as it's light. The dog will let us know if there's anything out
there.'

'Tuzik,' Anna said, making the dog look up. 'His name is
Tuzik.'

'Well, that makes it all right.' Lyudmila's voice was heavy with
sarcasm. 'We'll be safe for sure, cooped up in this house with

those people next door, not knowing what's outside, because Tuzik is here. The wild dog that doesn't belong to anyone.'

'Of course he belongs to someone,' Anna said. 'He's mine and Kolya's dog. Any idiot can see that.'

Lyudmila's head snapped up, her face a picture of surprise and indignation.

Anna took a step back, one hand going to her mouth as if her thoughts had betrayed her and the words were never meant to have been spoken. 'I'm sorry.'

Lyudmila took a deep breath and shook her head. 'It's all right. Don't worry.' And for a moment the briefest smile touched her lips and the hardness in her eyes softened. Then she cleared her throat as if to shake the weakness away, and her sullen expression returned.

'We stay, then,' I said. 'But we keep the door bolted and we take turns to keep watch.'

Lyudmila made a face and looked at Tanya. 'It's the wrong decision, for the wrong reasons.'

'We should get some sleep,' I suggested.

Lyudmila stood and stretched her back. 'I'll take first watch.'

# 30

Tuzik was the first to hear it.

Anna and I had taken separate berths, but it wasn't long before she came to join me, lying protected between me and the wall. She was far braver than I had expected, but when the night closes in and the darkness falls and everything is silent, that's when the demons come. That was the time when *I* was most tormented by my fears and burdens, so it was no wonder to me that it was also the time when Anna found it most difficult. She had grown brighter over the last day, but lying awake in the dark, her mama and papa dead in her past, she hadn't been able to sleep, so she had come to me, looking for someone to be her parent. Beside me, she had fallen asleep while I stroked her hair and let her know she was protected.

I had lain awake in my berth running through the events of the past days, imagining Krukov splitting his unit three ways, taking one ahead to burn and torture his way north to whatever mysterious destination he had planned, while leaving another to lead its prisoners to . . . where? And of course, I had come to the conclusion that there was that third split: the seven riders who were on my trail.

The old man and his family troubled me too. There was something in their manner that put me on edge. It wasn't unusual for my countrymen to be afraid at the mere mention of the word 'Cheka', so I attributed their behaviour to that fear, but there was something else I couldn't quite put my finger on. Something deeper. The glances they exchanged, Sergei's inability to look me in the eye. It was almost as if he were ashamed of something more than robbing bodies.

Anna had told us not to stay just because of her, but that's what we had done. Neither Tanya nor I would have remained here with the reservations we had, if we had been without her. We would have disappeared into the forest and made it our shelter for the night, but Anna had swayed our decision. We were bound to the girl, and I had promised to be her protection, but she weakened us. She made us more vulnerable. She would have survived in the forest, but we had chosen to stay. And when I saw Tuzik lift his head and prick up his ears, I hoped we had not made a mistake.

Lyudmila was a shadow, sitting motionless in a chair at the table, her rifle over her knee. She didn't notice Tuzik, but she heard his growl a fraction of a second before the tapping came at the door. A gentle but insistent sound, as if someone wanted to be heard by those inside but not those outside.

I was sitting up when Lyudmila turned to look in our direction, and I could tell she was surprised to see I was awake.

'Someone at the door,' she whispered.

'I heard. Wake Tanya.'

Tuzik padded across to the door, sniffing along the base of it, stopping to listen, his ears turning in much the same ways as Kashtan's did.

I shook Anna, putting a finger to my lips as soon as she opened her eyes.

'Put on your coat and boots,' I told her.

'What is it?'

'I don't know yet. Just do as I say.' I grabbed the revolver from the floor beside me and put on my own coat and boots. If we had to leave in a hurry, I didn't want to come back for anything.

Again the gentle tapping at the door.

As Tanya slipped from the berth on the other side of the room, I crossed to the front wall, treading as quietly as I could, and pressed myself against the blackened wood. I edged to the window beside the door and pulled the curtain just a fraction to one side.

Everything was black outside, so I leaned closer, my nose touching the glass.

A pair of eyes was looking back at me from the dark and I reeled in surprise, lifting my revolver without thinking.

'What is it?' Lyudmila said, coming to my side. Tanya was just a few steps behind her, already wearing her boots and slipping on her coat.

'Someone's there.'

'Who?'

'Only one way to find out.' I readied the revolver in my right hand and reached up with my left to draw back the top bolt.

'Lie flat on the berth,' I said to Anna, and I waited for her to do as I asked, the tapping coming once more.

As soon as she was lying so flat she was almost impossible to see, I worked the bolt, moving it up and down before it finally came back with a heavy thump. With that done, I crouched and took hold of the lower bolt.

Lyudmila had taken a position behind the table. She was on one knee with her rifle across the tabletop, ready to shoot at whoever was outside. Tanya had retreated to the far end of the room, hidden in shadow but with a perfect view of the door. Anna remained flat on the berth, Tuzik standing at my side.

I prepared myself for whatever was to come and drew back the second bolt. It released with a click of iron on iron.

I stood to one side as I opened the door and let it swing inwards, raising my revolver to the expanding slice of night that appeared.

And then she spoke.

'You have to leave,' she said. 'You're in danger.'

# 31

Oksana was afraid. She held her hands together as if in prayer, clutching them close to her chest, and her whole demeanour was withdrawn. Her shoulders hunched, her head lowered, her eyes turned down.

She refused to come into the house, staying on the threshold, trembling with the cold. It was clear that she had come out in a hurry and had not intended to be long.

I took a tentative step outside, glancing around the yard as I came closer to her. 'What kind of danger?' I asked.

'Sergei's gone for the Cheka. Svetlana said you were deserters and made him go.'

'The old woman?' I realised it was the first time I'd heard her name. 'For the Cheka? What are you talking about?'

'Please,' she said. 'You have to leave.'

Behind me, Tanya and Lyudmila were moving through the house, coming to stand behind me to find out what was happening.

'What's this about the Cheka?' Tanya asked.

'The other farm . . .' Oksana's throat was dry and the words didn't come easily to her.

'The one we saw from the woods?'

'Yes. There are Chekists there.'

'*Chekists?*'

She nodded.

'The ones who were following you?' Tanya looked at me.

'They couldn't be . . .' I looked down at Oksana and let her see my anger. 'When did they get here? *When?*'

'Yesterday morning.' She cowered away from me.

'It's not them.' I shook my head at Tanya. 'It can't be. It's someone else.'

'I knew there was something wrong here.' Lyudmila stepped closer to Oksana and leaned right in to stare at her. 'I—'

'Is it him?' Tanya said to me, her face draining. 'Do you think it's him?'

Lyudmila stopped mid-sentence and stared. She turned her head slowly, all three of us looking at one another. Tanya hadn't needed to say the name.

'Did we . . . ? While he was so close?'

The thought of it was like a thousand cannons firing in my head. It was almost too much to comprehend – that we might have found him. That our search might be almost at an end. That we might have been sitting in the *izba* sharing our food with Oksana and her family while Krukov was so close.

'It can't be . . .' I shook my head. It was too hard to believe.

'We stay,' Tanya said, hefting her rifle. 'Let him come. Kill them all.'

I imagined us barricading ourselves in the tiny *izba*, with its broken roof, waiting for Krukov and his unit of well-trained soldiers to arrive, but all I saw was bloodshed and death. Ours. 'We wouldn't have a chance.'

'We have rifles,' Lyudmila said. 'Pistols and enough ammunition to kill a hundred men. Will they *have* a hundred men?'

'They'll have explosives,' I told her. 'Gas. Maybe a Maxim gun.'

'Please,' Oksana said. 'My children.'

'And we have Anna. We can't . . . We don't have a chance. We should get the horses ready, go into the forest.'

'Run away?' Tanya said. 'After all this?'

'We can fight from the forest if we have to,' I said. 'And remember, I need to know where my family is. I need him alive.'

Tanya said nothing. She looked out into the darkness and said nothing.

'We don't have a chance,' I told them again. 'If we stay here, we'll die. We need to get the horses ready and leave. Now.'

'There's no time for the horses,' Oksana said. 'They'll be here any minute. Please just go.'

'We'll *find* time.' It would take a few long minutes to saddle the horses, but there was no question of leaving without them. We needed them. Without Kashtan, I would probably be dead in the forest already; I had no intention of leaving her anywhere. 'Take her.' I pushed Oksana towards Tanya, who gripped her tighter than necessary, and then the three women hurried towards the outhouse where the horses were stabled.

I ran back to the *izba* and called to Anna, telling her to help me carry the few belongings we had brought inside, then she and I followed the women, Tuzik on our heels.

The door to the barn was open and we rushed inside.

The animals were agitated; that was clear straight away. They had moved to one side of the barn, shying away from the place where Tanya stood, pressing Oksana against the wall.

Tanya had taken the front of Oksana's dress in her left fist, twisting to cut off her breath and pushing her forearm against her chest. In her right hand, she held a pistol, the barrel forced so hard into the soft tissue on the underside of Oksana's chin it was pushing the woman's head back. I had been on the receiving end of Tanya's temper when we first met in Belev, so I knew how fierce she could be.

As soon as she saw, Anna tugged on my coat. 'Make her stop.'

I understood Tanya's reaction. I knew how she felt because I felt that way too. We had compromised ourselves for the promise of some little comfort, for the protection of a young girl, for the slightest sense of humanity, and our decision to let down our guard had been rewarded with *this*. And if this kind of betrayal was the result of placing even the slightest faith in other people, then what hope was there for any of us?

There was also the thought of our proximity to Krukov. The soldiers in the nearby farm might not be Krukov and his men, but there was a good chance they were. We had been following them for days, and everything had pointed us in this direction. The temptation to stand and fight was a powerful one, and our decision to leave, right though it was, was a difficult one for any of us to stomach. The thought of letting him go was like a pain in my heart, and I knew it would be the same for Tanya, perhaps more so. If it weren't for Anna and for my need to have Krukov alive, Tanya might have chosen to make a final stand against him. With nothing to lose, she might have taken that risk. Tanya, though, was not as filled with the need for vengeance as she wanted to be, and she had a small chink in her armour. She had us. Or, rather, she had *Anna*.

'Please,' Anna said, and her single word cut through my own anger like a light splitting the dark. In that moment I saw one thing more clearly than anything else. She needed my strength to reassure her. She needed the father in me as much as my family needed the soldier.

I took a deep breath and banished my rage to its dark place to fester for a while longer, but I knew that when it finally came – when I finally allowed it freedom – the soldier in me would surface and my rage would be colder and blacker than it had ever been before.

'Leave her,' I said to Tanya. 'We don't have time for this.'

Tanya heard me but didn't respond right away. Whatever questions she had been asking Oksana now stopped, but the pistol remained against her skin.

I looked down at Anna, seeing the expectation in her face. She believed *me* to be the strong one. She wanted *me* to stop this. I couldn't let her down, and that in itself was another source of anger and frustration for me.

'We don't have *time*,' I said, striding across the barn.

Lyudmila tried to stop me. She saw the nature of my intent, if not exactly what I was going to do, and she stepped between me and Tanya, but she was neither powerful nor quick enough and I pushed her aside. She stumbled and fell as I grabbed Tanya's arm and tore it away from Oksana, who sank to her knees in the straw.

Tanya had allowed her anger to take control of her, as my own had threatened to do, and now she wheeled round, raising her pistol to point at me.

Arm outstretched, barrel against my cheek, her eyes like a demon's. She couldn't focus on me, such was the intensity of her feeling, and she was taking long breaths, sucking the air into her nostrils as if trying to calm herself. But her arm was like iron. Unmoving. The barrel of the pistol unwavering.

My own revolver was less visible, but just as deadly. I'd had no intention of using it against Tanya, but her action had triggered my reaction and now I held it at waist height, aimed at her stomach.

Lyudmila tried to get to her feet beside me, to protect her comrade, but Tuzik stood over her, and when she tried to back away from him, he showed her his teeth.

'Look at yourself,' I said. 'Save your anger for *him.*'

Tanya stared. For a moment she struggled to speak, and when she finally did, the words were spat through gritted teeth. 'They betrayed us.'

I looked down at Oksana, but she had lowered her gaze. She remained on her knees, head bowed as if in prayer.

'I know.' My eyes met Tanya's. 'And I know how you feel. After everything. All this way. All the things we've seen and done, and all that came before. But this is not the end, Tanya. This is *not* where it ends. We still have further to go.'

'They betrayed us.' It was as if the treachery stood in front of her, blinding her to everything else.

'Oksana *warned* us.'

'Kill him and have done with it,' Lyudmila said. 'We have to go.'

Tanya's eyes flicked in her direction, almost imperceptible, and the idea in her mind grew larger. Shoot and be gone. But I was armed too, my revolver pointing at her stomach, angled upwards for maximum damage. If there were to be shots tonight, there would be more than one.

'She changed her mind,' I said. 'She warned us, gave us a chance. Let's not waste it.'

'They betrayed us,' Tanya said again, quieter this time, and pressed the barrel harder.

'Leave him alone,' Anna said, and I heard her coming forward, but I held out a hand and told her to stop.

'Stay back. Don't watch.'

Now Tanya's eyes went to Anna, just for a second, but it was long enough for a new image to burn itself into her mind. The image of herself murdering me in front of this child. Perhaps the irony of that was not lost on her, that she should become the hated aggressor.

'She's afraid,' I said. 'Oksana is afraid like everyone else. And you're just making it worse. I want to hurt someone as much as you do, but this is not the right person. We don't have time for this. Krukov might be coming across the field right now. Do you want him to find us in here? Like this?'

Or perhaps she *did* want that to happen. Maybe that's what this was about – delaying our escape so that she could meet Krukov face to face.

'If he comes here,' I said, 'we'll all die. You, me, Anna, the children in the farm. He'll kill everyone and burn this place to the ground. We've seen that everywhere we've been.' But something in those words didn't ring quite true; a big question whispered quietly at the back of my mind, like a bad seed planted in a dark corner. If Krukov was here, why hadn't he already killed Oksana and her family?

Tanya lifted her left hand to the grip of the pistol and altered her stance. She set her jaw tight, but I knew there was a shift in her resolve. It was a sign of her doubt.

'So what are we going to do? Shoot each other?' I kept my eyes on her and lowered my revolver. 'What then? Who will punish Krukov then? Who will look after Anna?'

Tanya blinked.

'We have to go,' I said. 'We have to live. If there are men coming, we have to go. Now. This woman is not worth dying for.'

Tanya said nothing.

'Let's ride into the forest, disappear, find the right moment.'

She stayed as she was, trying to calm herself.

'We don't have much time,' I told her. 'Save your bullets for when we need them most.'

Tanya looked away now. She let herself see Lyudmila lying on the floor with Tuzik standing over her. She saw Anna, small and vulnerable and needing our help, and she turned to look at Oksana kneeling in the straw, shamed by her actions.

'If we wait much longer,' I said, 'we'll all be dead.'

When Tanya lowered her weapon, she said nothing.

She collected her rifle from the floor and walked away from me, holstering her pistol.

'Get this damn dog away from me.' Lyudmila stole my attention and I called to Tuzik, unsure if he would even listen to me, but he came as soon as I spoke his name, and Lyudmila jumped to her feet, casting a hateful look at me.

On the other side of the barn, Tanya lifted her animal's bridle from the beam where it was stored and began securing it over her horse's head.

'Help me with Kashtan,' I said to Anna.

Anna seemed to deflate then, as if she had been holding her breath for a long time.

'Quick,' I told her, feeling the urgency return. This was not over yet.

Kashtan was a little agitated by what had happened and she moved away as I tried to put the saddle onto her back, so I soothed her as gently as I could, feeling the time draining away, imagining the approach of the soldiers.

'Have you done this before?' I asked Oksana as I struggled to fit Kashtan's bridle, my fingers moving as quickly as I could make them. 'Taken people in like this? Betrayed them to—'

'Yes,' Oksana replied. She was still on her knees, in the gloom at the back of the barn. 'I'm so sorry. I . . .' She didn't know what to say. She couldn't explain the wickedness of what they had done to us. 'That's why I came to warn you. I . . . Anna. The child. The *children*. I don't know what I would do if someone took my *children*.'

My fingers fumbled with the buckles, my hands shaking.

Anna reached up to take the fastenings in her small hands, saying, 'I'll do that.'

'You're lucky they *haven't* taken your children,' I said, taking my saddle and hefting it onto Kashtan's back.

'Perhaps they still will,' Lyudmila said.

Oksana looked over at her, and the realisation was clear in her eyes. Her children were no safer than ours were. Reporting and trapping deserters might earn her a few favours, but there was no guarantee.

'What have they given you in return?' I asked, pulling the straps tight under Kashtan's stomach and tightening the buckles. The fixings were larger and my fingers managed them well enough. 'The Chekists? What have they given you?'

Oksana shrugged and shook her head.

The saddle was secured, the bridle on, and I straightened up, running a hand along Kashtan's smooth coat, feeling some of the anger and tension drain away. As always, there was something about her that calmed me, the sense that no one would ever be as in tune with me as she was.

'Good girl,' I whispered, patting her shoulder. 'Good girl.' Then I handed her reins to Anna, while Tanya helped Lyudmila to finish tacking her horse.

'How many are they?' I asked, drawing my revolver and heading towards the door. 'The Chekists?'

Oksana thought for a moment. 'Five or six, but they come and go. Sometimes there are more.'

'Have you seen any of them with prisoners? Women and children?' I stopped and looked back at her. 'Tell me the truth.'

Oksana lowered her head again and cowered against the wall of the outbuilding as if she wished the earth would swallow her whole.

'The truth.'

Tanya and Lyudmila had finished now and were preparing to lead the horses from the barn, but they too stopped to hear Oksana's answer.

'Yesterday. There were more here yesterday.'

'With prisoners?'

'I think so. We didn't see them, but—'

'Didn't see them? Then how can you be sure?'

'Not close, I mean. There were *people*, not soldiers – I saw that, but not who they were. Not really. They stayed at the other farm. They didn't come here.'

'Are they still there?'

She shook her head.

'And you kept that from us?' Tanya said. 'You kept that from us and you were going to let the Chekists come and drag us out in the night?' She looked at me. 'You should have let me put a bullet in her.'

'She's protecting herself,' I said, looking at Anna, knowing the depths to which people would sink in order to keep themselves and their family safe.

'You're wrong,' Tanya said. '*She's* wrong. Nothing would make me betray someone like that.'

'Not even for your own children?' I asked her. 'Would you not have done *anything* to protect them?'

Tanya stopped and stared at me, knowing I was right. We lived in times that made people do things they would never have considered before.

'Come on,' I said, crossing the short distance to the door and looking out to check it was clear for our escape. 'We need to leave.'

But we were already too late.

# 32

To my right was the dark shape of the *izba* from which we had run a few minutes ago. To the side of that, overshadowed by the trees, only the slightest hint of light was visible, nothing more than slashes of orange round the curtained windows of the old woman's house, as if cut into dark cloth by a sharp sword. Above, the sky was blacker than Koschei's heart, but all around, the air was sprinkled with a gentle fall of snow, the delicate drops sinking to the shapeless dirt at our feet.

To my left, though, looking out at what should have been a never-ending sea of night, something was moving.

'They're coming.'

Tanya and Lyudmila released the reins of their horses and came to the door. Anna did the same, but she was a part of me now, just as Kashtan and Tuzik were, so she came closer, fitting herself under my left arm, looking for my protection.

'Is it them?' she asked. 'Is it *him*?'

Nothing could have prepared me for the shocking beauty of the approaching evil.

Lamps danced in the gloom like fallen stars, floating first this way, then that. Stopping, starting, raising and lowering. Small patches of the field were brightened as they came, revealing snatches of hedgerow, casting shadows in the furrows and making giants of even the smallest thistles.

'Looks like we fight,' Lyudmila said, working the bolt on her rifle, then pushing past me for a better look.

'I count five,' I said, watching the mesmerising motion of the lights, slow and illusory, moving like spirits coming at us across the field. Demons risen from the broken, frozen soil, spilling from the forest to come and claim us. But these were not the demons Marianna told about. They were not the kind that inhabited the stories Babushka used to spin. These devils were real.

'Shoot at the lights.' Lyudmila pulled the rifle butt into her shoulder and aimed into the night.

'No.' I put my hand on the barrel and pushed it down. 'We have to get away. Save it for when we need it.'

'What?' Lyudmila snatched the weapon away.

'They don't know we're here. They think we're in the house, asleep. They can't see us—'

'So we shoot . . .'

'No. So we head into the forest. We disappear where they won't follow, and then we come back. When it suits us. When we have a plan.'

'Don't need a plan.' Lyudmila raised the rifle once more. 'We shoot.'

'No, we have to leave,' Tanya said. 'Come on, get the horses.'

'Don't lose your nerve,' Lyudmila argued.

'I haven't,' Tanya replied. 'There might be two men for every lamp. Three men. Five. As soon as we fire the first shot, they'll put the lamps out and we'll have no idea where they are or how many they are. If we let them trap us in here . . .'

'No windows, only one way out,' I said. 'We'll be blind in here and they'll burn us alive. At the moment, as far as they know, we're fast asleep. It's better to keep it that way, keep them slow and quiet.'

Lyudmila hesitated. She knew we were right. We weren't running to escape but to fight better and on our own terms.

'*Horses*,' Tanya ordered, and Lyudmila lowered her rifle, shaking her head. Her face was a picture of frustration.

I glanced down at Anna. 'Bring Kashtan. I'll watch.'

But even as she turned to go, the front door to the *izba* opened, light spilled into the yard, and the old woman came out onto the step.

'They're getting away!' she shouted. 'Hurry! They're getting away.'

For a heartbeat, the lights stopped. They hung in the air amid the snowflakes falling around them as if through a dream.

'Hurry!' the old woman shouted, and her voice broke the trance.

The lights began to move again, faster now, the men running.

I looked from the old woman to the lights and back again, knowing they would be here in just a few seconds. Those once-mesmerising lights were now frantic in their movement, jerking from side to side, accompanied by the swish of material in the grass and the thump of boots on the ground.

In the darkness, where the trees stood tall and thick, it would be safe, but we didn't have time to reach them. We probably wouldn't even clear the fence before the men were on us.

There was only once choice for us now.

'Into the house,' I shouted, grabbing the sleeve of Anna's coat and pulling her backwards, spinning her round. 'Everybody get into the house.' It was the most secure place for us, with its thick walls, sturdy roof and front-facing windows.

I pushed Anna into the yard, yelling at her to run, Tanya and Lyudmila spilling out after her. Kashtan snorted in confusion, the other two horses shying backwards, stamping their feet, beginning to rear, spooking her further. Tuzik, too, was troubled by the commotion and he brushed past my legs, slipping out into the yard ahead of me. Oksana remained at the back of the barn, cowering in fear, blocked by the horses.

'Come on,' I shouted to her. 'Run!'

She hunched her shoulders as if she was trying to make herself small enough to disappear. The horses moved backwards and forwards in front of her.

'Now!'

But she stayed as she was, giving me no choice. The thought of abandoning her passed through my mind, but I couldn't leave her alone at the mercy of the approaching devils. If they were the men we had been following, they would show her no compassion.

They would use her against us, leaving her with a red star of her own. And her children were in that house. Two more children who would be left without a mother.

With time running out, I dashed across the barn and took hold of her wrist, dragging her to the door, dodging the movements of the horses. Kashtan was the calmest of the three, but the actions of the other two had troubled her and she turned and turned, moving from one side of the barn to the other, needing my calm words. There was no time for words, though, and as we came to the half-open door, Lyudmila's horse bolted, heading for the opening, its hooves skidding on the cold ground. It lost its footing, striking its shoulder on the wall and bouncing off as it found its balance and forced its way outside. Tanya's horse followed, eyes wide and rolling with fear as it thundered past, bursting into the night and rearing onto its hind legs.

'Faster!' I pulled Oksana hard now, not caring that my fingers were crushing her wrist. Almost *wanting* to hurt her, to punish her for betraying us.

I pushed her out in front of me, sending her stumbling into the yard, where Tanya and Lyudmila's horses ran round in circles, following the line of the fence. As soon as Oksana was clear, I placed both hands against the door and used all my weight to swing it shut, keeping Kashtan inside. It cost precious seconds to drop the latch and secure it, but I wanted to keep her safe.

When I turned, Oksana was already rushing through the gentle snowfall towards the *izba*. Out in the field, the lights were coming closer, swinging and lurching like demons in the darkness. The devils were cutting through the night towards us, but I didn't stop to watch them. I bent low, bracing for the incoming volley of shots, and sprinted for the protection of the *izba*.

Lyudmila had already reached the house, the old woman backing away from the door when she saw us coming, wanting to slam it shut, not even caring that Oksana was out here, vulnerable, but the old woman was slow and Lyudmila's foot was in the door before she could retreat.

Tanya followed on her heels, holding Anna's hand in one of

her own and her rifle in the other. Oksana went into the house just a few seconds behind her, and I was last, slamming the door shut behind me and throwing the bolts across.

# 33

So it had come to this.

After countless hours on horseback, innumerable desperate nights in the forest and more red stars than I wanted to remember, it had come to *this*.

I had achieved nothing more than ground. I had moved from one place to another, collected a ragged group of people with either vengeance or grief in their hearts, but I was still as far away from what I wanted as I had ever been. When Alek and I had left our unit, all we wanted was to find some normality, to enjoy the peace of our families and escape the fire and blood of war, but perhaps that was my destiny. Fire and blood. To be a soldier first and a father second.

I went to the window and lifted the corner of the curtain to look out.

Tuzik was nowhere to be seen. Not even a hint of his lithe shape skulking in the yard. He had disappeared in the commotion, probably slipping through the fence and heading for the trees to find safety. He was a strange mix of wild and tame, but he was a hunter and he would survive. I wished him luck, wherever he went.

Tanya and Lyudmila's horses weren't easy to make out, but there was a dark form at the far right corner of the yard that moved in a manner I recognised. They had become calmer now and I suspected they were standing together, keeping close to one another for comfort and warmth, facing out into the field as if trying to ignore the men who occupied the yard with them.

It was those men who now demanded my attention.

Almost invisible in the night, there were two soldiers behind the cart, no doubt with rifles resting across the back of it; another two crouched behind the far fence. One more stood at the corner of the outbuilding, and his weapon would be pointed in our direction, but the expected attack did not come.

Not a shot. Not a word.

An eerie silence fell over the scene.

Inside, it was the same.

Sergei had returned home before the soldiers set out for the farm. He and his wife had now retreated with Oksana and her children to the back of the *izba*, close to the *pich*. Anna lay on the floor behind the overturned table, just as I had instructed her to do. Tanya crouched beside me at the window, rifle ready; Lyudmila watched from the other.

But all was still and quiet, as if the world had stopped moving around us. I had expected shooting, shouting, fire and blood, but there was nothing.

Only waiting.

It confirmed to me that these were not the men who had been following me. Men who had trailed me that hard and for that long would not have hesitated to kill everyone here. Instead the men in the yard had put out their lamps, just as we had, and they were little more than shadows in the falling snow. The soft flakes floated among them, settling on everything they touched. The gathering whiteness cast a beauty in the night. It softened and brightened everything, making the events being played out around the farm incongruous. These things should not happen amid such beauty.

Snow does that. It covers everything, from the autumn mud and the flame-coloured leaves to the sounds of the forest and the bodies left in the wake of armies and oppressors. Marianna always told me that God sent us the snow to make our country beautiful; to hide whatever ugliness we created for ourselves. Right now, it would be falling on the dead men of Belev. Erasing them. It was as if we had an unwritten law that we should find beauty and poetry in the white landscape, but the truth was that the winters were harsh and the beauty belied its cruelty. Winter was a difficult time for everyone and we all celebrated its passing, no matter what ugliness might be revealed when spring came and melted the snow as surely as a warm heart had melted Snegurochka, the Snow Maiden.

'Snegurochka' was just another of the *skazkas* Marianna told our children – she was the daughter of Spring and Frost who could never love until her mother granted her the ability, but the gift was fatal, and when Snegurochka fell in love, her heart warmed and she melted into nothing, just as the spring sun took away the whiteness. For all Marianna's talk of the snow hiding the ugliness, we had always drowned a straw figure in the river to signify the death of the Snow Maiden and to herald the spring.

Now that image brought new connotations for me.

*He likes to drown the women.*

I saw the white face of a woman squashed into a barrel. I saw Galina breaking through the paper-thin ice, sinking beneath its water. I saw the faces of men I knew as they threw the women of Belev into the lake. They were laughing, putting their boots on their heads to keep them under, firing their rifles into the water, the surface erupting in a mosaic of splashes and ripples as the women begged and struggled and died. And I saw the men, stripped of skin, nailed, cut, beaten, shot. Branded with that terrible red star. Men who would still be there when the snows melted.

The winter didn't change anything; it didn't make it go away; it *preserved* it.

I closed my eyes and tried to see something else. I put my hand over them and rubbed, but the images remained.

'You all right?' Tanya looked away from the window and watched me.

'Fine. I'm fine.'

She studied me, perhaps wondering if I could be relied upon, if the waiting would unnerve me. The whites of her eyes were clear in the semi-darkness. 'You think it's him?'

'I don't know.'

'How many do you count?'

'Five.'

'That's not many,' Lyudmila said. 'I would have expected more.'

'But if we're right, if Krukov split his unit . . . maybe this is part of it.'

We were all thinking the same thing. Five lamps, five men. We could have made a stand at the barn.

'I want him alive,' I said.

'If it's him.'

'Yes. If it's him.'

'What's stopping them from just shooting this place apart?' Lyudmila asked. 'From just killing us all?'

I glanced back at Oksana and the shadows sitting with her at the far end of the room. The iron door of the *pich* beside them was closed, but the glow of the fire within was visible in the cracks round it. The children were hidden above the oven now, just as they had been when we arrived.

'Women and children wouldn't stop them,' Tanya said, as if trying to read my thoughts. 'We know that. It must be something else. Maybe it's not even him.' But she shook her head and answered her own suggestion. 'No, that wouldn't matter. Chekists are Chekists, whatever their name is.'

'So why don't they just do something?' There was tension in Lyudmila's voice. 'Why don't they try something? I don't like this.'

'Stay calm,' Tanya told her.

'I *am* calm, but why—'

'*Something*'s stopping them,' I said.

'But what? It doesn't make sense.'

'This is worse than fighting,' Lyudmila said, getting to her knees and looking out of the window again. 'We should—'

'Do nothing,' I said to her. 'We should do nothing.'

'But we have to do something. Why don't we shoot at them? Anything is better than waiting. Who knows what they're doing out there while we sit in here like idiots.' The edge in her voice heightened; her words came faster. 'Maybe they're planning something. Getting ready to—'

'No shooting,' I said. 'Not yet. I need them alive.' I couldn't risk that we might kill the only people who could lead me to my family. And there were children in here. If we provoked the men outside, maybe they would change their minds. If they decided to be less passive, there were many ways they could force us into the open. Fire, gas, grenade.

'Why should I take orders from you?' Lyudmila raised her rifle and smashed the barrel into the corner of the window. The glass withstood the blow, but the sound was abrupt and unexpected.

'Stop,' I hissed at her. 'You'll—'

When she hit it a second time, the glass cracked, hair-thin fractures spreading like opening fingers across the pane.

'Stop!' Tanya went to her, scrambling across the floor, keeping low, putting her arms around Lyudmila and pulling her to the floor.

Outside, the dark shapes remained still, silhouetted against the soft whiteness of the fresh snow. It was undisturbed. A perfect covering in the yard that bore not a print. Not a sign that anybody had been there.

Lyudmila pushed Tanya away, rifles clattering where they fell, and then the two women were sitting on the floor, a few paces apart, staring at one another, knowing there was nothing to be gained from fighting each other.

'We have to stay calm,' Tanya was saying. 'Please, Lyuda. We have to stay calm.'

'Like you did in the barn?'

'That was a mistake,' Tanya said. 'My temper got the better of me.'

'Then let it again.'

'No.'

'Why?' she asked. 'We have to shoot them and get out of here.'

'There are children,' Tanya said. 'Children.'

'But—'

'*Children*, Lyuda. Isn't that what this is all about? The children?

And if there's any way to get them out alive, we have to find it. We can't let those . . .' Tanya shook her head and looked to the back of the room. 'We can't let those people out there do . . . what they did to me and you. We can't be responsible for that. *I* can't be responsible for that.'

With no lamp, I couldn't see Tanya's face, but her sobbing and the strain in her voice relayed the desperation well enough.

Lyudmila said nothing, but she crawled to her comrade and put her arms around her in as firm a show of solidarity and love as I had ever seen.

I watched them find comfort in each other, rocking together in the darkness, like children afraid of the forest terrors, and I turned my mind to other things. I ran through a thousand possibilities for the soldiers' actions, mulling them over, dismissing them, reassessing them and dismissing them again. Nothing made any sense, but I had the feeling that the answer to the Chekists' hesitation was right in front of us, hiding in plain sight.

'You think they're waiting for something?' I thought aloud. 'Reinforcements?' It was possible they had found out who I was and had chosen to wait for more men, but I could think of no way *how* they would have found out. I had only given my first name to Sergei, and even if they did know who I was, a single grenade would clear the *izba* in one easy throw.

The women had separated now, Lyudmila returning to her post by the window. Tanya remained where she was, but now she shifted to make herself more comfortable. She sniffed and wiped her coat sleeve across her eyes, then reached for her rifle. She made no apology for her actions or for those of her comrade. She made no attempt to offer an explanation. Instead she reverted to the thing that had kept her moving ever forwards in the hunt for Krukov. She went back to thinking like a soldier. Like a commander.

'Maybe they're conscripts,' she said. 'Maybe they don't *know* what to do.'

The change in her impressed me. The way she could switch from one thing to another, it was as if the past few minutes had never happened. I wondered which was the real Tanya, but I didn't insult her by asking if she was all right. She and Lyudmila were thinking straight again and that was all that mattered. We each had our burdens, things that tugged us towards our own madness, but we had to stay strong.

'Conscripts?' I said. 'Without a commander? I don't think so.' I edged back from the window and stretched my cramping legs out in front of me. 'It has to be something else. Keep watching.'

I crawled to the heavy wooden table that lay on its side, top towards the front of the house. We had turned it over when we came in, knowing it would give us some protection from the bullets of the men outside. We could shoot from the windows and retreat behind its solid shield if necessary, providing as good cover for us as the brick front of the space above the *pich* was for Oksana's children. For now, though, the only person behind it was Anna.

'Are they going to kill us?' she asked, as I slipped in beside her.

'No.' It was a lie and Anna knew it. I had no idea what the men were going to do or what they were waiting for.

'I'm scared,' she said.

'Me too, but we'll find a way out of this.'

Anna looked at me with expectation, as if she thought I was going to divulge a foolproof plan for our escape, but I had nothing to tell her.

'You know, she's not a witch,' I said, looking over at Sergei and his wife.

The old woman was sitting on one of the chairs that had been at the table. Her husband sat beside her with his hands on her forearm. Oksana sat on a third chair, all of them at the back of the room, arranged round the base of the ladder to the top of the *pich* where the children were hiding. It was odd that they had chosen not to avoid the soldiers' guns by taking cover behind the table with Anna, but were sitting as if protecting the children from *us*.

'I know that,' Anna said. 'There's no such thing as witches.'

'No.'

'But there's worse things, aren't there? There are things *much* worse than witches.'

'Yes, there are.' And maybe I was one of them. Those men outside instilled the same fear that I had instilled in people. If Anna knew who I was, what I was, would she be afraid of *me*?

Anna sat up and crossed her legs. 'Maybe they were just scared,' she whispered.

'Hmm?'

'The old woman. Maybe she was afraid *not* to tell them we were here. Afraid of what would happen if they found out.'

'You could be right.' But I was sure it wasn't her fear of the Chekists that had made the old woman inform. It was more likely to be her patriotism. The way she acted when we ate with them – clipping sentences, covering things up, silencing the boy, Nikolai, when he mentioned his father – and then she had been prepared to close the door on Oksana, to leave her out in the cold to face the Chekists alone. She wouldn't have done that unless she didn't care about Oksana or . . . or unless she thought she wouldn't be in any danger.

Tanya came and crouched beside me. She leaned close and spoke into my ear. 'I need to talk to you.'

'Then talk.'

'Over here.'

There was concern in her voice; something was bothering her. She wanted to speak to me where the others wouldn't hear, but we needed to watch the old woman. Neither of us trusted her, and she had made it clear what she thought of us, so we couldn't risk letting her out of our sight. Lyudmila's attention was focused on the windows, watching the men outside.

'They can't hear us,' I said, 'and we can trust Anna to keep a secret, can't we?'

'Of course.' Anna sat up a little straighter, displaying the importance she felt at being included.

'All right. I've been thinking about why they haven't done anything . . .'

'Me too.'

'. . . and the only thing that makes any sense is that there's something important inside this house,' Tanya said. 'That's why they're just sitting out there. They're trying to decide what to do.'

'Or maybe they made some sort of agreement with these people?' I gestured at Oksana and the others.

'Agreements can be broken,' Tanya said, 'but if there's something here they want . . .'

'Something important.' I nodded, glancing around the room. 'But what? It would have to be something that can't withstand bullets, otherwise they'd kill us and come in to get it.'

'I'm not sure, but it's the only explanation. There's something here, something we're not seeing.'

# 34

'They're calling,' Lyudmila said. 'They want to talk.'

While Tanya and I were discussing her idea, the men outside gave the first indication that they were even there. Until now, they had remained quiet. We had not attempted to speak to them, nor they to us, but now a voice shouted out in the night.

To my ears, the words were muffled and I couldn't make them out, but as soon as I heard them, both Tanya and I stopped.

'Sh.' I put a finger to my lips and looked at Anna. She had pushed back her cap and her hair had fallen from beneath the cloth in places, greasy and matted. In the gloom of the *izba*, I could see it was twisted and clumped, as if it hadn't been washed in a long time. Her pale face was streaked with dirt, and there was a dark band round her forehead, left by the ancient cap.

Lyudmila was closer to the window, able to make out the words. She beckoned us over.

'Stay here,' I told Anna.

Tanya and I returned to the window. The men were in the same positions as before. They had made no attempt to retreat or attack. They had not laid down their weapons, nor had they used them against us.

'What did he say?' I asked. 'Exactly?'

But before Lyudmila could reply, the voice shouted again.

'Send out the family,' the man said. 'Send them out and I'll let you go.'

Tanya opened her mouth to reply, but I stopped her, saying, 'Don't answer. Don't communicate with them at all. We need to think about what we're going to do.'

I sat on the floor and rested back against the wall, hearing the man shout again.

*Send them out and I'll let you go.* There was something odd about that. It wasn't what I had expected. A demand for us to surrender made sense, but these men were calling for us to release the old woman and her family.

'They think these people are our hostages,' I said.

'What are you talking about?' Lyudmila watched the yard, ready to smash the cracked glass in an instant. Ready and willing to kill.

'They think these people are our hostages,' I repeated. 'That's why they haven't done anything. They're protecting *them*.' I looked at the far end of the room where Oksana and her family remained quiet.

'Them?' Lyudmila asked, turning round. 'Why?'

Outside, the voice called to us again, but we refused to answer.

'I don't know.'

'Maybe they're not Chekists out there?' Tanya suggested. 'Maybe they're Blues . . .'

'Oksana called them Chekists,' I said. 'I don't think she was lying.'

'Maybe she was wrong.'

'Or maybe there's something important about these people,' I suggested. 'Maybe *that's* your "something valuable".'

All three of us now turned to look across the room at the family. Oksana held her hands tight together, one clasping the other as she stole glances at the top of the *pich*, where her children, Nikolai and Natasha, were hiding. Sergei still sat with his head hung low and his shoulders hunched. He looked even older now, as if the last few hours had stolen years from him. He kept his eyes to the floor.

His wife, though, sat upright, her head turned in our direction, glaring at us.

'What's so important about you?' I asked. 'What do you mean to those men?'

Her lips parted in a grin that would have sickened Baba Yaga's stomach. Dry and thin and cracked, they peeled back to reveal her blackened teeth and empty gums. 'You can't stay in here for ever,' she said with a sneer. 'You'll have to leave sometime, and they'll be waiting for you.'

'You might be right,' I said, getting to my feet. 'We *can't* stay in here for ever, but those men out there don't want to hurt you, so maybe you can help us get out.'

'I won't help you,' she said. '*We* won't help you.'

'You don't have any choice.'

'Wait,' Tanya stopped me. 'What are you talking about?'

'We'll use them as cover,' I said. 'If they're important in some way, let's use it to our advantage.'

'We can't—'

'I agree with him,' Lyudmila interrupted.

'Twice in one day?' I said.

She ignored me. 'Take them with us until we're out of danger. It's the only way.'

Tanya looked at the floor for a moment before turning her attention to the family at the back of the room. 'If we do that, we'll be no better than Koschei. Using women and children.'

'We're not going to hurt them,' I told her.

'But we're going to use them as a shield. And how do we even know it will work? You really think they'll just let us go because we have them?'

'We *don't* know.'

'So we just take a risk? We just put their lives in danger?'

'Their lives are already in danger – that was their doing, not ours.'

Tanya pushed to her feet and stood in front of me, a head shorter than I was, but she seemed taller when she turned her face up to look into mine. We were close enough that I could feel her breath on my skin when she spoke, her voice an urgent whisper but growing louder. 'What if it's nothing to do with these people, Kolya? What if . . . ?' She put out her left hand and touched the revolver in my right. 'What if you're wrong?' She kept her hand there as if to stop me. Her skin was clammy, her temperature raised by the warmth inside the room, coupled with the tension in her body. Her voice was pleading. 'What if you're *wrong?*' She was feeling doubt now; it was consuming her. The family, the mother, the children, they were all worming into her thoughts and making her doubt; weakening her. 'What if it doesn't stop those men out there? What if they . . . ? Lyudmila –' she turned to her comrade for support '– you have to know this is wrong. You *must*. We can't do this.'

But Lyudmila shook her head. 'I'm sorry.'

With my free hand, I peeled Tanya's away from mine. She didn't resist much, just enough to register that resistance, and I knew what she wanted – for this to be my decision. She knew that using the family was the only option left open to us, but she couldn't bring herself to do it. She had come here for revenge, but there were lines she was not prepared to cross. If something happened to any of them, she didn't want it to lie on her conscience.

My conscience was already as black as the darkest corners of the forest, though. A few more lives would make little difference to mine, and I had come here for more than revenge. I was here to find my family, and I would do whatever I had to, anything to stay alive long enough to find Marianna and the boys. I would kill anyone who stood in my way. And there was Anna too. If I let this family walk out of here, as the men were demanding, there might be nothing to stop them from burning the *izba* to the ground and shooting us like a farmer shoots rabbits running from the burning stubble of last year's crop.

'There's only one way for us to find out if we're wrong,' I said, still holding her hand, looking into her eyes.

'We'd be no better than them.'

'But I'm *not* any better than them, so you can blame me if anything goes wrong.'

She looked at me for a long while, as if she was trying to see something she had missed before. 'Who are you, Kolya?'

'I just want to find my family,' I said.

'And you're prepared to do anything to find them?'

'Anything.'

I saw in her face what a detestable notion she thought that was, and I even felt it myself, but I saw something else too. Understanding.

I let go of her hand and went to Anna.

'I want you to stay where you are,' I told her. 'Don't come out unless I or Tanya tell you to. Do you understand?'

She nodded and I began to turn, but stopped.

I crouched down and brushed a stray hair from her face. 'I'm going to do something not very nice, but whatever happens, I don't want you think badly of me. I'm doing this for us. To get us out of here. Can you understand that?'

'The men outside,' she said. 'They'll kill us, won't they? If you let the family go, they'll kill us.'

'Yes.'

Anna threw herself forwards as if unable to control herself. She wrapped her arms around me and pressed her face into my chest. The movement took me by surprise and I raised my hands to either side, keeping the revolver away from her. When she didn't let go, I placed the weapon on the floor by my knee and returned the embrace, putting one hand on the top of her head.

If there had been any doubt in my mind about what I was going to do, this swept it all away. I had to look after Anna. I had to get her away from here. Oksana and her family had betrayed us. They had displayed their intent and now I had to display mine.

I broke away from Anna, holding her at arm's length and forcing a smile. 'Stay here.'

'Be careful,' she said.

I leaned forward and kissed the top of her head, then collected my revolver and got to my feet. I cast one more glance down at Anna, then I hardened my resolve and turned towards Oksana, raising the weapon.

Oksana was on her feet before I reached her. Sergei and the old woman were slower, their muscles weaker and their bones more frail, so they managed little more than to sit up straighter before I reached them.

'Please,' Oksana said, backing against the short ladder up to the sleeping berth above the *pich*. 'Please.'

But I had hold of her arm, harder than necessary so she knew I was determined.

'Mama.'

I looked up to see the faces of her children peering over the side of the *pich*, frightened faces that I had to ignore. I could not allow myself to be swayed by their pleas. I had no desire to harm them or their mother, but I had to make them believe I did. 'Get back,' I snapped. 'I don't want to see you.'

'Papa will come.' The boy tried to look brave. 'He'll kill you and—'

'Get back now!'

'Leave them alone.' The old woman tried to get up, but I pushed her back down with little more than a slight shove.

'Sergei, do something,' she said, knowing she was too weak to resist me.

The old man looked up at me, began to rise from his chair, so I shook my head at him and he hesitated, half sitting, half standing. I aimed the revolver at his face and waited for him to make his decision.

'There's nothing you can do to stop me,' I told him. 'Nothing.'

Above the *pich*, the children's faces had withdrawn, but their crying was loud and they continued to call to their mother while she called back, telling them everything would be all right.

'You coward,' the old woman hissed in the chaos. '*Coward.*'

Who she was talking to, I don't know, but Sergei looked at her with disdain and said, 'You should have let me send them away.'

'Coward. Do something.'

'The only thing he *can* do is sit there,' I said.

Sergei eased himself back into his seat and hung his head once more, putting his hands over his ears as if he might be able to block out the world and all the horrors it held.

'You devil!' The old woman tried to stand again, reaching out with her gnarled hands to grab at me. Her nails raked along the sleeve of my coat, rasping as the rough edges scraped through the weave of the heavy wool.

She was like a possessed hag, One-Eyed Likho screaming and cursing as she clawed at me, but she was no fairy-tale witch. She was just an old woman, and although she broke my grip on Oksana, one shove was all it took to send her sprawling, knocking away the chair. She fell sideways, twisting, awkward as she hit the floor, and her shrieking became howling as the pain coursed through her brittle bones.

I grabbed Oksana's arm once more as the old woman tried to sit up, saying, 'What are you doing? What are you going to do to her?'

At the window, Lyudmila and Tanya alternated between looking out and watching the chaos unfolding inside, neither of them making any attempt to help me. I was terrorising an old woman, frightening a mother and her children. They wanted no part of it.

Behind the table, Anna sat hugging her legs, just as she had done that night we spent in the forest, and her fear was palpable, but when my eyes met hers, I knew that her trust in me was implicit. She believed I was doing this to make her safe.

'I have to know,' I said to her as much to the old woman or to Oksana. Or perhaps it was for my own benefit, just to voice my thoughts, to persuade myself that what I was doing was the only thing left for me. 'I have to know how far this can go.'

'What . . . ?' Oksana tried to break my grip on her, but I jerked her towards me and jammed the barrel of the pistol under her chin.

'And you all have to know I will do whatever it takes.'

If I were to have squeezed the trigger, the bullet would have passed through her head from bottom to top and the two children above the *pich* would be motherless. A fraction of a second, nine grammes of lead, and a pinch of gunpowder was all it would take.

'You asked me a question before,' I said to Tanya as I brought Oksana forward. 'You wanted to know if they would let us go just because we have them.' I pushed Oksana forward, making her move towards the front door. 'Well, now it's time to find out.'

'You know this makes you just like him?' she said. 'Like Koschei. You're no better than him now.'

'I'll do anything. I told you that.'

'You're mad,' Tanya said. 'You can't just go out there.'

'Can't I?' Still holding Oksana, I forced her across the room and stood a pace away from the front door. 'Open it,' I said to Tanya.

'At least take the old woman instead. Don't take *her*.' Tanya saw herself in Oksana, just as I saw Marianna. A mother with children, desperate and afraid, but that was what made her more valuable, more emotive. Who would care about an old woman already ancient and close to death?

'Open the door.'

'I won't do it,' Tanya refused.

'Just open it.'

'What if they—'

'Open it!'

It was Lyudmila who drew back the bolts. She gave Tanya a brief glance, then stood and pulled them back.

'It's the only way to know,' she said, as she threw the door open.

I pressed the revolver tighter against Oksana's skin, and we stepped out into the night.

# 35

The atmosphere in the house was thick with emotion and tension. There was a smell of fear in there that I almost didn't notice, because I had become so accustomed to it, but when I took the first breath of the fresh winter air, I wondered how I could have allowed it to become so familiar. I felt a jab of disgust with myself that it had passed me by. I should *never* be able to ignore it, and yet here I was, spreading that fear, amplifying it. I had come so far and sunk so low that I had become numb to the terrible feelings in that house. My mind had learned to ignore such things and I hated myself for that. I had been away from home for too long. I needed to be back with Marianna.

I took a long, deep breath of air that was so cold it hurt when it touched my lungs. It made my chest ache, and I reminded myself I had to be tough. I didn't have time to hate myself or what I was doing. I had one purpose. Nothing else mattered. Everything else was just a distraction.

The air bit at my ungloved hands as I tightened my fingers on the revolver and pushed Oksana forward. I stood directly behind her, covered by her body, and kept my head behind hers as much as possible. Only the side of my face was visible to the men in the yard.

We came out on the step, the gentle white flakes unchanged by our presence. Like the forest, they were unaffected by the small matters of the lives played out beneath them. They fell with consistency and grace, wisps that floated with the occasional flurry, settling on my shoulders, melting on my eyelids, painting the land a glorious, brilliant white that would cover the fallen men in the fields, making winter's own cairns.

I surveyed the yard, the snowflakes impeding my vision as I picked out the men, still in their places. That they hadn't moved told me much about their discipline and resolve – or perhaps their fear of their leader.

I took Oksana down the step, the revolver firm under her chin, and when we reached the bottom, standing on the thin layer of snow, the mud almost covered, I stopped and spoke aloud. 'Who's in charge?'

It was quiet out there. The night had settled and nothing stirred in the forest. Not even the wind wanted to blow. And though it was only sparse, the fresh fall cushioned everything.

'Who's in charge?' I asked again. 'Come forward.'

Still no one spoke. The men remained in their positions, motionless. They didn't even look to one another. They were like statues, frozen in time, with only their heads visible above the cover they had chosen.

'Speak now,' I said, 'or I'll take this woman back inside and kill her in front of her children.'

'You wouldn't do that.'

I looked in the direction the voice had come from. By the cart. The last remnants of steamy breath hung in the air like a ghost before breaking up and fading to nothing.

'You want to test me?' I asked. 'Very well.' I began to move backwards, pulling Oksana, keeping the barrel of the gun tight under her chin.

'Wait.'

I stopped.

'You don't need to kill her.' The plume of steamy breath from the cart.

'That's right,' I said. 'I don't.'

There was a pause. Just long enough for a heartbeat. Long enough for a hesitation. Then the owner of the voice moved, shifting and standing.

'What do you want?' he asked.

'Come into the centre of the yard.'

Again, there was a pause before the man shifted, walking slowly, holding himself upright, a little stiff as if he carried the ghost of a limp. He came round the cart and moved towards us, boots squeaking on the snow. His rifle was pulled to his shoulder, ready to shoot. He was not much more than the silhouette of a man in a heavy coat and warm *ushanka*.

All that was visible of the moon through the clouds was behind him and I wished it had been better placed. I wanted to see the man's face, to see if I knew him, but one thing I did know – this was not Krukov. This man did not have the lean, gaunt profile of Koschei the Deathless.

When he reached the centre of the yard, I spoke to him, saying, 'Stop there. Put your weapon on the ground.'

He stood watching me, rifle aimed, wondering what I was going to do.

'Put it down,' I said. 'Last chance.'

His arms relaxed and he lowered the rifle, crouching to place it on the ground in front of him.

'Now step back.'

This time he complied straight away.

'Tell the others to do the same,' I ordered.

'I can't do that.'

'Then the woman dies.' I began to shuffle backwards, taking Oksana towards the door, moving into a faint semicircle of orange lamplight that washed across the snow at my feet.

'He'll do it,' Tanya said from behind me, and there was something in her voice, something that told me she really believed I would. She wasn't just saying it to make him comply.

'All right.' He put up his hands. 'Wait.' He turned his head to speak to the men behind him. 'Come out. Everyone come here and put down your weapons.'

None hesitated. They did exactly as commanded and I knew this man was in charge.

In a short time, the men stood in a line, five of them, with their weapons on the ground in front of them.

304

'Everybody take two steps back,' I said.

As soon as they did as I had asked, the light moved behind me. It became more concentrated, the semicircle receding as Tanya placed the lamp on the floor, then she came out of the house behind me, her footfall soft, just the slightest creak of snow in the tread of her boots. She moved past me, glaring, and collected the rifles, taking them inside the house before returning to inspect the men for more weapons.

We stood in silence as she moved among them, pocketing what they had. Oksana had relaxed a little in my grip, but it was cold and she was without a coat and had begun to shiver. I was reminded of the moment I had found Marianna's winter coat at home, still hanging behind the door in the bedroom. If she were outside without her coat right now, she too would be shivering. Or perhaps she was beyond needing it; beyond feeling anything.

'That's it,' Tanya said, coming to my side. 'They're harmless. Well, less dangerous.'

I nodded. 'Do any of you men know where Koschei is?'

No one answered.

'I'm looking for Arkady Krukov. Where is he?' I raised my voice, feeling my anger threaten to get the better of me. I was close now. So close. If Krukov was not here, at least these men might tell me where he was.

'*Where is he?*' Without realising it, I jammed the revolver harder into Oksana's throat, eliciting a small cry of pain from her.

'Don't . . .' The words escaped Tanya before she could stop herself, and at the same time, the soldier who had first come forward held out a hand.

'No,' he said.

'Why not?' I asked. 'What's so important about these people?'

Tanya said nothing. The man said nothing. Instead he cocked his head to one side as if he had heard or seen something he wasn't expecting.

'Who are they?' I repeated, moving my left hand up and taking a fistful of Oksana's hair, tugging her head back so they could see the revolver pressed hard against the underside of her chin. Just in case there was any doubt about what was going to happen to her.

'Please.' The man held out both hands and took a step forward, coming closer to where the light was more concentrated. 'I—'

'Stay there.'

Again he cocked his head to one side as if listening, one foot forward, his body weight shifting in my direction.

'No closer,' I said, but already he was close enough for me to recognise him. His voice hadn't given him away, and nor had mine, but his face was familiar. I knew this soldier and he knew me. We were not friends, we had not served together for more than a few days, but I knew him nonetheless.

'Levitsky?'

The name sent a jolt right through me, just as it had on the train when Commander Orlov had identified me. I sensed Tanya stiffen beside me. Oksana tensed under my grip.

'Is that you?' the man said. '*Nikolai Levitsky?*'

'I . . .' But it was too late for me to hide it; I could not deny who I was. There was nothing I could say. There was nothing I could do.

'We thought you were dead.'

'Do you know this man?' Tanya said, taking a step away from me.

'Do I know him?' the man replied as he stood to attention. 'Of course I know him.' He raised a hand to his brow in salute. 'This is Commander Nikolai Levitsky, rightful commander of this unit.'

# 36

Tanya was lost for words. She looked from me to the unarmed men standing in a line, then back to me again. She leaned away as if she was seeing me for the first time. Seeing who I really was.

'*Commander?*' She knitted her brow and narrowed her eyes. 'No, that can't . . . I . . . You're a Chekist? A *commander?*'

I opened my mouth, wishing there was an easy way to deal with this. Everything was going to hell now, and it felt like there was no way to stop it. There would be blood. I could see it coming as sure as I could see that winter was on us.

'We should never have trusted him,' Lyudmila said from the doorway behind me. I didn't dare turn to look at her, but I knew she would be pointing her rifle at me.

'Tell me it's not true,' Tanya said.

I shook my head.

'Tell me.'

'Let me shoot him,' Lyudmila called. 'Let me shoot them all.'

I knew she would do it if Tanya allowed her. She wouldn't care that Oksana would probably die too, that in death my finger might tighten on the trigger.

The soldier was confused. This wasn't what he had expected, dissent in our own ranks, and he dropped his hand, looking at each of us in turn, trying to decipher our relationship.

'I *was* a Chekist,' I said.

Tanya took another step back. 'I *knew* there was something.' She shook her head as if she didn't believe it, or didn't want to.

'I'm sorry.'

'And now?' she asked. 'What are you now?'

'Just a man who wants his family back. You know that.'

Tanya stood with her mouth open and shook her head at me. She didn't know what to do. She had always struggled to trust me, but somewhere inside, she had come to respect me at least. She had always suspected I was a Communist, a Red Army soldier, but she was prepared to put up with that because we shared a target and, I guessed, because she saw how I took care of Anna. She had not expected this, though. Now I represented everything she hated. I had moved from the countless ranks of the Red Army to the Cheka; the state security organisation that was the elite enforcer of Communism. And it was men like that, *Chekists*, who had murdered her family.

'These are your men?' she asked.

'In a way.'

'And Krukov? He was one of yours?'

'Yes.' I felt my grip relax a little on Oksana. She was unmoving now, seeing a possible reprieve, and my attention was elsewhere.

'You were his commander?' Tanya asked.

'Yes.'

She shook her head in disbelief. 'So it could have been you who came to my home? You might have—'

'No.' I stopped her as soon as I realised what she was about to say. She was imagining me in her village, seeing me murdering her children, her husband. 'Not me,' I said. 'I never did that. Not *that*. It was Krukov, remember. *Krukov*.'

'I should kill you right now.' She raised her pistol and put it to the side of my head.

'Kill him,' Lyudmila urged.

'Commander?' The soldier began to move forward.

'Move back,' Tanya told him. 'Now.'

The soldier stopped, looking from Tanya to me and then at Oksana. There was no hiding his anxiety, but I couldn't be sure it was for me. He seemed more concerned that something might happen to Oksana. I still had the revolver to the underside of her chin.

'What is this?' he said. 'I don't understand. Who is this woman, Commander? I thought she was with you.'

'She *is* with me,' I told him.

'But—'

'Just do whatever she says.'

The soldier put up his hands and hesitated before stepping back. 'Just . . . be calm.'

'Killing me would achieve nothing,' I told Tanya. 'All that would be different is that I wouldn't be here. It wouldn't change anything else.'

'I could live with that.'

'Could you?' I asked. 'After what we've been through? To-gether? And what about my family?'

'You might be lying about them.'

'And Anna? Is she a lie too?'

'You would do the same to me,' she said.

'No.' I looked at her. 'No, I wouldn't.'

She kept the pistol steady, arm outstretched, the cold metal pressed to my head.

'I'm on your side,' I said to her. 'That's why I didn't tell you who I am, because you'd never have trusted me—'

'I'd have killed you the day we met.'

'I didn't harm your family,' I said.

'How can I believe you? Why shouldn't I just kill you now?'

'Because you won't leave my wife without a husband and my children without a father. Because that would make you just like *Krukov*. Because you won't leave Anna with no one to look after her. Because we are friends.' I fixed my eyes on hers. 'And because we're going find to Krukov together. Is that enough reasons? And there's another – if you kill me now, you'll have to kill all of these men too.'

Tanya glanced away and closed her eyes. When she looked back at me, the disappointment was clear, but she took the barrel of her pistol away from my head, letting her hand fall to her side. 'So what now?' she said.

'What are you doing?' Lyudmila asked from behind us. 'What—'

But Tanya lifted a stiff hand at her, a frustrated and angry gesture telling her to stop.

When her comrade fell silent, Tanya tightened the hand into a fist and put it to her mouth, nodding at me to go on.

'We carry on just as before,' I said. 'You, me, Lyudmila and Anna.'

'But these are your men.'

'I don't even *know* these men.'

'But he said—'

'I know what he said, but my unit was small, depleted like this man's unit was, and we were only merged with another one after . . . after what happened at . . .'

'After your heroism at Grivino.' The man who had saluted puffed out his chest with pride.

But I felt no pride. The massacre at Grivino had sealed my decision to desert.

'For which you were awarded the Order of the Red Banner,' he went on. 'We *are* your men, Commander Levitsky.'

He had a good-looking face with high cheekbones and fierce eyes. It was too dark to see their colour, but I imagined they would be pale and cold and blue. He might have been a little younger than me, but the difference in the years between us was emphasised by his clean-shaven skin. I remembered him as an eager soldier trying to impress me, always following my orders to the letter, but that was as much as I knew about him. By then, most of my comrades-in-arms were killed, and the ones who remained were the ones I kept close – Krukov included, which was what made his viciousness all the more distressing. But this man was one of a number who had joined my unit shortly before I chose to become a fugitive. I hadn't fought with them or formed any bond with them. They were nothing to me but men in uniform. I couldn't explain that to Tanya right now, though, and hoped that she would trust me a little longer.

I watched him, all of us standing in the falling snow, trying to get some measure of him, but he gave little away. I wished I could see his eyes more clearly, but the darkness conspired against me in that. I felt that if I could look into his eyes, I would know him better. Standing to attention and saluting was not enough to guarantee loyalty. I had known soldiers inform on soldiers, commanders shot simply because one of their comrades accused them of unpatriotic thoughts. This man was as likely to deceive me as he was to support me.

'You'll have to earn my confidence,' I said. 'I don't know you, and trust is hard to come by. So for now we'll keep your weapons, and this woman and her family will remain my hostages. You will do as I order.'

'Of course, Commander.'

I took a few paces back, keeping Oksana in front of me, still believing that she might be the only thing keeping me alive. These men had proclaimed their loyalty to me, but words were easy to say and this was the time of lies. I couldn't believe anything anyone told me, and if these men were my enemies, they would say and do anything to get the better of me. I couldn't take any risks. They would be well trained and vicious.

When I reached the bottom step of the *izba*, aware of Lyudmila behind me, I stopped and turned to Tanya, speaking in a quiet voice so the soldiers wouldn't hear. 'You have to believe me. Whatever he says, you *have* to believe me. These are *not* my men. My unit was small, and I lost soldiers in battle, others by transfer. I was given what was left of another unit in the same state, one that had been operating for several weeks without a proper commander. *These* men. But I only knew them a matter of days, and even then it was a confusing mess. Things were complicated.'

It had been hard after Grivino. All that killing on my conscience and being called a hero for it.

'We were given fresh orders,' I told her. 'Orders to . . . to do . . . terrible things.' Worse than I had done before. Not just requisitioning food, taking conscripts and executing deserters, but to spread terror. To torture and kill and burn. To propagate fear and drive the enemy into the shadows.

'Is that why you deserted?'

311

'I don't know these men any more than you do. I trust *you* more than them. Is my trust misplaced?'

'Don't pretend you didn't hear me. *Is that why you deserted?* I have to know. I have to believe there's something good in you.'

A few weeks ago, I wouldn't have cared what Tanya thought of me, but now I felt a pang of disappointment. 'Have you not seen any good in me? None at all?'

'Answer my question.'

'Yes. Yes, it's why I deserted.' The word was not easy for me to say. For Tanya, it just meant I had abandoned a heartless regime, but to me, it meant something else. It meant disobeying orders, accusations of cowardice, acceptance that my loyalties had been given to a belief I could no longer embrace. And it meant that I had forsaken my own comrades, leaving some to do terrible things, while others hunted me down.

Receiving those orders had been a trigger for all the disillusionment and exhaustion that had been building in me. The yearning I'd felt last time I was with my family. The appalling thought that my own son, Misha, wanted to follow in my footsteps. The guilt of the countless lives I'd taken, including those at Grivino. And my elevation to heroism because of it.

So I deserted not because I was a coward, but because I wanted to escape the horror, to be with my wife and sons, to protect my family from men like Koschei; men who revelled in their new orders. So while Koschei had pressed his burning, five-pointed star to the skin of helpless people in his quest to proliferate the Red Terror, so I had chosen a different path.

Tanya thought about it, looking from me to the soldier and at the revolver I still held beneath Oksana's chin.

'Now it's your turn to answer *my* question. Can I trust you?' I pressed her. 'I need to hear it.'

'No,' Lyudmila said, and that half-whispered word was heavy with disbelief, making Tanya look over her shoulder to see Lyudmila standing in the open doorway. She took a deep breath and something unspoken passed between them. An apology perhaps, or a plea for understanding. Then Tanya shook her head once at her comrade and looked at me.

'Yes. You can trust me,' she said. 'For now. But when this is over, you will be Red again.'

'And you will be Green or Blue or whichever. I understand. All scores will be settled.' That was good enough for me. I knew that, for the moment, I could rely on Tanya.

I turned back to the soldier and raised my voice. 'Where's Koschei? Where's *Krukov?*'

He hesitated, glancing around at the others.

'Don't look at them. Where is he?'

'He's . . .' He seemed almost reluctant to tell me.

'*Where?*'

'He's delivering prisoners, Comrade Commander.'

'Delivering them where?'

'There's a camp—'

'You know where it is?' I couldn't help but feel I was getting closer.

'No. He doesn't tell us everything.' He looked back at the others again. 'But I think it's nearby . . . He's returning in the morning. I . . . Yes. Tomorrow.'

'What's your name, soldier?'

'Ryzhkov. Grigori Ilich Ryzhkov. Our unit joined yours just a few days before you were killed. Or that's what we thought had happened to you.'

'I remember you.' But I knew almost nothing about him.

'Thank you, Commander.'

'Tell me, Ryzhkov, why are you guarding this house? What's so important about these people?' I remembered the look on his face just a short while ago when Tanya threatened to kill me. I was sure his concern had been for Oksana's life rather than mine.

'I don't know. All I can tell you is that Krukov ordered us to protect it with our lives. To protect the people, otherwise he would take our heads.'

'You're afraid of him?' It would explain his earlier fear, his concern for Oksana, but it also brought his loyalty to me into even more doubt. How could I compete with a man who instilled this kind of reaction even in hardened soldiers?

'Everyone is afraid of him,' Ryzhkov said.

'So why haven't you run? He's not here.'

'Because that would make us deserters. And he always finds deserters.'

# 37

Aware of Tanya's eyes on me, I asked the rest of the men to step forward one at a time and introduce themselves. I recognised some of the faces, but like Ryzhkov, they were strangers to me.

'What about the others?' I asked.

'Gone,' Ryzhkov said.

'Following me?'

'Some.' He didn't pretend to be surprised that I knew about them, but he didn't offer any more information than he had to and I realised I had already told him more about what I knew than I should. I decided to keep everything else I had seen and heard to myself.

'They volunteered?' I asked. He already knew I was aware of my hunters, so it was in my interest to gather as much information as I could.

'Some of them, Comrade Commander. Others were ordered.' He gave me no names and I asked for none.

'So Krukov took over right away.' It was more a thought spoken aloud than a question. Krukov was a serious man of few words and capable of acting without any display of emotion. He'd been a reliable comrade to have at my side, had fought with me and Alek at Grivino. Alek never liked him much, but I had always thought I could trust him. This war, though, it had taught me new things about conviction in others. Now I couldn't tell the truth from lies anymore.

'Yes, as soon as you were gone. He had enough loyal men, and anyone who questioned his orders . . .' He shook his head. 'The only way to stay alive was to do what he said.'

'You didn't think about reporting this?'

'To who? There's no one to tell. Other units do the same thing. I've seen . . .' Once again he let his words trail away.

I remembered what Stanislav had told me at the train before he died – that I had created Koschei – and now I understood what he meant. When Alek and I had left, we had given Krukov free rein to command the unit. We had made it possible for him to carry out our new directive in as efficient and brutal a manner as he could. We had unleashed Koschei, and in his rampage across the country, he had found Belev.

My head spun with the implications. If Alek and I hadn't run, the medic, Nevsky, might have saved his life. My brother might be alive, and I would still be in command of my unit. And if I were still in charge of my unit, Marianna would be at home. My *boys* would still be at home. I would have been able to protect them better as commander of a Cheka unit than as a miserable fugitive hiding in the forest, fleeing from those who hunted him. My mistake in deserting was monumental, almost too much for me to bear.

Galina driven to insanity; flayed hands and branded stars; my brother, cold and dead in the grave; Lev, lying broken on the forest floor; Anna left fatherless. All these things would have been undone if I had stayed with my unit. Everything was my fault. I had caused it all, and now the faces of the dead filled my mind.

And that thought. *He likes to drown the women.* That thought was ever present, always echoing.

'Kolya.' Tanya's voice breaking through the clutter. 'Kolya.' An arm on my shoulder. 'Kolya.'

'What?'

'What do we do now?' Tanya asked, lowering her voice. 'You still want to leave?'

I tried to show no sign of my confusion as I concentrated on one thing only. I had to be single-minded. Hard. Cold. Cruel. I needed to be the soldier now. The Chekist commander. It was the father who had sparked this terrible chain of events, so now it was time for the other part of me to take control.

'You say he's coming here?' I asked Ryzhkov. 'Tomorrow?'

'Maybe tomorrow, maybe later. I can't be sure.'

'But he took prisoners? Children?'

'Boys of fighting age.' There was a hint of indignation in his voice. He would have had to vindicate his actions to himself, just as I had always done, and when you tell yourself enough times that something is justified, you begin to believe it.

'And women?' I asked. 'There were women too?'

'Some.' I didn't ask about Marianna, didn't even try to get any intimation that she was still alive. Partly because I didn't want to know right now – I wanted to maintain enough hope to keep me going – but also because I didn't want him to know about Marianna and the boys. And I wanted to keep my knowledge of Belev to myself.

'But he told you to guard this house? These people?'

'Yes.'

There was only one reason why he would have done that. Krukov had done the one thing I should have done, and I finally understood his reason for pushing north.

His family lived here.

He had been coming here. Not just north, but *here*, to this farm, to protect his own family from the Red Terror that gripped the country. He came here to shelter them from men like himself.

I beckoned Tanya closer and whispered in her ear. 'Krukov's coming. I think we should prepare to meet him.'

Tanya called Lyudmila from the *izba* and ordered her to return the horses to the barn, but she was reluctant to go. She didn't want to leave Tanya alone with me or the other soldiers.

'Don't do this,' she said, coming close to Tanya and speaking with some urgency. 'Don't trust him. Don't make me leave you alone with him.'

'I'll be fine,' Tanya told her.

'He's one of them.' She glared at me with disgust and there was poison in her words. It was Tanya who had lost her family at the hands of Bolsheviks, but she was prepared to work with me. Lyudmila, on the other hand, was not so forgiving. Something

317

had happened to give her unwavering hatred, but I doubted I would ever know what it was. We all had our secrets, and we all told our lies. Such a web of deceit was spun round us that it was impossible to see the world as it really was.

'Get the horses, Lyuda, please. Put them in the barn. When Krukov comes, we don't want him to know we're here.'

Lyudmila backed away a few paces, making her disapproval clear before she turned and trudged into the darkness, leaving a line of prints in her wake.

Tanya returned to the *izba*, ensured the weapons were secure in the second room, and when she was ready, she called to me and I told the men to go inside.

Once Oksana and I were alone in the yard, I released her, taking the pistol away from her throat. My arms were stiff, my hands aching.

'I'm sorry,' I said.

She didn't look me in the eye. She hung her head and rubbed at her neck.

'You have nothing to be ashamed of,' I said.

'Can I go back to my children now?'

Of course she wanted to see them. It was the most natural thing in the world. I wanted to see mine. 'No,' I said. 'I want you to stay with me.' If something were to happen tonight, I wanted to be sure that Oksana was close to me. As callous as it felt, I had a suspicion I might be able to use her as protection.

I stood for a moment, Oksana breathing heavily beside me, trying to find some calm in the quietness of the night, but there was none to be had. I let my breath steam around me, and I tipped back my head to look at the sky. The snow had thinned, the flakes becoming smaller and smaller so they were tiny flecks spiralling and dancing in the air. The grey clouds had dissipated, revealing the outline of the moon; a silvery spectre, more than half grown, trying to spill its light on a sombre land. It was quite beautiful, the kind of night Marianna would have loved.

'Come in,' Tanya called, interrupting my thoughts. 'We're all waiting for you.'

'You first,' I told Oksana, and suddenly I wanted to be inside, to see Anna.

They had lit more lamps, filling the room with light, and they must have fed the oven because as I moved closer, I felt the warmth spilling from the room. I glanced in the direction Lyudmila had gone, seeing glimpses of her in the moonlight as she rounded up the horses, then I followed Oksana over the threshold and closed the door.

The table was no longer overturned but stood in its original position in the centre of the room, and now Ryzhkov and the other soldiers were sitting at it. Tanya had instructed them to pull the chairs as close to the table as possible, so the soldiers were wedged in place, making any sudden movement difficult. They sat with their hands on the tabletop, fingers laced together.

Tanya stood by the door to the second room in the house – the place where she had stored their weapons out of reach. Her own rifle was over her shoulder, her pistol in her hand. She did not trust the men, and was wise to keep them under watch.

The old woman and Sergei had hardly moved – they remained on the chairs at the side of the *pich* – and neither of them spoke when they saw me. Sergei only looked down at his feet, while the old woman, who was watching the men at the table, glared at me as if she wished it would boil my blood.

As soon as I was inside, I allowed Oksana to go to the back of the room. She hurried straight to the ladder and spoke to her children. Their worried faces appeared at the edge of the berth over the *pich* and Oksana reached up to touch each of them. She whispered reassuring words, and as I watched, I felt the wickedness of my actions. Instead of Oksana, I saw Marianna, and I knew how I would feel if such a thing had happened to her. What I was doing was monstrous – using women and children as a shield to get what I wanted – and the only way to crush the guilt was to tell myself I had no choice. It was the only option left open to me.

Oksana looked back at me with hate in her eyes, an expression that warned me not to underestimate her. She had expected the surrender of the soldiers to result in her freedom from me, but I wasn't going to release her just yet. That would have to wait until tomorrow, until I had finally confronted Krukov and learned the whereabouts of my family. While I waited, I would have to contend with not just the soldiers, but also an angry and desperate mother.

Anna had retreated to the far corner of the room, the only place where the light did not fully reach. She must have sought refuge there when the men righted the table, and she sat on the floor, arms hugging her knees. As soon as our eyes met, there was a noticeable change in her demeanour. She sat straighter, raising her head, widening her eyes in a more hopeful attitude. She changed from a frightened child to a more confident, expectant one. She was a spirited and resilient girl.

I went to her, crouching beside her so that I was facing into the room. I didn't want to display too much affection or she might be seen as my weakness, so I resisted the urge to put my arm around her, just as I had resisted the urge to hurry to her when I entered the house. With my back to the others, though, my left hand was out of sight, and I let it brush against hers in an act of reassurance.

'Are you all right?' I asked, whispering so the Chekists would not hear my concern.

'Yes.' Anna responded to my attempt to comfort her by pinching my fingertips in her own. She held them lightly, as if she understood that I wanted to conceal it, and turned her face to look up at me. 'Are *you*?'

I was warmed by seeing her face. Looking into her eyes like that made me feel less cruel. More justified.

'I'm fine,' I told her, feeling a vague smile cross my lips. It was such a simple thing, for her to ask me if I was all right, but it meant so much. No one had asked me that in a long time and it made me feel good. 'Thank you for asking.'

She smiled back, but it was not a natural smile – it was an expression of support and communication, and I couldn't help but reach out and put my hand on the back of her head. It was instinctive and felt right, but as soon as I realised I had done it, that I was about to take off her cap and kiss the top of her head, I took my hand away and glanced at the soldiers sitting at the table.

Ryzhkov was facing us, watching us like a snake, and he nodded once in acknowledgement.

'No one hurt you or said anything to you?' I asked, eyes still on Ryzhkov.

Anna shook her head.

'Did you see what happened outside?'

'No.'

'And did you hear anything we said?'

'Not really. Some. Who are those men?'

'Soldiers.'

'I can see that.'

Again, I felt myself smile and I looked down at her. 'I think they might be able to help me find my family.'

'Marianna,' she said. 'That's good.' Then her face fell as though she was thinking about something serious.

'What is it?'

'When you find them . . . will you still . . . ? What will happen to me? Will you still want me?'

I felt a fist tighten round my heart for this poor, lonely child. 'Of course I will. There's no question about that. You're my daughter now.'

Anna turned her eyes to the floor and nodded to herself as if arranging her thoughts. She was tough, but she was young and saw the world in a different way. She didn't understand the conflicts of adults. She knew right from wrong, good from bad, but the shades of the many colours that lay between were difficult for her to fathom. Experience told her that adults could lie; that they could do awful things.

'I'm telling you the truth, you know that, right?'

'Yes. I know,' she said.

There was movement by the *pich* and I glanced up, seeing the children's faces still at the edge of the berth. Just below them, Oksana was looking in my direction, watching Anna and me. Her expression had changed now; it was no longer laced with hatred. There was something else there instead, but I wasn't sure what it was. It might have been pity or even sadness, but there was also a trace of what looked like guilt. The same expression that had been on Sergei's face.

There was still something I was missing. Something was happening here that I hadn't understood.

'Why is he staring like that?' Anna whispered.

'Hmm? Who?'

'That man,' she said, leaning in to me. 'The soldier.'

I turned my attention to the main part of the room and saw right away what she was talking about.

The men at the table said nothing. They sat with their hands on the surface, as Tanya had instructed, and they each had their faces turned to Ryzhkov. They waited for him.

But he was watching us.

When our eyes met, he nodded as he had done before, but there was something different about him now. Perhaps it was a trick of the flickering lamplight, but there was a hint of malevolence in his face and an intensity to his stare. Something about the unblinking way he watched us reminded me of Tuzik when he had caught the scent of new prey.

He was alert but relaxed. Confident. There was an air of superiority about him that I hadn't seen before, and there was a hint of a smile on his lips.

'I suppose he's curious about us,' I said. 'About me.'

'Are you going to hurt him?'

'I don't think so, but don't you worry about that.' I started to get up. 'You just stay here and keep out of trouble.' I touched the tip of her nose. 'Can you do that?'

She put a hand to her head and saluted, saying, 'Yes, Commander,' and I felt a stab of panic. She told me she hadn't heard what we said outside, that she hadn't seen what happened.

'Why did you say that?' I asked. 'Why did you salute?'

'I don't know. I just . . . Should I not do it?'

'No.' I relaxed. It was just a childish action, nothing to do with who I was. 'No, it's fine. Just stay where you are. Keep safe.'

She showed me that smile again before I left her.

The men at the table had the quality of battle-hardened soldiers. Outside, they had been concealed in darkness, but now, in the light, they couldn't hide themselves. Their tunics were ingrained with the blood and dirt of war, but their faces were wiped clean and scrubbed hard, as if they'd recently had the opportunity to wash themselves. Their beards were scraped away, leaving pale patches around their cheeks and chins where they had been protected first from the sun and then from the bitter winds of early winter. But despite their cleanliness, they carried the look of men who had seen fighting. Not as the ordinary soldier might have seen it, but something much more sinister. It might have been because I already knew that they had followed Krukov and because I had witnessed what they had done, but they had the distant, uncaring and arrogant look of men who had known the worst humanity had to offer. I had witnessed the same bearing in small units that had committed some of the basest atrocities. Inhuman men who had lost any notion of right and wrong. Men on the verge of insanity.

These men here were the men who had flayed skin from flesh, crucified and tortured. These were the men who had pressed the branding iron bearing the red star, and it had all been done under Krukov's orders.

I wondered which of them had been in Belev, which of them had branded the people I knew, and how it must have been for them to follow a man like Krukov, to obey his orders for fear of the most terrible punishment, to kill until they became numb and uncaring. Perhaps even until they came to enjoy it. I could not trust these men, would *never* be able to trust them. They were Krukov's; bound to him by their actions, and nothing I could do would break that bond.

And now they sat and awaited their fate, all eyes on Ryzhkov, the man who had assumed leadership of this part of the unit while they waited for their commander to return.

'So what's your plan?' Ryzhkov asked as I approached. His voice was even, and still he watched me with that hungry look. I hadn't noticed it outside, where the light was sparse, but now I wondered how I could have missed the intensity of those fierce eyes. There was a sense that he was brooding beneath the surface; that his compliance with me was only temporary and that he would strike as soon as he saw an opportunity. 'You must have a plan, Commander.'

Tanya stood by the door to the room where the weapons were stored, watching me with a disappointed look in her eyes.

'What would *you* do?' I asked him, trying not to be distracted by the way Tanya now felt about me.

Ryzhkov answered without hesitation. 'I'd make myself as strong as possible – arm your men and wait for Krukov to come back.'

'You mean you?'

'Of course.' He said it as if there could be no question about it. 'Arm us, ambush him when he returns and find out where he took your family.'

'My family? What makes you think I'm looking for my family?'

Ryzhkov raised his eyebrows. ' "I'm just a man who wants his family back." That's what you said to her before.' He nodded at Tanya. 'Or something like it. And when you asked about prisoners, you mentioned women and children, so . . . I put those things together and . . .' He opened his hands and smiled.

'Fingers laced together,' Tanya said.

'Oh. Sorry.' Ryzhkov clasped his hands and smiled, pointing one of his fingers at her. 'You, on the other hand, are looking for something else. You didn't ask about prisoners, but you wanted to know about Krukov, and the look on your face when you found out about *him* –' his finger moved in my direction '– well, I'd say you're not keen on Bolsheviks. Revenge? Is that it?'

'Don't arm these men,' she said to me. 'You can't arm them. It wouldn't be safe.'

'How do I know I'm safe from *you*?' he asked, keeping his gaze on her. 'You're the one who's armed. You're the one who hates Bolsheviks.'

'You don't know anything about me.' Tanya bristled, her knuckles white round the handle of her pistol.

'That's right – I don't.' Ryzhkov addressed me now, speaking in that calm tone, as if trying to hypnotise me. 'Who is this woman anyway, Commander? She doesn't look like a patriot to me. Do you trust her?'

'More than I trust you.'

Ryzhkov smiled and shook his head. 'I'm your comrade,' he said. 'We're brothers.'

'No, we're not brothers.'

The smile fell away in an instant. 'Where *is* your brother?' he asked. 'Did he die in Ulyanov, or did he run with away with you? Alek. That's his name, isn't it?'

It took me by surprise to hear him talk about Alek and I felt at a disadvantage. Ryzhkov knew more about me than I did about him.

'*Did* he die?' Ryzhkov stood, pushing back his chair. 'Is that what happened to him?'

'Sit down.' Tanya stiffened.

Ryzhkov snapped his head round to look at her. His expression intensified, becoming angry. He lifted his hands, still clasped together, and pointed at Tanya. He stood that way for a moment, arms trembling, before he controlled himself and lowered his hands.

'Don't let her give me orders,' he said. '*You're* my commander, not her. *You* are in charge, not this woman.'

'Sit down,' I told him.

He ignored me, leaning forward and separating his hands to put his palms flat on the table. 'They all said you were such a good commander. Fair, they said. It's what I expected from you.'

'Sit down.'

Ryzhkov stood straight and stared right at me, raising his voice, challenging me. 'Why won't you trust me? We're brothers.'

'You're not my brother.' I felt my anger rise. I had kept it inside for so long, suffered every mental and physical hardship, trying to keep it all at bay while I did the right thing for Anna, for Tanya and Lyudmila, and for my family, but now I felt it consuming me. It burned in me, and Ryzhkov's words only fuelled that fire. The way he looked at me, the way he spoke, everything about him needled me, pushed under my skin. 'You could never be my brother. The things you did for Krukov. You might have been one of the men in Belev. Maybe you murdered those men and threw the women into the lake. Maybe *you* dragged my wife from our home.'

'We had no choice,' Ryzhkov argued.

'There's always a choice.'

'You're wrong. With Koschei, there was never a choice. If you disobeyed . . .' He shook his head and grinned as he drew a finger across his throat. 'You know how easy it is to do that? Well, of course you do. There's a war; people die all the time. You've killed your share.'

'Women drowned?' I said. 'Children taken away? That's not war. That's just—'

'*You* did those things.'

'No. Not like that.'

'What about all the people you killed at Grivino?'

'I was fighting for my life. I never skinned a man alive, never branded anyone, never—'

'Then why did you join the Cheka? You always knew what it was.' He made a fist and held it out to me. 'Fear. That's what the Cheka is. Fear. To drive the enemy into the shadows.' His face reddened as blood flowed to his cheeks.

'The enemy?' I said. 'No one knows what that even means anymore.'

'*I* know,' he said, slamming his fist on the table. '*I know*. Anyone who opposes the revolution. We are the heroes who keep it from failing.'

'The revolution? The revolution was supposed to make us all equal. That's what we forgot. The same people still suffer. And there's nothing heroic about taking food from the mouths of children. What kind of shit has Krukov been spinning for you? Can't you men think for yourselves anymore?'

Ryzhkov fell silent, the colour fading from his face. He sighed and shook his head. 'You disappoint me, Commander. I thought you were better – a true patriot.'

'I *am* a patriot,' I said, 'but men like Krukov are tearing this country apart, using the war as an excuse to commit the worst crimes. You think calling himself Koschei is patriotic?' My anger was hitting its peak now. 'You know how far I've come? What I've seen?' My voice was growing louder. 'How my eyes have been opened? I've seen the trail of horror men like Krukov leave behind them. The things he gets his men to do – men like you and the four at this table. My wife and sons taken away. So many dead and . . . I saw a woman stuffed into a barrel and left to drown. Did you put her there? Did you . . . ?' I took a deep breath and closed my eyes tight as I tried to calm myself. I knew how Commander Orlov felt now. Useless. Unable to change anything.

When I looked at Tanya, she said nothing, but her surprise was undeniable. She had never seen me like this. Anna cowered in the far corner as if seeing me as a new person. Sergei and his wife sat with confused expressions on their faces, but they were not looking at me; they were looking at Ryzhkov. Oksana appeared horrified by what I had said, disturbed by the monstrous things she now knew these men had done.

Ryzhkov stared past me, looking at Oksana, shaking his head. Then he smiled at me. He stepped back from the table and rubbed a hand across his head. 'You know what I remember about you?' He looked at the men seated round the table. 'You know what I remember about this man? About Nikolai Levitsky?' He waited, as if he expected one of them to reply, but they remained silent.

'We were tracking deserters,' he said. 'Someone reported a deserter in some shitty village in the middle of nowhere. This was my first day with him. The great Nikolai Levitsky. Order of the Red Banner. The deserter who hunted deserters.' He stood with his back to the front door and looked at his boots as if trying to order the story straight in his mind.

'You should sit down,' I said, feeling the weight of the revolver in my hand.

'Should I?' Ryzhkov raised his voice and snapped his head up, taking me by surprise. 'Should I? No, I think I'd rather stand when I tell this story. You're disappointing me, Comrade *Commander*. I expected more from you. The way you're judging me after the things you've done. Don't you remember how you shot that old man? Sitting up there on your horse and the old man came forward, pleading with you, and you shot him in the face. It was magnificent.'

'He was armed,' I said.

'I don't remember it that way. I remember a poor old man begging you to spare his son, and you shot him like you were swatting a fly. And what was it you said after that? Oh yes. "Hang his son." You were magnificent. *Magnificent.*'

'No. I was doing my job. The old man was armed, and his son was a deserter.'

'Yes, you were doing your job, and it was an inspiration to see. You said that we had to pull out the weeds to make the crop grow strong – that's what you told us – and I knew exactly what you meant. You were so right, and it felt good when I threw the rope over the tree. And when we hauled that boy up and watched him struggle at the end of the rope, his feet kicking, didn't you feel it too?'

'He was not a boy; he was a soldier,' I said.

'A deserter, like you. A weed that needed to be pulled out. He struggled for a good few minutes, you know. It wasn't quick.'

'He was a deserter who murdered two men. Two good soldiers with families.'

'What difference does that make?'

'It makes all the difference.' I stared at him, this vile and misguided creature, wondering if it really could have been me who created the man who led these soldiers to Belev. But he had made me look at myself again, reminded me who I had been, who

328

I was now and how my beliefs had changed. The anger slipped away, smothered by other feelings of guilt and denial and realisation. I was questioning myself, my former actions, knowing I had found excuses for them then, just as I was trying to do now. I didn't know if I was a product of my time or if my time was a product of men like me, men like Krukov and these soldiers in front of me. Men who can use twisted and misinterpreted beliefs to vindicate their most base actions. 'It makes—'

'No. A deserter is a deserter. That's why I was so let down by you. When we realised you weren't dead, that it was all a trick . . .' He sneered at me. 'You were such a disappointment. I thought you were so *righteous*, so *solid*. Such a patriot. The things you said, the things I'd heard about you. I was honoured to join you, *honoured*.' He spat the word, then stopped. He looked down and sighed. 'But in the end, you were nothing more than a coward and a traitor who lied about what he believed in.'

I couldn't accept what I was hearing. Had he admired me so much that he had taken my words and applied them to justify so much violence? Had I really given him the excuse to do the things he had done? Had he murdered and burned according to a doctrine he had learned from me? There had to be more to it than that. There *had* to be.

As I reeled at the horror that he could rationalise his actions using words and beliefs he had learned from me, some other words echoed in my mind: the words the young soldier from the train had heard from Stanislav. That Nikolai Levitsky had created Koschei. That Nikolai Levitsky had let him loose.

And then I knew the truth.

I raised my pistol and pointed it at Ryzhkov. 'It's you,' I said. '*You're* Koschei.'

# 38

The room was silent. The accusation of Koschei's identity was like casting a spell inside the *izba*, As if time had stopped to allow us to process this new revelation. No one spoke; no one moved; hardly a breath was taken.

Marianna. The boys. I was close now. So close. I had to keep my nerve. I couldn't fail now. Not now.

'You?' Tanya broke the silence. '*You're* Koschei?'

Ryzhkov inflated before me as he sucked a long breath into his nostrils. He held it for a moment, then let it out as the grin returned to his lips. He kept his eyes on me, only me, and there was a disturbing glint in them, which he had hidden well when we met. He had played the part of the honourable soldier; the man who had followed the orders of a maniac because he was too afraid to disobey, but he had been unable to maintain the charade for long. He was too full of conceit, and now the spark was there that made him more alive than any of us. *My* eyes felt dull and tired and weary of the things they had seen, but his were glittering with expectation and excitement. He was glad to be himself again, the perfect tool of the Cheka. A man who enjoyed his work.

He straightened, throwing back his shoulders and lifting his arm. He raised it slowly, finger and thumb formed in the way a child would pretend he was holding a pistol. When the finger was level with me, he was a mirror image, standing with his make-believe weapon outstretched, as I stood with my real one.

His sudden composure was chilling. One moment he was raising his voice and ranting like a lunatic, and the next he was almost serene.

'No. *You're* Koschei,' he said, dropping his thumb to fire an imaginary bullet into my head. 'And him. *He's* Koschei too.' He aimed at one of the men at the table and did the same. 'And *him*.' He pointed at another, firing a third, silent, invisible bullet.

'Where is my wife? Where are my sons?' My words came out as a whisper, but they were easily audible in the quiet room.

Ryzhkov spread his hands wide. 'We're *all* Koschei. Don't you see that? Every one of us tasked with spreading the terror that keeps the enemy in the shadow is Koschei. We're a whispered promise of death.'

'Where are they?' I asked.

'I'm a *monster*, and you are too. Don't you understand that? That's what they want us to be, the men who give the orders. They want people to tell stories about us for years to come. They gave you a *medal* for it.'

'Tell me where you took them.'

Ryzhkov rolled his eyes in exasperation as if his mask of calmness were about to crack and fall from his face to reveal the true evil beneath.

'Think about it, Nikolai. Mothers and fathers tell their children the *skazkas* to teach them not to go into the woods, not to steal, not to curse, to . . . to do as they are told.' He waved a hand. 'To obey. And that's what we do for the people – we give them a symbol of what can happen if they don't obey. They'll be afraid for a long time – for years to come. They'll talk about us in whispers, Nikolai. We make them afraid. *You* make them afraid.'

'Where are they?' I thumbed back the hammer of my pistol, aware of the men at the table. They were unarmed, but they were still dangerous. Four loyal, well-trained, experienced and obedient men. I could not afford to dismiss them as subdued.

Ryzhkov shook his head in disappointment. 'You can't shoot me, Nikolai, you know that. Kill me and you'll never know where my prisoners went. Or . . .' the grin returned, '. . . or maybe you *can* just shoot me. I mean, how do you even know they're still alive? Maybe they're dead already. I've killed so many people I've lost count and probably wouldn't even remember which village it was. Isn't that a wonderful irony? That I found your family without even knowing it?'

It was clear that Ryzhkov was a madman. Whatever he had done, whoever he had been and whatever he had believed, it had driven him to this. Turned him into *this*.

'One of your men will tell us,' Tanya said.

'Perhaps they don't even know.' He turned to Tanya with an expression of mock sympathy. 'Sorry. It looks like we've reached a stalemate. There's nowhere to go from here. So what do we do? What do you want to do?'

Tanya didn't reply. Instead she approached Ryzhkov, coming close enough to press the barrel of her pistol against his heart. 'I want my husband and my children back.'

Behind me, Oksana and the old woman said, 'No,' in unison, and the men at the table made a move to rise, but Ryzhkov held out a hand to them, signalling them to stay where they were.

'Tanya.' I called her name, letting her hear the warning in my voice. I needed Ryzhkov to tell me where Marianna was.

Ryzhkov pushed against the pistol, forcing it harder into his chest as he leaned his face close to Tanya's. 'Did I take them too? Your husband and children. I've taken so many, you know.'

'You murdered them.'

'Oh well, I can hardly bring them back from *that*.'

Her left hand darted out and gripped his throat, her fingers tight. Her face was a tortured picture of pain and fury.

Ryzhkov didn't flinch. 'Are you going to let her kill me, Nikolai?'

'Tanya,' I warned her again.

'You hear how afraid he is?' Ryzhkov said, staring into Tanya's eyes. 'How desperate?' The sinews bulged in his neck.

'Tanya.' I shifted my pistol to aim at her now, then at Ryzhkov once more. There was so much confusion in her, so much conflict. I understood what she was feeling, but I couldn't let her do this. 'Tanya, please.'

'You kill me and he might never see his family again. Would you do that to him?' His eyes slipped to the side so he could look at me and I saw that, despite his predicament. he was enjoying this.

Tanya squeezed harder and Ryzhkov's face began to change colour. Her fingertips dug into his skin as if she intended to tear out his throat, but Ryzhkov did nothing to prevent it. He let his arms hang by his sides as she crushed his life.

'And then you'll be just like me.' Ryzhkov's voice came in a hoarse whisper. His breath was failing, his life hanging on the edge. 'You will have condemned Nikolai's family. You will be like us. You will be *Koschei* too. Just another monster.'

'She's killing him,' the old woman said behind me. 'Don't let her kill him.'

I heard Oksana saying something too, but the words were lost on me. There was too much happening, too much to think about. Ryzhkov was letting Tanya choke him – he was far more powerful than she was, yet he did nothing to retaliate. He was using his own mortality to manipulate us.

'Are you going to let her do this?' Ryzhkov asked me. His voice was tighter, and his eyes were wide and red.

I trained my gun on Tanya now, began to tighten my finger on the trigger. It wasn't what I wanted. I didn't want to kill her, but I would have to.

'You have to stop,' I warned her. 'Please. If you make me do this, he's one step closer to getting what he wants.'

Ryzhkov dropped to his knees now, his face bright red, his mouth open in a desperate attempt to draw breath. Still his men did nothing. They obeyed his order, sitting by and watching as Tanya squeezed with one hand and held a pistol to his heart with the other.

'Don't make me kill you, Tanya. Don't let him use me to do this.'

Finally I broke into her rage and she turned to me as if woken from a dream. She blinked, looked down at her hands, at Ryzhkov's bloated face, then released her grip.

Ryzhkov bent double, head to the ground, coughing and gasping for air, but as soon as his lungs were full, he pushed Tanya's pistol away and got to his feet in front of her. The redness began to drain from his skin, and he lifted a hand to his throat, rubbing at the spot where Tanya's fingers had marked him.

His grin returned and he looked from Tanya to me and then back again. 'You can't kill me,' he said, voice rattling. 'I'm deathless.'

I remembered that Galina had put her knife in him and all he carried was the ghost of a limp.

'No one's deathless,' Tanya replied.

'But you can't kill me. You can't let me live, and you can't kill me, so what do you do?'

Ryzhkov had backed us into a corner, but he had a weakness. I had seen that already, and I wondered if we could play him as he had played us.

'You found my family,' I said, 'but you're forgetting that I found yours too. Maybe we *can't* kill you –' I stepped to one side and swivelled to point my pistol at Oksana '– but I can kill *her*.'

Immediately the smile dropped from his face.

Oksana was standing at the base of the ladder to the place where her children were hiding, exactly as she had been since I had allowed her back into the house. She had hardly moved. The old woman, though, was on her feet, hands to her mouth, and I realised the question of whose mother she was had been settled. Her fear was for Ryzhkov: he was her son.

The old man remained in his seat, head bowed as if he was trying to ignore it all, and now I understood the reason for his behaviour. While the mother was proud of her Chekist son, the father was ashamed. The revolution had split this family as easily as it had split the country.

'Come here,' I said to Oksana.

She hesitated, looking at her husband. 'Tell them it's not true,' she said to Ryzhkov. 'Tell them they're wrong. You didn't do all those things.'

So now I knew.

'Come here,' I said again, and this time she shook her head.

'Would you rather I used one of your children?' I asked, hating

334

the dreadful nature of my threat. Ryzhkov had forced me to behave like him and I couldn't help looking over at Anna, sitting in the corner watching me. I wished there was a way to let her see that I wouldn't do it. I wanted her to know I would never hurt Oksana's children, but there was no way to do it without warning the others too.

'Which one will it be?' I asked.

'I'll come,' Oksana said, and when she was at arm's length, I reached out and pulled her towards me, jamming my pistol under her chin as before.

I looked at Ryzhkov. 'Your wife, I presume?'

I saw from his expression I was right.

'Tell them it's not true, Grigori,' she pleaded with him. 'Those things they say you did. Tell them it's not true.'

But he couldn't deny it. Not in front of his men, not in front of us. And when I looked back at the old woman, I saw sorrow replace pride, as if she had rejected the possibility of her son's madness until this moment, but *now* she knew the reality of what he was.

Beside her, Sergei had his head in his hands.

'Your mother and father,' I said. 'See how ashamed they are of you.'

'They should be proud. I'm making our motherland better. More powerful.'

'No, you're just a murderer.'

'I'm a *patriot*.'

'Who drowns women and beheads old men.'

'Enemies,' he said. 'The ones who can't be taught. They have to be rooted out like weeds – you said so yourself. The weak and the unwilling. The others, I send for labour so they can learn to love the revolution; to fight for it.'

'You didn't do this for the revolution,' I said. 'You did it for yourself. Because you enjoy it. Because you're a monster.'

'Grigori,' Oksana said, 'tell them it's not true.'

He turned up his lip at her. 'Are you not a good Communist?'

'Of course, but—'

'Then you'll find nothing wrong with what I'm doing. It's these people who are killing our country with their false ideas and desertion.' He looked right at me. 'Kill her. I don't care.'

Oksana tensed and then slackened in my arms as if she had been slapped. She couldn't believe what her husband was saying. The father of her children.

'Do it,' he said. 'Go on.'

I tightened my grip on Oksana and pressed the gun barrel harder, but my finger froze on the trigger.

'Do it,' Ryzhkov said again. 'See what *I* will sacrifice for the cause.'

'No,' Oksana begged. 'Please.'

I looked across at Anna, seeing how afraid she was of what I was doing.

'Do it.' Ryzhkov's demand made me turn my attention back to him and I could see from his expression that he thought he had won. 'You can't,' he said. 'Can you?'

I wasn't going to murder Oksana, and Ryzhkov had known that right away. He had seen my care for Anna and the way I had allowed Oksana to go to her children. He knew I was incapable of killing her. I was not the man he was, and now Oksana was of no use to me as a hostage because he understood that. There was nothing to stop him from doing what he wanted. I had no hold over him. Unless I told Tanya to do it her way.

'Shoot him,' I said.

'What?'

'Shoot him. Make it hurt, but don't kill—'

'That damn dog of yours wouldn't let me into—' Lyudmila was saying as she pushed the front door inwards, bumping against Tanya's shoulder.

Distracted for a fraction of a second, Tanya flinched and began to turn her head towards the intrusion, but Ryzhkov saw his chance.

It was all the edge he needed.

# 39

Raising his left arm, Ryzhkov pushed Tanya's hand to one side, brought up his right elbow and slammed it hard into her nose. She fired but was too late. The deafening shot cracked in the dead air of the *izba*, filling the confined space with sound, releasing a cloud of acrid smoke that dispersed around them. The bullet went wide and low, thumping into the man who had been sitting beside Ryzhkov. At almost point-blank range, it hit him under the right armpit, knocking him sideways. He put his hands out to stop himself from falling off his chair, but already the bullet had done its work. He would be dead in a few minutes.

Tanya stumbled backwards, reeling from his blow, but Ryzhkov gripped her arm in his left hand and swung her like a rag doll, turning her so she was in front of him, obstructing my aim. He balled his fist and hit her a second time, then a third and fourth in quick succession, his knuckles pounding her face, her head lurching with each blow. When she stopped resisting, he kept Tanya between us, using her as a shield, tearing the pistol from her limp fingers.

As he did it, he gave the order to his men.

'Kill them.'

Ryzhkov was quick and strong. He had overpowered Tanya in just a few seconds and then he was raising the weapon to point at Lyudmila, who'd barely had time to register what was happening.

But I saw no more, because by then, the three other men at the table had knocked back their chairs and come at me in one swift movement. They were quick to their feet, blocking my view and preventing me from finding a clear shot at Ryzhkov, so I shoved

Oksana away from me and swivelled at the waist, redirecting my aim.

My first shot caught the man nearest to me in the hollow of his throat, the bullet passing through the soft flesh, shattering the vertebrae in his neck as the lead struck bone. His head snapped back, and his hands went to the place where the blood now drained from him. He didn't fall immediately, but the impact unbalanced him and he stumbled, blocking the path of the second man, who bumped into him, giving me time to adjust my aim before he pushed his comrade aside and came at me. The second shot I fired hit this man in the cheek, turning his head as it tore through his face just below the cheekbone. The lead drilled up and out, taking tissue and bone with it when it burst from his skull and spun out towards the corner of the room. He straightened and toppled sideways like a felled tree, and then the third man was on me.

He was a short man, much smaller than me but quick on his feet. He stepped over his fallen comrades and put his head down, throwing his full weight at me before I had time to adjust my aim and shoot again. His shoulder hit me hard in the stomach and he wrapped his arms around me, lifting me high, then half throwing, half dropping me. My back slammed against the hard wooden floor, my grip breaking on the pistol, which skittered away across the room as a sharp pain fired like a hot iron along my spine and the breath rushed out of me.

As I went down, I caught a glimpse of Ryzhkov with Tanya's pistol in his outstretched hand, pointed at Lyudmila's head, but I was on my back when he shot her.

The soldier who had overpowered me didn't take even a moment to recover. Right away he raised his fists and began hitting me, endless punches to my head, breaking my nose, clattering my teeth, smashing my ears, filling my mouth with blood. Then he put his hands to my throat and pushed his thumbs hard, trying to crush the life from me. I turned my head this way and that, raised my hands and took hold of his arms, trying to break his grip, but I hadn't taken a full breath since

338

hitting the floor and I was weakening. My face hurt, my back hurt, and my chest was burning. My mind was burning too, with desperation and anger and disappointment. I had let everyone down.

I had come so far, so *close*, and now I was dying.

My thoughts became less coherent. A whiteness was seeping in at the edges, threatening to envelop me like an unstoppable snowstorm. Consciousness was leaving me and there was nothing I could do about it. Maybe it was the best thing for me. Maybe it was the only way to find any peace: to simply give up. To let my arms relax, let my body be still and allow the man to crush my life away.

To leave Anna to their mercies. To abandon my wife and my sons.

'No,' I said. 'No.' This wasn't how it was supposed to be.

I released my grip on his arms and put my hands to his face, pushing my thumbs against his eyes. In his panic, he squeezed my throat harder, turning his head this way and that, trying to stop me, but I only pushed more, feeling his eyes begin to give beneath the pressure. He gave one more concerted effort to strangle my life away before I could take his eyes, but as he did so, my thumbs slipped in towards the inside corners of his eyes, gouging deep so that my nails scraped against bone.

The soldier screamed and released me, putting his hands to his face. He was heavy and I was too weak to push him off me, but I saw my opportunity.

My only chance.

I reached down to unfasten one coat button, fingers moving quickly. No more than a second and my hand slipped inside, reaching for the knife secured there in its sheath. I pulled it out, holding it high and to the side.

Then I drew on all the strength I had left and thrust it into the soldier's neck.

His body stiffened, his screaming stopped, and when I pulled the knife free for a second attack, blood arced high and wide, and I plunged it into him once more. This time it was as if I had let

339

the air out of a balloon. His entire body relaxed and he slipped sideways, life evaporating into the warmth of the *izba*.

I lay on my back as the whiteness began to recede. I opened my mouth wide and gulped at the air, feeling the pain returning to my neck and face. I became aware of someone shouting, but everything was confused, the sounds dull and echoing. Sergei, I think, the old man shouting, 'Grigori.' I tried to remember who 'Grigori' was, my mind sluggish, taking too long to connect the name to Ryzhkov. Then a woman was shouting too. No, *screaming*. Oksana, or perhaps the old woman, I couldn't tell which, the voices melting into the pounding and ringing that already filled my head. But I heard no children's voices. No sound from Anna.

Anna. The name repeated in my mind and I was filled with a sudden dread. I needed to see her, to know that she was all right.

I brought my knees up and tried to push onto my elbows, but I was weak and my muscles burned. Nothing worked as it should. My arms trembled. The pain in my back intensified; my chest ached; my vision blurred; my hearing was muted. My body was fighting to recover from the punishment it had just taken and I trembled as I willed myself to move first one arm, then the other, and when I finally managed to prop myself up and look towards the door, I saw neither Tanya nor Lyudmila.

Close to me, the bodies of three men lay sprawled on the floor, but beyond them, by the door, I saw only Ryzhkov standing with Tanya's pistol at his side, his face glistening with sweat and dotted with flecks of blood. His shoulders were hunched the way Tuzik's hunched when he was issuing a warning or about to attack. His head was dropped so that his chin was almost touching his chest and he was staring at me.

Ryzhkov did not have the gaunt and bony figure of Koschei the Deathless. He did not have the long beard or the sword at his side, but he did have the crazed and savage look in his eyes.

When he raised the pistol and shook his head, I lifted one arm in a useless but natural gesture.

'Please,' I tried to say.

And he hesitated.

His eyes shifted to focus on something behind me just as a shot cracked, dull and flat and undramatic to my damaged ears. Ryzhkov flinched, but the bullet missed by a hand's width, burying itself in the wall beside the front door.

A shadow of surprise and confusion crossed his face, and he twitched again as another shot followed immediately after the first, this one striking the wall on the other side of him. Then he scowled and started to adjust the aim of the pistol away from me, to point at whoever had demanded his attention, but his movement was never finished.

Third and fourth shots came in quick succession, one of them finding its mark, and Ryzhkov lurched when the bullet struck him. He bent at the waist as if punched and took a step back to steady himself. His arms dropped as if suddenly heavy and Tanya's weapon slipped from his fingers.

I saw my chance for life. Whoever had fired those shots had given me precious seconds. I pushed harder with my shaking arms, summoning what little strength I had left to turn onto my front so I could struggle to my feet, and in that movement, I caught a glimpse of what was behind me.

Everything had happened so quickly that no one had moved much. The few seconds it had taken for the violence to play out were barely enough for them to do much more than watch in horror. Oksana was still beside the *pich*, her children still out of sight, but the old woman was closer, as if she had tried to come across the room. What she thought she might achieve, I couldn't tell, but Sergei had both hands on her, gripping her upper arms as he held her back. There was no need for that now, though, because they were all motionless and silent.

The old woman was staring at her son, horrified, but both Sergei and Oksana were looking at the far end of the room.

Anna was sitting with her back to the wall, arms outstretched. Her small hands still clutching my revolver. Her fingers still working the trigger, firing on empty cylinders.

341

# 40

Koschei was not dead.

He was in pain. He was losing his lifeblood onto the floor of his own home, but he was not dead.

'Where is my wife?' I mumbled as I struggled to my feet, fighting the dizziness. I felt drunk, as if I had lost control of my muscles. Nothing worked the way it should. 'Where are my sons?'

He ignored me, head down, searching around him for a weapon. He turned on the spot, looking for the pistol he had dropped.

A part of me wanted to go to Anna. I wanted to comfort her and make her feel secure. I wanted to hold her and thank her for my life, but I knew that the only way for her to be safe was to eliminate the threat to her. I had to reach Ryzhkov before he could arm himself again. He had information I needed. I had to make him tell me.

'Where are they?' I took a stumbling step toward him, putting my hands out, reaching for anything to hold on to. 'Where did you take them?'

I was slow, but some of my strength was coming back. My neck was throbbing and my face aching. Pain fired up my back, exploding from the base of my spine with every step, but I had something to drive me on, something to numb the pain for me.

I had Koschei. Right in front of me.

As I took another step, he looked up at me and stared. His face was white, the spots of Tanya's blood standing out against his skin. He was hunched, both hands crossed over his stomach, but there was nothing he could do to stop his slow death. Anna's bullet had cut into him just above the belt, and while his blood emptied from him, so his ruptured insides were poisoning him. His life was ebbing away.

'It's over now,' I said. 'Just tell me where they are.'

'No,' he managed. 'It's not over yet.' He looked down at the knife in my hand, then scanned the floor one last time before raising his eyes to meet mine. He knew I was recovering now, regaining my strength, but there was a defiance in him, a refusal to accept his situation. He was Koschei. The Deathless One. He could not be killed.

But nor could he kill. Without a weapon he was defenceless against me and there were few options left for him. He could try to arm himself before I managed to cross the room and get round the table. He could wait for me to come to him, to force the information I needed from him. Or he could run. The bullet had weakened him, but he was a strong man. If he could make it to the darkness of the field or forest, he might have a chance.

And that is what he did.

He turned and fled.

He was faster than I had expected, quick on his feet for a man who had been shot, and by the time I had taken another faltering step, he was out of the door.

'No.' I felt my desperation grow now. 'No.' I was determined that he shouldn't escape. He knew where my sons were. He knew what had happened to Marianna. I needed to know. I couldn't let him get away.

No sooner than I had taken another step, I heard a terrible screeching, like something from a child's nightmare. I half turned, cringing, to see that the old woman had broken from her husband's grip and was coming at me, wailing like a demon, arms outstretched, gnarled fingers hooked into claws. She let out a terrible shrieking that made me want to reel in horror, and I had a flash of the image that I'd conjured in the forest – of the *rusalka* coming at me, hungry for vengeance.

I put out my hand, bracing myself to meet her.

She hit me as hard as she could, her chest colliding with my outstretched hand, striking me with more strength than I had anticipated. Weak as I was, she pushed me back against the table, which squealed as it scraped across the floor.

Then she was raking and clawing and screaming, her rotten nails scratching my cheeks, ripping into my skin, trying to find my eyes as she wailed like a vengeful nightmare.

Leaning back, supported by the table, I raised my arms to protect myself and lifted one leg, planting my foot against her pelvis and shoving. I didn't have much strength in me, but she was light and I kicked her away hard enough to knock her off her feet, not stopping to see what happened to her. I had controlled her and that was enough. I was single-minded now.

Koschei was escaping.

Bent at the waist and leaving a trail of red spots in the snow, Ryzhkov had reached the barn and had lifted the latch. The door was now swinging open. He had seen the horses when he came up from the nearby farm, and that was what he wanted. That was how he intended to escape.

'Where are they?' I shouted, but the words were muffled, as if my mouth were stuffed with cotton.

Ryzhkov didn't stop. He didn't even register that he had heard me.

'*Where are they?*'

As I blundered into the yard, Ryzhkov pulled the barn door wide and began to make his way inside, but already the horses were agitated by the commotion inside the *izba*. Now they smelled the blood and death on Ryzhkov and it sent them into turmoil, desperate to escape.

Tanya's horse came out first, brushing past him as it trotted into the yard, snorting and swishing its tail. Its ears were back flat and it tossed its head as it searched for safety.

The second to burst into the yard was Lyudmila's, close on the heels of the first horse, the pair of them feeding off each other's fear, becoming more and more agitated. They came together, careering into one another, Tanya's horse colliding with

344

the cart, hooves skidding and kicking up the powdery snow before the pair of them turned and galloped towards the fence. They followed the line of it towards the far end of the yard, rearing back in panic as a black shape streaked past them, low to the ground.

Tuzik's legs were a blur as he darted across the snow, snarling, launching himself at Ryzhkov, snapping for his throat. Ryzhkov put up his arm in defence and Tuzik's teeth clamped onto it, working through the sleeve of the coat as the dog braced his feet on the ground and tried to pull Ryzhkov down.

The two of them turned in an unnatural and freakish dance as they writhed together, and I moved as quickly as I could, shouting at Tuzik, trying to make him stop. I needed Ryzhkov alive. I couldn't let him die, not yet, and I was afraid that if Tuzik brought him to the ground, he would tear out his throat.

I was halfway across the yard, shouting, watching the struggle, when Kashtan emerged from the barn. She was almost in a frenzy, overwhelmed by the blood and commotion, and her exit was blocked by the snarling, screaming mess of man and dog that amplified her distress. Unable to escape, she showed the whites of her eyes and bared her teeth, reared and stamped her feet in a display of aggression, but when it had no effect, she made a break for safety.

As she barged past, Ryzhkov reached out for her reins, perhaps hoping she would save him from Tuzik's jaws, but it served only to unbalance him, dragging him off his feet. As Kashtan made it past him, she bucked her rear quarters, lashing out with her hind legs.

Tuzik yelped, legs flailing as he was knocked into the barn, but the impact was far worse for Ryzhkov. There was a sickening crunch as one of Kashtan's hooves made contact with the commander's skull. His head jerked back, his body arched, and he crashed onto the snow, where he lay twitching for a moment before becoming still.

Kashtan trotted to the far end of the yard, huddling with the other two horses by the fence, and Tuzik scrambled to his feet, dazed but ready to fight again. I staggered across to where Ryzhkov lay, reaching him before Tuzik could get there.

'No.' I pointed at the dog, then fell to my knees beside Ryzhkov.

'Where are they?' I said, grabbing the front of his coat to pull his head from the ground. 'Where are they?'

Ryzhkov's left eye was smashed and bleeding where Kashtan's hoof had struck him, and the skin round it was split and bleeding. His right eye was open, but it seemed to have a life of its own, rolling up first, then down and looking about as if trying to find something to focus on.

'Don't you die on me.' I shook him hard. 'Don't die on me. Not now. Not after all this.'

'What happened?' he asked.

'Where are they?' I said. 'Where is my family? Where did you send them?'

'Nikolai Levitsky? Is that you?'

'Where is my family?' I said, pulling him up further so that my nose was almost touching his. '*Where are they?*'

Koschei said nothing more. His good eye rolled up, and his body relaxed.

'No. You can't die.' I shook him hard. Over and over. 'You can't die. You have to tell me where they are.'

But Koschei the Deathless was already gone.

# 41

The interior of the *izba* was like a battlefield. Bodies. Blood. The dead, the confused and the walking wounded.

Ryzhkov lay in the snow, his secrets unspoken, and I propped myself in the doorway feeling cheated and helpless, wondering how it had come to this. I had left my unit to escape the war. Alek had given his life for us to avoid it, and yet here it was, right here in this house. I realised then that it was everywhere. That there was no way to escape it. It touched every corner of our country. The distrust and the separation and the violence were everywhere. It was plain to see on the battlefield, but it was in our homes too. It was thick in the air that we breathed and I understood that it was a part of us now. We had come too far; there was no way to turn back. Whoever won this terrible war, it wouldn't matter.

The old woman was wailing when I came in, but when she saw me, she stopped. She knew her son was dead, and now she didn't know what to do or how to feel. She had protected him as any mother would protect her child. Even a grown man. She wouldn't want to believe my accusations, to accept who her son had been and what he had done, but in her heart, she knew it was true. Ryzhkov had kept his madness from his family, but it was there, raging beneath the calm demeanour, and when I had pushed him, he was unable to deny it. The old woman couldn't deny it now either.

Sergei, though, he knew. I think he had known all along that his son was out of control; that's why he had warned us to leave. Now the shame was more than he could bear. He sat motionless on the floor beside his wife, holding one of her hands in his own, but he stared at the wall seeing nothing. His face showed no emotion, as if his senses had all but deserted him, and he gently patted his wife's hand over and over. It wasn't that he didn't care if his son was dead or alive – I think he just didn't want to know. He didn't want to be a part of it. And for now he was going to deny us all.

Oksana was nowhere to be seen, but I knew she would have retreated above the *pich* to be with her children, keeping them safe and out of sight. Where else was there for her to go but to her children?

Anna was sitting where she had been when I last saw her, my revolver still in her hands, but she placed it on the floor as Tuzik brushed past my legs and went to her, a slight awkwardness in his step. She threw her arms around him and hugged him tight, pushing her face against his neck. When she looked up, our eyes met, a silent acknowledgement passing between us, and it was that which gave me strength. Were it not for Anna, I think I might have sobbed at my misfortune. I had come so far, followed Koschei's trail of destruction for so long, and all the time I had fixed my hope on the information he would give me. But he had given me nothing and now all seemed lost.

I had Anna to make me keep going, though. She depended on me and I on her.

The old woman stood and came across the room, leaving her husband. She stepped over the bodies and I moved aside to let her out into the yard. I didn't watch her cross to her son and fall to her knees at his side, but I knew it was what she would do. No matter what he was, she would mourn him. He was, after all, her son.

At my feet, Lyudmila lay dead.

'Kolya.'

My name whispered.

'Kolya.'

Tanya was on her side by the table, her face bloody.

'Kolya,' she said again. She was looking up at me through half-open eyes. She raised a hand and made a weak, beckoning motion, so I crouched beside her.

'You'll be fine,' I said.

Tanya shook her head and put her hand on her stomach. It was only then that I realised she had been shot. There was already so much blood on the floor I hadn't noticed that a lot of it was coming from the wound in her abdomen.

I put my hands to her injury and pressed hard.

'Is he dead?' Tanya asked. 'Koschei?'

'Don't talk,' I said. 'You'll be all right.'

Tanya managed a gentle shake of her head. 'Is he dead?'

'Yes.'

'Did he tell you?' Tanya asked. Her voice was weak and I could almost hear the life leaving her.

'Yes,' I said, running my hand across her brow, moving aside the blood-matted hair. 'Yes, he did.'

'You can find your family.'

'We'll find them together.'

She lifted her fingers to my face, touching my cheek, and our eyes locked together. 'Find them,' she said.

They were her last words.

I sat back, turning my face to the sky and closing my eyes, but allowed myself only a moment. Other things were more important. The living had to take precedent over the dead.

I left Tanya where she lay and went to Anna.

The old woman was still outside when dawn broke. She remained at her dead son's side, stricken despite his crimes, and the day renewed about her, unmoved by the night's tragedy.

No more snow fell, and that which had settled became a crystalline crust that hardened on the frost and decorated everything from the frozen mud in the yard to the narrow fence tops and the field beyond. The morning light glittered in the countless angles of the flowering ice with an incongruous beauty.

Dragging the bodies from the house was hard work, but had to be done. I couldn't leave them where they had fallen; Sergei and the old woman wouldn't be able to move them, nor would Oksana, and I couldn't leave them in the *izba* with the children.

With a frankness that saddened me, Anna offered to help, but I couldn't allow it. If anything ever taught me that our country was hard on people, it was that a twelve-year-old girl could offer to help drag dead men from a family home. She needed to do something, though, so I pointed to the horses, who shied away from the ugly tableau, huddling at the far end of the yard, and I told her to take them back into the barn to shelter. There was hay and warmth for them there.

'You look bad,' she said. 'Does it hurt?'

'I'll live. Go on. Take the horses inside.'

She went without question, ignoring the old woman and going to Kashtan first.

Tuzik divided his time between us, patrolling from one to the other.

'You're a Bolshevik.' They were Sergei's first words.

I was by the door, the night behind me, bent over the corpse of one of the Chekists as I struggled to pull him outside. I looked up to see the old man watching me. His beard was thick over pallid skin, and his red eyes were watery and sad.

'What does it matter?' I asked.

'Were these men your brothers?'

I glanced at the body of the man who had tried to strangle me. He was stiffening now, the side of his neck plastered with drying blood. 'These men passed beyond being anyone's brother. They weren't Bolsheviks. They were. . .' I shook my head and looked for the right word, but I wasn't sure what it was. 'They weren't Bolsheviks.'

'What does that mean, anyway?' he asked. 'Perhaps it means something to the men in Moscow, but here?'

I didn't reply.

'Perhaps we've just forgotten what we're fighting for.'

I stared at the old man and wondered what he must be feeling. His own son was a monster.

'So what are *you* fighting for?' he asked me.

'Then? For the revolution. But now for my family.' I remembered what Commander Orlov had said to me. 'Nothing else matters now.'

The old man looked over at his wife mourning their son and I understood the irony of what I had just said. I could not tell him I was sorry, though. My only regret was that Ryzhkov had died before I could learn what he had done with Marianna and Misha and Pavel.

Sergei sighed, and his eyes shifted so he could see beyond the yard. He watched the sparkle of the rising sun on the field and I knew our conversation was over. He reached into his pocket to take out his pipe, and when he began to pack it with tobacco, I continued with the task at hand, dragging the body the short distance to the cart, moving it just a few paces at a time before I had to rest, and then struggling to load it on with the others.

The old woman paid me no attention, sitting beside her son with her head hung. The air was bitter and yet she hardly seemed to notice.

Taking the coat from the Chekist's body, I draped it over her shoulders and drew it around her.

'Stay warm, grandmother,' I said. 'Enough people have died here already.' She didn't even acknowledge I was there.

By the time I finished loading the cart, Anna had stabled the horses and remained in the barn, petting Kashtan, but she didn't take her eyes off me. Tuzik lay in the straw by the door, head up, watching.

I went back to the old woman, touching her shoulder.

'Time to go inside,' I said. I had one more body to deal with, but to her, I wasn't even there. She didn't move, didn't even acknowledge my presence. Nothing existed but her and her son's body, and I think she might have stayed there until she wasted to nothing or froze in place if it hadn't been for her husband.

The old man came out and crossed the yard, boots crunching on the ice. He reached down and took his wife's hand in his own, then put another under her arm to help her to her feet. Now she

351

complied as if in a daze, and the vagueness of her expression reminded me of what I had seen in Galina's face when I had been in Belev.

'He's gone,' Sergei said as she stood. 'He's gone now.' He turned her round and guided her back to the house.

When they had left, I went to their son's body and took the papers from his pocket. I checked the uniform beneath his coat and kept anything that might be of use, then I hauled him onto the back of the cart with the others, taking my time and resting often.

Piling the men like that had been a great effort and had taken me over an hour. My muscles protested, my back screamed in pain so I could hardly stand straight, and my face throbbed, but I had to keep going. I wanted to finish, so I gathered an armful of split logs from the woodpile and went to the cart, packing them around the bodies. I would not allow these men to have anything. Not even six feet of land. I would burn them and let them scatter to the wind.

When I returned for more wood, Anna was waiting for me.

'Let me help,' she said.

I considered for a moment, then reached out to put a hand on her shoulder. 'Aren't you cold? It's warmer in the barn with Kashtan.'

Anna responded by turning to the woodpile and grasping a log in each hand. 'This will keep me warm.' She offered them to me.

I took the wood from her, seeing that she wanted to be with me, and I smiled at her. It was not a smile of happiness, but one of understanding and togetherness.

'Thank you,' I said.

So Anna lifted the wood from the pile and I took it to the cart, and when there was enough, I covered the bodies with dry straw from the barn.

With that done, Anna and I returned to Kashtan, who nickered and came to me, putting her nose against my chest. I looked into her soft brown eyes and rubbed her neck.

'Stay with her,' I said to Anna. 'There's one last thing for me to do.'

'What is it? Can't I come with you?' she asked.

'I need you to keep Kashtan company. Don't worry. You're safe.'

'I don't feel safe.'

'I know.' I turned to Anna and opened my arms to her and she stepped against me. I embraced her and held her tight, putting up a hand to stroke her hair. 'But I have to bring Tanya and Lyudmila out.'

'I don't want to be alone.' Her face was pressed against my coat and her voice was muffled.

'You won't be. I'll be close. And Kashtan is here. Tuzik too.'

Inside, the old woman was sitting at the table, and Sergei had put water on to boil. He made tea while I took Tanya and Lyudmila into the yard, but I didn't put them in the cart with the Chekists. They deserved better than that. They deserved the land, so I laid them on my tarpaulin, one at a time, and wrapped it round them before I returned to the barn to collect some tools.

'I'm going to take them to the edge of the forest,' I told Anna. 'To bury them. It may take a little while.' I glanced over at the *izba*. There was a glow at the window and it would be warm inside.

Anna saw me looking and began to shake her head. 'Don't leave me.' There was desperation in her voice. 'Please don't make me go—'

'I want you to come with me,' I said, removing one glove and putting my hand to the side of her face. 'I won't let you out of my sight.' It was the only choice I had. I couldn't leave her out here in the barn, and though it would be warm in the house, I couldn't send her inside to be alone with the old woman, the mother of the man she had helped kill.

Anna's relief was clear. Her shoulders slumped and she closed her eyes, releasing her breath.

'Come on,' I said, putting my glove back on. 'You can bring the tools.'

I gave her an axe and a shovel from the back of the barn and we went to the wrapped tarpaulin at the far end of the yard. I took the end in both hands and walked backwards, dragging it through the gate, to the edge of the trees.

Anna walked beside me while Tuzik followed, and when I broke the ground with the axe and dug a shallow grave, they watched in silence, Tuzik sitting motionless, Anna standing beside him with one hand on his head.

As I dug, I remembered how I done the same thing for my brother not long ago. I had broken the ground as the sleet came down, and the two women had watched from shelter. It occurred to me that I knew so very little about them.

When the grave was deep enough, I checked their pockets, removing all papers and belongings and putting them in my satchel. Then I rolled them into the hole to lie side by side under the trees. They looked small and insignificant like that, as if they didn't matter. I wondered who would miss them or if they'd even know they were gone.

The cold, black, rich soil was like heavy rain on their clothes as I shovelled it onto them, and when all I could see were their dead, white faces, I paused. I closed my eyes and touched the *chotki* round my wrist. I said a small prayer and wished them luck wherever they were going, then I threw the last of the soil over them and they were gone.

# 42

When we returned to the house, Oksana and her children were at the rear of the *izba*. Sergei and the old woman were at the table.

I stopped in the doorway, Anna beside me. Tuzik pushed past, coming into the warmth, and grunted as he lay down. He kept his head up and opened his mouth. The sound of his breathing filled the room.

I scanned the *izba*, my eyes meeting Oksana's, but Sergei and the old woman kept their heads bowed.

'We'll take some of your food,' I said, going to the cupboard, 'but not everything.'

I gathered some pickles, bread, sausage, *kovbyk* and a hessian bag filled with sunflower seeds. I stuffed what I could into my pockets and handed down supplies for Anna to carry.

'What will you do now?' Oksana's voice was quiet and husky, but it took us all by surprise.

I stopped with my hand still in the cupboard and turned to look at her. Tuzik was on his feet immediately. Anna inched closer to me.

'Just leave?' Oksana asked.

'Yes.'

'And do what?'

'Look for my wife and sons.' It wasn't Oksana's fault. She had not been responsible for her husband's madness, had even tried to warn us, but I couldn't hide the animosity in my voice. She was connected to him and he was no longer here to accept my anger.

'What about Anna?' She looked at the girl, who now moved so she was partly behind me. 'What will happen to her?'

'She'll come with me.' I took my arm from the cupboard and put it down to shield Anna.

Oksana took two hesitant steps towards us and stopped. She ran her hands down her apron. 'With you?'

'Yes.'

'Winter is almost here. How long do you think it will—'

'As long as it takes.'

She clasped her hands together, a troubled look on her face. 'It's no place for a young girl, out there in the cold with a man like you.'

'A man like me?'

'At least let her stay here for now. Come back when you've—'

'She's coming with me,' I said.

'But we can feed her, keep her warm. It'll be so cold soon; the snow has already started. You have to let her stay.'

'Do I?'

'She's just a child.'

'She's stronger than you think, and she knows her own mind.' I looked at Anna. 'What do *you* want to do?' I asked her.

'You were his wife,' Anna said, looking at Oksana. 'And she was his mama.' She pointed at the old woman without taking her eyes off Oksana. 'I'm not staying here. Not with you. I don't want anything from you. I want to be with Kolya.'

Oksana lowered her head and tightened her mouth and nodded once. She didn't speak again. She went back to her own children as we finished gathering what we needed.

Anna and I took a fair amount of what we found, leaving Oksana and her family enough to survive. Then we left the *izba*, with Tuzik following on our heels.

We went to the barn, and I lit a lamp and eased down to sit on a pile of straw and lean against the wall. My whole body ached and it was good to take the weight off my feet. I wanted to put my head back and close my eyes, but didn't dare, in case I fell asleep.

Anna sat beside me, stretching out her legs, and Tuzik came to lie along the side of them. Kashtan and the other two horses watched us as they chewed the hay Anna had put out for them earlier.

'How are you feeling?' I asked her.

'I'm all right.

'You sure? What you did—'

'What about you?' she asked. 'Doesn't it hurt?'

'Don't worry about me.' I put a hand to my nose, feeling the dried blood and realising what a mess I was. 'It probably looks worse than it is.' When I ran my tongue round my mouth, I felt the jagged edge of a broken tooth. 'But maybe we should talk about what hap—'

'I don't want to talk about that,' she said. 'Not now.' There was almost no expression in her voice. 'I was thinking there might be clues at the other farm,' she said. 'Where the soldiers were. There might be something there to tell you where they took your wife.'

I was taken aback. I had expected something else. A different reaction. This must be her way of putting it behind her, pretending it hadn't happened. Sooner or later, though, she would have to talk about it. She couldn't keep a thing like this inside her.

'Is it not a good idea?' She stared ahead and put out a hand to scratch Tuzik behind the ear.

'Yes. It is.' Then I thought about what we might find at the other farm. There wouldn't be more soldiers – I was certain that if there had been, they would have heard the shooting last night – but there might be something else. More bodies. The five-pointed brand Ryzhkov had used to mark his victims. The sword he had used to take their heads. This was not something I wanted Anna to see. She didn't need any more of this; she needed a home; she needed someone to look after her.

'We can take their equipment,' Anna suggested. 'It might help us.'

'I don't . . .' I searched for the right words. 'Do you . . . ?'

Anna continued to scratch Tuzik's ear.

'You don't like Oksana,' I said.

'No.'

'What about her children? Nikolai and Natasha?'

Anna shrugged.

I sighed. 'What I'm trying to say is, maybe she was right. Don't you think you might be better off without me?'

'Without you?' She turned to look at me, worry in her eyes. 'Why? What do you mean?'

'It's dangerous what I'm doing, where I might have to go. It's no life for you.'

'Don't you *want* me to come with you?'

'It's not that . . .'

'You promised.'

'I know, but don't you think you'd be safer here? With Oksana?'

'And the witch?' Anna glanced at the barn door as if she expected the old woman to come flying in like Baba Yaga.

'I don't think they'd hurt you. I think they're—'

'No. I want to go with you.' She shook her head with short, tight movements. 'I'm safer with you.'

'I hoped you would say that.'

'You can't go without me. Wherever it is. I want to help you. Promise you won't go without me. *Promise.*'

There was a desperation in her voice that I couldn't ignore. 'I promise,' I said.

Anna's relief was evident and I leaned over to kiss the top of her head. 'We'll find them together.'

'When will we leave? We should go soon, shouldn't we?'

'Yes. Soon.' I took off my satchel and put it on the ground between my outstretched legs. I opened it and removed the things I had taken from Tanya and Lyudmila's pockets.

'What's that?' Anna asked.

'They never told me who they were,' I said, staring at the papers, wondering if I wanted to look, if I wanted to know who they were. I didn't know if it would change what I thought of them. 'It doesn't make any difference,' I said under my breath.

'What?' Anna asked.

'Nothing.'

Tanya's belongings consisted of a tin containing only three cigarette papers and a pinch of tobacco. There was also a stripper clip of ammunition for her pistol, a folding knife, a small piece of cloth wrapped into a tiny bundle and tied with a piece of string, and her papers. The papers had been folded into a small rectangle and pushed to the bottom of her inside coat pocket and had been difficult to find. It seemed that she, unlike me, had been unable to part with them.

I placed the bundle of cloth on the ground and picked at the string to loosen it. I opened it out in front of me.

The glow from the lamp glinted on the matching pair of gold rings.

'Wedding rings,' I said, looking at Anna. 'Expensive too. Real gold.'

I pinched one of the rings between my finger and thumb, holding it up to the light and turning it before placing it in Anna's palm for her to see.

'Did she have children too?' she asked. 'Did that man . . . Is that why she wanted to kill him?'

'Yes.' I took the ring when she handed it back to me, then tied it back into the piece of cloth.

Next, I unfolded Tanya's papers and opened them out in front of me to look at what was left of her.

'Tatyana Maximovna Tikhonova.' I smiled to myself and tapped the paper. 'You see what it says here? She was gentry.'

Anna leaned over to see.

'Can you believe it? She was gentry. I knew she was educated, from a good family, but . . .' I put my head back and thought about when Tanya told me what had happened to her family. I had imagined she had lived in a good village, but the details in her papers said otherwise. Tanya was from a wealthy family; she wouldn't have lived in a village. She would have lived in a big country dacha, or a many-roomed house in one of the towns, depending on the season. She would have worn fine dresses and attended parties and talked about the latest poets and writers. That explained why Koschei had taken no prisoners. As an over-zealous revolutionary, he would have hated her privilege more than anything.

I realised how the revolution must have changed Tanya. It had not been kind to her and her family. She would have suffered even before Koschei descended upon her family, perhaps for years, and then he had come, and I would never know how she had survived *that* horror.

Tanya had never been a soldier. She was just a woman looking for revenge because she had nothing else left. Koschei had taken everything from her.

He had even taken away who she was.

I put the papers aside and turned my attention to the belongings from Lyudmila's pockets. Like Tanya, there was little there: a tobacco pouch, a smooth stone, a few coins, some pistol cartridges, her papers.

And a small fold of cloth tied with a piece of string.

I held the bundle in my open hand, reflecting that I knew even less about Lyudmila than I did about Tanya. She had never told me her motive for chasing Koschei, and I had always assumed it was from some allegiance to Tanya, but the fold of cloth suggested otherwise.

'Are you going to look?' Anna said.

I pinched it with my finger and thumb, feeling what was inside.

'Is it rings?' Anna asked. 'Like the other one?'

I picked away the knot and opened the bundle to reveal two gold rings. They were fine and expensive, just like Tanya's were.

'She was married too,' Anna said. 'Did *she* have children?'

'I don't know.' I retied the rings and placed the bundle beside Lyudmila's other belongings.

I studied the small collection of bits and pieces, sad to think how little it was to account for a person's life, and yet it had given me a greater insight into Lyudmila's truth than the woman herself had ever given me.

When I opened the tobacco pouch, and tipped it into the palm of my hand, something hard and yellowed poked from the small pile of tobacco. I picked it out between finger and thumb, and held the tooth up to the light. It was too small to have come from an adult and I knew it was a memory of her child. Lyudmila was cold and distant, and I had never liked her much, but as I held that tooth up to the light, I felt a tightening in my heart when I realised how wrong I had been about her. I had seen some evidence of softness when it came to Anna, but I had thought her childless and unable to understand my predicament. In fact, it was me who was unable to understand hers. There was a lot the three of us had not shared with each other, but there was one more surprise still to come.

I returned the tooth to the pouch and opened the papers that she, too, had folded into a small rectangle and hidden in her pocket. When I read her details, I understood what had brought the two women together.

Lyudmila Maximovna Morozova.

*Maximovna.*

It was too much of a coincidence for them to share a patronymic. As different as they seemed, they were bound together by blood.

Lyudmila and Tanya were sisters.

# 43

Anna and I returned to the edge of the forest. We went to the place where the sisters lay side by side, and we buried the rings and the tobacco pouch in the hardening soil.

I put my arm around Anna's shoulders and we stood side by side for a moment, neither of us speaking. I felt her breathing falter, coming in short gasps and I knew the tears were for her father. For me, there were no tears, but my heart was heavy with thoughts of my brother and Lev, and of the two women who had no one to mourn them but us.

Coming back to the barn, I led Kashtan out into the cold. She was eager to leave that place, but I had one last task for her.

'I'm sorry,' I told her, 'but I need you to do this for me. You're much stronger than I am.'

Anna helped me with the age-worn harness we found. Kashtan was not unaccustomed to pulling a load – she had pulled *ta-chanka* machine-gun carriages before – but this cart was loaded with the dead and she baulked as soon as we brought her close enough to smell the blood. Her muscles flexed and bulged under her taut chestnut coat as she backed away, but between us, Anna and I managed to keep her calm.

Anna had hitched a cart before, so she helped me hook up Kashtan while Tuzik sat on the ice and watched.

'It's not far,' I told Kashtan once we were ready. 'Just away from the house, that's all.'

Kashtan nuzzled at me and complied, as if telling me it was only this once, then Anna and I walked either side of her as we led her into the field. As soon as the cart was a safe distance from the house, I unfastened the harness and we led her back to the outbuilding, where we resaddled her and prepared her for the journey ahead.

I took from Tanya and Lyudmila's supplies whatever I thought we would need and put Lyudmila's rifle across my back.

'We'll leave the rest for Oksana and the others,' I told Anna. 'They'll need it now.' Without their son's protection, they were as susceptible as anyone else to the terrors of the war.

'What about the other horses?' she asked.

'Can you ride well?'

'Yes.'

'Then choose one and we'll leave the other. It'll only slow us down if we have to lead it.' I had a fleeting memory of leaving my brother's horse behind, but brushed it away and took out my tobacco pouch to roll a thin cigarette from the remnants I had found in Tanya and Lyudmila's belongings. I put it between my swollen lips and mounted up, feeling good to be on Kashtan's back. It meant we were, at least, moving again, leaving this place behind.

Anna inspected the other two animals, going to each one and rubbing its nose, looking over the tack before she decided which she was going to take.

'Are you sure you can manage that horse?' I asked, as she pulled herself into Tanya's saddle.

She shifted, turned the animal towards the door and looked at me.

'Of course you can,' I said.

'Do you know what its name is?' she asked.

I shook my head. 'We'll have to think of one.'

Anna and I crossed the yard, Tuzik trotting behind, and passed through into the field without looking back at the *izba*. We stopped when we reached the cart and I leaned down to dust away the frost in a small place at the back of it – just enough for me to strike a match against the coarse wood. As I blew the first lungful of smoke into the early morning air, I touched the tiny flame to the straw that covered the men and waited for it to take

363

hold. The fire needed no encouragement to devour the dry strands, and once the flame had grown, it spread and spread, catching on the men's clothes, dancing over their bodies. Black smoke, with sparks glowing and spitting in its heart, was snagged by the breeze and whipped low to the ground, thinning, moving over the field like a grey snake. Beyond it, over the distant farm, the low winter sun poured light through cloud and smoke and fire, reddening and casting a crimson glow across the yard and the field beyond, where the frost glistened red as if each crystal had been formed with the blood of men.

And in that unearthly hue, a shape began to form.

# 44

'There's something there,' Anna said.

'I see it.'

It was difficult to make it out. Maybe five hundred metres away, it blended well against the dark tangle of hedgerow behind it, and the sun was in my eyes, the colour dazzling. The smoke, too, was drifting about us now; the breeze was breaking it up as it came through the trees, catching the dark clouds in places, scattering the snake in swirls and twists.

Four hundred metres.

I put a hand to my brow and squinted to see the shape move, split, become more than one.

'Riders,' I said.

They had been moving in a column but had now separated, moving out in a line across the field.

Kashtan shifted, moving sideways.

'I know,' I whispered, and patted her neck.

'Should we run?' Anna asked.

'There's nowhere for us to go. We can't outrun them. We can't go back to the *izba*. We'll have to meet them; see what they want.'

'Are they the ones who were following us?'

The smoke thinned, the grey and black mass weakening. I didn't dare take my eyes off the shapes as they moved towards us across the field.

Three hundred metres.

'I think they might be. How many do you count, Anna?'

'Seven.' She controlled her horse well, keeping beside me.

Two hundred metres.

'It's all right, Anna. We're going to be fine.' I pulled the revolver from my pocket and held it resting along my right thigh.

One hundred metres.

The pounding of hooves on hard ground joined the cracking and popping of burning wood behind us.

'Stay calm,' I told Kashtan, and I forced my fear deep, pushing it away for all of us. If I was confident, Kashtan and Anna would be too.

The riders were easier to make out now. The smoke still drifted, the sparks still danced, but now the men were men rather than just shapes in the distance.

The rider in the centre raised a hand and the line of riders came to a halt just twenty metres from our position. Each of them was holding a rifle pointed forward, and as soon as they were still, they released the reins of their mounts and steadied their weapons with both hands.

The air was quiet but for the crackle of the fire and the breathing of the horses. They had ridden hard across the field and their hot breath came heavy, drifting from flaring nostrils like the smoke that swirled about them.

The rider who had raised his hand nudged his horse forward. He was a lean man, tall enough to look strange in the saddle, as if his horse were too small. He was gaunt, with yellowish waxy skin over drawn features, and his eyes stared in a permanent bulge from their sockets. He wore a thick, dark winter coat over his Chekist uniform, and on his head was a fox-fur hat. The breeze rippled in the soft fur, blowing through the dark hairs to the white below. His rifle remained on his back, but in his hand he held a pistol. At his waist, he wore a sword. If ever a man had been born into the image of Koschei the Deathless, it was this one.

Krukov.

He brought his horse forward so its nose was alongside Kashtan's, and when he stopped, he spoke to me without expression. 'Commander Levitsky. You're a hard man to follow.'

'I tried.'

'What happened to your face?'

'It's a long story.'

He looked me up and down. 'For some of the men, it was easier to believe you were dead. They didn't want to believe you were a deserter, but I never doubted that you were still alive.'

'How did you know?'

'You forget I've known you a long time. It was me who cut the bullet from your wound.' He touched a finger to the soft part of his stomach, just below his ribs. 'The bodies we found might have had your papers and uniforms, but they didn't fool me for a second.'

'And you've been following me all this time?'

Krukov looked at Anna for the first time. He showed no emotion, but studied her as if she were a curiosity. He nodded. 'All this time.'

Anna stared at him, showing no hint of backing down. When faced with the kind of hardship she had endured, there comes a point for every person at which they must make a choice: to give up or to dig in. Anna had chosen to dig in.

'To what end?' I asked. 'What happens now?'

He stroked his beard with a gloved hand but said nothing as he watched her.

'Koschei is dead,' I told him.

He was not surprised. 'On the fire?'

'Yes.'

'And the others?' He turned back to me, his expression still devoid of emotion. Krukov was a proud and principled man, and I had seldom seen him let down his guard. He never gave anything away that he didn't want to. 'Dead too?'

'Yes.'

'They were not good men.'

'You're in charge of this unit now, Commander Krukov. That's how it should be.'

'No. It should be you.' He fixed his eyes on mine.

'It's not how I thought it was. I've seen things that change it all.

We're not saving our country; we're killing her. Men like Ryzhkov are killing her. Do you know the things he's done?'

'Yes.'

'And you didn't try to stop him?'

'I thought about it, but then I was following *you*.'

'On *his* orders?'

'We had both lost our commanders; he was the senior soldier. I never wanted to take orders from him.'

'But you had to.' I had heard that sentiment before. Commander Orlov had been the same. He followed orders because it was his duty to follow them and because there were consequences for men who did not. 'And he wanted you to come after me.'

'Yes, and I wanted to come. Some of the men too. We talked; they volunteered.'

'What about Ryzhkov's comrades? Any of them come with you?'

'Two of them. They aren't good men either.'

Only two of them were with Krukov. Including the four who had been at the farm, that gave him only six men from his original unit, but there had been more when we merged. The rest must have been with the prisoners, taking them to a holding camp. At least Ryzhkov had only been half lying about that. I wondered if they were due to return at any time soon.

'You know what happens to deserters,' Krukov said.

'I know.'

'It would have been easier if you had died.'

'I am dead. At least, I *can* be. If you would let me be.' Deserters could be hunted. Dead men could only be mourned and forgotten.

Krukov blinked hard and tightened his mouth further.

'My family was taken from a village called Belev. If you've been following me, you will have seen it.'

'There have been so many villages.'

'My wife and sons were there. Ryzhkov took them.'

'Where is Alek?'

'Dead.'

'And Ryzhkov took *your* wife and sons?' Krukov looked me up and down once more, then nudged his horse even closer. 'Are they alive?'

'I think so. I hope so.' I gripped the revolver harder, my finger tightening on the trigger.

'I'm sorry, Commander.'

'It's just Nikolai now. Kolya.'

Krukov backed away, keeping his eyes on me, then he turned his horse and rode to the other men. He spoke for some time with the two men in the centre of the line, while the others maintained their positions facing us.

When he had finished his conversation, Krukov rode along the line, going to one of the men at the end and speaking briefly before the man passed something to him. Krukov set the object on the saddle in front of him, then turned his horse in our direction.

As he returned, the two riders from the centre of the line broke away and followed, coming either side as he reached us. They were the two men he had spoken to at length, men whose faces were in shadow beneath hats, but as they came closer, I wondered if I had seen them before. Something about them was familiar.

Both men wore a winter coat, and each of them had a leather cap pulled low on his brow. The front of each cap bore the red star. The same image I had seen branded into my children's eyes in my nightmares.

The older of the two men had a weather-beaten face, and a look of boredom about him, the way he slouched in the saddle. A scar ran from his left eye and disappeared at his cheekbone, where it was covered by a beard that had been allowed to grow wild. The other was clean-shaven and thick-featured with a firm, square jaw. He was a good-looking man, the kind whose representation wouldn't look out of place on a propaganda poster.

It was the bearded one who spoke first as he caught up with Krukov, saying, 'What's going on, Commander? Why did you want to know about—' As soon as he saw the revolver in my hand, he raised his rifle and pointed it at me. 'Drop your weapon.'

Krukov was sitting still in the saddle, one hand on the reins, the other holding his pistol, resting on the item he had brought: a large bag, shaped like a sack but made from stout green canvas, tied with a piece of frayed cord.

'Drop it *now*,' said the scarred man.

'Who are you?' I asked him. 'You're not in charge.'

'This is Stepan Ivanovich,' said Krukov, tilting his head to the man at his left, 'and my other comrade is Artem Andreyovich.'

'Ryzhkov's men?' I asked. That's why I had recognised them.

'We are all of the same unit,' Krukov replied. 'These men volunteered to join the search for you.' When he said the word 'volunteered', there was a hint of sarcasm in his voice. Krukov was not an emotional man – he gave little away in his expressions and intonation– but I had known him long enough to understand that he didn't like Stepan Ivanovich and Artem Andreyovich. Krukov would have preferred to lead just the men he knew. Like me, he would have felt uneasy having strangers at his side, especially ones who were loyal to a man like Ryzhkov. Krukov would see them as spies in his ranks. He would not have liked having them in his unit.

'Why didn't you take his weapon?' Stepan asked Krukov. 'And where's Koschei?'

'Ryzhkov's not here,' Krukov said.

'He's gone ahead to the camp, you mean? That's where he is?' Stepan's words made me look to Krukov.

'Exactly. He's taken the prisoners to the holding camp.' Krukov spoke slowly and with emphasis.

'So what are we waiting for?' Stepan Ivanovich snapped the rifle tighter to his shoulder and glanced sideways at Krukov.

Neither Krukov nor I spoke.

'You want me to get a rope,' asked Artem Andreyovich, 'or you want to shoot him?'

'Wait.' Krukov raised his left hand and made a circling motion in the air. Immediately the other riders came forward.

For a moment the approaching men were silhouettes against the sun. They moved well in the saddle as they crossed the blood frost, and like the others, I saw their faces only when they were almost upon us. They were four faces I recognised: Bukharin, Manarov, Repnin and Nevsky. Four men who had served with me for many years. Four men whom I had loved like brothers but now thought me a traitor and were bound to execute me for treason.

When they were almost upon us, they split, riding in pairs to either end of the line and moving inwards to form a semicircle round Anna and me. We were hemmed in now. No escape.

'We have a choice to make,' Krukov said. His voice was hoarse, as if he needed to clear it.

'You mean bullet or rope?' Artem Andreyovich smiled at the prospect.

'We should wait for Koschei,' said Stepan. 'Or take him to the camp. He'll want his head.'

Now Krukov took his eyes off me. He shifted in the saddle and turned first to look left along the line, then right along the line. When he faced forwards once more, he took a deep breath. 'Koschei is dead.'

'What?' There was a flash of confusion in Stepan's eyes, followed by a glint of understanding, but before he could react, Krukov raised his pistol to point directly at his chest.

As soon as he did it, the two men at either end of the line turned their weapons on Stepan and Artem.

'What is this?' Stepan demanded. 'What the hell is going on?'

'I don't trust you men,' Krukov said. 'I never did. You are no longer needed in this unit.'

'You can't do this.'

'Who's going to stop me?'

Stepan tore his eyes from Krukov and looked at me along the barrel of his rifle. 'I could kill him now. I'd be a hero.'

'No, you'd just be a dead man,' Krukov said. 'Or you could ride away. Right now.'

'And you'd just let us go?' Artem asked.

Krukov thought for a moment. 'No,' he said. 'No, I wouldn't.' And he shot Stepan through the heart.

# 45

Krukov was quick. He didn't wait to watch Stepan's death. As soon as he fired the first shot, he swept his pistol across his body, bringing it round to aim at Artem, who was so surprised that he'd barely moved. Without wasting a second, Krukov pulled the trigger, jolting Artem's head back as the bullet tore into his skull.

The suddenness of the gunshots unnerved the horses. They were hardened animals, all of them accustomed to the crack of gunfire, but they still moved beneath us, forcing us to bring them under control. I didn't want Anna to see such things, but if it bothered her, she didn't show it. She just lowered her head so she didn't have to look, and she concentrated on controlling Tanya's horse.

With no living riders, Stepan and Artem's animals bolted away from us. Stepan's forced its way between Anna and me, racing off in the direction of the *izba*, while the other went round us, galloping off towards the forest. I didn't turn to watch either of them go; they were of no consequence. What mattered now were the remaining soldiers.

But none of them made a move to turn his weapon on me. Each of them settled his horse as if rider and animal shared a firm bond, and when all was still, Krukov holstered his weapon and came forward.

'I've been with these men a long time, just as you had. I think I know their minds well enough to speak for all of us.' He took a folded document from his pocket and held it out to me. 'Whatever your reasons for leaving, there isn't one of us who would call you unpatriotic.'

'Never,' said Bukharin, and the others nodded in agreement.

I took the document and unfolded it to look at the identity papers I had left on a disfigured body in Ulyanov a thousand years ago.

'I kept them for you,' Krukov said. 'And these belonged to Alek.' He passed my brother's papers to me, but I didn't open them. That was for another time.

He took the bag from the saddle in front of him and passed it across to me. 'Before he died, Stepan Ivanovich was good enough to tell me that a day's ride north from here is a ruined village called Nagai,' he said.

I took the bag and opened it to find it filled with clothing.

'In the forest just north of Nagai, there is a holding camp for conscripts and exiles,' Krukov went on. It was usual for Cheka units to set up temporary camps to contain prisoners before allocation to units, deportation or transportation to labour camps. There was one such labour camp near Kaluga, but this area was much further north than I had operated as a Chekist. I was unfamiliar with the camps here.

I took the first garment out of the bag.

'It's my thinking that a Chekist commander could go into that camp and take away anybody he wanted.'

I looked up at Krukov.

'For any purpose,' he said. 'As long as he has papers and a uniform.'

I held up the uniform and studied it for a moment. When I lowered it, Krukov and the other men were watching me.

Krukov cleared his throat and spoke again. 'When do you want to leave?' he asked. 'Your men are waiting for your orders, Commander Levitsky.'

# 46

It felt strange to be on the open road with a small company of men behind me. For so long I had kept to the forests, stealing across the country as a fugitive, but now I was a soldier again. There was no reason not to keep to the roads now, and our progress was swift as we moved from road to field, heading towards Nagai, our horses scattering the thin layer of snow and ice underfoot.

Anna rode beside me, more resilient than I could have imagined, but her manner both uplifted and saddened me. She was tough, and that would serve her well; she would not be a burden to me or the other men, but she was a child. A twelve-year-old girl who should have been playing with her friends, arguing with her mother and twisting her father round her little finger. She shouldn't have been riding with a company of armed men.

Yet I was as proud of her as it was possible to be. I would protect her as I would protect my own child, and I was glad she had not stayed behind with Oksana and the old woman. Anna and I had been together a few days that had lasted a lifetime, and the prospect of never seeing her pale face again was one that haunted me when I allowed my mind to linger on it.

Krukov rode on the other side of me, stiff-backed in the saddle, gaunt and bearded as if I was crossing the country with Koschei the Deathless himself. But Koschei was a fairy tale. A myth. He didn't exist; at least not in that sense.

Ryzhkov was close to the truth when he said that we were all Koschei because we were all capable of terrible things, but he had tried to take the name for himself and was now turning to ash in a nameless field. There had been nothing arcane about finding the key to his death. Ryzhkov had died like any man dies. Just as Koschei always died in the *skazkas*.

We stopped by a river at midday to eat and to rest the horses. My wife and sons were almost within reach now, but the horses were tired, and Anna was beginning to look as if she might fall asleep in the saddle.

The steppe was open in all directions, dull now that the sun was lost behind another wall of grey cloud, which threatened to bring more snow. Grass grew thick and long around the river-bank, but the ground was at a gentle slope and the water was shallow, so we led our horses to drink. It was the first time we had dismounted since meeting Krukov, and Anna positioned herself so she and I were side by side, sandwiched between our horses, and she could take the chance to speak to me alone.

'I don't trust them,' she whispered. 'And that man Krukov is more frightening than the old woman at the farm.'

'I don't think they mean us any harm.' I stopped at the edge of the river and watched the current swirl and eddy. 'They would have done something already if they were going to.' I felt as if I was trying to persuade myself.

'So we're staying with them?'

'I've known these men a long time – we've been through a lot together.' Two of them had been at Grivino with Alek and me. Krukov and Bukharin had stood by my side.

She made a face and released her horse's reins so it could dip its head to drink. 'Well, it makes my back tingle, having them behind us.'

I smiled. 'I know what you mean.'

'So can't we ride at the back?'

As Kashtan drank, I scanned the steppe behind for any sign of Tuzik. He had kept pace with us for a while, but he didn't have the strength or stamina of a horse so he had soon fallen behind.

'He'll catch up,' Anna told me. 'He always does.'

I nodded. 'You're right.' I squatted and dipped my hands into the icy river, downstream from the spot where the horses were drinking. I scooped the water and splashed it onto my face, rubbing away the dry blood and letting the cold numb my nose and mouth.

'How do I look?' I turned my face towards Anna.

'Not good. Your lip's fat, and you have a black eye. Your nose is bruised too.'

'It feels worse,' I said, standing and taking a cloth from the saddlebag to dry my face. If I left it, the water would most probably freeze.

'So *can* we?' she asked.

'Hmm?'

'Ride at the back? It would be safer for us to be behind them.'

'The thing is, Anna . . .' I looked about. Krukov was no more than a couple of metres away on the other side of Kashtan, so I lowered my voice further. 'I'm their commander. They expect me to lead from the front.'

'But *are* you, or are they lying?'

'Well, I don't think they're lying. I've known these men a long time.'

'But they might be. And if you're the commander, you can do what you want.'

'If only that were true. No, if I ride behind them, they'll think I don't trust them and so they won't trust me. It's . . . complicated.'

'Well, I don't like it.'

'Then we need to remain alert and keep watching. And stay close to me. Don't ever leave my sight. Here.' I took Tanya's folding knife from my satchel and held it out to her. 'Put this somewhere handy. Just in case.'

I didn't anticipate that she would ever need it, but it would make her feel safer, and soon, there might come a time when I would have to leave her alone with some of these men.

Anna took it without hesitation, turning it over in her hands and slipping it into her pocket.

'You know what I was, don't you?' I said.

'You mean a soldier?'

'But you know what *kind* of soldier.'

376

'Yes.'

'But I'm not a bad person. I don't want you to think I'm a bad person. I've done—'

'I know what you are,' Anna said. 'You're not a bad man. Papa liked you.'

'That's good,' I said. 'I liked him too. Very much. And thank you.'

'For what?'

'For what you did in the *izba*.'

'I don't want to talk about that,' she said.

'All right. I understand.'

The men had few supplies, so when we rejoined them, Anna and I shared what we had. They took the opportunity to speak with me, shaking my hand, patting me on the back and saying how good it was to have me as their commander once again.

'But you've been hunting me all this time,' I said.

'You were in no danger,' Bukharin said. 'Not from us.' He was one of the men I had known the longest – a subordinate, but with as much experience as I had. Bukharin fought in the war before the revolution, joined the people's army rather than be conscripted. He was more a soldier than anyone I knew, but had always shown more loyalty to his unit than to Moscow. He had been a good man to have with me at Grivino.

'You could have just let me go. Gone back to Ryzhkov to tell him I was dead.'

'He wanted you alive,' said Manarov. 'Or proof that you were dead.'

'What kind of proof?'

The men looked around at each other.

'Your head.'

Then I understood how truly afraid my men had been of Koschei. Now there was an air of relief about them, as if a burden had been lifted from their shoulders, and I imagined them pursuing me, all the time wondering what they would do if they caught me.

'Did you let me get ahead?' I asked. 'You let me escape you?'

377

'Not really,' Manarov said with a shrug. 'Sometimes you were clumsy, but mostly you were almost impossible to follow. In the forest, you were like a ghost.'

I smiled and clapped him on the shoulder. 'You're too kind.'

The men tried to talk to Anna, showing a kindness I had hardly known in them, reminding me that they were also brothers and father and sons. As a unit, we had taken our job seriously and had gathered conscripts and punished deserters just as we were supposed to, but we had not been animals. I had become caught up in my duty, as these men had, but I had woken to the horror of what was being done across our country and I wondered if these men's eyes had been opened too. Perhaps they had seen enough to instil in them a little compassion. Or perhaps they were just loyal men taking care of their commander's ward.

Even so, Anna did not speak to any of them. Not a single word.

They put down a tarpaulin for her to sit on, but she refused to leave my side, sitting only when I did. When they made a fire to boil tea, she drank only when I did. One of the men, Nevsky, even brought a medical bag, offering to check her over, but she refused, staring at him and narrowing her eyes in distrust.

Krukov sat beside me, the breeze ruffling his fox-fur hat, and watched her without expression. 'She's the child from the farm?' he asked.

'That's right.'

'We thought she was a boy. What happened to the man who was there?'

I shook my head.

Krukov adjusted his hat. 'I'm sorry.'

'I didn't leave because I'm a coward,' I said. 'I'm not a coward.'

'I know that.'

'I shouldn't have gone, though. If I hadn't, none of this would have happened.'

'Or perhaps it would have happened in a different way,' Krukov said. He removed his gloves and tore a chunk of bread in two, offering one of the pieces to me.

I took it and stared at the river. It was beautiful, the sun reflecting from its surface, the water still chasing through the wide channel. A few more weeks and the worsening weather would freeze it right down to the bed. The cold would halt all nature but man.

'Why did Ryzhkov send you after me?' I asked, still watching the water. 'Why not come himself?'

'He did.' Krukov took a bite of the bread and reached for a piece of *salo*. 'At first, anyway.'

'You told him I was still alive?'

'It was my duty.'

I took my eyes off the river and looked at Krukov sitting beside me. His sunken cheeks were corpse-like, tight around angular cheekbones. His eyes were almost too large for their sockets, bulging, and his lips were thin. If any one had told me this man was Koschei, I would have believed it. He had the look, the cold disposition, the literal interpretation of orders. For a moment I felt uneasy in his presence, wondering if I had been fooled. It wouldn't be the first time I discovered that someone wasn't who they said they were. Perhaps Ryzhkov had lied. Perhaps he had been protecting Krukov's true identity. Perhaps it was *he* who was afraid of Koschei.

My mind spun as it tried to follow the endless strands woven into the blanket of deceit that smothered us. I felt as if I would never be certain of anything again. Everything was a lie. Everything was shrouded in dishonesty. Everyone was hiding something.

'Are you all right?' Krukov asked.

'Of course.' It was a ridiculous notion. If Krukov was Koschei, he would have killed me by now, and the deception would be too elaborate. I couldn't let go of it, though. Everyone was someone else. It almost hurt to think about it. All I wanted was to be alone with my family, to put the world behind me and find a place where a man is just a man. A friend is a friend.

'I had to tell him,' Krukov said. 'Without you, he was my superior.'

'I understand.' Disobeying orders was a capital offence.

379

Ryzhkov had been commander of his unit before it was attached to mine, so when I was no longer there, leadership fell to him. The Red Army had done away with rank and title, but it could not do away with leaders. Without leaders, an army was just a rabble.

Krukov studied the bread in his hand as if he were thinking hard about something, and when he looked back up at me, his expression had softened.

'All my life I followed orders,' he said. 'I was never in command . . .'

'You're a good soldier.'

'Let me finish.' Krukov reached into his pocket and took out a flask, which he opened and raised to me. 'Alek,' he said. Then he put it to his lips and drank. He grimaced and offered it to me. 'Vodka.'

'Alek,' I toasted, and drank. It stung the cuts and swellings in my mouth, burned as it went down, but it spread a good warmth in my chest. I passed it back and bit into the black bread as Krukov returned the flask to his pocket.

'I always followed orders,' he said, 'always trusted my senior officer, so when I realised it wasn't you in that ditch in Ulyanov, it was like you'd betrayed me. I was angry, so I reported it to my new commander, Ryzhkov, and we came after you right away. Ryzhkov was . . . His behaviour was strange. He was like a man whose wife has cheated on him. I had never seen anything like it. I think he admired you.'

I remembered what Ryzhkov had said to me in the *izba* last night. It felt like it was a long time ago, but it was only a matter of hours since he had told me how I had disappointed him.

'We received orders to crush the local peasants,' Krukov said. 'There had been resistance to grain and animal requisitions, and the Bolsheviks were afraid the uprising was spreading.' He took a deep breath. 'So we went into the first village we came to.' Once more he reached into his pocket for the flask and I noticed his hand was shaking when he drank from it and offered it to me.

'That's when we saw what kind of man Ryzhkov was; what kind of unit he was leading.'

'It wasn't your fault,' I said. 'You didn't know.'

'We should have stopped him.'

I realised that the other men had grown silent and were listening to Krukov. When I glanced around at them, none of them would meet my gaze. The river, the open steppe and the road cutting through it had become fascinating to them.

'They took the boys and some of the women. Others they . . .' He looked at Anna, then lowered his voice and leaned closer to me. 'They raped them. Shot the men, hanged them . . . Ryzhkov himself flayed an old man's hand. And there was that brand. The star that—'

'I've seen the things they did,' I told him.

'But you didn't see their faces when they did it. You didn't hear them laugh. I couldn't believe what I was seeing, couldn't believe that my commander would . . . He was like an animal. Like the devil. Like—'

'Koschei,' I said.

Krukov shook his head. 'He was worse than that.'

He held his hands out in front of him, fingers outstretched, as if he had just noticed they were shaking, then he clenched them into fists and held them tight to his thighs. 'When we left the village, I told him it was wrong, so he went ahead to the next village and sent me to find you alone.'

'You're lucky he didn't try to kill you.' I kept my tone flat, so he didn't hear the question in it. If Krukov had disagreed with a man like Ryzhkov, I was surprised he had just let him go.

'I think he wanted to. I saw him kill one of his own men for disobeying an order to . . .' He noticed Anna watching him. 'Well, it doesn't matter.'

'So what stopped him?' I asked. 'From trying to kill you?'

Krukov looked at the others sitting with us. 'Loyal men, I suppose. He knew these men might support me, and he didn't want to fight soldiers – that wasn't his style.'

'But he sent a couple of his men to watch you?'

'Yes.'

'He should have sent more.'

Krukov allowed a wry smile to show, the first sign of emotion, but it was gone in a second. 'Some of the men were taken in by him and stayed. Dotsenko—'

'I saw him. After the farm, there was a train in the forest.'

'We saw it too. All those wounded men. How was Stas?'

'Dead.'

Krukov sighed. 'It was as if Ryzhkov had put a spell on them, convinced them they were doing revolutionary work.'

'But not you?' I asked. 'He didn't convince you?'

Krukov shook his head. 'Not me.' He looked around. 'Not us.'

I hoped he was right. All it would take was for one of them to share his twisted idea of patriotism, for one of them to turn his weapon on me.

'I never had any intention of executing you as a deserter,' he said.

'You're sure about that?'

'Maybe at first. It was a crime. I thought you were a coward, but then . . . the more we saw . . .' He shook his head. 'You're a better man than he ever was. You're the commander of this unit, and now you're back where you belong.'

It took a moment for his words to sink in.

'You want me to take command of this unit again?' I couldn't quite believe what he was saying. I couldn't let everything turn in a circle; all that death and nothing gained.

'Of course. If you come back now, no one need ever know you left. Ryzhkov and the others are dead now.'

I swallowed my words. This was not the best time to tell Krukov I had no intention of commanding this unit again. I wanted a life of peace; to forget the things I had done, to atone for them by taking care of my family as a father and a husband. I wanted to leave the soldier behind, but I didn't know how Krukov would react. He was giving me a chance to come back, but if I refused, perhaps he would turn on me as Ryzhkov had done.

My trial wasn't over. I wasn't done with the soldier just yet, and it was likely there was more blood to be spilled.

'Maybe we should go,' I said, standing up.

Krukov stood too, coming to attention. 'It's time to put on your uniform,' he said.

# 47

Nagai was barely recognisable as a village. There was no life there. Not even a dog strolled in what was left of the street, but it was not like it had been when I arrived in Belev. Not one of the houses here was intact, not a wall left standing. The husks of the buildings were blackened, collapsed in on themselves or blown out into pieces, and there was rubble all about: cracked stones, crumbled bricks, charred beams, broken fences. The ground was a mess of craters big enough to swallow a man, and the air was thick with the scent of old smoke. Last night's snow had settled in places, stark against the burned wood that lay all about.

'Shellfire,' Krukov said, as we rode among the ruins, sweeping our eyes around the destruction. 'They didn't stand a chance.'

'I wonder which side it was,' said Nevsky from behind me.

'What difference does it make?' I asked. 'People are people.'

Krukov glanced across at me. 'Those who oppose the revolution must be . . .'

'Crushed?' I said.

He clenched his teeth and the muscles at the side of his jaw bulged.

'Would it not be better if we could just live in peace?' I suggested.

'Once the counter-revolutionaries are quiet, then there will be peace. We remove the weeds and the crop grows strong, right?'

I sighed and shook my head. 'That's too much black and white.'

'No, for him there's only red,' Bukharin said, making some of the men laugh.

Krukov cast a stern look at them. 'I saw the wrong in Ryzhkov,' he said, looking at me once more. 'The war is only against those who bear arms.'

'And those who refuse to give up their grain?' I asked. 'Do they not need to be crushed too?'

'They need to be educated,' he said. 'Not crucified and tortured.'

'And how can they be educated?' I asked.

'Labour. It's the great leveller. No man is better than another when there is sweat on his brow and he's working for the good of the people.'

'Like my family?' I asked. 'They should be in a labour camp, should they?'

'No, I . . .' He shook his head. 'Everything used to make sense.'

'Yes, it did,' I agreed.

We came to a halt among the ruins, where what remained of the road cut through them, passing back onto the steppe and curving round the forest to the north.

'It should be in there,' Krukov said. 'Among the trees.'

Among the trees, I thought. Would I ever get away from them?

'All right, then,' I said, feeling my anticipation build. 'Repnin and Manarov, you come with us. Bukharin, I want you and Nevsky to stay here with Anna. Guard her with your lives.'

'I won't stay with them,' she said, refusing to dismount. 'I won't let you leave me.'

'Anna.'

'You can't go without me.'

So I asked her to ride to the end of the village with me, alone.

'This is going to be dangerous,' I told her.

'I don't mind. As long as I'm with you, I'll be fine.'

Her confidence in me made me feel good, proud even, but this was not a time for pride.

'What I mean is that *you'll* make it dangerous. You see, a commander riding into a camp is one thing, but a commander riding into a camp with a child is something else altogether. People will wonder why you are there. They may ask awkward questions. Remember when I spoke to the Cossacks? This is no different.'

'You're a Chekist commander,' she said. 'You can tell them whatever you like.'

'No one is immune,' I said. 'No one is safe. You have to stay. I'm sorry.'

Anna said nothing. She pouted and stared ahead, reminding me she was only twelve years old.

'I'll be as quick as I can. The camp won't be far into the forest. It won't take long.'

'I won't talk to them.'

'You don't have to. In fact, I don't want you to.'

She looked at me like she didn't understand.

'I want you to keep away from them, and I'll tell them to keep away from you.'

'Why? I thought you trust them?'

'I do. I *want* to. I *think* I trust them, but they want me to lead them again and—'

'You're not going to, are you?'

'No. And I don't know what they'll do if they find out, so you keep apart, and if anything happens, I want you to ride away as fast as you can. I'll find you.'

'Out here?'

'Tuzik will help me. He'll catch up soon.'

'What if he follows me?'

'He won't. He'll be looking for me.'

Anna bit her lip as she thought about what I'd said. 'You *will* come back?' she asked.

'I promise.'

She closed her eyes and nodded. 'All right.'

With that settled, we turned and headed back to where the others were waiting. I was eager to find the camp, and the day was drawing to its close. We had to leave soon.

'How many will there be?' Anna asked as we rode. 'How many prisoners at the camp?'

'I don't know.'

'Where will they all go?'

At first, I didn't understand her question and I repeated it to myself, wondering what she meant, but then it struck me that my intention today was not exactly what Anna thought it was.

I stopped Kashtan and leaned back to look at the sky. I took off my hat and ran a hand over my head before turning to her. 'I won't be bringing everyone out. Only Marianna and the boys.'

'You mean you're going to leave everyone else? That's . . .' she searched for the right word, '. . . that's unfair.'

'Yes, it is, and I'm sorry for them, but it's the way it has to be. I can't save everyone, Anna.'

'*I* would try.'

'That's because you're a better person than I am.'

The sun was setting over the forest as we approached the trees, and when we rode into the woods, following a narrow trail, everything darkened around us.

An eerie silence fell over the world as the clouds thickened and the second snow of winter began to fall. This time it was heavier, though, the flakes softer, like countless feathers filling the air between the trees. They rode the gentle currents, settling on naked branches, cheerful against the darkness of the oak and chestnut and maple, beautiful against the stubborn colours of the evergreens.

I glanced back at Krukov, his horse just a length behind Kashtan, Repnin and Manarov following, and I wondered what he was thinking. It occurred to me that he could be leading me into a trap, enticing me into the forest to take my head or nail me to a tree. Krukov was a soldier and a patriot. He might not have considered himself a thinker or a leader, but he was a true believer. He still saw righteousness in the war. He still thought a deserter was a deserter rather than a man who had seen and done enough to want just a little peace.

Then I told myself that if he was going to kill me, he would not have come this far with me. No, he wanted to help me. He wanted to assist in putting Marianna and the boys in their rightful place so that he could see me put in mine: at the head of this unit. I only hoped that once I had found my family, I could persuade him to see things differently.

I didn't want to have to kill him.

No more than three hundred metres inside the forest, the camp had been invisible from the ruins of Nagai. As we drew nearer, we heard sounds of life – the low hubbub of voices, the occasional shout or the clatter of metal on metal – and I formed a picture of what this place would look like. I had seen many transit camps and they had all been similar: small, squalid affairs more fit for animals than for people. The prisoners they housed were criminals, enemies of the state who deserved no better.

Or so I had always thought.

This camp was new, though, much larger than I had expected. It must have taken a great team of labourers to fell so many trees and turn them into the log cabins that stood here in the forest. The inner compound, surrounded by a high wire fence, contained eight buildings large enough to house twenty people each. They were arranged in two rows with a cleared area in front of them that was now filled with prisoners milling about in the falling snow, huddled together for warmth because they would be locked out of the huts for most of the day. I sat a little higher in my saddle as we approached, trying to spot Marianna among them.

I touched the *chotki* and prayed she was here.

*He likes to drown the women.*

My heart was beating as hard now as it had ever beaten in battle. I could feel it racing in my chest, forcing blood to every part of my body so that my muscles prickled with anticipation. I fought to keep calm, to keep from spurring Kashtan into a gallop.

I was moments away from what I had longed for.

*If she's here.*

*Please let her be here.*

Directly outside the secured inner compound, two more snow-capped buildings provided barracks for the soldiers who were posted here to guard the camp, and there was a smaller cabin for the commander. The whole area was then surrounded by another fence, at least ten or twelve metres high, that ran in a square round the entire camp. Outside the fence, the trees had been felled so that none overhung the fence, and at each corner, a watchtower stood half as tall as the trees. In each tower, a guard stood watch.

'All this for a few harmless peasants,' I said.

'What's that you said?' Krukov asked.

'Nothing.'

The entrance to the camp was made up of two gates, one at either end of a ten-metre run that served as a corral. Anyone coming in had to pass through an outer gate, which was then closed behind them before the final approach to the second gate that gave access to the camp.

This final approach was overlooked by guard towers.

The path we were following through the forest began to widen, and I followed it to the outer gate, beside which there was a small guardhouse.

'I want you to follow my lead,' I said to Krukov as he came alongside me. 'Is that understood?'

'Of course, Commander.'

'Stay calm,' I whispered to Kashtan, reaching down to pat her neck. 'Stay calm.'

I rode straight to the front gate and stopped, Krukov beside me, Repnin and Manarov behind.

Before I could call out, a guard emerged from the hut, dressed for cold weather in a coat and *budenovka* hat. The material was as black as poppy seeds, not at all faded, and the star on the front of it was red like blood. In his hands, he held a Mosin-Nagant dragoon like the one I had given to Lev.

'Comrade Commander,' he said, looking me over, taking note of my uniform.

No longer was I dressed as a peasant, trying to remain unnoticed. Now I wore the uniform I had left on the body of a disfigured man in a distant and unwanted past. The uniform Krukov had returned to me and wanted me to wear as I led him through the remainder of this war.

The brown coat was much warmer than the one I had taken

from the peasant, but it felt wrong to be wearing the insignia of the Red Army, which was sewn on the arms and lapels. It reminded me of the raw and festering star Ryzhkov had branded into his victims. And the bright red button loops and lapel-tips seemed to draw attention to themselves, like blood in the snow.

Beneath the coat, I wore the uniform and long, black boots I had thought never to see again, and over it, I wore a Mauser pistol, which denoted my position, holstered in its wooden case and clipped to the leather strap that crossed my chest. Rather than a red-starred *budenovka*, I wore a black leather cap with a short peak, which dipped to a spot just above my eyes. The leather was old and faded, and the star adorning it had lost its lustre.

'We weren't expecting anyone today,' the guard said, putting a hand to his brow to keep the snow from his eyes. 'Shit. What happened to you?'

'Do you always know when someone is coming?' I replied, looking down at him. I was a Chekist commander now, not a nervous husband or a worried father.

He hesitated. 'No, comrade.'

'Then stop talking and let me in. Or do you want to join the prisoners inside?' I stared down at him, and Krukov did the same. I could only imagine how we must have looked to the young man. Battle-hardened Cheka soldiers, weary from a long ride, expressions that allowed no dissent.

Even so, it would only take one wrong move, one word out of place to raise suspicion. And we were surrounded by soldiers who would kill us with almost no hesitation.

The guard nodded, then remembered himself. 'Y-your,' he stuttered, 'your papers, please, comrade.'

I paused, staring hard at the young man for a moment as if to ask him how he had dared to request such a thing, then I looked at Krukov and sighed so the guard could see my contempt. 'Why do they post boys in positions of responsibility?' I said.

When I turned back to the guard, I unfastened one of the buttons on my coat and pulled my papers from the inside pocket.

I held them out without leaning down, forcing him to come closer.

He hardly dared to look me in the eye as he reached up to take them.

'Well, hurry up,' I said.

His hands were shaking when he unfolded the documents. He scanned them, glanced up at me, then looked back at the papers again. 'I-I'm sorry, comrade. Just one moment.'

And with that, he disappeared back into the guardhouse.

I turned to look at Krukov, who shrugged, just a slight movement of his shoulders, and then a different guard emerged from the hut. This man was older, sterner, but he still had trouble looking me in the eye.

'Grigori Ryzhkov,' he said.

'*Commander* Ryzhkov,' I said, before I turned to Krukov with a subtle warning glance. 'Where do they find these people? They wouldn't last more than a day out there.'

Krukov could hardly hide his confusion, wondering why I had shown Ryzhkov's papers and not my own. I was a decorated soldier – Nikolai Levitsky should command more respect than Grigori Ryzhkov, but I had my reasons for the deception.

'My apologies, Comrade Commander,' the man said, before looking over the papers he held in his thick hands. He pursed his lips, his moustache rising so the bristles touched his nostrils. 'I have to ask . . . what is your business here?' He looked back at the soldiers behind me.

'We're taking some prisoners away,' I said.

The guard took off his hat and scratched his balding head as he went back to staring at my papers. 'I—'

'Just open the gates.'

He nodded at me and shifted his attention to Krukov. 'Papers?'

Krukov passed his documents to the guard.

'I know you have a job to do, comrade,' I said, 'but you *do* you know who I am?'

'Yes.'

'Then I suggest you give me access to your prisoners right

away, or when I speak to your commander, I will ask him to give you to me for punishment. Comrade Krukov here is particularly good at flaying a man's hands while he's still alive. He can peel away the skin like a glove.'

Beside me, Krukov remained expressionless.

'All right.' He swallowed hard and handed back the papers, waving us forward. 'Let them in.'

The younger man ran to the first gate and opened it, signalling to the towers to let us through.

I looked down at the guard for a long moment, then nudged Kashtan forward into the corral between the two gates. 'You think we're safe?' I spoke under my breath.

'I can't be sure,' Krukov said. 'Why did you use Ryzhkov's papers?'

I ignored his question and rode on as the first gate closed behind us, the barbed wire rattling as it banged shut. The older guard followed us into the corral.

We were trapped now, hemmed in between the two gates, with towers ahead of us. If they'd wanted to kill us, now would be the best time. The four of us wouldn't last more than a few seconds.

As we reached the main gate, though, it drew back in front of us, rolling away to one side, and I felt my heart beating hard as we crossed the groove it had left in the dirt.

I had a better view of the prisoners in the inner compound now. There were more than two hundred of them at first sight, milling about in front of the huts, but there may have been more, obscured by the buildings. Mostly they were women and children, some of them hardly more than babies, but there were some men too. Boys, really. Boys destined to be soldiers.

*Please be here. Please be here.*

Most of them watched us enter the camp. Undernourished, tired and afraid, they could only wonder what we might have in store for them. They would be accustomed to soldiers arriving and taking people away to labour camps or Red Army units, and already groups were forming, families closing together, hoping they would not be separated from their loved ones. I watched those groups, looking for any sign of Marianna and the boys, but saw nothing.

As soon as we were all in, the soldiers drew the gate closed behind us, and the guard jogged past, heading for the building closest to the entrance. He didn't need to knock on the door, because as he reached the building, the door opened and the prison commander stepped out. The two men spoke, and then the guard returned to the gate, calling for the men to let him back out to his post.

The commander of the camp smoothed his uniform tunic and came towards us, his gleaming black boots stark against the thin layer of snow.

I remained in the saddle, giving myself a position of superiority, making the man look up at me when he spoke.

'Comrade Ryzhkov,' he said with an officious smile. 'I am Commander Donskoy. I didn't know you were coming.' He couldn't help looking at my bruises, staring at my swollen lips.

'Why *would* you have known I was coming?'

The smile fell from his face. 'Your men are still here. Shall I call for them?'

'My men?' I couldn't help but glance at Krukov, whose face remained blank. I searched his eyes for any clue that he knew about this and it crossed my mind that he had planned it. He had brought me to a place from which there would be no escape.

'Commander?'

I looked down at Donskoy and tried to give nothing away in my expression. I was thinking quickly, trying to see a way through this. If Krukov was betraying me, I had no chance, but if not, I had to stop those men from seeing me. As soon as they saw me, they would give up my real identity. I had men at my back, men who I hoped were loyal. They were experienced and quick, but we would be outnumbered if we had to fight. Too many possibilities were presenting themselves to me.

I had to just fix on one.

'Where are they?' Krukov asked.

'In the barracks.' The commander pointed to the building

closest to the camp entrance. It looked like all the others, but instead of housing prisoners, it housed the men who could identify me as Nikolai Levitsky. Something in Donskoy's voice, though, and in the twist at the corner of his mouth suggested that he disapproved of the men who were now his guests.

'Doing what?' I asked, risking a quick look at the building before pulling my cap further down on my brow and allowing Kashtan to turn so that my back was to it. If any one were to look out of the window, they would see only a man on horseback.

The commander's eyes turned down for a fraction of a second before he spoke again. 'They're sleeping, Comrade Commander.'

'Sleeping?'

'They said your orders were to rest once the prisoners were delivered, so they've been drinking all day. They had some of the women in the barracks too.'

'The women?' I tried not to clench my fists as anger began to replace fear. 'And you disapprove?'

The camp commander looked to one side and clenched his jaw.

'I understand,' I said. 'They're not fit to be part of my unit. Have your men arrest them.'

Donskoy could not hide his surprise.

'Do you know who I am?' I asked him.

'Only by reputation, Commander Ryzhkov.'

'Good. Because those men in there,' I said, 'have not only brought you the wrong prisoners, but they have taken advantage of that reputation.'

'The wrong prisoners?'

'Have your men arrest them, Commander. They're to be sent to Ryazan. Perhaps a few years of hard labour will remind them how to be patriots.'

'You don't want them shot?'

'Let them labour for the glory of the revolution,' I said. 'The motherland always needs more workers.'

'I'll prepare the papers.' He looked disappointed to be denied a shooting.

'Sign them yourself,' I said. 'In the meantime, I want you to

394

give me access to the prisoners. Some of them will be leaving with me today.'

'If you give me the names of the ones you're looking for, I'll have my men—'

'If I wanted to do that, I would have done it. Do you know the names of every prisoner you have here?'

'No, but we can—'

'Unlock the gate.'

'Of course, Comrade Commander.' Donskoy took a step back, saluted and turned to summon one of the guards. He issued his orders, and when the guard hurried back to the barracks, the commander went to the gate and unlocked it, pulling it wide for us to enter.

I glanced at Krukov and dismounted, feeling my heart thumping.

Closer.

*Please be here.*

I had to control myself, stop myself from hurrying into the compound and calling out Marianna's name.

Krukov and the other men also dismounted, and we stepped into the compound.

The commander came in behind us and called to the prisoners, ordering them to assemble in front of us and form a line.

*Please be here.*

They were a ragged bunch, shivering in clothes that were dirty and torn, many of them thin, as if they hadn't eaten properly for a long time. They were like animals kept in a cage, thrown scraps of food and forced to sleep piled on top of one another. I remembered what Anna had said about wanting to save them all, but I couldn't do it. No matter how wrong this was, I was one man. I would struggle even to save my own; I couldn't begin to think about taking them all with me. A child's world is so much simpler.

*Please be here.*

I saw Marianna straight away. She was unmistakeable. She stared at the ground, as if afraid to look up, and she held our sons close to her, pulling them against her almost as if they had become a part of her.

My heart stopped. My eyes took in every detail.

The shabbiness of her dress, the way she shivered without her winter coat, the split boots that barely covered her feet.

She kept my sons near, both for hopeless protection and to share their warmth. Her face was thinner than I had ever seen it, engrained with dirt, and the tangle of her hair had lost its winter-wheat shine.

Misha was hunched in his coat in a way that was unnatural for one so young, and his features, too, were sharper than I remembered them. The weeks of hunger had not been kind to him. Nor had they been kind to Pavel, who looked smaller than he was in my memories, so that his winter coat swamped him, hanging off his thin shoulders. His head was lowered so that he stared at the ground, and I longed to bring him to me, to put my face to his hair.

They were alive.

The look of despair about them was almost too much for me to bear. I wanted to cry out their names and throw my arms around them. I wanted to rage against those who had harmed them. I wanted to fall on my knees and thank God they were still alive.

But I had to be calm. I had to act the part I was playing.

Marianna looked up to see who had come; at first, she just saw a soldier with his cap pulled low, so she averted her eyes, not wanting to draw attention to herself. But she had seen something she recognised. It was clear in her expression. A widening of her eyes. A loosening of her mouth.

And when she looked up again, our eyes locked.

For a second it was as if no one else were there. We were alone.

I stared into her eyes, the colour of the summer sky, and I longed to reach out and touch her. I wanted to put my hands on the pale skin of her cheeks just to be sure it was her, that she was really alive. It took all my strength and reserve to hide my emotions as I looked at my sons, desperate to put my arms around them, hold them tight. I yearned to press my face against

Misha's, to kiss the top of Pavel's head and breathe the scent of his hair I remembered so well.

'Comrade Commander?' Donskoy asked. 'Is everything all right?'

Then the spell broke. My heart lurched and Marianna began to open her mouth, as if to speak, but I shook my head in warning, sharp and quick.

I turned away, hoping she had seen the message I was trying to send.

It took all of my strength to look away from her. Every fibre in my body ached. When I went to the first man in the line of prisoners, I risked a glance back at her, seeing her whisper to Misha and Pavel. The boys lifted their faces to look at me, but Marianna put a hand on each of their heads and turned them with a quick jerk. Even so, their eyes slid to watch me and I prayed they would say nothing.

So I fought my yearning and began to walk along the line of prisoners, looking at the face of each person I would not save. I could hardly concentrate on anything. The prisoners in front of me were a blur and I had to stop my eyes from wandering, shaking my head each time.

When I came to Marianna and the children, my mouth was dry and my hands were shaking. I had to lace my fingers together to hide their trembling as I nodded and spoke to Krukov. 'These ones,' I said.

'Come forward,' Krukov ordered, and when they stepped from the line, he ushered them out of the compound before my sons could say anything.

'That's all?' Commander Donskoy said, and I could see that he wanted to ask. He wanted to know why I was taking these prisoners away.

'Secret business,' I said, lowering my voice. 'Orders from Moscow.' I looked along the line of other prisoners, thinking again about what Anna had said, but I could not help them. I had to leave them to their fate.

Donskoy straightened and stiffened his back. He put his feet together, throwing his chest out like a peacock. 'From Moscow. Of course, Comrade Commander. I understand.'

I let him have his moment of pride, then turned to watch Krukov leading my family away. As I did, I noticed soldiers coming out of the barracks in the outer compound. They were armed with rifles, five men, and heading towards the other barracks building where Ryzhkov's remaining men lay sleeping.

'You want to speak to them when they are arrested?' Donskoy asked, as we returned to the horses.

'No.' I put my foot into the stirrup and pushed up onto Kashtan's back. 'I have to leave.'

'So quickly? Let me offer you a—'

'Thank you,' I said. 'Moscow can't wait.'

'Of course. I understand.'

I nudged Kashtan into a walk and directed her towards the gate. Krukov fell in beside me, while Repnin and Manarov took their positions behind us. My prisoners – my *family* – walked in front of us, waiting at the gate for the guards to pull it open.

From the barracks came the sound of shouting. A mess of voices arguing and swearing. Then a single shot was followed by the crackle of several weapons firing at once.

The guards in the towers all turned their rifles towards the barracks, and the men at the gates unslung their rifles, working the bolts and preparing to fire. The commander of the camp drew his pistol and stood waiting to see what or who was going to emerge.

Repnin and Manarov behind me had also readied their weapons, while Krukov and I had drawn our pistols.

Then there was silence.

Not a sound from the barracks.

Everyone waited, the snow falling around us, thick flakes settling on our shoulders.

And in that moment when time seemed to stand still inside the camp, I spoke to Krukov, my voice barely more than a whisper. 'Get my family through that gate,' I said. 'Whatever happens.'

The door to the barracks opened and a soldier came out into the evening. He was barefoot and had his hands clasped together over his head. He was followed by a second man, then a third. Each one of them had nothing on his feet and held his hands on his head. The guards who emerged behind them organised Ryzhkov's men into a line and ordered them to their knees.

'What happened?' the camp commander asked.

'They shot Suvorov,' said one of the guards.

'So you killed him?'

'We had to. He would have shot us all.'

The commander turned to look at me. 'What do you want me to do?'

Ryzhkov's men all looked over at me. My cap was pulled low and the day was darkening and I hoped they couldn't see my face, but I couldn't take the risk. I couldn't let them identify me. I was too close now.

Too close.

'They're your prisoners now,' I said, kicking Kashtan forward. 'Do with them as you will.'

I trotted into the corral, side by side with Krukov, and when we were halfway through, the gate closed behind us and a volley of shots cracked the evening air.

When the outer gate opened, I trotted through it and felt nothing for the men who had just died. Nothing that was behind me mattered anymore – all that mattered now was ahead.

# 48

Marianna walked with one arm around each of our sons so they couldn't look behind them and raise the suspicion of the guards. Pavel tried to turn, but Marianna held him tight.

Side by side with Krukov, I followed the tracks they left in the snow. I stared at their backs and controlled myself, but tears came to my eyes no matter how hard I tried to hold them at bay.

I wiped them away with a gloved hand and turned to Krukov to acknowledge my thanks.

'What now?' he asked.

I cleared my throat, taking a chance to compose myself. 'I'm going home,' I said. 'I'm taking my family home.'

'And your unit?'

'I thought for a moment back there that you might betray me,' I said, watching my family once more and feeling a lump rise to my throat.

'It can be difficult to know who to trust,' he agreed.

'But I can trust you,' I said.

'Yes.'

'Even if I told you I have no intention of commanding this unit any longer?'

Krukov nodded. 'How could you command a unit when you're dead?'

His words surprised me, and without thinking, I turned to him.

My hand reached for my pistol.

Krukov saw the movement and shook his head. 'That's not what I meant. We're the only men who know you're alive. Anyone who accused you of desertion is dead. *That's* why you used Ryzhkov's papers in there. You don't want anyone to know that Nikolai Levitsky is alive.'

'*You* know,' I said. 'And the others too.'

'All of us loyal to you. All we know is that you're dead. We'll swear to it.'

And for once I believed it.

# 49

We maintained the pretence of a unit escorting prisoners until we were well out of the forest, and even then, I was afraid to believe that I had recovered my family and that no one was hurt.

When we were clear of the trees and came to the ruined town, concealed among the damaged buildings, Marianna stopped and looked back at me and I saw what was in her eyes. It was not happiness but immense relief. She had travelled here on foot, seeing the kinds of horrors I had seen. Perhaps she had witnessed Ryzhkov's brandings and torture, and wondered how long it would be before he did the same to her or to our sons. She had been imprisoned and starved and mistreated. She was awaiting deportation to a labour camp and would have known that meant certain death.

Now that she was free, the relief was overwhelming her.

When the children turned, Pavel called out, 'Papa!' and ran to me as I climbed down from Kashtan, the faithful friend who had brought me so far and never let me down.

Misha ran too, keeping up with his brother, and then my sons were putting their arms around me as if to test that I was real.

'Papa,' they said over and over, squeezing me tight and staring up at me.

I hugged them back and kissed them, and I put my face to Pavel's hair. And as I did it, I looked over the top of their heads at Marianna.

She was so much thinner than I remembered, but just as beautiful.

I took off my coat and held my hand out to her.

She began to cry, her face crumpling, her shoulders rising and falling with great sobs as she took my hand.

'Marianna.' I put my coat around her. 'I found you.'

'Kolya,' she said, touching her fingers to my face and staring in quiet disbelief. 'Kolya.'

I drew her closer so that we were all together and we stood as a family, holding one another as if we would never be parted again.

I closed my eyes and held them for a long time.

When I finally opened them again, Anna was standing close, waiting, with Tuzik at her side.

'This is Anna,' I said. 'She'll be coming with us.'

'Anna.' My wife repeated the name as if to test it. She spoke gently and looked at Anna.

'She's part of our family now,' I said, holding a hand out to her.

'Where will we go?' Marianna asked. 'Home?'

I had been so single-minded I hadn't given much consideration to what we would do when I had found them. Perhaps I had been too afraid that they might not be alive and that we'd have no future together. We couldn't go home, though, I knew that.

There was nothing for us in Belev anymore but the dead.

Then I remembered the last place I had experienced real warmth and comfort. I remembered Lev's friendship and how welcome he had made me feel.

'There's a place,' I said, as Anna put her hand in mine and I brought her to be with us. 'A farm that's far from the road. I think we'll be safe there for a while.'

'And then?'

'And then we'll be together,' I said, 'all five of us. Whatever happens.'

## About the author

Dan Smith grew up following his parents across the world. He's lived in many places including Sierra Leone, Sumatra, northern and central Brazil, Spain and the Soviet Union, but is now settled in Newcastle with his family. His debut novel, *Dry Season*, was shortlisted for the Authors' Club *Best First Novel Award 2011*, and was nominated for the *IMPAC Dublin Literary Award*.